REQUIEM

TOR BOOKS BY KEN SCHOLES

Lamentation

Canticle

Antiphon

Requiem

REQUIEM

KEN SCHOLES

TOR®

A TOM DOHERTY ASSOCIATES BOOK
NEW YORK

REQUIEM

Copyright © 2013 by Kenneth G. Scholes

A Tor Book
Published by Tom Doherty Associates, LLC
175 Fifth Avenue
New York, NY 10010

www.tor-forge.com

Tor® is a registered trademark of Tom Doherty Associates, LLC.

Library of Congress Cataloging-in-Publication Data

Scholes, Ken.
    Requiem/Ken Scholes.–First edition.
    (Psalms of Isaak; 4)
    "A Tom Doherty Associates book."
    ISBN 978-0-7653-2130-5 (hardcover)
    ISBN 978-1-4299-4797-8 (e-book)
    1. Fantasy fiction.   I. Title.
    PS3619.C45353R47 2013
    813'.6—dc23
                                2012043814

First Edition: June 2013

Printed in the United States of America

0   9   8   7   6   5   4   3   2   1

For those I've lost along the way

REQUIEM

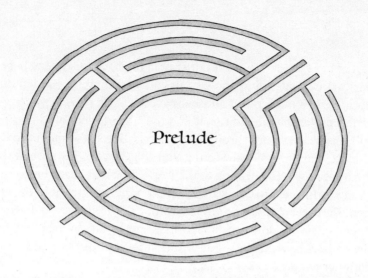

Prelude

A gibbous moon hung in the predawn sky, casting shades of blue and green over a blanket of snow. Fresh from the gloom of the woodlands behind her and not even an hour past the warmth of the thick quilts and crackling fire of her family's home, Marta clutched her stolen sling and cursed the rabbit for running so far and so fast.

She'd not meant to be gone so long. She'd only meant to quickly and efficiently do her part, proving to her father and her brother that she could. Still, if she caught it, skinned and gutted it, she could have it in the stew pot before the sun rose.

Marta moved slowly, following the slight trail the rabbit left in the thick snow, her sling loaded and ready in her left hand.

"Everyone," her father had said since her mother died, "must do their part." She'd been selling fresh produce in Windwir two years ago, same as she'd always done, when the ground shook and the pillar of fire rose up into a Second Summer sky to choke out the sun.

Everything changed that day. *And then kept changing.*

First, there had been the armies. Then, eventually, the soldiers had retreated and the Marshers had come, though now they wore black uniforms and called themselves Machtvolk. Now they built schools and encouraged the children to attend, though Marta's father had not permitted her to. Twice a month, the black-robed evangelist visited their doorstep and entreated Galdus to send at least his daughter so that she might be *properly educated.*

Part of her resented that her father held her back, relegating her to do *her* part, namely sweeping and cleaning and tending the garden during the spring and summer. But another part of Marta reveled in being one of the few children who did not attend the Y'Zirite school.

Still, she heard things through her friends. She knew about the Crimson Empress and the Great Mother and the Child of Promise and how their advent meant the healing of the world. She had heard bits of scripture and had listened to the evangelists expounding upon it in the village square. She'd even seen the Great Mother not long ago, just after the earthquake, riding south in a small company, fast as fast can be on magicked horses. And she'd guessed that the bundle she carried close beneath her winter cloak was the Child of Promise, Jakob.

They'd lined the muddy road to catch a glimpse, though her father's grim jawline told her that he did so with no sense of the faith or joy the surrounding villagers felt.

Everyone must do their part.

Marta pushed ahead and caught sight of movement near the tree line. Beyond it, she heard the quiet rush of water that marked one of the many creeks that ran into the Third River. She watched her breath gather in a cloud ahead of her face and measured the distance with her eyes. The rabbit was just out of reach.

Picking up her pace, she twirled the sling and listened to its buzzing as it built on the air.

She broke into a run as the rabbit moved into the trees, and gasping in frustration, she loosed the stone. It shot out and hummed across the clearing, cracking against a tree as she fitted another into the sling's pocket.

Overhead, the sky moved toward gray.

Then, something happened. There was movement—heavy movement—within the tree line and she heard the rabbit scream even as she heard the snap of breaking bones.

She felt a sudden rush of fear and tasted the copper of it in her mouth. But still, her feet carried her forward. She caught a glimpse of something in the trees moving with long, deliberate strides off toward the river. It was tall and looked like a man.

Marta glanced down, saw the speckle of blood on the ground and the large footprint. *I should go back,* she thought. *I should tell my father there is someone in the woods.*

But it would easier to go back with the rabbit in hand. And it would be more efficient to go back with some idea as to who hid in their woods.

It moved faster than a man and she jogged to keep up, staying well behind.

When it paused, she stopped in her tracks. And when it looked over its shoulder in her direction, she felt her mouth go dry.

Eyes that burned the color of blood opened and closed on her. "Do not follow me, little human," a wheezy, fluid voice said.

She swallowed, then summoned up her own voice, trying hard to not let it shake. "Give me back my rabbit."

It turned and moved off again. But now it slowed, and she drew closer.

It was a man made of metal, but no metal she'd ever seen before. It was a silver that reflected back their surroundings—the white of the snow, the blue-green of the moonlight, the charcoal shadows of the forest—and it moved with liquid grace, its joints whispering and clicking faintly as they bent.

"Who are you?"

They were near the river now and the cliffs it ran beside. The metal man paused, and she was close enough now to see tears in its red jeweled eyes. "I do not know who I am," he said.

"Where are you from?"

The metal man looked up, its eyes taking in the moon. "I do not know." It shuddered slightly as it spoke.

Marta took another step forward and the metal man spun suddenly, moving off in the direction of the cliffside, the rabbit hanging loosely in one slender, silver hand. Again, she jogged to catch up.

She'd heard tales of mechanicals though she'd never seen one, and an idea crept to mind.

"Are you from Windwir?"

This time, its movements were violent, and she leaped back when it spun toward her. "I told you I do not know, little human. It is not safe for you to follow me."

She gritted her teeth. "Then give me back my rabbit."

He looked down at the rabbit and then looked at her. "The human body contains on average two congius of blood." He leaned forward. "You are not fully grown, but you would suffice."

She felt herself go pale. She even willed her feet to carry her backward, to fly her home to the warmth of her waiting house and bed. But they refused her. Instead, she stood transfixed by the creature that towered over her now, the sling dangling powerlessly from her hand. She wanted to ask him what she would suffice for, but couldn't make her tongue work either.

When he turned away just as suddenly, she heard her breath release. Striding to the cliffside, he disappeared behind a boulder.

Shaking, she followed slowly this time.

When Marta reached the boulder, she saw that it hid a crack in the granite wall, and just within that crack, she saw the metal man crouching over a battered wooden pail. She winced as those bare metal hands ripped open the rabbit's throat and upended it so that its blood could drip into the bucket.

I should be silent, she thought. *I should flee now and get the others, tell them what hides here.* But as she watched, she saw the metal shoulders begin to shake, and she saw silver tears roll down silver cheeks to mix with the rabbit's blood.

"Why do you need blood?" the girl asked in a quiet voice, though she wasn't certain she wanted to know.

The metal man looked up and raised a tattered brush in his other hand.

"To paint the violence of my dreams," he said. And in the dim red light of his eyes, Marta saw the words and symbols that covered the walls of his cave and she gasped.

Outside, a cold wind picked up as the moon began its slow slide downward into the horizon and the sky went purple with morning.

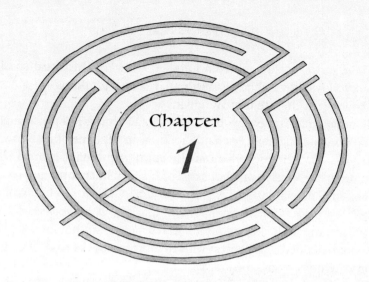

Chapter

1

Rudolfo

Outside, a cold wind muttered along the edge of the Prairie Sea, whispering over the canvas of a hundred tents. Inside, Rudolfo waited for a meeting he could not bear to hold but could not avoid.

"They are nearly here, General," said the Gypsy Scout at the entrance of his tent.

Rudolfo looked up from his work table. He'd reached his western border just three days earlier and had whiled away the days going through yet more reports and communications.

Much had happened since he'd left the north and their exploration of the Beneath Places. The magnitude of it all left his head aching.

First, there had been the earthquake. It was slight on the surface, but many of the tunnels far below them had collapsed. Tunnels that Rudolfo's scouts and miners had been mapping. The tunnels that Isaak and Charles had taken to follow the other mechoservitors west.

Next, Aedric's birds and runners had reached them with warnings about what they'd found in the Watcher's cave, followed soon after by word that Winters was returning with an unknown number of Marsher refugees. And though he'd assumed Jin and Jakob and their entourage would return with them, he'd heard no word from any of them, and that perplexed him greatly. Still, he'd convinced himself it had to do with the difficulty they'd had with the birds of late.

Then, most recently, all communication out of Pylos had suddenly ceased, followed by a flurry of birds that bore dark tidings of a desolation larger even than that of Windwir.

An entire nation lost. Every man, woman and child. *Gods,* he thought. It couldn't possibly be true. But Rudolfo knew in his bones that it was.

And now this. He looked up at the young lieutenant framed in the morning light. Nearly two thousand of his kin, his people, approached on foot, and he would have words with one of them. "When will they arrive?"

"Within the hour," the scout answered.

Rudolfo nodded. "I will meet with Kember alone," he said. "Bring him to the watchtower when he arrives."

The officer inclined his head. "Yes, General."

When he was alone again, Rudolfo turned to the plate his cook had left for him and scanned reports while picking at bits of chilled rabbit, pickled asparagus and rice. Between bites, he sipped cold, sweet chai and tried to imagine what he would say to the man who'd been a father to him since the first days of his orphanhood.

He waited until the last minute to dress, then slipped out of his tent to stride through frozen blades of grass and snowdrifts to the skeletal wood tower that stood watch over the Western Steppes. Around the tower, hasty structures and tents formed a small town with the first soldiers of his standing army taking up their posts to guard the closed borders of the Ninefold Forest, there at the edge of the Prairie Sea.

Rudolfo climbed the stairs, his Gypsy Scouts behind and before him as he went. He slipped through the heavy oak door and into a cold room furnished simply with a table and chairs. He sat and waited.

When the door opened, he looked up as his second captain ushered Kember in.

The forced winter march had not been kind to the old man, and it pleased Rudolfo to see it in the hollowness of his eyes and his weeks-long growth of beard. Behind him, Philemus stood by silently.

Rudolfo did not invite the former steward of his Seventh Forest Manor to sit. Instead, he met his stare coolly.

"How long, Kember?"

The older man said nothing.

"Damnation," Rudolfo roared, his fist coming down upon the table. *"How long?"*

"Fifty-three years," Kember finally said.

More than a dozen years before Rudolfo's birth. He didn't want to believe it. "Show me the mark."

Kember shook his head. "I was not permitted the mark. Most of us weren't. It was your father's—"

Rudolfo cut him off. "Did my father take the mark?"

Slowly, Kember nodded. "He did, Lord. And his fondest desire was that in time, you would, too."

The Gypsy King felt rage twisting in his gut like a blade. "That won't happen." He leaned forward and let the rage settle into his voice, chilling his carefully chosen words. "But I will tell you what *will* happen," Rudolfo said. "You have one opportunity for grace. Otherwise, the Physician Benoit will be here tomorrow morning to assist in your redemption." Here, he nodded to his second captain. "Philemus will spend today and tonight with you, asking questions, and if he is satisfied with your answers, you and your people will leave and never return. Your properties will be forfeit and divided among the refugees *your* faith and treachery helped to create. The edicts are posted; this resurgence will not be tolerated in my forest."

Rudolfo paused and studied the man's face. It was too calm for his liking. "If Philemus is not satisfied with your answers, an appointment with my Physician will be arranged." Still, that calm remained, and Rudolfo forced a smile to his lips. "An appointment," he said slowly, "not for you but for Ilyna."

The mention of the man's wife was the first sign of his resolve slipping, and Rudolfo continued. "And for every answer you do not give with promptness, accuracy and sincerity, Benoit will cut a piece of her away. If necessary, you will be afforded the opportunity to watch and hear this redemptive work."

The blood drained from Kember's face. "I will answer your questions, Rudolfo. Certainly I will." His voice caught, and it pleased the Gypsy King to see the man's composure dissolve. "But hear this: what is coming is a work carefully conceived for your benefit and for the healing of the world. Your father would be ashamed of you for your actions today."

"My father betrayed us all," Rudolfo said, "and I am ashamed of *him* for his own actions." And for the first time, he understood the sharpness of those feelings as that betrayal cut its own mark above his heart. He stood. "And I am ashamed of you, as well, Kember."

He turned his back upon the old man, and left his second captain to the work of interrogation.

Reports of Philemus's progress trickled in throughout the day. Rudolfo tried to busy himself with work, but found his taste for it had gone sour. He sat and stared into nothing, his hands still upon the pile of papers.

Finally, as afternoon became evening, he stood, put on his coat, and slipped out into the cold.

At first he wandered the camp under the pretense of inspecting his men, but despite his best efforts, he felt his booted feet pulling him beyond their military outpost to the large cluster of mismatched tents that formed the exiles' camp. His Gypsy Scouts, bolstered by two companies of his Wandering Army, stood somber watch over the ragged group of frostbitten Y'Zirites.

Rudolfo walked that perimeter, his eyes intentionally meeting those of the exiles. Most looked away beneath the hardness of their king's angry glare. Some met his eyes with quiet resolve. Rudolfo was careful to keep his stare level, though he was not sure why he'd come here. It was not as if he would understand any better from the exercise or that if he did somehow gain knowledge, that it would change the course of action he'd committed to.

Their faith is a poison laced with sugar. He thought of his father and felt the grief again. A question arose within him that he'd asked many times these past two years. "Why?"

He heard footfalls behind him and turned to see Lieutenant Daryn—the Gypsy Scout from earlier—approaching. His face was grim.

"General," he said, "the Marshers have reached the western watch."

Rudolfo quickly calculated distance. They'd arrive within the next two hours. He felt relief building in him. Sending his wife and son into the enemy's den after the explosion had been the best course of action at the time. But now, with his borders guarded and with the surgical knife-work with which the conspiracy had been cut out of the Named Lands by Ria's people, it was time to have them at home. In the midst of the madness his life had become, Jin Li Tam and Jakob were what anchored him.

"Excellent," he said, and gave a tired smile.

But the smile faded at Daryn's troubled face. The lieutenant looked away quickly; then he met Rudolfo's eyes. "Charles and Winters are with them," he said. "Lady Tam and Lord Jakob are not." He paused. "Isaak and Aedric are also missing."

Rudolfo felt it like a fist in his gut, and his knees went weak. "Where are they?" But before the man could answer, Rudolfo was racing toward camp and shouting for his fastest horse.

Winters

The moon was a smudge of blue and green behind a veil of clouds, and Winteria bat Mardic walked beneath it, forcing each step despite the protest of every muscle in her body.

It had been a long ten days, moving from village to village on foot. Exhaustion saturated her. She spent her days putting one foot in front of the other, moving among her people as they made their way southeast. And she spent her nights tossing and turning, struggling beneath the weight of bad tidings she knew she must soon share with Rudolfo about Jin and Jakob, about Isaak and Neb.

Neb. She'd been terrified of him. Something had changed the boy into . . . what? She didn't know. But after healing her cuts with a touch, he'd gone out to face the Watcher, and he'd held his own against that ancient metal man in a battle that left a wide path of ruined forest behind them. And he had not come back. Neither had Isaak or the Watcher.

She glanced over her shoulder to where Charles sat upon the back of a tired pony. His face had paled at the earthquake, and he'd said fewer than three words to her in the days since. But she'd seen him wiping tears from his eyes from time to time, and she suspected strongly that he knew what she feared most—that Isaak was not coming back.

And Neb may not be either.

She shook the thought away, refusing it. She needed to believe that he somehow escaped. That somehow, he was doing what her people's dream had called him to, seeking their Home, and she wanted to believe that maybe Isaak had escaped with him. And that maybe, somehow, they'd wrested the final dream from the Watcher before they fled.

But she saw no evidence of that, and she'd left with her people the morning after the earthquake, even while the Machtvolk scouts and soldiers scoured the forest for some sign of where Neb and the mechoservitors had vanished to.

Scout whistles ahead startled her and she stopped abruptly, hearing the sound of fluttering feathers grabbed from the air by catch nets. She knew they were close now, and soon Rudolfo would demand answers of her.

She sighed and steeled herself, adjusting the knives she wore at her hips before hurrying ahead.

She heard the pounding of hooves first, followed by a whispering wind that betrayed the approach of magicked scouts.

Winters reached the front of the caravan even as a dark mare and turbaned rider crested the rise of frozen scrub ahead of them. There was something different in his posture now, but it was unmistakably Rudolfo. His head moved from side to side, taking in the scattered line of refugees.

"Hail, Lord Rudolfo," she shouted, stepping out in front of her people. The Gypsy Scout Aedric had left in charge materialized beside her. "I've brought more orphans for your collection."

He didn't answer. Instead, Rudolfo whistled the horse forward and toward them, letting the beast pick its footing carefully on the snowswept slope. As he drew closer, she saw his eyes narrow at the sight of her scars, his lips pursed in anger.

When he spoke, there was a cold edge in his voice that she was not accustomed to. She could feel the weight of his stare. "Where is my family?" Then, his eyes shifted to the Gypsy Scout. "And where is my first captain?"

She watched the man try to meet Rudolfo's gaze and fail, hanging his head in wordless shame. "Perhaps we should discuss this matter in private, Lord," she said.

He turned on her quickly, moving the horse in close. "Where," he asked again, this time slowly, "is my family?"

She swallowed. "They have left the Named Lands," she said, then glanced over her shoulder at the people who stood nearby. "It is a matter we should discuss *privately*, Lord Rudolfo."

He looked away from her and to his scout. "And Aedric?"

The scout reached toward his sash. "I bear a letter from the captain addressed to you, General."

Rudolfo raised his hand. "Enough," he said. The rage Winters saw in his eyes startled her and she would have looked away, but he did first. He scanned the crowd. "Where's Charles?"

"I'm here," the old man said.

"What of Isaak?"

Winters turned in time to see Charles meet Rudolfo's stare. "Lady Winteria is correct," he said. "We should speak privately. These are sensitive matters."

Rudolfo took a long, deep breath. *He's wrestling with his anger,* she realized. "Very well," he said. Then he dismounted and handed the reins over to a scout who materialized at his arm. He looked first to Charles and then to Winters. "Walk with me. Both of you."

They set out at a brisk pace, their breath frosting the night air. Rudolfo set that pace with long, deliberate strides, and when they were sufficiently away from the others, he slowed them. "Tell me," he said.

Winters started at the beginning, updating him on Cervael's death and the Mass of the Falling Moon, through Neb's appearance and then disappearance with Isaak and the Watcher.

Rudolfo listened intently, his hands folded behind his back as he walked, and occasionally he interrupted to ask questions. When she reached the part about Jin Li Tam's sister, he raised his eyebrows.

"A Tam in the Y'Zirite Blood Guard?"

"Yes," Winters said. "Lady Tam said the woman told her to go with the regent when he asked."

He nodded. "Continue."

This is the part I dread telling him. She did not know why, but the thought of it knotted her stomach. Winters took a deep breath and continued. "Lady Tam also bid me tell you that she loves you and that you bear her grace above all others but your son. And that she would see him back to you."

She saw him flinch at the words, and when he turned his eyes upon her, she saw anguish now mixing with his rage. "And you've known this ten days gone but did not send word of my wife and my son? Nor send word about my first captain?"

Winters looked away. "I did not, Lord."

"Why?"

Look him in the eye. She forced her eyes toward his. "Aedric bid me not to. He knew you would try to pursue them. It's in his letter."

Now Rudolfo drew in a breath and slowly let it out. He turned away from her and toward Charles. "And tell me what you know about Isaak," he said.

Charles looked at Winters, then back to Rudolfo. "I fear he is dead, Lord."

Dead. Winters blinked back sudden, unexpected tears. This was what she'd feared, and hearing him say it aloud hollowed out a part of her.

"What leads you to believe that?" Rudolfo asked.

"I believe his sunstone overheated, Lord, during his fight with the Watcher. I think the earthquake was an explosion underground—a large one."

How large, she wondered? Her mouth went dry, and Rudolfo asked before she could find the words.

"What about Neb and the Watcher?"

Yes. What of them? Charles glanced at her before answering, and she knew from the look on his face that she did not want to know what he was going to say.

He looked away from her. "I don't see how they could have survived if they were nearby. Especially underground."

No, Winters thought. Neb left the way he came. He went to do what needed doing. *He went Home-Seeking.* Isaak went with him. "But we can't know for sure," she said. "Neb was . . ." Her words trailed off as she thought about them. "He was *different* when we saw him. He came out of nowhere and he was stronger." She shuddered at the memory of his choked voice, feeling the heat of his hands upon her body. *Be whole.* "He was faster." She looked to Charles. "You saw it?"

"Some," Charles said. "Mostly, we heard it. But she is right, Lord. Neb was holding his own against the Watcher."

"That is curious." Rudolfo stopped and stroked his beard. He looked at Winters. "You're right. We cannot know for sure what's become of them."

But his eyes told her that he wasn't hopeful. When he started walking again, he turned them back toward the scattered line of men, women and children who stamped their feet in the cold. "I will send scouts to your young officer with an offer of aid," Rudolfo said. "I'll have them gather what information they can."

She blushed at the mention of Garyt ben Urlin, then willed the heat from her cheeks. "Thank you, Lord." She paused, thinking she should say more but unsure of what that more should be.

They walked quietly, and when they reached the caravan, Rudolfo paused. "We have tents and food," he said. "And when you reach Rachyle's Rest, my new steward, Arturas, will help you find housing and work for your people."

New steward? When she'd left with Lady Tam, Kember had been steward. And though she wanted to ask, she knew from the way he said the name that this was not the time. Instead, she inclined her head. "Thank you, Lord Rudolfo."

He looked at Charles next. "And you have work waiting for you," he told the man. "We've recovered an artifact from one of these Blood Scouts. We're not sure what it does, but it's been stored in the Rufello vault in your office."

Charles bowed. "Yes, Lord. I'll look at it." He moved back into the line and recovered his pony from the woman who held its reins, but Winters stayed, still looking for the words.

Rudolfo spoke first, his voice so low that none could hear but her. "My disappointment is profound," he said. "By withholding this information until now, you've robbed me of choices regarding my family . . . my son." She forced her eyes to his and saw the anger and pain there.

"You are a queen, Winteria, and one who understands what it is to have your power and your choices taken away." He paused and held her gaze. "I expected better of you."

The heat on her face was different than earlier, and it arrived accompanied by a lump in her throat. She opened her mouth to answer him, but what could she say? She had wondered a hundred times whether or not she made the right decision. Before she could speak, Rudolfo climbed into the saddle and looked at the Gypsy Scout again. "I'll have that letter now," he said.

The man drew it from his sash and passed it up to his king. Lines of grief stood out on the scout's face.

Rudolfo took it, tucked it into a pouch at his belt, and turned the horse. When he rode away, his back was straight.

Winters blinked tears of powerlessness and frustration. *I did what was best for all of us.* She knew when Aedric came to her that Jin Li Tam would've concurred as well.

Still, watching the result of that choice in the angry posture of the man who'd sheltered her, aided her since that dark night Hanric fell, Winteria bat Mardic felt a blade sharper than the Y'Zirite knives that had scarred her flesh.

This blade cut deep and cold.

Petronus

Petronus felt the heavy wooden crate crash against him, and he clung to the safety harness with white knuckles, trying to shout over the sound of shrieking metal and hissing air that filled the cargo bay.

The floating crate traveled the length of him, and he deflected it as best he could with his free arm. Across from him, he saw Rafe Merrique groping for purchase on one of his crew. Beads of blood floated on the air, bubbling out of a gash on the crewman's head. All around the metal room, anything that wasn't strapped down drifted. Grains of rice from a burst sack, beads of water from an open canteen. A medico kit moved past Petronus, and he snagged it then pushed it across the room toward the old pirate.

Rafe cursed and stretched out for it. "What in the hells is happening?"

"I don't—" The weight of a mountain fell upon him before the words were out, and all around Petronus, everything that had hung suspended suddenly dropped as the ship bucked and shimmied.

The ship pitched starboard, and Petronus found himself pressed hard against the metal wall. As he rolled along with the vessel, the cargo bay filled with light and he saw a bright blue sky through a crystal porthole that slid by beneath him as he tumbled about.

He heard the sound of metal on metal and looked in the direction of the ladder that separated them from the pilothouse above and the engine room below. A mechoservitor moved down the ladder, steam rising from its exhaust grate. The metal man reached the deck, and another began its descent.

What are they doing? There were four of them now. The ship steadied, and the metal men moved across the deck quickly, pulling their way along the line of safety harnesses. The vessel shuddered, and the shrieking rose to a new and frenzied pitch. One of the mechoservitors staggered, steadied itself and moved quickly to Petronus.

"What's happening?" he shouted as the mechoservitor lifted him to his feet.

"We've been attacked, Father Petronus. We are attempting to land."

Attacked? He flinched when the metal man's arm encircled his waist, but the sharp pain he felt in his left leg convinced him to accept the offered help. The mechanical man lifted him easily. Behind him, he saw Rafe Merrique and two others also being carried toward the ladder.

The ship pitched again, and he felt the gears grinding beneath his ear as the metal man staggered and then compensated.

When they reached the ladder, Petronus scrambled up it and into waiting metal hands that pulled him up and strapped him beside a still form. *Neb.*

He twisted in the harness to look at the boy but found the view beyond too compelling to resist. Two metal men worked the wheel while another sat in an odd contraption of levers and pedals. Just past them, through a wide crystal window, Petronus saw wisps of low-lying clouds shrouding a green carpet of jungle, interrupted occasionally by patches of blue water.

Something large and silver flashed by, and once again, the ship shuddered and then dropped suddenly. He heard a thud to his left but couldn't turn to see what had happened. Rafe Merrique's cursing was explanation enough.

"We are landing in the southern lunar sea," the mechoservitor who worked the pedals and levers said, its voice booming in the confined space.

Petronus saw it now, rising up at them faster and faster as the ship continued its descent. He tried to force himself to watch, but in the end, he shut his eyes against it and held his breath.

When they hit the water, it knocked the wind out of him, and light exploded behind his closed eyes. His awareness shrank to a single point of focus—clutching at the harness against the tossing and bucking and shaking of the vessel. Everything else faded, and even the roaring around him was shut out.

He became nothing but fists hanging on until he felt a sharp pain in the back of his head and gave way to the gray that swallowed him.

When awareness returned, he once more found metal hands pulling at him. Watery light washed the cabin, and the air had changed. It was fresh and heavy with salt, nothing like the stale air he'd been breathing since they left the Named Lands, and all around him, he heard the rush of water.

The mechoservitor before him was dented. One of its eyes hung useless and dark, and the other guttered. It lifted him up, and Petronus felt other hands taking hold of him as he was passed along a chain of mechanicals and eventually laid out upon a twilight shore. He tried to roll over and found the light erupting behind his eyes again.

"I have you, Father." It was Rafe.

The old pirate carefully turned him over, and the first thing he saw was the massive brown-and-blue world that filled the sky and painted the landscape with an ethereal twilight.

Petronus lay still and blinked until the familiarity of that vast world registered. He could see the two mountain ranges he'd grown up with— the Dragon's Spine marching across the northern reaches of the continent and the Keeper's Wall running north to south, carving the Named Lands off from the desolation of the Churning Wastes.

"Gods," he whispered. "I'm on the moon."

"Aye, Father," Rafe said.

Petronus took his eyes off the sky and looked to the pirate. "What happened?"

"I know what you know. We were attacked and crashed in the sea."

Petronus forced himself to sit up, threads of light spider-webbing his field of vision as he did. Shaking it off, he looked around. They were on a strip of beach, and to the right, a mechoservitor bent over a still form.

"Neb?" The boy didn't move, and Petronus felt fear rising in his stomach. He tried to stand and Rafe steadied him.

"The boy's asleep, Father. He slept through it all."

Asleep? He'd not seen Neb since the day they loaded him into the vessel, naked, burned and unconscious. But the boy had spoken into his mind, and his words were full of despair. *We've failed. Isaak is dead. The dream is lost. The staff is lost.*

And now, Petronus thought, *this.* He limped to Neb and crouched. The metal man looked up briefly, its eye shutters flashing open and closed, then returned to checking the boy. From what the old man saw, there were no obvious injuries. The hair was growing in where it had been burned away, and the boy's left hand and arm were covered in the pink of new skin. Anyone else would've died from the shock of the burns he'd sustained, but Petronus knew now that Neb wasn't anyone else.

He'd heard *that* voice, as well, dropping into his mind, commanding him to fall back and accompany Neb. It was a voice that started his nose to bleeding and his head to pounding.

It was the voice of the Younger God, Whym, declaring himself Neb's father and with that pronouncement challenging everything Petronus had ever believed.

He reached a hand out to touch the boy's cheek. It was warm. "Neb?"

The mechoservitor looked up again. "Lord Whym continues to regenerate."

Lord Whym. When he'd met Neb, the boy was nearly mad from the loss in Windwir's pyre. Petronus had watched him rise to the challenge of leadership in the grave-digging camp. He'd never imagined this. "Is he okay?"

Billows wheezed. "He is functional," the metal man said.

Petronus nodded and looked back to the water. Rising up from it, half buried, lay the massive hulk of the ship that had carried them here. Five metal figures formed a line, passing what could be salvaged out of the ship and onto the sand. The others—two scouts and a sailor—gathered around two forms now covered with wool blankets.

We've dead to bury. And one of them was his friend, Grymlis, killed by kin-wolves as they raced to board the ship. Petronus felt the grief of that loss. It was a fog that hemmed him in, and not even the wonder and fear of being shipwrecked on the moon could lift it.

What now? He stood and went to stand with the others. They looked to him, their bruised faces pale and expectant in the light of the world that hung above them.

As a boy, he'd spent hour upon hour playing out the apocryphal *One Hundredth Tale of Felip Carnelyin,* he and his boyhood playmates turning the backwoods of Caldus Bay into a vast lunar jungle filled with new smells, new sights and dangerous beasts. And now, he stood upon the shore with that jungle stretching out behind him, smelling salt, ozone and the sweet scent of flowers he did not recognize on the midnight air. This wasn't how he imagined landing upon the moon, back when he was young and playing out Carnelyin's adventures.

Still, for now they were alive and safe enough, though he wondered what manner of mechanical or magick could bring down a vessel such as theirs. And more importantly, he wondered if it might return for them.

Regardless, he realized, there was work that must be done, though it grieved him that it was their first work in this new place.

He looked down at the bodies of those they'd lost and then turned to the growing pile of boxes, crates and barrels. He walked to it, and dug around until he found a shovel still wet from the sea.

"We'll need white stones," he said.

And then, once more, Petronus set about the task of burying his dead.

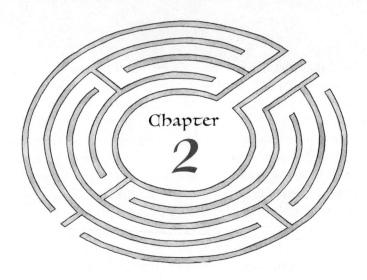

Chapter

2

Neb

Neb floated in gray silence, sliding in and out of awareness until he heard the singing. He recognized the song instantly, and with it, he recognized the scent of lilacs and lilies on a warm breeze. He sniffed at the air tentatively and then drew in a great lungful of it before opening his eyes.

Vertigo rushed at him and he tottered for a moment, taking in the rich green jungle far below him. Beyond it, a green-tinged sea glinted in the sunlight. He closed his eyes against the impossible height he stood at, counted silently to ten, and then opened them again.

I've been here before. He recognized it from his dreams, though the vastness of it had never struck him as it did now. Here on the tower, he stood above the wisps of morning cloud and watched a flock of silver birds move across the surface of the jungle canopy, their backs and wings reflecting back the blue sky.

And this tower was different than the one in his dreams. It wasn't the ancient bone-white material he remembered standing upon with the mechoservitors, but instead, this surface was a garden—a grassy man-made ridge that encircled a stand of fruit-bearing trees and a pond. He stood on the ridge now, the grass warm beneath his bare feet, and wondered how it was he came to be here.

Am I on the moon then? He thought he must be, and he reached back into himself to find some sense of how he'd arrived. The last thing he remembered was metal hands pulling him up and lifting him, the sharp odor of his charred skin and burnt hair choking his breath. Prior to that . . . He felt his muscles seize with the memory of violence. Other metal hands upon him, pummeling him, tossing him with ease, as he tried to escape the Watcher. The smell of ozone and oil filled his nostrils, and the shriek of tearing metal and grinding gears drowned out all other sound as a smoking, wheezing form toppled the Watcher into the bargaining pool.

The singing grew louder, and Neb turned in the direction it came from just as the music stopped abruptly.

The girl stared, her mouth hanging open and her eyes growing wide. And if the look on her face wasn't enough to convince him, her emotions rushed him, pushing into his mind. *Fear. Confusion.* His head hurt from the force of those sensations, and he pushed back at her until she blinked. She took a step back and frowned.

"What are you doing here?"

"I don't know," he said.

She was older than he was by a few years, he suspected. Her blond hair was long and braided with unfamiliar flowers that set off the silver of her robes. She took another step back. "How did you gain access?"

Neb shook his head. "I don't know that, either."

The girl wrinkled her nose. "Do you happen to know," she asked, "where you might have misplaced your clothes?"

Neb blushed, feeling the heat of it move over his body. He turned away and tested the instinct that suddenly prompted him. "Clothe me," he said in a quiet voice.

Mist lifted from the garden and moved over him, forming itself to him until he wore a robe like hers.

"That's better," she said. "Now who are you?"

"I'm Nebios ben Heb—" He cut himself off when he realized he was answering by habit. *That is not who I am anymore.* He swallowed. "I am Nebios Whym," he said.

"Nebios Whym." She cocked her head to the left. *Curiosity.* "Are you kin then to General Whym?" She paled. "Do you bring word of the Downunder War?" *Dread.* Her voice lowered. "Did my father send you?"

Neb bit his lip against the intensity of the emotion and intent she pushed at him along with her words. "I don't know about the war," he said. "But Whym is my father. I do not know if he is a general. And I don't know who *your* father is."

"I am Amylé D'Anjite," she said.

He recognized the name and reached for the recollection. D'Anjite was the Younger God who had bridged the chasm that divided the Churning Wastes thousands of years earlier—the very bridge where the mechoservitor had broken Renard's leg and taken Neb to Sanctorum Lux. "I've heard the name D'Anjite," Neb said.

"My father is a captain in General Whym's army." She moved closer to him, regarding him with brown eyes that pulled at his own. "Where are you then? You must be nearby."

Where am I? What kind of question was that? He blinked at it. "I'm here," he said, "with you." Neb looked around them. "On the Moon Wizard's Tower."

"The what?"

He repeated himself. "The Moon Wizard's Tower."

She laughed. "There is no such thing as wizards."

Neb flinched at the sudden, stabbing memory of Windwir—handiwork of the Wizard King Xhum Y'Zir. Once more, he saw the ships that sank burning in the river as fire rained down upon the city. He thought about correcting her, telling her there certainly *were* wizards, but didn't. Instead, he took in the garden around them and the vast carpet of jungle below. "Then what do you call this place?"

She chuckled. "It's the Firsthome Temple. How can you not know that?"

Firsthome Temple. The meaning was lost on him, but when she said it, the words were accompanied by an emotion akin to reverence and longing that settled into his mind alongside it. "There are a lot of things I don't know," Neb said.

Once again, he felt his muscles seizing, and the force of the tremor staggered him. Something like panic knotted his stomach, and he closed his eyes against it until her voice brought them open. "Are you okay?"

Neb saw the girl had taken a step forward. He found himself stammering, blushing once again. "I'm . . . I don't know."

The smile she offered held sympathy in it. "These are hard times for us all. But my father says the thief Y'Zir will not prevail, no matter how much he stirs up the 'unders."

Neb pulled what meaning he could from her words but found her difficult to follow. He reached back into the mythology he'd spent his childhood studying in the Androfrancine Library. "You mean Raj Y'Zir?"

She shook her head. "Not Raj . . . *Tal.* I've never heard of Raj Y'Zir.

But I'm sure they must be kin." She studied him again, biting her lip. "Well," she finally said, "I'm not quite sure what to do with you, Nebios Whym. You're the first of the People I've encountered here in more years than I can count. When did you arrive?"

"Only just now," Neb said.

"Hopefully," she said, "more are coming. It's been so long that I thought maybe I'd been forgotten." He wanted to ask how long she'd been here and who exactly she thought might be coming, but she moved past him before he could speak, calling to him over her shoulder. "Still, at least *you're* here, Nebios Whym. So come along or you'll miss it."

He turned to follow her. "Miss what?"

"Something beautiful," she said.

She moved quickly now and he followed her, feeling the wind move through his hair. The sensation startled him, and he raised a hand to his head, running it through his thick silver mane. He remembered the smell of it burning what seemed like hours ago. Was it possible that it had grown back so fast?

He pushed the question aside and focused on the girl's back. Her shorter legs carried her forward with deliberate purpose, and he relaxed into a stride that caught up to her easily as they skirted the grassy ridge. He wasn't certain what direction they faced when they finally stopped, but when she sat down quickly in the grass, he did the same.

He was surprised but did not resist when she reached over to hold his hand. "Sing with me," she said in nearly a whisper.

But as she started singing that familiar song again, Neb found he had no voice for it despite the emotions that flooded him from her. Joy. Hope.

It started far out beyond the jungle on a horizon that glinted in the afternoon sun. At first, there was a sliver that slowly grew as a massive world rose to fill the sky. Only this world was unlike the scarred and dying planet that he'd seen in his dreams. It rose, blue and green, and as it did, Neb saw once more a geography familiar to him.

Only this world is whole.

The girl must've heard his sudden, indrawn breath, because she stopped singing and squeezed his hand. "Are you okay?"

Neb felt his lips moving, but no words came out. He swallowed, tried to take his eyes off the place that had so recently been his home. Finally, he found his voice. "It's . . . beautiful."

Yes, the girl whispered in his mind with a warmth that he felt beneath his skin as she squeezed his hand. They sat in silence for a time, and Neb felt a calm settle over him even as the sky grayed toward twilight. Finally, the girl spoke again, and when she did, Neb found his mouth opening suddenly with the quiet force of her familiar words.

"This dream," she said, "is of our home."

Vlad Li Tam

Hot wind pulled his tattered robes and shaggy hair as Vlad Li Tam stood in the surf and watched Behemoth descend back into the sea. His beard and hair, now longer than he remembered ever having them, stank of dried seawater, and he felt the breeze moving through a dozen tears in the light cotton fabric he'd worn nearly bare over the weeks. He could feel the dark sand beneath his toes, the warm water against his legs, and he could taste the bitter smell of salt—and some unidentifiable other scent—on the air.

He kept his eyes on the metal serpent until it was completely submerged, and then he turned back to the shore to take in this new place.

The sun had barely risen though the temperature already had him sweating. The beach was a ribbon of black at the base of high dark cliffs that ran east and west as far as the eye could see. Overhead, wisps of cloud raced past, and the absence of birds was noticeable.

Were these the Barrens of Espira?

He wasn't sure how many days had passed; he'd spent them underwater as the Behemoth steamed south. But not long ago, the ghost of Amal Y'Zir, his inexplicable beloved, had told him the metal beast would bring him here, her father's staff in hand, to find her father's spellbook.

Much of what she'd told Vlad was lost on him, and he wished Obadiah were with him so he could ask the metal man. After all, he was more familiar with the dream they followed. He'd known about Behemoth, after all. But would that dreaming mechoservitor have known anything about the Continuity Engine of the Elder Gods? And who was the heir of Whym that the staff was meant for? Cryptic, unfamiliar terms that were compelling when combined with the urgency in her voice. What was it she had said there near the end?

We have bargained in the Deepest of Deeps that the light once more be sown in the darkness that contains us all.

Regardless of understanding, Vlad knew he would let the Moon Wizard's staff lead him where it would, fueled by the conviction of a love so deep that it ached in his veins and bones.

The sun rose higher now, and the sky went from mauve to blue as Vlad approached the shade at the base of the cliffs. Here along the rocky wall, there was little in the way of tidal debris and nothing at all that spoke of life. He stood there looking east and then west, uncertain of what to do.

The staff will lead you to it.

He extended the staff out ahead of him but sensed nothing—not even a tingle—as he turned each direction. Vlad scratched his head and then nodded slowly.

He placed one tip of the staff in the sand and stepped back as he let go. For a moment, it stood straight and then began to lean to the west.

Vlad smiled, took back the staff, and started walking.

By noon he'd covered a dozen leagues, the landscape around him never changing. Heat shimmered off the dark sand as bitter-tasting winds blew in from the north over the water. Overhead, the cliffs continued their jagged march.

I should be thirsty. But he wasn't. And now that he thought about it, he'd felt nothing he would normally feel. His muscles didn't ache, and his breathing wasn't labored after hours of walking in unrelenting heat. It made no sense.

Yet nothing has made sense these last few months. He'd chased a ghost across an ocean to find the Moon Wizard's Ladder, and then he'd descended into the basement of the ladder to confront his grandson, Mal Li Tam, and be commissioned by his water ghost to come to this gods-forsaken place.

He looked at the plain silver staff in his hand and remembered what she'd told him about it. *Use the staff to aid you; but use it with care. For the tools of the parents are not made for the hands of their infant children.*

He suspected that somehow Y'Zir's staff aided him now, extending his stamina far more than any scout magicks he could use.

Using the slender, lightweight rod as a walking stick, he continued west along the shore.

This place was familiar, though he knew he was far from home. It reminded him of the Churning Wastes, only much older. The air here had a deadness about it that tasted like dried blood on his tongue, much heavier than the air of the Desolation he was most familiar with. And there was still some life there in those wastelands beyond the Keeper's Gate. Here, nothing moved and nothing grew and there was no sound but the waves and wind moaning over dark stone.

A tomb at the bottom of the world.

Two hours later, he saw the kin-raven.

There was no doubting it—the bird was massive and dark, soaring high above. Vlad moved toward the shade of the cliffs, extending the quicksilver staff ahead of him to get it out of the sun.

The kin-raven circled once and then descended quickly. For a moment, Vlad thought the bird might be diving on him, and he pressed himself against the cliff, the hot stone burning his back.

It landed heavily in the sand and regarded him with a dead glassy eye. It cocked its head and took a step forward, its beak open.

Vlad raised the staff, keeping it between him and the kin-raven. He was far better with a knife than a staff, but the massive talons that now tore up sand were such that he'd want to keep his distance. The bird took another tentative step, its head still cocked.

It's only a bird, he thought. Then, he took a deep breath.

"Be gone," Vlad shouted, lunging forward with the staff. The bird scrambled and then hopped backward, its wings unfurling. When it was well out of reach it closed its beak, cocked its head the other direction, and opened it again.

"Be gone," the kin-raven said, and Vlad realized the voice was his own.

He'd not seen one this close before, and the decaying smell of it was heavy on the air. It hopped from left to right now, its eyes never leaving Vlad.

He knew little about this species. They'd been considered extinct for two thousand years and had only recently begun to appear—not long after Windwir's fall. At first they'd appeared in the Wastes. And then at sea. Nothing good ever followed the sighting of a kin-raven.

"Be gone," the kin-raven said again.

Vlad Li Tam thrust the staff forward again, and once more the kin-raven hopped back. Then, Vlad leaned on the silver rod and studied the bird.

"What brings you here?" he asked.

Once more, the beak snapped closed, the head tilted, and it repeated back Vlad's question. "What brings you here?"

Love or madness, he thought. Or both.

Turning west again, Vlad Li Tam set out, and the enormous bird took flight, racing low and ahead of him down the narrow, dark ribbon of beach. It pounded its wings against the wind and sped west a league, becoming a dark speck before banking out over the ocean and gliding back.

Vlad kept moving, his eye following the bird's antics as it repeated its flight out and back, staying well below the cliff line. As the hours slipped past, the kin-raven stayed near him, and each time the old man paused, the bird would land nearby and ask once again why he was here.

Sunset found him still pressing westward into the gloom, accompanied by his dark companion. Still without hunger, thirst or weariness, he gave himself to walking. When the stars guttered to life and the blue-green moon pushed up behind him, the bird vanished, rising up and over the cliff top and vanishing to the south.

"Love *and* madness," he whispered to the night that he suddenly found himself alone in.

Then, with the moon casting his shadow long upon the dark beach and reflecting back to him in the silver of his staff, Vlad Li Tam walked toward whatever waited ahead.

Jin Li Tam

A cold wind whispered across the deck, and Jin Li Tam pulled her coat tight around her as she paced fore and aft along the rail. They'd lowered their sails sometime in the night, and the ship now moved forward, the deck vibrating from an engine somewhere below and aft that she suspected was much like those that powered her father's iron armada. The clouds that had hemmed them in two hours ago were breaking open as the wind rose, letting the moon and stars cast dim light over the quiet ship and the ocean that surrounded it.

When she'd slipped from her cabin below deck, she'd checked Jakob in his crib after casting a glance toward the narrow bed where Lynnae slept. Her hosts had tried to give her and her son separate quarters—the captain's quarters, no less—but she'd refused and had insisted that the three of them share a single stateroom and displace as few of the ship's crew as possible. The regent, Eliz Xhum, had not seemed surprised by this. But the crewmen, already gazing upon her with something akin to adoration, now looked upon their Great Mother with a different kind of respect.

As I intended, she realized. She needed their respect and any favor it might purchase her; she would bend their worship of her and her son into whatever tool or weapon she might use to accomplish the work she was made for. And beyond that: She needed to keep Lynnae near. It was bad enough, a mother bringing her child into this situation. She would not leave him unsupervised among these blood-loving savages.

Not that she could stop them if they chose to take Jakob from her. She'd known this when she agreed to leave the Named Lands in the regent's care, but she also believed her sister—the long lost Ire Li Tam—when she assured Jin that the boy would be safe. And her grandfather's voice, tinny and far away, offered her a measure of confidence as well when it whispered from the beak of the golden bird.

No such assurances for me. And yet, she stood here, committed to a path now difficult—if not impossible—to retrace, hundreds of leagues from home and sailing toward an empire she could only imagine . . . in order to kill its Crimson Empress.

She paced another hour as the sky grayed with morning. As she walked, she counted the steps and quietly noted the few sailors that worked the deck. She'd already mapped most of the vessel, familiarized herself with most of the crew, and inventoried most of its armaments without effort. It was an instinctive hypervigilance drilled into her by her father and his siblings during a preparation that had begun before she had conscious memory. Each Tam was shaped to be an arrow fired into the heart of the world to do their father's work, even as her father had been trained to do the same by her grandfather.

Obedience without question; trust without doubt. Only these past two years, since Windwir's fall and since becoming a parent and a wife, she'd questioned and doubted a good deal.

"And yet I'm still here," she whispered.

"Yes," a voice whispered near her elbow, "you are." She jumped at the sound of it and spun, reaching for knives she did not carry. "And now I am too, gods-damn it."

She knew that voice, muffled though it was by scout magicks. "Aedric?"

"Aye," he said.

She felt her jaw go slack from the surprise of it, but only for a moment. Then, she felt anger spark. "Why aren't you with Rudolfo? He needs you now more than ever."

She heard his own anger in the careful clip of his words. "I serve my king by watching over his son," he said slowly. "And if I'd not been harried by their Blood Guard I'd have taken him from you before you boarded this ship and returned him to his home."

She willed ice into her voice but couldn't find it within her. She could hear the fear at the edge of his rage and knew why: His father's closest friend—a man who'd been an uncle to him his entire life—had lost his son. It wasn't lost on her that he referred to watching the son. *Not the wife.*

She took a breath, and when she spoke, the words were quiet. "You should not have come."

"I will see my king's son safely home."

She heard the resolution and love in the man's voice, lending the words a heaviness that made her momentarily sad. Her choice to strike out on her own without even discussing it with Rudolfo was unconscionable. At the very least, he deserved the respect of knowing where she went with his son. She'd have been furious at any less from him, and she knew that by now he had to know and had to be enraged.

Her romance with the Gypsy King had been a strange partnership initiated by strategy, sealed with passion, and then broken by betrayal. Jakob had given them a shared focus, and a type of love had taken root in the midst of the events since his birth. But there was also the hard truth that she'd spent most of Jakob's life separated from Rudolfo.

She forced her attention back to the ghost that shifted before her. "Aedric," she said, "we will both see him home. You have my word."

"And you," he said, "have my word as well. The first sign of danger and I will take him from you without hesitation and I will cross any waste, any ocean, to return him to his father. You should never have left with him."

She heard boot heels on the deck and looked up quickly. Eliz Xhum, wrapped in a heavy red robe, made his way toward her. She felt the faintest brush of wind as Aedric slipped away into the gray of morning.

"Good morning, Great Mother," the regent said. His smile was genuine, wide upon his scarred face.

She inclined her head. "Good morning."

"You've the look of someone who's paced the moonfall."

She nodded. "I have." She decided to be forthright. "I couldn't sleep."

"Perhaps the sea disagrees with you."

"Perhaps," she said. "You're up early as well."

Now he nodded, looking out over the water. "Yes. Well, I often rise early for prayer. But this morning is actually somewhat special."

She felt her eyebrows rise. She'd watched the Mass of the Fallen Moon and had read of other holy days within the Y'Zirite faith. "Really?"

He offered her his arm. "Walk with me and I will show you."

She suppressed a shudder as she took his offered arm and let him set the pace as they moved forward. When they reached the bow, he placed his hands upon the railing. "This," he said, "is a historic moment for us all."

She stood beside him and looked out and ahead but saw nothing initially. "I can't—"

He lifted a hand. "Wait."

She waited as minutes crawled by, and then she saw it in the distance. At first, she thought perhaps clouds rose on the horizon, dark and moving rapidly toward them. But she realized quickly that wasn't the case. The sound of wind moving over canvas and water slapping against wood betrayed the truth, and she felt her stomach sinking into nausea at the sight that unfolded before her.

Hundreds of ships took shape on the ocean before her, at first ahead and then suddenly surrounding her own ship. They moved past relentlessly, and on the decks she saw soldiers in formation all facing her own ship with hands upraised in salute.

At first, she thought they saluted her, but when Eliz Xhum raised his own hand to return the gesture, she realized it was the regent they honored.

It took several minutes for the armada to move past them, and when it did, Xhum lowered his hand. "It's begun," he said in a quiet voice.

She wanted to ask what had begun, but she already knew the answer, and she knew there was nothing she could do about it.

Jin Li Tam closed her eyes and swallowed against the lump that grew in her throat. And in that moment, she wished she were a woman of prayer, that she might bid someone help her people in the hour of need that now fell upon them.

But at the deepest core of her, she knew it wouldn't have mattered, and she knew that even if the Named Lands could rally itself, a foe approached that they could not long withstand.

So she closed her eyes instead and willed them strength—willed herself strength—for the dark days ahead.

Chapter

3

Winters

The sky was crisp and blue and the wind was down when Winters stomped across the muddy snow to the gathering of wagons covered in drab tarps offset by the bright colors of the Gypsy Scouts' winter uniforms.

She'd not seen Rudolfo again after their meeting outside camp, and she felt the sting of his displeasure though his personal quartermaster helped her collect supplies. His anger toward her would not keep him from making sure her people were fed and reasonably warm until they arrived at Rudolfo's Seventh Forest Manor in the growing city of Rachyle's Rest. Winters had heard Lady Tam say a few times of the Gypsy King that he always knew the right path and took it. She could see that clearly in this and in a dozen other instances.

I wish I had a compass so sure. She was anything but sure of the path ahead. And she could only see the week ahead. When they arrived, she would help her small tribe get settled into the transitional barracks that had grown up in answer to the Entrolusian refugee problem. There was plenty of work to be had at the library between reproducing its holdings and constructing that receptacle to house the vast collection. And despite the town's rapid growth prior to Rudolfo's closing of the borders, that library had created a demand for labor, skilled and unskilled.

And then what? She glanced up, though the moon was not out. She'd done that more since she learned that it was the home her people had awaited all this time. She had no idea exactly how or when Neb would take them there, but she knew that somehow he would. Until then, she supposed she would wait at the library and use her time there to learn what she could about their new home.

She reached the wagons and met the young scout lieutenant Rudolfo had assigned as a part of her escort. He inclined his head as she approached, and Winters returned the gesture. "Lieutenant Adrys," she said. "Are we ready?"

He looked up and down the line. "Nearly, Lady Winteria. We still have some people rotating through the galley tent."

She nodded. They anticipated one hot meal per day for the last leg of their journey—more than they were able to do for the first leg. "Good," she said. "Starting out well fed will carry us farther today."

"Aye," the scout answered.

"Perhaps," she said, "I'll join them." She turned and crunched through the frozen mud, the smell of roast lamb soup and baking bread growing in her nose as she approached the large tent.

She slipped inside, savoring the warmth of bodies and stoves as she made her way through the line to emerge with a bowl full of stew, a chunk of sweet black bread and a tin cup of hot chai. She quickly scanned the tables and spotted an old man hunched alone in the corner. She made her way to him. "May I join you?"

He looked up, and she blinked when she saw it was Charles. "Certainly," he said.

She sat and studied his face. His beard had grown out more full than in his days at the library, and his eyes were red-rimmed and empty.

As mine were for Hanric. No, she realized, not just Hanric. But also her father, Mardic, taken from her too soon. And the others she'd lost along the way. Her mother, though she'd never known her. Tertius, the old Androfrancine who'd tutored her at her father's insistence.

And Isaak. She sighed and forced herself to sip her chai. He went back to eating, and she joined him, unsure of what to say. They ate in silence, and just as he started to rise, Winters reached out and grabbed his hand. "How are you, Charles?"

"How am I?" He chuckled. "Tired of snow. Tired of walking. That's how I am."

She lowered her voice. "You know what I mean." He looked away, and in that moment she saw his face awash with sorrow.

"I'm . . ." His eyes returned to hers, and she saw the control he tried to exert in keeping them clear and focused. His jaw went firm, but his voice cracked. "I'm unexpectedly lost," he said. "But I will move forward through this loss like I have all the others."

Yes. There had been plenty of loss before Windwir and vastly more with that city gone now from the world. It was hard for her to acknowledge that given her people's history with the Androfrancines. But for Charles, he'd lost what came closest to being his family in that genocide. And now, he'd lost a son.

The old arch-engineer continued. "We've all lost. And we've more loss ahead," he said. "The best we can do is to serve the memory of those we've lost by serving the light. Though there are times that I do not understand what that means."

No, she realized. She didn't understand it either. Not everyone could know the right path. Perhaps in those times, the path was made by striking out where no path had been before. She leaned forward. "Are you certain then that he's gone?"

He nodded and their eyes met. "I think they *all* are, though I know you do not want to believe that."

He was right; she did not want to believe that. But he did, and that gave her some pause. "I have to believe that Isaak and Neb escaped somehow with the final dream."

"Because your Homeseeker's Dream compels you to believe that or because it makes sense?"

She paused. "I trust the dream," she said. "I don't know why, but I do. I trust Neb. I trust Isaak. They've a part in this that is unfinished."

"Sometimes," Charles said, "things are left unfinished, Winteria." He stood, collecting his half-empty bowl and cup. "I'll hope against hope for your Neb, but I'm certain Isaak is lost. His sunstone ruptured in the fight with the Watcher; we all felt the explosion." He looked away again before meeting her eyes once more. "But this I'll say; I know he knew the risk to himself when he went out into the fight to protect your so-called Homeseeker. And I know he believed in your dream as well as his own. In the end, he gave himself for it, and I honor him best by serving the light he was in service to—the library he loved so well."

She understood that, and for the briefest moment she wondered what she would do if Charles was right and they were gone—Neb, Isaak and the Watcher along with the final dream he claimed to have. What if Rudolfo's Ninefold Forest and his library were the closest she would come to the Home her people had been promised? Thousands of years of dreaming come to nothing. She couldn't fathom it, and she involuntarily shook her head to cast off her doubt. "My dream and Isaak's were bound up in one another," she said. "And I have to trust it."

"I know," Charles replied. "But my faith was never in Isaak's dream. It was in Isaak." Then, he gave her one final, anguished look and turned, depositing his bowl and cup in the waiting bucket of wash water on his way out of the tent.

Winters finished her stew despite the tangle of worry in her stomach. She ate it quickly, and left still chewing the bread. When she reached the caravan, she noticed all eyes turned to the north, and she turned to see what everyone was watching.

Walking across the snowy plain, surrounded by mounted soldiers and Gypsy Scouts, marched a column of people. They struggled toward a solitary figure sitting, straight-backed, atop his horse at the crest of a hill. The green turban of the Gypsy King's office was bright in the winter sun, as were the rainbow-colored scarves of his houses as they ribboned on the wind.

She reached Adrys and saw the look of anger and sorrow in his eyes as he watched. She came alongside him and turned to watch them as they approached Rudolfo. "Who are they?"

He glanced at her. "Y'Zirites," he said. "From the forest."

Y'Zirites? At first Winters wasn't sure she'd heard him correctly. They looked like any other band of refugees, only moving away from the Ninefold Forest rather than toward it. She could pick out elderly couples and young families with children in the large crowd that moved slowly toward Rudolfo. "How have they come to be in the forest?"

"I do not know. But they've been there, secretly, for years. Building shrines and holding their blood-loving ceremonies beneath our very noses."

"And now where do they go?" But even as she asked the question, she wasn't sure she wanted to know the answer.

The scout shrugged. "I do not know where they'll go. But the general has ordered them from his lands. I suppose the Machtvolk will take them in."

If she hadn't personally witnessed the brutality of the Moon Wizard cult firsthand, she might've felt sorry for them. But she found she grieved instead for Rudolfo. Beset on all sides and wronged by many, saturated by losses among his friends and his family . . . and now his people. Her eyes went to the man on the hill, and she wondered how a life shaped by loss over so many years could retain such strength. Even the strength for something such as this.

As much as she hated knowing, she suspected she would learn that answer on her own if her life continued the path begun with her mother's death so long ago. Sighing, she gave one last glance to the shuffling group of refugees and their waiting, brooding king. Then Winters whistled her people forward to begin the last leg of their most recent journey through losses of their own.

Rudolfo

They gathered around him, shivering in the cold, and Rudolfo forced himself to make eye contact with as many of them as he could from where he sat in his saddle. His dark mare stamped and snorted, steam jetting from her nostrils.

He knew everything now. At least everything that Kember knew.

It really didn't change anything.

They'd been in the forest in small numbers since before Rudolfo's birth, quietly living their faith with ritualized cuttings using paints and inks so as to not betray their practice with their scars. They still held secret bloodletting ceremonies for the Mass of the Fallen Moon, where a proxy was chosen by lottery to take the Y'Zirite gospel upon their skin in payment for the sins of many. His father—but not his mother—had converted before Rudolfo and his brother Isaak were born. Kember thought the faith came to Jakob through Mardic or through Vlad's father, Ben Li Tam. Rudolfo's father had never talked about the experience, but the house steward had seen the scar; and soon Jakob was gathering small groups together to study the gospel of Ahm Y'Zir. The faith had taken root quietly and had become what it needed to in order to survive in the Named Lands. According to Kember there were quiet pockets of worshipers all over the northern regions. But he'd sworn over the blood of his wife that he knew nothing of Windwir or of the darker conspiracy that brewed throughout the Named Lands—the intricate Tam-influenced plot interwoven through the houses to bring down the Androfrancines and sow discord among the nations in preparation for what Rudolfo thought surely must be an invasion.

There was no doubt now that his father had betrayed his kin-clave with the rest of the Named Lands and—directly or not—had participated in the Desolation of Windwir.

"None of us knew of Windwir," the sobbing house steward had insisted during his final interview with Rudolfo.

And I believe him. But that, too, changed nothing.

He saw Kember now, shaken and hollow-eyed from his interrogation, and when their eyes met, the old man's filled with tears before he looked away. Beside him, Ilyna stood, her face a mask of white rage but for a single red line running along her jaw.

Rudolfo drew in his breath and then released it in a shout. "I am Rudolfo, Lord of the Ninefold Forest Houses and General of the Wandering Army. By my edict, the Y'Zirite faith is unwelcome within my forest, and those who practice it are beyond my grace." He let the horse step to the right and then to the left as he took in the crowd. "To be beyond the grace of your king is to be removed from his territories, and so I utter now this Writ of Banishment upon you."

He waited then and let his lieutenants and sergeants, distributed throughout the crowd, repeat his words. The faces below him looked up, some broken in sorrow and others livid with rage. He studied them, bidding himself to not forget this moment.

"You are to leave my lands," Rudolfo said, "and you are not to return. Should you return, you will be killed. Let any among you who do not understand this writ say so now."

He heard the thunder of quiet gasps and sobs; somewhere beyond that he heard a voice shouting. "Bring him in to me," Rudolfo shouted, and watched as armed men waded through the crowd to escort the young man to the front.

He couldn't have been more than fifteen—not much younger than the boy Neb was when Rudolfo had met him. Rudolfo could see the fear on the boy's face, widening his eyes and flaring his nostrils. There were white streaks from tears recently cutting across the grime of his face.

"What have you to say?" Rudolfo asked, and as he did, he felt the stirring of sympathy and did his best to quell it.

The boy's lower lip quivered. "I said I wish to recant."

Rudolfo blinked. *Recant.* He'd wondered if any would, and for a moment, he hated that it was this boy in particular. Still, he knew that how he responded would send a far stronger message than even his earlier words. "No," Rudolfo said in a loud voice. "There is no recanting."

The boy lunged forward. "But Lord, I—"

He nodded, and a Gypsy Scout shifted, knife in hand, to block him. "Telling me you no longer believe a thing is not a fact I can verify. I could never know for sure that it was so."

The boy burst into tears and tried to fall to his knees, but the scout held him up and pushed him back into the crowd.

"Anyone else?" Rudolfo shouted, and he stared at Kember as he did.

Kember met his glare, and his hands moved and posture shifted. *This is the wrong path.*

Rudolfo took the man and his wife in one last time and tried not to remember how like parents they'd been to him when he'd been orphaned. They and Gregoric's father had been his family during those first critical years beneath the turban. He forced himself to meet Kember's eyes and give no acknowledgement of his message. And he kept the eye contact until Kember finally looked away.

Rudolfo raised his hand to the sky and called down a pronouncement that had not been uttered in the forest in well over a thousand years. "Be gone," he cried out. "You live now beyond my grace. You are no longer welcome in my house."

Then, he waited there upon his horse and watched as the Y'Zirites were marched across his border by fresh-faced recruits of the new Forester army.

When they were well across, he dismounted and whistled for an aide to take the reins. "I'm not to be disturbed for the rest of the day," he said. The man nodded his understanding and left with the horse.

Rudolfo took the most direct route back to his tent, and this time, he went to the palatial tent he'd been more accustomed to rather than the command tent he'd taken to sleeping in. Another aide met him at the entrance, and Rudolfo told him the same thing he'd told the other. "And find me a bottle of firespice," he added.

He went inside, kicked off his boots and untied the rainbow-colored scarves of rank—one for each of his nine Forest Houses—from the sleeves of his long coat. He was peeling off the coat when the aide arrived with the bottle and a single cup. The aide placed both on the table near Rudolfo's reclining pillows, inclined his head, and then left.

When Rudolfo was certain the young man was out of earshot, he drew in a long, ragged breath and let it out. He could feel the anger shifting now back into the sadness it covered, and he kept his eye on the bottle as he slowly reached up and unwound his turban of office, draping it over his coat. He followed it with the matched set of knives—the ones his father had carried before him—and he paused there, contemplating them. Then, he continued stripping until he was down to nothing but his silk undertrousers and tunic, pushed his feet into waiting wool slippers, and walked to the large pile of pillows. He stretched out on them and took another deep breath.

He felt the tears now, and he reviled himself for them, reaching for the bottle and then pausing, his hand poised above it. It was the same bottle he'd requested for the last several nights, and still it remained unopened.

Rudolfo sighed and rubbed his eyes. "Gods," he whispered. "What have I done?"

"What you've needed to, Lord." Rudolfo started, his hand already sliding beneath the pillows to the small but sharp knife he kept hidden there.

It was a woman's voice, and his first thought was that it must be Ria again violating his borders. But he'd heard that voice under the muffled blood magicks of her people, and this voice was different—oddly accented and slightly higher of pitch.

Blood Guard, then? He'd seen their handiwork in the north and had taken one of them prisoner after they'd mowed through his best men in their pursuit of Isaak and the other mechoservitors. They were a tough lot; the prisoner had proved resistant to their more polite interrogations, and in the end, Rudolfo had killed her with his own hand, finding a type of satisfaction the bottle couldn't give him as he watched her die.

His voice was taut with rage. "Who are you?"

"I am Ire Li Tam, thirty-second daughter of Vlad Li Tam," she said. "Your sister by marriage."

Winters had told him of this woman; she was the one who'd compelled Jin Li Tam to take his son and leave in the care of Eliz Xhum for reasons unknown. His eyes narrowed. "My borders are closed," he said. "Your presence within them is unacceptable." He paused, slowly easing the knife free of its sheath beneath his pillows. "And coming magicked into my tent further compromises your position with me."

He felt the breeze shift, and he realized she moved closer, not farther from him. "I realize this," she said, "and I offer my deepest apologies for this intrusion. It would have been . . . *imprudent* . . . for me to approach you in any other way."

He measured the distance between them by her muffled voice. Scouts knew to change position as they spoke, never within reach unless they intended harm. But this woman was not following typical scout protocol. He licked his lips and chose his words carefully. "I'm told that you approached my wife as well and that you are responsible for her departure with Xhum."

Another step closer. "She also did what was needed. What she was made for. Just as I have." She paused. "Just as you have, too, Lord."

Rudolfo lunged forward, the knife up and ready. He felt himself collide with a solid form. His free hand sought her throat even as his left foot hooked behind her and toppled her.

She did not resist, not even as he put the tip of his knife to her throat. "Where," he said, his voice a low growl, "is my son going?"

"He travels by ship to Y'Zir," she said slowly.

"Why?"

She lay still beneath him, and he became aware suddenly of her warm, muscled body. "I do not know," she said. "I only know it was my life's work to bid her take him and go."

"And to await further instructions from Tam's metal bird?"

"Yes," she said.

She is not going to resist. Yet he knew she could've easily tossed him aside if she were under the same blood magicks as the others he'd encountered. It perplexed him, and he relaxed his grip upon her throat. "And why are you here in my presence after sending that which I cherish most from my sight?"

"I have come, Lord," she said, "to pledge my strength and my blades to your service and protection."

An unexpected reply. He thought for a moment, shifting his weight carefully. "And why should I wish your strength or your blades?"

"Because," Ire Li Tam said, "you will need them in the days to come."

"I doubt that very much," he said.

And when she moved, she was as fast and as strong as he'd expected, lifting him easily and throwing him into the pile of pillows. "They are yours regardless of your doubt, Lord." She was on him, her hand easily twisting the knife from his wrist even as she pinned him soundly.

He puckered his lips to whistle third alarm, and he felt her breath in his ear. "Don't," she said. "I don't wish to fight my way out of your camp." Her hands were strong upon his wrists as she shifted on him. "And how many more scouts can you afford to lose, Rudolfo?"

I've lost too many as it is. Rudolfo lay still, now feeling the firmness of her as she lay over him, feeling her breath hot upon the side of his face, and he found his body's unexpected response to her alarming. "How do I know you are who you claim to be? How do I know your pledge is true?"

She released him and moved away. "The Y'Zirite emissary is near," she said. "Accompanied by a squad of Blood Guard. They await the last sign fifteen leagues south and west, just out of reach of your patrols. The honor guard is magicked, armed with knives and dreamstones for casting in the aether. When the last sign is given, they will approach you."

"What is the last sign?" Rudolfo asked.

Now the voice was by the flap at the tent's entrance. "Empty skies," she said simply.

And Rudolfo knew it would do no good to ask what she meant, because she was already gone, slipping like a ghost from his tent. Instead, he would simply summon Philemus and have his second captain send a magicked half-squad southwest to verify what his heart already told him must be true.

Sighing, Rudolfo looked to the bottle but—once again—refused to reach for it.

Petronus

Petronus crouched at the shore and scrubbed the dirt from his hands and forearms while he contemplated the massive, dead world that hung above him. Its presence prevented true night, the darkest point being a shadowy twilight. The temperature dropped, but the jungle never quieted. Throughout the dusk in which they buried their dead and spoke over them, the sounds of birds and monkeys and animals Petronus couldn't identify played in the background.

What now? Their dead were buried, and what could be salvaged from the ship had been gathered and sorted by the mechoservitors and the last of Rafe's men.

He heard footsteps behind him and rose to his feet, turning to watch Rafe Merrique and two Gypsy Scouts approach.

The old pirate spoke first. "So what now, Father?"

Petronus saw weariness in the man's face, and Rafe's eyes were dark from lack of sleep. The Gypsy Scouts fared no better. "I think we need to get some rest," he said. "In the morning, we can decide our next steps." He paused, scratching at the scar on his throat. "Perhaps by then our boy will be awake."

And, Petronus thought, *be able to tell us exactly what we're meant to do here.*

The highest-ranking scout—a sergeant named Olynder—nodded. "Very well. Shall I organize a watch?"

Petronus shook his head. "No," he said. "I'll ask the mechoservitors to establish a perimeter. I'm sure they'll see the value of letting us get our wits about us."

He took another look at the vast world above him and then turned back to the crash site, making his way across the sand and up into the grass-covered dunes that marked their makeshift camp. The others followed, and when they reached the collection of crates and barrels and piles of salvaged gear and tools, the metal men had already started erecting small field tents.

Petronus approached the two metal men who stood over Neb. They looked at him, their amber eyes glowing dully in the twilight as their shutters flashed open and closed. He reached for the word they used and formed his question. "Is Neb still regenerating?"

Bellows wheezed before the first spoke. "Yes, Father."

"The rest of us need to do the same if we're to be of any use to you," Petronus said.

The other mechoservitor spoke. "Forgive my forthrightness, Father, but even regenerated, you are of little use to us. The parameters and outcomes of this expedition were not calculated with your participation taken into account."

Petronus felt a momentary surge of anger but held it in check. "Regardless," he said, "I'm certain you also heard the voice that compelled us to join you."

The metal man nodded. "Yes, Father. It is a curious development outside the framework of our dream."

"Yes," Petronus agreed. Even he was uncertain why the ancient god Whym would send him here, and until he'd heard the voice, he'd not even believed in gods that could speak much less direct. "It is curious indeed. But we are here and we are in your care. And we need rest."

The mechoservitor inclined his head. "My brothers and I will keep watch."

Petronus returned the gesture. "Thank you."

He was turning to leave when the quietest of whispers brought his head around. Neb's lips were suddenly moving, and Petronus strained to hear even as the two mechoservitors leaned in.

Beautiful? He tried to push closer to the boy, but the metal men blocked him. He raised his voice. "Neb? Can you hear me?"

"He is dreaming," one the metal men said. "That is a good sign."

"Dreaming?" Petronus glanced to the boy's burnt hand and saw the fist was tightly closed. "Is he . . ." He'd heard the word from Hebda or from one of the mechoservitors. *What was it?* "Is he in the aether?"

Petronus had first encountered the aether when Hebda had made contact with him. The arch-behaviorist had been able to infiltrate Petronus's dreams in the early months of his exile from the Named Lands and had eventually been able to induce dreaming even while the old man was awake, stretched out upon a massive black stone in some underground place. A small kin-raven carved from a similar stone had allowed Petronus to reach the mechoservitors and bid them admit his tattered band to defend the Antiphon.

"If he's in the aether," Petronus said, "we should be able to reach him."

Both mechoservitors released steam from their exhaust grates at the same time. One of them spoke. "Yes, Father," it said, its voice wheezing from a leak in its bellows. "But even if we did, that would not change his need for regeneration." The metal man stood and faced Petronus. "You also require regeneration. Tell your men to sleep, and we will watch over you."

Petronus glanced to Neb again. He'd spent days pondering the ramifications of who this boy really was. *Nebios Whym.* Kin, it seemed, of P'Andro and T'Erys, the brothers who'd forged the Order, shepherding the earliest years of the refugees who wandered the ashes of the Old World. Neb, the orphan boy, somehow caught up in the roles of Homeseeker to some and Abomination to others. He didn't know how it was possible, but he believed it; and that faith disturbed him.

He looked to Rafe. "Bring the men in," he said. "Tell them to get some sleep."

Petronus then turned to the small pile of belongings he'd salvaged from the larger pile of cargo. He pulled free his bedroll and opened it, spreading it out in the soft green grass. He left his clothes on and stretched out with his hands behind his head, gazing up at the sky. That broken world hung low now, and he saw unfamiliar seas and large islands scattered over it. In the middle of the sea, something white caught his eye.

His mind went back to Neb. He wasn't sure what the mechoservitor meant exactly by "regenerating"—he suspected in Neb's case it was about more than sleep—but he did understand the dreaming. And if Neb dreamed in the aether, there was no telling what the boy was experiencing. Petronus's own forays into that surreal space had reproduced his papal office, had shown him things he should not be able to see.

And voices I should not hear.

The old man tossed and turned, the itch of the scar on his neck unbearable and his mind racing. Finally, he sat up and reached for his pouch. He rummaged through it until he found the wad of cloth and drew it out carefully. Then, he unwrapped the tiny black kin-raven slowly. Glancing once more toward the mechoservitors who kept watch, Petronus slipped the token into his palm. He felt the slightest tingle as it touched his skin, and he shivered, suddenly chilled despite the heat of the night. He forced his fist to close around it and lay back down.

He bent his mind forward and focused on the sharp-edged carving in his hand. *Neb.*

Nothing.

Squeezing his eyes shut, he tried again. This time, he whispered the name as he thought it. *"Nebios."*

When it happened, it was sudden and jarring. He found himself suddenly surrounded by hot wind, his robes flowing around him. He stood upon the top of a tower the color of bone, a dead world suspended above him, casting a dim light over a jungle far below that whispered as it was savaged by the storm. The first warm rain began to fall.

A woman's voice, flooded with rage, rose above the roaring of the rising typhoon. It was nearly a shriek, and he jumped at it. "You do not belong here," she said.

Petronus spun around reaching for a sword he did not have, and he saw her. She was at least ten years his senior, her white hair wild and tangled, her skin sagging with age. She wore a tattered robe that hung loose over her bony frame, and it took no Franci training to recognize the madness in her eyes. "You do *not* belong here," she said again, pointing a long crooked finger at him.

Petronus took a step back, raising his hands. He opened his mouth to speak, and she cut him off.

"You have no right," she said. Then she raised her finger until it pointed at the dead world above. "Behold your home, Downunder. Behold your handiwork."

He forced his eyes back to hers. "I'm looking for a friend," he said. "Nebios Whym."

Her eyes widened at the name. "Whym." The anger drained from her voice until it was a whisper. "She told me one day Whym would come."

Petronus blinked. "Who told you?"

But she didn't answer; instead, her whisper became a singsong murmur. "Whym will come in the last days of Lasthome. A dream within a song shall bear him." Then, her eyes came back to him. "Where is he? He must come to me. He must—"

A howling rose from far below them, cutting her off. The sound of it widened her eyes and dropped her jaw. "Clumsy Downunder," she said. "They've smelled you in the aether."

More howls joined the first. "Who?"

"The Hounds of Shadrus," she said. "They hunt you now."

The noise grew in his ears, and Petronus felt his head throbbing. A wave of nausea washed over him, and then there were metal hands forcing his fist open.

"You should not have used the dreamstone," the mechoservitor said, taking the kin-raven from him. Around him, Petronus was suddenly aware of the pandemonium and clamor as they hurriedly struck camp. "What's happening?" he asked.

But a moment later, he needed no reply. The distant sound of howling told Petronus all he needed to know.

Chapter 4

Vlad Li Tam

Vlad Li Tam walked for another day and night before he found himself growing weary and thirsty. The kin-raven followed, racing up and down the beach repeating back any words that Vlad shouted after it.

As the sun started its slow climb into the morning sky, he paused and wiped sweat from his brow, startled by his perspiration. "I need water," he said.

"I need water," the kin-raven repeated, beating its wings as it landed on the black, hard-packed sand.

But from where? Vlad looked around and saw the same beach stretching east and west, running along the base of the same dark cliffs and lapped by waters washed purple in dawn. In two days and nights of walking, he'd seen nothing but the kin-raven, who left at sundown and returned just before dawn.

There'd been no other sign of life. Even the water here seemed dead.

And I would be, too, without the staff. He looked at it in his hands, cast red now in the growing light. It had carried him this far, but he could tell that whatever magicks it bore were only for a season. His muscles were growing aware even as his thirst grew, and he knew he needed to rest soon.

"Water and shelter," he whispered. The bird was out of earshot, but he felt a tingle in his palm—the slightest *thrum*—that brought his eyes back to the staff. For a moment, it went dark as dried blood, and then it became silver again. And even as it did, he felt the strength going out of him. It was as if what little he had left rushed out, and he felt his breath rushing out with it.

The kin-raven was back now, and repeating words it should not have been able to hear. "Water and shelter," it said, turning quickly, wings beating against the hot air, as it shot west again. "Water and shelter."

Only it wasn't Vlad's voice, he realized. It was a woman's . . . and he recognized it. He felt a rush of emotion at it. *Beloved?*

Vlad squinted and saw something in the shadow of the cliff ahead. He forced his feet back to their work, taking the staff in both hands now. As he drew closer, his nose picked up the scent of something foreign in this place, and it took him a moment to find a word that aptly described it.

Life.

The sun lifted higher, its light dispelling the shadows, and Vlad staggered from what he saw ahead of him.

Rising up at the base of the cliff was a patch of green—thick, high grass and a scattering of palm trees unlike any he'd seen before, heavy with an unfamiliar purple fruit. A murmuring sound reached his ears, and his stomach responded to it before he recognized it. He saw the glint of sunlight from its surface and moved toward it—a narrow creek that flowed out from the oasis to hiss into the hot ocean.

I am mad, he thought. But he knew if that were so, he'd been mad for a while now. From the time he'd fallen in love with a ghost in the water and found meaning in its song.

"Water and shelter," the kin-raven said again. This time, it was Vlad's own voice, barely a whisper.

"Yes," he said. He smiled, feeling a sudden lightness in his step even as every muscle and bone he had protested these final steps. Still, he moved forward until he felt the cool water flowing over his feet and the soft green ferns brushing against his arms and hands.

He followed the water to its source—a crack in the side of the cliff—and only then did he lie down in the shade and drink with cupped hands. He took the water slowly, waiting to see what his stomach would do with it, and then he sat, leaning against the cliff, cradling the staff in his arms.

I am mad, he thought again. Yet he'd felt the power go out from him, felt the staff respond to him and then . . . *this*. Water. Fruit. Shelter. What had she said about the parents' toys in the hands of infants?

Vlad shook his head. "Not possible," he said.

The kin-raven settled down before him, but this time, the large bird regarded him without speaking. Vlad studied it, cocking his head. How long would it shadow him? And who bid it do so?

He'd heard Amal's voice clearly from it; he'd swear to that. Of course, that was another impossibility. Like this island of life in the midst of nothing but scorched earth and dead water. He looked away from the bird and back to the staff. It felt heavy now, but he couldn't bring himself to put it down. He stood, refusing to lean upon it. And then, he stretched his aching muscles and picked some fruit.

An hour later, he lay in a pile of ferns in the shade, licking dried juice from his fingers, his stomach full and his eyes heavy. The kin-raven had sped off again, and Vlad suspected the bird kept vigil, flying up and down the coast, even as this unexpected place gave him shelter from the heat of the day. He smiled at the thought and felt his body relax. This, he realized, was the most at ease he'd felt in a good many months.

And cared for. He didn't understand how, but he thought he grasped who. Some part of her, he suspected, lived within the staff he had carefully tucked beneath him. And she would not send him here and let harm befall him.

Somehow, Vlad trusted that and let sleep take him someplace cool and far away.

When he awoke, he found himself sprawled in the sand, clutching the staff, the heavy weight of the kin-raven pressing down upon his chest. The sun was down, and his body felt strong, rested, and ready once more to walk.

"Be gone," he told the kin-raven.

It hopped from him to a rock. "Be gone."

Vlad chuckled and sat up. When the moon rose, he watched, stretching the staff out toward it and feeling the silver pulse in his hands. The moon was particularly clear this night, and he could see the slightest white scar upon its surface that marked the Moon Wizard's Tower.

"Be gone," the kin-raven said again as it took to the night sky, moving eastward up the beach.

Vlad Li Tam inclined his head in the direction of the tower, though he was not sure why he did so. Then, he turned and followed his dark companion along the cooling beach.

Neb

A warm wind rose up from the jungle below, and Neb heard the whispered name it carried even as it pulled at his hair.

"Neb."

He heard Amylé gasp beside him and looked over his shoulder. The voice was familiar but out of reach, and it evoked a mixture of emotion. Anger, sorrow and relief all wrestled for primacy, and the girl's eyes widened.

She sees it on my face, Neb thought.

"Neb." This time, the voice was stronger, closer. He closed his eyes and stretched toward it by instinct, leaning into the dream with his mind. What had the Blood Guard who'd captured and cut him called it? *Casting in the aether.*

"Father?" Three faces flashed across his mind, and he finally registered which one spoke to him now. Petronus.

Yes. The old man had been at the ship, holding off the Y'Zirite soldiers as the metal men prepared for departure. And he'd heard the other voice—Whym's voice—speaking to Petronus, though he couldn't pick out the words. And now, the former pope called to him.

He saw the old man stretched out upon his bedroll, eyes rolled back in his head, fist clenched and held tight against his chest.

"Father?" He tried to project the word, but the rising wind pulled it away from him.

There were hands upon his shoulders now, pulling him back. Even as they did, he felt something cold and dark moving between him and the old man, impenetrable as a wall. "No," Amylé D'Anjite cried out as he staggered in her grip. "You can't let her find you," she said.

Petronus was gone now and so was the wall. All that remained was the girl limned in the light of planet, bright with life, that hung above them. "Who is she?"

The young woman shook her head. "Do not go to her when she calls for you, Nebios Whym. Do not heed her lies." She backed away from him. He could feel the fear pulsing from her. "I have to go. You should go, too."

He stepped toward her. "But why—?"

A lone howl lifted from the jungle below, and the wind rose with it. Even as he turned in the direction of it, another joined in. And then another.

"Because the hounds have your scent," she said. "Fly away home and tell my father to come for me soon." She moved quickly, her long legs stretching out into a sprint. He tracked her course and released his held breath as her intentions became clear. He called after her as she raced up the slope of grass and spread her arms wide. But she did not stop and did not heed his call. When she leaped, it was high and arching, graceful as a swimmer's dive that carried her over the railing.

Neb turned to face the howling, feeling the robe around him constricting, conforming itself to his body in a protective sheath. *The hounds have my scent.*

Even as he thought it, their howls ceased and the wind dropped. He glanced over his shoulder to where Amylé had jumped. Something told him that were he to do the same, no harm would come to him. Not in this place. He turned back in the direction of the hounds. But that same instinct told him that it wasn't true of the hounds.

He heard them before he saw them, the sounds of their claws grinding on stone as they dug into the wall of the tower. When their long, dark faces rose over the balustrade, Neb stepped back. There were five of them, and they were easily the size of kin-wolves—maybe larger. But these were sleek and black, rippling with a liquid flow that was neither fur nor skin nor scale. The largest stepped forward, tearing chunks of sod as it moved.

A new voice fell into his head even as he felt the cold presence he'd sensed earlier. *Yes. They* can *harm you. They were bred to hunt our kind.*

"Abomination," the first hound hissed. "You should not have returned. The time of your kind has passed."

Even as it gathered itself up to pounce, Neb closed his eyes and poured his attention away from the tower and the hounds. He focused it upon the sole sensation of sharp stone in a soft fist somewhere far away where his body lay and forced himself to open a hand that he'd clenched tightly since they'd pulled him from the quicksilver and loaded him into the ship.

The vertigo that seized him was staggering, and even as he started to fall backward, he felt the dual sensation of bolting upright from his bedroll on the hard ground.

Neb blinked. Around him, men and mechoservitors bustled, strapping what they could to the metal men and shoving the rest into overflowing backpacks.

In the distance, he heard the baying of the hounds.

He tried to stand, and his legs gave out as a weariness washed over him.

"He's awake," he heard someone say.

A familiar face appeared over his own. Worry showed in Petronus's eyes and jaw. "How are you?"

"I'm . . . weak." His limbs were heavy, and he could hear the slur in his speech.

"We'll carry you," the old man said. He wrapped the kin-raven in a scrap of cloth and tucked it into Neb's shirt. "You'll also want this, I'm sure."

Neb heard the song even as Petronus passed the pouch to him. He felt the urge to open it, to hold the silver crescent within to his ear and be soothed by the dream it held. But the dream had become a nightmare, it seemed.

Metal hands swept beneath him, and Neb was lifted into the air and swung around over a metal shoulder. Another mechoservitor bound him in place with a cargo strap.

Petronus was moving among the gathered men, and another man barked orders. He was perhaps as old as the former Pope and wearing tattered Androfrancine digging dungarees and a loose-fitting silk shirt that had seen better days. There was a long cutlass tucked into the sash wrapped around his waist.

As they lined up, Petronus made his way back to Neb's side. He leaned in, his voice low. "They're waiting for you to tell them what to do," he said, nodding to the other metal men. "We are, too."

Neb swallowed. Behind him, he could hear the howling grow closer, though it was still far off. "I don't know," he said, his voice a whisper. He felt the muscles spasm in his feet and legs.

Petronus's voice lowered even further. "That is not an option now," he said. "If you don't know, then guess and convince us you know."

Neb closed his eyes. "We flee along the coastline," he said. "Away from the howling."

The old man nodded. "Then say so."

Neb raised his voice. "We'll follow the coastline."

Petronus offered a tight, grim smile and nodded. "Good," he said. "For now." As they started to shuffle forward, he kept pace beside Neb, opening a canteen and holding it to Neb's mouth for him to drink. "But we're going to need to hide somewhere and rest at some point."

The water was warm and metallic in his mouth. Neb swished it around his teeth before swallowing it, and felt his stomach gurgle both protest and a desire for more. He took another drink and glanced in the direction of the howls. "We have to stay ahead of them."

A cloud passed over Petronus's face, and Neb read in it that he had more to say that he struggled with. Finally, the old man looked away. "I think I woke them in the aether," he said. "They're called the Hounds of Shadrus."

Shadrus. The Marshfolk—now returned to their older name of Machtvolk—referred to themselves as the House of Shadrus. But all Neb knew of that mythic figure was that he'd brought his people, then the servants of House Y'Zir, down the Moon Wizard's ladder with Raj Y'Zir and his silver army over four millennia ago. Something Petronus said suddenly registered, and he wished he had a hand free to pat the man's shoulder. "They don't hunt you, Father," he said. "They hunt *me*. She told me they had my scent."

He heard Petronus's intake of breath and saw the furrowing of his brow. "She?"

Neb nodded. "A girl in the aether. We . . ." Already, the memory of it tried to fade as he put more distance between himself and the dream. "We were on the tower, watching the world rise." He hesitated, uncertain if he should say more. "Only it was whole," he said. "Blue and green and . . . beautiful."

Petronus's brow furrowed even more. "I was on the tower, too," he said. "There was a storm and an old woman. But the world was as it is now." He paused. "She blamed me for it. And for waking the hounds."

The old man's eyes told him there was more that he wasn't saying, but the exhaustion that rode Neb grew heavier. His eyelids were weighed down, and his mouth slow to find words.

Questions for another time, he thought.

"Try to rest. We're going to need you." He felt Petronus's strong hand squeeze his shoulder once, and then the old man shuffled off ahead.

Sleep pulled at him, its argument strengthened by the rhythmic back and forth of the mechoservitor's shoulders as the metal man strode along the sand. Neb resisted, forcing his eyes open for as long as he could. Behind him, he heard the baying of the hounds. Around him, he heard the whisper of waves and the constant chatter of the lunar jungle.

He glanced to his left, looking out across a twilight sea that grew darker as a brown and dying world slowly sank into its horizon. He'd seen it in his dreams over the last two years, certainly, but that had not prepared him for the weight that fell on him now as he saw it descending.

I may never return. The thought expanded, and the full realization of it made his mouth dry. *None of us may. Because they followed me here.*

Try as he might, Neb could not push the foreboding away, and when sleep took him, the howling followed him into that restless, dreamless place.

Jin Li Tam

Jakob laughed and clapped his hands before the rocking of the room tumbled him to the deck, and Jin Li Tam willed herself to laugh as well, applauding his tentative steps alongside a flushed Lynnae.

"Learning to walk at sea is hard work," the younger woman said.

Jin nodded, feeling pride grow in her as she watched the little boy grab hold of a nearby chair and pull himself back up, his face fierce with a determination she'd seen a hundred times.

He is his father's son. The realization brought a reminder, and she swallowed against the lump in her throat, forcing herself to speak instead. "You can do this, Jakob."

He smiled at the mention of his name. Then, biting his lip, he let go with one hand and then the other, tottering as he found his balance.

But the knock on the door startled him and he sat heavily, his mouth twisting into a frown that signaled tears. As Lynnae moved across the room to scoop him up, Jin went to the door and opened it. "Yes?"

Eliz Xhum stood with a woman she had not seen on the ship during her time aboard. She was tall, her hair the color of iron, straight and long. Her dark robe was tied off by a silver chain, and Jin could see the Y'Zirite runes in the white lattice of scars that covered the woman's face and hands. Jin found herself staring at the woman until the regent spoke.

"Good afternoon, Great Mother," Eliz said with a wide smile. He craned his head to scan the room for Jakob. "How are you and our Child of Promise today?"

Jin inclined her head. "We're well, thank you."

Eliz Xhum nodded. "Good. I'm glad to hear that."

The woman said something to him in Y'Zirite, and Eliz chuckled. "Yes," he said. "She does indeed." He looked back to Jin. "She says you have your grandfather's eyes."

She flinched at the words, losing her composure and feeling the heat rising to her cheeks. She took a breath and chose the best path she could. "I'm sorry? She knew my grandfather?"

The woman nodded, inclining her head as she spoke. "I did, Mother.

He would have been so proud to see all of his hard work bear fruit in you and your son."

Jin Li Tam had no words. Instead, she continued to stare until the regent spoke again.

"This is Mother Elsbet," Eliz Xhum said. "She is the Chief Mother of the Daughters of Ahm Y'Zir—a position of great honor among our people. She came aboard this morning to begin her work with you."

Her work with me? Jin Li Tam once more had to work to keep her face calm as the woman extended a scarred hand to her. "What work is this?" Jin asked as she took the hand and held it briefly before releasing it.

Eliz shrugged. "Primarily language and eschatology. But she can also assist you in Y'Zirite history and custom."

Jin opened her mouth, but the woman, Elsbet, spoke first. "I personally requested this assignment, and the regent was gracious enough to permit it." She bowed her head toward the man, who returned the gesture. "I couldn't bear to send someone else. I've waited so long to meet you, Great Mother."

Jin Li Tam forced her eyes down, followed by her head. "I am honored," she said. Already, she was forming her strategy for this woman. Reading in her face and words and posture exactly what path was best used to approach her, to gain her trust and then ascertain her best use. She smiled.

"Well," the regent said, "I have other matters to address. I'll leave you two to discuss the work ahead." A look passed between him and the woman; then he turned and moved down the narrow passage.

Elsbet glanced again over Jin's shoulder, and Jin followed her gaze. Behind her, Lynnae held Jakob's small hands above his head as he practiced awkward steps. "He's beautiful," the Y'Zirite said.

Jin nodded. "And strong."

Elsbet looked from the boy to the mother. "May I hold him?"

Jin Li Tam forced her mind away from the growing ache in her stomach. "Certainly," she said. Standing aside, she held the door open for the woman. "Please come in."

Lynnae shot her a questioning look, and Jin nodded. Then, Elsbet was scooping up the boy, holding him aloft to cluck and coo at him as he first smiled and then giggled.

While the old woman fawned over the child, Jin counted the places on her turned back where a well-placed blade might be most effective. She pushed her anger aside. "You'll forgive me," she said. "But I'm unfamiliar with how you knew my grandfather."

Holding the child close, Elsbet turned. "We were lovers," she said. "A long time ago." Her voice was so matter-of-fact that it caused Jin to blink. "I would have gladly been his kin-healer as well, but the kin-healing was reserved for your father once we knew the time of the Empress was at hand."

Kin-healing. She'd talked little with her father since he was captured and tortured by Ria, but she knew that was what the woman had called it. That, along with the systematic torture and murder of most but the youngest members of her family.

"There is much I do not yet understand," Jin said.

"Yes. That is to be expected." The woman held Jakob with one hand now, tickling his chin with the other. "Everything that transpires now is a product of prophecy and meticulous planning. Your grandfather, when he came to the true faith, was an integral part of that planning." Her smile showed teeth now. "It is a strength of the Tams."

Yes. And the resurgence that brought down Windwir was carefully planned, Jin knew, with many hands in the stew pot. Most of those hands were her brothers and sisters, nephews and nieces, though she suspected now that there were also others involved, likely from the heretofore hidden Empire of Y'Zir.

And certainly the Watcher played a role. She suppressed her memory of the ancient mechoservitor, resisting her body's urge to shudder, before returning her attention to Elsbet.

The woman placed Jakob into Lynnae's waiting hands. Her eyes were wet with tears. "I'm so very pleased to meet you, Lord Jakob," she said, kissing his forehead. Then she turned to Jin. "I've a chest of books for you—some you can read and some you'll be able to read shortly if you're diligent in your studies. I'll have one of the men drop them by later. And tomorrow morning, we'll start your language lessons. I taught your grandfather Y'Zirite, and he learned quickly." Here, she winked. "I suspect it will be the same for you."

"I hope so, Sister," Jin said.

The woman moved to the door and paused with her hand on the latch. "It was good to finally meet you," she said. "I've longed for this day my entire life. Your grandfather longed for it as well."

Jin forced herself to nod, remembering his words—spoken decades ago and carried to her by way of his golden bird. Whatever this woman thought, her grandfather had died believing her faith was madness and executing a plan that spanned three generations to end the resurgence by killing the Crimson Empress. "I look forward to your tutelage," she said with a final smile.

Sister Elsbet let herself out, and Jin locked the door behind her. When she looked to Lynnae, she saw the girl's face was pale and her eyes wide as she held the squirming prince. She could see the fear there and wished for a moment that she could just bare all, lay the truth out on the table, and have at least one person in her confidence. If it were Winters here with her, she might be more tempted to. But Winters was a girl who could now dance the knife with the best of Rudolfo's scouts. There was a strength about her that Jin trusted, though she suspected it was because she knew the girl better. Lynnae had accompanied her and shared in the care of her son for nearly two years, yet the young woman largely remained a stranger.

Because I've kept her apart; I've not let her near. Somehow, Winters had slipped past her gate, but Lynnae had remained shut out. And even with the young queen, Jin knew she'd frequently withheld her trust, holding back information that might've benefited the girl.

Moreover, she'd done the same with the man she claimed to love— the father of her child. And it took her no effort whatsoever to dispel all of it under the guise of that love. A love that protected and guided by what it gave or took, shared or kept. It was an equation she could run with nearly all of her choices and in the end, justify them.

How very Tam-like of me, she thought.

Swallowing her remorse, Jin Li Tam reached for her child and held him tightly even as he squirmed and pushed at her. "No, Mama," he said, but the words weren't what caused her mouth to fall open. It was the look of fierce anger in his eyes, so much like Rudolfo's, that caught her off guard.

Putting Jakob on the floor, she watched him crawl quickly back to the chair to pull himself up once again, seeking first to stand and then to walk.

She knew there was something buried in his resolve that held some kind of meaning for her, because she felt it in the form of tears that pushed at her eyes.

But Jin Li Tam did not fathom what exactly that meaning was.

Chapter 5

Rudolfo

Twilight stilled the thin forest surrounding them, and Rudolfo crawled carefully beneath his snow cloak, moving slowly until he lay between Philemus and his first lieutenant.

The second captain pressed words into Rudolfo's shoulders. *The monoscopes are effective.*

Rudolfo smiled. In Charles's absence, the mechoservitors had provided six of the devices, and this had been their first opportunity to test them in the field. His own fingers found the man's forearm. *Excellent.*

Downslope and upwind from them, in a small clearing, burned a single fire. Beside it, a solitary form sat eating from a metal tin near the mouth of a small, open tent. Nearby, a horse chewed at its feed-sack.

Philemus pushed the cold, metal monoscope into Rudolfo's waiting hands and Rudolfo held it to his eye, disregarding the leather harness designed to strap the device onto his head. As he panned the hollow below them, he held his breath. In the wavering image that the Firstfall steel reflected, he counted four—no *six*—figures that formed a perimeter around the man. The people were slight—probably women as the other members of the Blood Guard had been—and they crouched low to the ground, heads moving back and forth.

Philemus's fingers were light on his shoulder. *What are your orders?*

He frowned. The woman who'd met him in his tent—the so-called

Ire Li Tam—had been truthful about this much. He knew that meant little when it came to validating her other claims or proving the devotion of her blades in his service. Still, Rudolfo would take whatever intelligence he could get. He stretched out a hand, holding it over his second captain's forearm before finding his words. *Pull back for now.*

Soon enough, this man would find him, and Rudolfo need do nothing now. Ire had told him that the Y'Zirite emissary would not approach the Gypsy watchtowers until the last sign was given. He glanced up at a somber, gray sky that seemed empty enough and puzzled again at her cryptic words. Then, he pushed the monoscope back toward Philemus's waiting hands and slowly scooted backward on his belly, the snow cold against him, until he was beneath the ridgeline and could risk rising to a crouch. They moved even farther down the hill, ghosts brushing evergreen branches over their footprints, wiping the snow clean.

"There are only six of them," Philemus whispered nearby. "And we have the advantage."

Rudolfo shook his head. "No. This war has changed for us before it's even started. We bend to this wind and find a different path or we risk breaking."

The faintest change in the captain's breathing told Rudolfo what he needed to know about the man's thoughts on the matter. But he put that information aside, laying it next to Philemus's disapproval of the enforcement of Rudolfo's Y'Zirite edict. In earlier days, he'd have removed the officer and replaced him. But Philemus's willingness to question—even challenge him—was a trait he'd grown to value.

I learned it from Gregoric. The memory of his fallen friend stabbed at him, and he felt his jaw growing firm. That man would have taken an even firmer hand with Rudolfo, he suspected. And the second captain might disapprove, but Rudolfo had no doubt that the man would do as he was ordered, with or without a given reason.

Still, he continued. "You and Lysias told me yourselves that we are spread too thin. How many more are we willing to throw at these Y'Zirite knives?" He leaned in close to the vague shimmer that marked where his captain stood. "Do not misunderstand me, Captain," Rudolfo said. "I intend to win this war. But we will not win this one by striking first and fastest." He paused. "This will require patience . . . and precision."

Philemus's eyes flashed for a moment, and then he looked away. "Aye, General," he said. "What would you have us do?"

Rudolfo smiled at the evidence he heard of the efficacy of his words.

The edge in Philemus's voice already softened. Because men were eased by the confidence of their king even when that king felt uncertain.

And because they know you've never chosen the wrong path. Even as he thought it, a choice he'd not considered presented itself and he smiled at it.

"Perhaps," Rudolfo said, "we should invite our visitors to return with us."

Philemus made no attempt to hide his astonishment. "General?"

His smile widened.

Yes, Rudolfo thought. *A simple gesture.* Something to show that he still made his own choices, despite those others had made for him. "I know better than to tell you not to follow," he said. "But follow at a distance and do not interfere. Stay clear of the Blood Guard and do not let them see you." He waited, and when he heard no acknowledgement, he spoke again. "Do you understand?"

The doubt was back in his second captain's voice, and the words were clipped. "Aye, General."

Rudolfo nodded in the direction of his magicked officer. Then, he turned and set himself to climbing the hill, making no effort to conceal his approach. He took the slope with long, deliberate strides, his breath clouding around his face. The forest grew darker as night fell around him, and he whistled into that dark, choosing a cheerful tune. When he crested the ridge, he raised his right hand, pausing before he continued his descent. "Hail the camp," he shouted.

The sitting figure shifted, turning, and Rudolfo kept his eyes upon him as his feet chose their path down the snowy hill. By now, the Blood Scouts would be moving toward him, and he willed his men to obey him and hold back. He had a great deal of confidence in his own safety in this moment, but they were another matter. "Hail the camp," he said again. "Rudolfo approaches." He kept talking as he walked, his voice ringing out into a silent forest. "Lord Rudolfo of the Ninefold Forest Houses to some," he said. "General Rudolfo of the Wandering Army to others." He smiled as he approached the bottom of the hollow and his shadow twisted in the light of the fire. "That damned Rudolfo to those I've bested in battle or bed."

He was close enough now to see that it was indeed a man who sat at the fire on a large chunk of wood. The man was younger than Rudolfo but not by much, and his hands and face bore the scars of Y'Zir. His heavy winter cloak was of a dark fur that matched his boots, and beneath the cloak was a dark uniform much like those he'd seen at the Blood Temple where he'd found Vlad Li Tam.

And like those the Machtvolk now wore. But unlike the others, this man appeared unarmed, holding only a tin plate and spoon in his hands. A cooking pot sat to the side of the fire, where some kind of stew simmered.

The man paused and continued eating without a word.

Rudolfo stopped just a few spans from him. "Have you no words for me?"

Still, nothing. He felt the stirring of anger and forced it aside. He stepped closer, keeping his hands well away from the knives that hung from his hips. He leaned in, pausing to listen and hearing nothing but the sound of the man chewing. Then, he walked slowly around the fire.

"I'm perplexed," he finally said. "I'm told by kin-raven to expect an emissary; I ride league upon winter league to meet him. Yet when he arrives, he hides from me in a hollow. And when I approach, he ignores me."

Silence.

Rudolfo continued. "Regardless, you and the women who travel with you are welcome. There is warmth and comfort yonder. And much, I'm told, for us to discuss." He waited, though he expected no answer. "So come when you will. I will be waiting."

With that, Rudolfo turned and strode from the camp, returning the way he had come. The man's silence surprised him. There was strength in it. And focus. Rudolfo pondered it as he made his way slowly up the hill until a thud to his left brought him to a sudden halt.

He looked in the direction of the sound and saw a small, dark form lying in the snow. As he approached it, he recognized it at once as a bird. It lay unmoving on the ground, and as Rudolfo grew closer, he saw the blue thread of inquiry upon its foot and the scrap of paper it held in place.

He looked up to the sky, then back to the fallen bird.

Could that be it? But of course it could, though Rudolfo knew not how or what kind of dark magick could do such a thing. Somewhere in the distance, he heard another thud. And then, behind him, he heard the crunching of boots in snow.

Rudolfo turned, his suspicions now confirmed.

"Well met, Lord Rudolfo," the emissary said where he now stood below. "I bid you greetings on behalf of the Empire of Y'Zir and her regent, Eliz Xhum." The man inclined his head, and his next words were a knife Rudolfo did not expect. "I also bear word from your father."

Somewhere far off in the forest, Rudolfo heard another thud and released his held breath as the skies of the Named Lands emptied themselves, paving the way for conquest.

Charles

Shivering, Charles pulled himself out of his sweat-soaked bedroll and
cursed the cold as he wrestled out of his wet clothing. He rummaged
through his pack, pulling out a dry pair of woolen trousers, socks and a
shirt, the last of the images he'd just seen already vanishing from his
mind, though the memory of them remained in his body.

Soon all he would remember was the vague memories of blood and
fire and words whispered too quietly for him to understand. And beneath it all, a song that played itself in a loop.

Of course, he knew what was now happening to him. It was perfectly
reasonable, given the strain and loss he'd endured. Isaak, after all, had
been a son to him. And this was how that Fivefold Path of Grief carried
him through it. Terrors in the night. Hollowness in the day. A war he
could not win.

Because of all the things he'd made with his hands, that robed and
limping mechoservitor had been the only one to ever raise affection
from him. An affection that quickly became love. The idea that Isaak
was no more desolated him, and yet part of him scoffed at himself as a
foolish old man. "You built him. You can build another," he chided himself. "He's a machine made from a schematic."

No. He was more than that. And Charles knew he was done with
building. Isaak could never be replicated, nor should he be.

Those we lose are lost, he thought. He believed that truth despite his
fondest wish otherwise.

And I cannot bear that I believe it. So he warred against himself, even in
his sleep, and lived his days in the fatigue and despair of that conflict.

Charles tugged on his boots and coat, then worked the flap of the
tent and slipped out into a night that danced with the shadows of two
dozen campfires, all surrounded by tents and shelters of various shapes
and sizes. A scout caught his eye and nodded. He returned the gesture
and moved to the fire.

Charles didn't see the girl until she spoke. It wasn't the first time, he
realized. "Hello, Charles."

Winteria smiled up at him from where she sat on a round of wood, scarred hands extended toward the flames. She nodded to another round, and he tipped it up to sit on it beside her. He tried to smile, but he was certain it showed as a grimace. "You're not sleeping either?"

She shook her head. "No."

In the firelight, he could see the circles beneath her eyes. In addition to her own losses, her encounter with Rudolfo—and more, her betrayal of him, despite her good intentions—was added weight to young shoulders. "You could see the medico. Maybe find some kallaberry in the camp."

She nodded her head toward him. "So could you."

He chuckled. "I could."

But something in him resisted it, even though he knew there were a half dozen herbs or berries that could induce a dreamless sleep. *Because I need to walk this path.* And in realizing it for himself, he knew it was true for her as well.

A quiet whistle drifted over the tents—at first, he thought it was second alarm, but it shifted quickly to third. Winters recognized it at once and stood, turning in the direction of the noise. Charles did the same.

It was a soft whistle, with the obvious intent of rousing only the attention of the scouts, and they passed it around the camp in the span of moments. He saw an officer moving quickly through the camp and watched as Winters fell in beside him. "What is happening, Lieutenant?" she asked.

Charles caught up to them just as the young man answered. "There is a problem with the birds," he said.

They wove their way between fires until they reached the birder's wagon. The birder, wearing only his uniform trousers and the winter-issue woolen undershirt, waited by the cages, and Charles heard Winters gasp. Charles stepped up beside her and saw the piled bodies of dead birds. She looked from the lieutenant to the birder, then glanced to Charles. "They're all dead?"

The birder nodded. "And not just these, sir."

Charles followed the man's line of sight to one of the scouts who stood near the wagon. Upon his belt, he wore a small cage for the birds they used for sending coded messages in the field. Inside that cage, he saw two limp piles of feathers.

Winters's voice was incredulous. "Every messenger bird in the camp? What could do that?"

"Poison, perhaps," the lieutenant said, but the birder shook his head.

"Not here," he said. "I'm the only one that feeds them."

"Perhaps," Winters said, "they were poisoned elsewhere."

Charles thought of the birding station he'd seen in the Watcher's cave. Somehow, that mechoservitor had drawn birds from all over the Named Lands, forging notes and monitoring communications in the execution of an elaborate plan that had begun, it seemed, decades before Windwir fell. It was no stretch to believe that a capacity of that magnitude could engineer a poison that killed on delay.

The lieutenant whistled two of his sergeants forward. "I want runners, under magicks, back to the Seventh Forest Manor and to Philemus. We need fresh birds."

Charles's fear found words, and he heard them as if he were far away. "There may be none," he whispered.

Winters looked at him, their eyes meeting. "I hope you're wrong."

Me too, Charles thought. But it would be the ultimate tactic and one that would easily cripple the Named Lands by shutting down communication. Only it would best be used just before . . . He forced the thought away.

The two sergeants left quickly, whistling for their squad leaders. When they were gone, Charles looked at the young officer. "You may want to reach further," he said. "If I'm not wrong, Rudolfo's going to need a line of couriers connecting his key assets."

The scout lieutenant nodded. "Noted."

As he moved off with his men, Charles and Winters found themselves alone with the birder. Once more, the girl surprised him. "Do you need help burying them?" she asked the man.

"No, Lady," he said. "We'll burn them to control any contagion."

She looked to Charles. "Are you ready to sleep yet?"

He started to shake his head, and as he did, a piercing bright light blinded him even as a ringing filled his ears. The force of it fell on him, wrenching his stomach and dropping him to the ground as his knees gave out.

The light was gone now, replaced by an utter darkness, the likes of which he'd only seen in the Beneath Places. Charles writhed in that darkness, feeling the hot blood as it leaked from his nose and into his mouth.

He felt hands upon him, fighting to turn him over, and the hands were so hot that they burned through his clothing. "Charles?"

He opened his eyes, and a little girl's face filled his view, illuminated by the small lamp she carried. "Are you awake?" she asked.

"I am functional," Charles heard himself say in a voice that did not belong to him. The sound of it set his stomach to cramping.

And then the light was back, excruciating in its brightness, and Charles heard an incoherent babbling that rose and fell in its pitch. That voice, he recognized instantly.

It was his own.

Forcing his eyes open, he saw the look of rapt surprise on Winters's face, her mouth hanging open even as she tried to hold him to the ground. She called his name again, and he barely heard it above the sound of the nonsensical words that flowed out of him. He tried to stop, and the effort of it made his body tremble. He was vaguely aware now of others gathering nearby, following the horrific sound that rose from him.

Winters repositioned herself to cradle his head in her lap. She brought her mouth to his ear. "Listen to me, Charles. This will pass. Relax into it."

He felt his muscles seizing and spasming, and he stopped fighting to close his mouth. He let the words pour out of him until finally, after what seemed like hours, he was spent and empty, sprawled in the mud and cradled gently by the Marsh Queen's strong and scar-latticed arms.

He panted for enough air to speak. "What happened?"

"It's hard to explain," she said, "but I've experienced it before. As have all the dreaming kings before me." Her brow furrowed. "Neb, too."

A medico broke through the crowd to kneel beside him.

"It's the dream," Charles said.

Winters nodded. "It is. What did it tell you? Usually they bear words or images of some kind."

He swallowed water from the canteen the medico offered. "I don't know," he said.

But he did know, and the knowledge made his head ache all the more.

"Are you awake?" the girl had asked him.

"I am functional," came the metallic reply. And it was a voice he would never forget.

It was the voice of the Watcher.

Winters

The jostling of the wagon was both jarring and lulling, and Winters found herself sliding in and out of a light sleep. She sat with her back to the sidewalls and canvas canopy, her body covered in wool blankets up to her chin, as she kept watch. Charles slept soundly, stretched out beneath another pile of blankets, surrounded by supplies that had been rearranged to make room for him in the wagon.

She'd lost count of the hours, but she was certain that they were nearing the end of the day. Soon, it would be time to stop and make camp. One of maybe four or five nights left sleeping in the snow before they reached the waiting beds at Rachyle's Rest.

Charles muttered something and twisted in his sleep. The kallacaine had kept him down all day, though she knew the burst of glossolalia also did its part. Those times that it had seized her had left Winters exhausted sometimes for days. Eventually, she'd grown used to it and came to expect it as part of her role as a dreaming queen. It was a documented occurrence among the ruling family, many of the written dreams coming from these ecstatic utterances. But before Neb, she'd never seen another person—especially not an outsider—experience it. And when the two of them had experienced it together, in the forests at the edge of Windwir's desolation, it had confirmed to her that he was the Homeseeker they awaited. It was the beginning of her love for him as well.

But Charles was another matter, and it puzzled her. She shivered, despite the warmth that wrapped her, at the memory of his high and cackling voice and the white of eyes as they rolled back into his head. For an old man, he'd fought her well until he realized she was there to help. And then, when he'd finally relaxed into it, his voice lowered to a quieter singsong pitch and the words poured out from him.

After, she'd seen the terror on his face, and she was torn between believing it was simply the unexpected experience or believing that he had seen or heard something within his waking dream that frightened him so. Regardless, he'd drunk down the kallacaine powders, and she'd sat watch over him from the time sleep found him until now.

Her own dreams had gone quiet of late. It wasn't the first time. They'd fled her until she returned to her homeland with Jin and Jakob, and then the dreams had guttered back to life. They'd become violent and shapeless memories before quieting.

But now this old Androfrancine dreams. Why?

She heard him stir, and she looked back to him. His eyes fluttered before opening, and she was pleased to see the dark circles beneath them finally washed clean by sleep. He licked his lips, and she reached for the canteen before he could ask.

Leaning forward, she propped up his head with one hand and held the canteen to his mouth with the other.

"Thank you." His voice was hoarse and gravelly.

She sat back. "How do you feel?"

He closed his eyes. "Like I've been run over by a herd of wild horses. Every muscle in my body hurts."

She nodded. "That's common. Especially if you resist it when it comes over you." She paused. "We should be stopping for the night soon. We can fetch you more kallacaine when we do."

Charles shook his head. "No. No more drugs. They dull my wits."

She chuckled. "You don't need your wits nearly as much as you need your rest right now."

He struggled to sit up, and she nearly prevented him but forced herself to let him discover for himself. When he fell back down into his pile of blankets, she stretched out a reassuring hand to touch his shoulder. "It will pass," she said.

He managed to roll onto his side, facing her. "You told me you've experienced it before. What is it?"

"I do not understand it exactly," she said, "but I know it is the dream manifesting itself during waking hours."

"The Homeseeking Dream?" he asked.

She nodded. "Yes."

He sighed. "So many dreams. Your dream. Isaak's dream."

"They are the vehicle of heaven," she said, reaching back to her father's words to her on the morning after her first night of dreaming.

Charles looked away. "I do not believe in heaven," he said.

Not even when it seizes you, has its way with you? The words formed for her, but she did not speak them. Androfrancines eschewed such primitive notions. Metaphysics and mysticism, they called it. Instead, she offered him a weak smile. "Apparently," she said, "belief is not required for your participation in its workings."

"Apparently," he said.

She offered him more water, then helped him drink it. After, she repositioned herself so she could better see him. They were quiet for a space, though she saw from his face that he was deep in thought.

"You've experienced this before," Charles said. "Neb, too."

"Yes." The sudden memory of sharing dreams with the boy brought about the ache of loss. When those dreams had stopped, after he left the Named Lands to run the Churning Wastes, she'd been beside herself, cut off from him. She'd dreamed alone her entire life, and when he'd joined her there, it brought about a sense of completeness and understanding she'd not felt before. Something she'd not felt, at least not in the same way, in a goodly stretch now. "Usually," she added, "there is an underlying message, though it is not always easily discerned."

A cloud passed over the man's face, and his mouth tightened.

He saw something. Whatever it was disturbed him. She waited, and when he said nothing further, she gently prodded. "What did you see, Charles?"

He looked at her. "I saw a girl," Charles said. "A young girl." He paused. "She asked me if I was awake."

"Did you recognize her?"

He shook his head. "No."

She could see the uncertainty in his eyes. "Did you answer her?"

Charles sighed. "I did." There was hesitation in his voice. "I told her. . . . I told her I was functional."

I've heard those words before. Many times, she realized. It was a common response among the library's mechoservitors. A response Charles also had heard, probably since long before her birth, back in the days when he'd first re-created the metal men from Rufello's *Book of Specifications*. His furrowed brow told her there was more. "What else?"

His face was white now. "I recognized the voice I spoke with." When his eyes met hers, there was a fear in them that she could not place. As if what he'd seen and heard was not nearly as frightening for him as what it represented. "I think . . ." He paused again, looking away. "I think the Watcher survived the explosion."

The words struck her, and she could not comprehend the fear he felt in the swell of hope that she experienced. If the Watcher lived, the Final Dream lived, too. Those pages, carefully cut from the Book of Dreaming Kings by that ancient mechoservitor, that together formed their last Homeward Dream. The dream that would open the tower to Neb and ultimately, would open the path for her people to return to their promised home.

Back to the moon. Though she did not comprehend how such a thing could be possible. "That is a fortuitous dream," she said.

He stared at her, blinking, and she suspected in that moment that she knew what he was afraid of. He would not say it himself, so she gave words to it. "Don't you see, Charles? If the Watcher survived, it's also possible that Isaak and Neb were spared as well."

"Those we lose," he said, breaking off eye contact, "are lost."

Winters shook her head. "And yet you've seen one of those believed lost in a dream."

And despite his best Androfrancine training, he believed what he saw and it frightened him. It is a hard thing, Winters realized, to lay aside one truth and take hold of another.

He mumbled something, and she didn't catch the words. "I'm sorry?"

He drew in a deep breath, released it, and brought his eyes back to hers. "I have to know," he said.

Yes. Of course he did.

The wagon lurched to a stop, and she heard voices shouting orders. Soon a perimeter would be set and the people she'd bought with her blood would go about the work of establishing yet another camp. Until now, she'd longed for the comfort of a bed and roof, the quiet familiarity of the library.

But this changed things. And Winters suddenly suspected that perhaps that bed and roof would have to wait to another time at least for her and the old arch-engineer. It was too soon to know for certain, but if the Final Dream was out there, it had to be found; it had to be dreamed.

And it didn't matter to her what required it—heaven or prophecy or simply a longing for those they'd lost to have been suddenly found. What mattered was that they listen and respond.

She looked at Charles. *Such an unlikely messenger,* she thought. But then again, she'd thought the same when she'd met Neb two years earlier. And, Winters realized, she'd thought it each time she met her own reflection in the mirror.

Unlikely, she thought, was perhaps heaven's most fluent language.

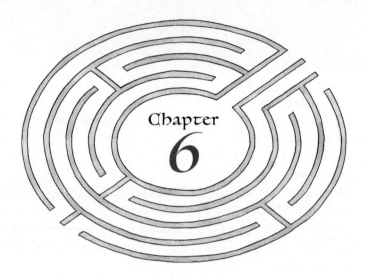

Chapter 6

Marta

Marta stepped back as the metal man's eyes opened, red and cold, upon her.

"I am functional," he said. He swiped a hand over his face and stared into the water in the palm of his metal hand.

"Were you dreaming?"

"Yes."

She nodded to the entrance to the cave behind her. "I brought you a cow. That's a lot of blood to paint with."

The metal man stood, and she watched as the light from her small lamp played out over its silver skin. "Thank you, little human."

It was still dark outside, though the moon slowly made its way to bed for the morning. In the last few days she'd become quite adept at slipping out. And at stealing her brother's sling so that if she were caught, she could claim hunting as her excuse.

Of course, she realized, if Dagya's father discovered that she'd stolen one of his cows, she'd have no excuse to fall back on. But it was bound for the tithe caravan leaving tomorrow for the Machtvolk Territories; another practice her father would not abide, garnering stares from the others. Still, it would be missed and possibly searched for. "You'll want to bury it when you're done," she said.

The metal man's bellows whispered in and out, powering his voice as it inclined its head slightly. "I will do so."

This was her third visit. She'd brought a lamb the last time—one she'd found wandering—but it wasn't until now that she felt a stab of guilt over it. Her father had taught her throughout her life that the only killing that was condoned—and even that with remorse at times—was for food or for the protection of one's family. She could only imagine his reaction to this kind of killing. It wouldn't be favorable.

Marta followed the metal man out to the front of the cave where the cow awaited, its lead tied to an outcropping of rock. "Do you remember who you are yet?"

He glanced down at her. "I do not."

She thought about the last two years of her life, living in the shadow of her mother's loss. Marta looked down and away. "Sometimes," she said in a quiet voice, "I wish I couldn't remember who I am."

She jumped at the loud crack of the cow's neck breaking. Her eyes wanted to wander up to see just how he did it, but she forced them not to. "It isn't very pleasant," the metal man said.

And like him, you'd never escape the dreams. Marta bit her lip. Nothing had been the same since the day that ash rained down and her mother did not come home. But her dreams, bad as they were, didn't need to be painted with blood. She thought about his answer. "I imagine it depends on what you're forgetting."

He lifted the cow onto his shoulder and glanced briefly to the southeast. "Yes," he said.

She followed his eyes. "I would only want to forget the bad things."

"I do not know how I know or if my speculation is correct, little human, but I suspect the bad things are as important to remember as the good things."

She thought about this for a moment and found she really had no reply. So she walked with him as he took the cow back into the cave. She'd brought him more buckets with the lamb, and she wasn't sure exactly how he would handle something as large as a cow. She wasn't sure if she wanted to know. She watched as he laid the dead animal aside.

"I have something for you," he said. He moved deeper into the cave and came back with something dangling from his hand. As he drew closer, she saw it was a rabbit. He extended it to her, and she carefully wrapped a hand around its feet. When he released it, she felt its weight pull at her arm.

"What is this for?"

"Dinner," the metal man said. "It seemed only fair that I compensate you for your assistance."

She looked closer at the rabbit. Its neck had been broken, and not too long ago. "Thank you," she said. "I'll try to find more buckets. Do you need anything else?"

The metal man looked eastward again, and she wondered what pulled him in that direction, even here in the cave. When he spoke, there was a sadness in his voice that made her feel sad as well. "Not anything that you can give me, little human."

He turned back to the wall, and she looked, too. The dark, dried blood was hard to decipher on the stone, especially with the scant light her lamp offered. But she could make out what looked to be spiders and a tower surrounded by words in an unfamiliar script. She knew that the pictures and words went farther back along the cave wall, and she wondered what other images he'd painted from his dreams.

"It will be light soon," the metal man said, turning to the cow.

Marta glanced over her shoulder to the soft disk of gray that betrayed the coming dawn beyond the cave's mouth. "I should go." She looked back to him. "I will come again tomorrow."

"I will have plenty of blood left for tomorrow," he said.

She nodded. "I know."

Then, before he could tell her not to, she turned and left, moving quickly out into the winter gray. She'd stayed out too late this time. *And the mornings are coming earlier.* Extinguishing her lamp, she picked her way through the snow in the long meandering path she'd made. She'd not worried about being followed the last two times, but the more she returned, the more she realized she was now keeping a secret that others would not approve of. And providing that secret with animals to kill.

Her stomach hurt at the thought. *And yet I will keep doing it.* But why? The strange mechanical man stirred something in her, and she found herself worrying about it, wondering about it during the day as she went about doing her part for the family.

After tracing and retracing her steps, she moved into familiar forest and merged her footprints with the rest of her village's hunters. She picked up her pace now, her breath billowing out from her mouth and nose as she broke sweat beneath her coat.

If all went well, she thought, she'd have the rabbit skinned and in the stew pot before her father and brother were awake.

Marta approached the house from the back, circling around to the shed where her father kept his knife, cutting board and whetstone. She had her hand on the door latch when she heard a clearing of the throat behind her.

"Martyna?" Her father's voice was controlled anger; using her full name was clear evidence of that. "What in the Younger Gods' Hell are you doing out here?"

She turned to face him. In the gray light, she could see the hard line of his mouth and jaw. She stammered at first, then forced her composure to return. "I'm . . . I've been hunting." She held the rabbit up.

His brow furrowed. "In secret?"

She cast her eyes away from his, her mouth suddenly more dry that it should be. The trick to lying, she reminded herself, is to let some truth in around it. "You told me hunting wasn't my part. I didn't think you'd let me go."

He growled. "Certainly not alone in the middle of the night." The anger was already fading, though, and she could see it. "Especially not in these times. It isn't safe."

She wanted to tell him that it seemed safe enough to her, but she knew better. Instead, she let him continue.

"We've got Marsh soldiers passing through daily on their way south. Jeryg's got a lamb that's come up missing. Thalnas is missing buckets. And Widow Tamrin's son swears he saw some kind of fearsome beast wandering the forest near Mayhap Falls. These are not safe times."

Mayhap Falls. That was only a sling-shot away from the caves where her metal man hid. Marta hoped that the alarm didn't register on her face. She looked back to her father. "I've been careful."

He nodded and took a step toward her. "Aye," he said, offering a forced smile. "And you've been successful, I see."

She returned the smile. "I have."

But her smile faded quickly as he closed the distance between them. "Let's see what you've brought home."

Marta's stomach sank as she tried to find another lie. He stretched out his hand for the rabbit. She willed herself to lift her arm, but it disobeyed, hanging loosely by her side. He took it from her and held it to the moonlight.

She saw the anger in his eyes as he nodded to the sling tucked into her belt. "You didn't kill this rabbit with that sling."

No. She couldn't find the right lie, so again, she opted for something closer to true. "I broke its neck."

Her father turned the rabbit over in his hands, now looking at its feet. "You didn't take it from a snare."

"I . . . I caught it."

Her father's eyebrows furrowed, and that controlled anger was back in his voice. "With your bare hands? In the dark?"

She nodded, but even as she did, she knew it was wasted effort.

He sighed. "Back to your room," he said. "When your brother's awake, you'll apologize to him for stealing his sling. And you'll be staying in until you learn truthfulness." He stepped back from her now to take her in. "Maybe keeping you out of the Y'Zirite school was a mistake."

The thought of that one-room building with its robed and smiling teacher twisted her stomach. "I don't want to—"

"And I don't want a daughter who sneaks about and tells lies," he said, his voice more firm and sharp than she'd heard it in some while. "At least those children are honest regardless of the madness they believe. Now off with you." He held up the rabbit. "I'll clean this when I get back. We're hunting the woods out by the falls to see if we can find any sign of Reyjik's so-called monster."

She felt a panic now, and it was all she could do to hold her breath and keep her eyes downcast. He stood still, and she could feel his eyes boring into her. Finally, Marta released her breath and made her way to the steps. She started knocking the snow from her boots and glanced up to see her father moving off in the direction of the village square.

She slipped into the warmth of the house and fled to her room, stripping down to her undergarments and crawling beneath the down quilt. She'd hoped to sleep but knew she wouldn't. Instead, she'd toss and turn and wonder about the metal man.

And she would worry, too, but not about him. She doubted there was much that arrows and knives could do to harm him. But the villagers were another matter.

If they did find him, she knew with certainty that they were the ones to be worried about.

Yet I said nothing.

She rolled over and faced the wall, but sleep still would not come. Finally, she cursed and blushed at the sound of her words. Then, she pulled her clothes back on and slipped quietly into her father's room. There, she found his largest shirt and trousers. In the hall closet, she tugged out his spare coat, a broad cloth hat and the boots he wore when he mucked the barn.

She crammed these all into a rucksack, picked up her brother's sling once again, and fled into the morning calculating the best route to get her to the caves before her father and his friends.

Neb

Neb moved from sleeping to waking as they slipped through the lunar night amid the sound of howling and the whisper of moving machine parts. It wasn't restful sleep, but it was all they could afford and more sleep than any of the other nonmechanicals were getting.

The rhythm of the metal man's long strides rocked Neb more gently than he thought it would, but there was still no way to find comfort strapped to the cold steel shoulders. His muscles ached from head to toe, and he suspected it was as much from the crash he'd somehow slept through as it was the hard steel that pressed into him.

And everything else I've faced. Much of it was a blur to him—the capture and cutting by Shyla and her Blood Guard, his rescue by Renard followed close on its heels by a flood of knowledge he wished he could forget. The very people he'd considered his family had left him behind to witness the fall of Windwir alone. And the power of the Seven Cacophonic Deaths had somehow begun his transformation into something far more than he'd imagined he could be, the result of some bargain he still did not fully comprehend. From that quiet cave and Neb's first encounter with his actual father, he'd flown quickly along the veins of the earth to Winters's side, lured into combat with the Watcher.

His body twitched as the sound of metal on metal flooded his ears, as the smell of pine trees and snow and ozone filled his nostrils.

Isaak. He'd watched the metal man tackle the Watcher and plunge into the quicksilver pool, saving Neb's life. He'd felt and heard the explosion. And now, not only was the Final Dream lost—supposedly the sole key to the tower—but so also was the staff and spellbook the metal men of Sanctorum Lux had set out to gather for this journey. And how many mechoservitors were now lost?

Neb pushed the grief away from him and it pushed back.

He tried to go back to sleep, but his mind would not slow. It raced, a dull hum behind his eyes that ached as all of his senses were ambushed by this new place.

He could smell the sweetness of blossoming fruit trees and wildflowers mingled with the scent of sea grass. He could taste the salt on the warm, moist breeze that moved over him.

And he could hear the baying and howling of the hounds.

At some point, Petronus settled in to keep pace with the mechoservitor, walking beside Neb. The man had to be past seventy, Neb suspected, and yet the old pope held his own. His breath was even and steady as they talked quietly, starting from the day they'd parted company in the Ninefold Forest nearly two years ago and filling one another in on all that had transpired in that time.

Neb watched him as they talked in quiet voices, noting each time the old man looked away or reached for the scar on his neck. And Neb especially paid attention to the line of Petronus's jaw—a trick Petronus himself had taught him. All of this unspoken language underlined the words themselves, giving him a broader picture. And punctuating it, Neb felt bursts of emotion at key moments, strong enough that he flinched at them.

Rage. Despair. Bereavement.

All feelings he knew well, but he knew this was not some empathic echo. These were Petronus's feelings. Products of his own path, not Neb's.

Neb blinked. *I can read him with ease.*

This was new. Certainly he'd done well enough in the Franci school, but this was beyond any skills he could have learned there and he suspected he knew why. What had Whym said? He would find his path by walking it, growing into the powers of an unexpected godhood.

He let the old man talk, closing his eyes and listening to the words even as he experienced the emotions that accompanied them. And not just Petronus's feelings about his own experiences, but also his response to Neb's. When Neb told him about the letter from Introspect III, rage of that betrayal rose up from Petronus like a fist. It nearly took the wind out of Neb, and when they finally ran out of words in the gray of morning, he found himself exhausted by the ordeal.

Neb felt a firm hand squeeze his upper arm, and he opened his eyes. "You've had more than a lifetime of sorrow," Petronus said. "Hells, we all have. Betrayal and loss on every side. And I don't know the why of it all, but I do know *some* things."

Neb met the man's eyes. "What do you know?"

Petronus smiled. "I know I've died and come back twice . . . once by my design and once by the dark design of others. I know I'm walking on the moon with a boy who now seems to be a god. I know we've come here, following a dream within a song, in a ship built by the metal men who heard it." He paused, and behind them a howl arose. "I know," he said, "that there is great purpose in all of this and I've no choice but to trust this bargain we're caught up in."

He squeezed Neb's arm again. Then, he slipped back to talk quietly with Merrique.

Neb closed his eyes again, letting the weariness wash over him and through him. His body craved sleep, but his brain resisted. The image of Amylé D'Anjite leaping from the tower and the hounds that scaled it haunted these quieter moments, chilling the warm comfort that slumber offered.

Instead, he pondered Petronus's story and his own—all of their stories, at least those parts he knew. They formed a tapestry stitched together by loss and hope, dreams and death. And always, his mind wandered back to Winters and the wideness of her eyes when she saw him in his translated form. He wondered what she was doing now and what her response was to the loss of the Final Dream he'd hoped to wrest from the Watcher.

And more than anything else, he wondered if she still loved him or if what he'd become lived beyond that kind of grace.

The pondering twisted to brooding easily, leaving him even more unsettled. Behind him, the howling drew slowly closer, and he tried to calculate how long they had before those large, sleek beasts overtook them. Probably by nightfall.

And what then? They had a half-dozen thorn rifles, a few men and a handful of mechoservitors. If he could somehow clothe himself in the blood of the earth that had he'd used to fight the Watcher . . . But the thought was stillborn. Even if he could find a source here in this place, his father had been clear: It would not serve him if it sensed his body wasn't strong enough to bear it. It might carry him elsewhere, traveling vast leagues in mere seconds through those silver veins that laced the Beneath Places. But it would not carry his companions, and he would not leave them.

And we can't outrun the hounds.

A glint of light to his left caught his eye, and he turned his head. The lunar sea shone white with the newly risen sun, and its brightness made his eyes water. The water stretched out away from him to a smudge of horizon indistinguishable from sky or sea. *If only we had a ship.*

"If only we had what?"

The voice startled Neb, and it took him a moment to realize he'd spoken aloud and Rafe Merrique had heard. "I said we need a ship."

Rafe Merrique chuckled. "Aye, lad. It would be a handy thing."

Neb nodded and pushed the thought aside. If he was going to wish for the impossible in the face of what pursued them, why not instead wish for a quicksilver vein in the earth or an access to Beneath Places that they could hide in? But instead of continuing that wishing game, he closed his eyes again and forced his breathing to find a rhythm in the steady pace of the metal man who bore him. Whatever did await them would require all of their wits and strength. So as much as he dreaded what might meet him in his dreams, Neb willed himself to sleep. And as he slept, he dreamed of a crystalline vessel, low in the water, racing seaward propelled somehow without sails.

It was a good dream.

He wasn't sure how long exactly his eyes were closed before the party's sudden stop brought them open. What he saw brought his mouth open as well.

Ahead of them, a scattering of glass structures stood above the jungle. Nature's resolve had left its mark upon the buildings but still, they stood. They scintillated in the light, reflecting back the blue of the sky and sea, the green of the foliage. Leftovers of some ancient city.

Neb's first thought was that perhaps they'd find shelter there, but then he realized that it wasn't the city that had captured everyone's attention. When he followed the line of their stares, his stomach twisted and he felt bile rising in his throat. There, just before the city, moored to an ancient dock set within a lagoon, lay a crystalline ship.

He felt Rafe Merrique's eyes upon him before he saw them. And when he met his stare he saw an awe that looked too much like fear in the old pirate's eyes. He wondered if the old man could see the terror in his own.

"Gods," Rafe Merrique whispered as he looked back to the waiting ship.

The still, small voice was a tickle beneath Neb's scalp. *Yes,* it whispered in reply.

Jin Li Tam

The galley was warm with the smell of fresh-baked bread and cinnamon-flavored chai when Jin Li Tam pushed her way through the door to take her seat at the table. A handful of crew and an off-shift Blood Guard with her close-cropped hair and her dark leather armor sat at the table for breakfast. The Blood Guard sat alone and silent. The sailors were rowdy—until they saw Jin enter.

It was early yet for breakfast—dawn still hours away—but she came here when there were as few people as possible. She preferred to take her meals in her room.

It was easier that way. The awestruck stares of the Y'Zirites unsettled her, and she wasn't quite sure how to act around them. Still, she could learn more by venturing out here and there. And the truth was the cabin left her feeling stifled, crammed into a small space on what seemed a small ship on such a vast ocean.

A serving boy, his scars white on skin red from the heat of the kitchen, raced out upon her arrival. His eyes were wide despite having served her a half-dozen times before, and his hands shook as he poured her chai. When he inclined his head, she returned the gesture, then sipped her tea while he hurried away to fetch food for her.

She breakfasted on fresh fruit and crisp bacon served with a sweet, dark bread and pears soaked in a sauce she did not recognize. Jin ate quickly and slipped out of the galley and moved aft to the prayer deck where Sister Elsbet awaited.

The woman looked up from where she knelt. Her hair was braided, hanging heavily over her shoulder to coil on the ground. "Great Mother," she said. "You're early."

Jin Li Tam nodded. "I rise early. I've already danced the knives and had breakfast."

Elsbet smiled and climbed slowly to her feet. "I used to watch your grandfather practice. The Tams have a distinct . . . style."

She mentioned Grandfather. It was the second time, and this told Jin it was an area she could drop her nets. "You were close," she said.

"Yes. Very. He and Jakob were the first to convert during the Watcher's Vigil. I met him when he made a pilgrimage to Y'Zir. I was assigned to tutor him, but things took . . . a different direction." The woman smiled.

"You said something about being his kin-healer?"

Sister Elsbet folded up her prayer mat. "If the Vessel had held, I would have. But it was not time."

They walked to the small chapel abaft and ducked through its small hatch. It housed a simple altar and two chairs. To the left of the altar sat an open Rufello lockbox.

Elsbet walked to the box. "Now," she said with a smile, "it's time."

She drew out a small phial and a wooden box and sat, pointing to the chair across from her. "Sit. We don't have much time. Maybe a week."

Jin sat.

Elsbet leaned forward, unstopping the phial. "Open your mouth and stick out your tongue."

Jin cocked her head. "I thought you were tutoring me in language and eschatology?"

"I am. This will help."

It was not in her nature to trust, especially when it came to matters concerning Y'Zirites. She forced her tongue out and watched as Elsbet drew out a glass dropper and touched it to her. The taste flooded her mouth, sour and heavy, and Jin's stomach clenched. Memories of breakfast gurgled in her throat. "Gods," she muttered. "What is it?"

Elsbet clucked her tongue. "Blood magicks. The mildest of doses. It's far better if we can start younger—Jakob's age even—but this will be fine for our needs."

Jin felt the nausea spreading out into the rest of her body, becoming a dull ache. She closed her eyes against the urge to vomit.

Elsbet patted her hand. "It will pass."

Jin felt the cramps now and gasped. "How is this helping?"

The old woman held up the box. "I'll show you." Opening the carved lid, she lifted out a leather cord. At the end of it, a small carved stone object dangled. "Now, lean forward."

Jin did and felt the necklace settle over her head and onto her shoulders. When the cold stone touched the skin of her chest, she felt a vertigo take her, and only the woman's steadying hands kept her from falling over.

"Steady." *Steady.*

Jin blinked. It was like an echo. The word in her ears followed close on the heels by the word in her mind. She forced herself to look at the woman across from her. "What is happening?"

"Close your eyes," Elsbet said. *Close your eyes.*

She did, and as she did, she felt the weather change. The cold, wet morning air was gone. Instead, Jin felt sunshine on her face, and the crash of waves had been replaced by birds singing.

She opened her eyes. They sat in a field now—a meadow of green speckled with purple flowers—on a rise overlooking a vast forest. She smelled summer on the warm wind. "Where are we?"

Elsbet smiled. "We're in the aether. The stone and the blood magicks can bring you there. But you've been here before without them."

Yes. She'd thought they were dreams—she'd visited the Plains of Wind-wir to find the bones had all been dug up. A kin-raven had quoted Y'Zirite scripture to her just hours before Jakob was born. "How did you know?"

"It was a likely outcome of your pregnancy," she said. "A side effect of bearing the Child of Promise." She stood up and stretched. "Of course, we need nothing so elaborate as this for our lessons. I just thought you might enjoy a momentary diversion."

Her stomach was settling, and the sunlight felt good. "How are you doing this?"

"It's like dreaming awake," the woman said. "The stone is a conduit. The blood magicks give you the ability to use the stone." She smiled. "If you start when you're small—say, as a young Daughter of Ahm just four years old—and practice your entire life, you can learn to shape things here."

Learn to shape things here. The echo was back, and she understood it now. "You're not speaking Landlish," she said.

Mother Elsbet shook her head. "I am not. I'm speaking V'Ral, the im-perial language of Y'Zir. You are gathering the meaning of the words from my thoughts."

Her nausea was forgotten entirely now, and she felt wonder pulling at her. It wasn't the first time. She'd seen miracles of blood magick both on the battlefield in the form of near-invincible scouts but also there on the ground, as they brought Petronus back from the dead, choking his way to life through a sliced throat even as the wound healed itself. She'd seen the miracle of that same blood magick heal her child after she'd begged for Jakob's life as she knelt and clutched at Ria's feet.

The memories brought back a rush of emotion. Gratitude and shame, anger and hope. Across from her, Elsbet flinched, and they were suddenly back in the room. "I'm . . . sorry," she said in a quiet voice. Her face was white. "You have strong feelings, Great Mother."

Jin Li Tam felt heat rising to her cheeks along with a sudden sense of violation. She instinctively reached for the necklace, but instead of claw-ing it off, she forced herself to breathe. She'd not just seen the woman flinch and heard her gasp, she'd felt Elsbet's surprise in those moments before the woman brought them back to this space and even now. "I do have strong feelings," she agreed. *And I am uncomfortable sharing them with you,* she thought. "How does the stone convey them?"

Elsbet smoothed her long robe as she sat. "Usually as vague impres-sions. But yours are quite powerful."

Jin's eyes narrowed. "And it lets me see thoughts."

"Yes. But only the ones I present to you. Trying to find anything else would be like searching for a flea on a sand dune." She held out her own hand, and Jin noticed for the first time that she also had a stone—carved into a tiny kin-raven—tied to a leather cord wrapped around her hand. "The stones—and the aether—are really intended for dreaming. They're much more effective if the user is asleep."

Jin reached down and lifted her own stone off her chest. It was shaped like one of those dark messengers as well. Most Tams were as well educated as any Androfrancine, but she'd never seen or heard of such a thing. "Where do they come from?"

"They're very rare. Mined from the Beneath Places."

Jin released it and felt the slightest tingle as it touched the soft skin of her chest. "I've never seen such a thing."

"No," Elsbet said. "You would not have. Even if those Deicides had known of them, it's not magick they would've deemed safe for you." She cleared her voice as if it might somehow dispel the air of disgust her words carried. "But to the work at hand. We'll meet each morning after prayer if you find that agreeable, Great Mother. I think you'll find that the stone will help you pick up V'Ral much faster. We'll study language in the mornings; eschatology and customs in the afternoons."

Jin Li Tam inclined her head. "Very well."

Elsbet smiled and returned the gesture. "Good." *Good.*

From there, the older woman started pointing to objects around the room, stating what they were in Landlish while Jin replied in V'Ral. But even as she parroted back the words, she was elsewhere, busy cataloging what she'd learned of the dark stone that dangled at her throat.

Jin Li Tam added that knowledge to her growing inventory. She would learn everything this woman could teach her, she would do the same with every person who crossed her path, and she would use that information to assassinate the Crimson Empress and bring this madness to an end. After, she would take her son home where he belonged.

And where I *belong,* she thought, hoping that it was true that the woman across from her could not read her mind or comprehend exactly why she smiled.

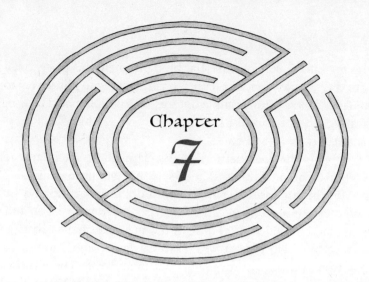

Chapter 7

Rudolfo

Rudolfo sat across from the emissary of Y'Zir and imagined the pleasure it would bring to kill the man. Still, there was a Franci proverb that suggested killing the bird because of the color of its thread was inefficient, and he knew that his mind wandered toward murder because of the document that he held in his hands—not because of the man who bore it to him.

The Gypsy King leaned forward and chose his words carefully. "Emissary El Anyr," he said, "I appreciate your assurances, but you can certainly imagine my surprise and consternation regarding this so-called treaty." Rudolfo looked down at it again, scanned the thirty-year-old parchment, shuffling its pages back to the last. The page that sank his heart into a sorrow that twisted itself into rage.

My father's signature and signet.

He knew both well. And the terms and conditions of the treaty staggered him. It named Rudolfo chancellor; it also called not only for the protection but also the promotion of the Y'Zirite faith within the Named Lands—and for the exile of any remnant of the Androfrancine Order.

As well as the establishment of a unified constabulary and educational system.

El Anyr inclined his head. "Yes, Chancellor Rudolfo. I completely understand. Regent Xhum has asked me to personally convey his regret that he could not be here himself to speak with you about these matters.

He also regrets the duplicity that has brought you to this place. But again, I assure you: These were your father's wishes for you. His legacy to you, if you will." When El Anyr smiled, it was wide and warm. "Your part in the healing of the world."

Chancellor of the Named Lands.

Rudolfo laid the document aside and clapped. An attendant stepped out of the command tent's shadows with a carafe of chilled peach wine. After both glasses were refilled, Rudolfo took a sip and savored the sweetness on his tongue. "And you wish me to go with you and your escort to the Divided Isle?" He scanned the document. "To negotiate the surrender—" The emissary's eyebrows went up and Rudolfo paused.

"Not to negotiate," El Anyr said, "but to facilitate. There is no other option for your neighbors but unconditional surrender. You will call together the council, present the terms and call for a dissolution of kinclave and a pledge of fealty to the Crimson Empress and her regent. General Yazmeera has established a command headquarters there, and she will work with you in the transition ahead."

Rudolfo put his glass down and rubbed his temples. The dull ache behind them was nearly constant now, with too little sleep and too much stress fueling it. He'd returned to camp with the emissary and the Blood Guard to find his worst suspicions true—every bird in the camp had died. Philemus had sent runners out to reestablish lines of communication, but it would be days—maybe weeks—before they would have any reliable news of what transpired in the lower Named Lands.

Still, it took little for Rudolfo to imagine it. Ria would certainly have brought her Machtvolk armies to her southern borders, creating a wall of swords and spears at the back of his neighbors in Turam and on the Entrolusian Delta. Pylos, already fallen, would no doubt serve as Y'Zir's foothold on the mainland, and if El Anyr spoke true, the Divided Isle and its loose affiliation of counties and volunteer militias would have quickly been overrun by an army they'd never imagined possible.

Rudolfo sighed. "Very well." He forced resolve into his voice, but beneath it, the anger coiled and his mind turned to murder again.

Why do I want so badly to kill this man? Was it the smug face? The assured tone of voice? Or was it simply that this was the man who had driven home the last nail into Rudolfo's heart, the one who had brought the last bit of evidence necessary for him to judge a father he'd revered his entire life.

I named my son for him. His stomach clenched at the thought.

He looked up and met the emissary's eyes. "I can arrange for us to leave first thing tomorrow morning."

The emissary nodded, and Rudolfo started to rise, then stopped when he saw his guest did not. "There are two other matters for us to discuss," he said, "though I fear they may be difficult topics."

Rudolfo settled back into his cushions. He lifted the wineglass and sipped. "Yes?"

El Anyr offered a nervous smile. "First, there is the matter of the mechoservitors. I understand that Lady Tam bore word to you of the regent's request? They are to be escorted to the Divided Isle as well."

Rudolfo nodded. "She did bear that word to me, though she told me it was a mechoservitor who requested it—an Y'Zirite mechanical called the Watcher." He noted the cloud that passed over the man's face when he mentioned the name; then he continued. "Of course, at the time I was unaware of the full nature of the relationship existing between the Ninefold Forest and the Empire of Y'Zir."

"Yes, absolutely," the emissary agreed. He opened his mouth to say more, but Rudolfo cut him off.

"And I'm certain you realize that they are actually essential to my work at the new library," he said with a smile. "Especially in light of the books destroyed in the insurgents' bombing."

El Anyr returned the smile. "Certainly. And to be perfectly honest, I believe we can accommodate your need if you would grant General Yazmeera the grace of a small complement of Blood Guard. The added security, I'm sure, would be welcome given your present standing in the Named Lands."

Rudolfo saw the pieces in this game of Queen's War as they moved over the invisible board between them. "I think the general's forces are far too valuable in the southern reaches at this time; however I'll gladly increase my own security."

The emissary's smile widened, and Rudolfo knew that now the net was laid out for him, even before the words were spoken. "I think that may be sufficient, Chancellor." He paused. "I have but one condition."

Rudolfo raised his eyebrows. "Yes?"

"There is a mechoservitor in your care that goes by the designation of Isaak. Regent Xhum was most insistent that this particular mechoservitor be brought south with haste. The others, I believe, can be left to their work, though I'll have to seek the regent's confirmation of this."

Rudolfo's eyes narrowed. "Let us be perfectly clear. You want Isaak because of the spell he bears."

The emissary shrugged. "Why the regent wishes this is not something I am privy to. But he was most emphatic that the mechanical enter into Y'Zirite care."

"I would gladly meet this request," Rudolfo lied, "but there has been an unfortunate incident involving the mechoservitor in question." He waited, watching the man's blue eyes for some betrayal of emotion. He saw nothing. "Isaak was destroyed in the Machtvolk Territories in an altercation with your so-called Watcher." He leaned forward and saw the first hint of those clouds regathering on the man's face. "I understand the earthquake from the explosion was felt for league upon league, well past the ruins of Windwir, so I'm certain your Watcher can confirm this fact." The man winced at that, and Rudolfo forced his smile to stay behind his camouflage of concern. "And what other matter did you have for us to discuss? I'm afraid I will need to excuse myself soon to make preparations for our journey south. . . ."

El Anyr cleared his throat. "Yes. Well, this other matter is too recent for Regent Xhum to have offered any instruction, but I understand that you've recently banned the practice of the Y'Zirite faith in the Ninefold Forest and have exiled its practitioners?"

Rudolfo nodded, knowing what came next after his reading of the treaty. "I have."

"An understandable decision based on the information available at the time," El Anyr offered. "But surely now you see the untenable nature of this choice given the terms of your father's treaty?"

The anger spiked, and Rudolfo wasn't certain that he could keep it in check much longer. "Tenable or not," he said slowly, "my orders stand for now." And to punctuate his words, he climbed to his feet.

El Anyr did not. He looked up, his own eyes wide at Rudolfo's careful words and sudden movement. And others in the tent—invisible Blood Guard that he could not see—must have also been surprised, because he felt the softest breeze of movement as they drew closer. The emissary's words were hurried, clumsy, betraying his surprise. "Regent Xhum will likely take great exception to this, Chancellor, and—"

Rudolfo's voice was cold. "And when he does, he may do so *personally.* I will gladly discuss it with him . . . and him alone." Then, he forced the anger aside. "And with that said, Emissary El Anyr, I believe our business here is completed. I will be ready to ride at first light."

Not waiting for a reply, Rudolfo inclined his head and strode past the man, brushing against the ghost of a magicked scout as he left the tent.

Once back in the wind-driven snow, Rudolfo turned north and made for the edge of camp. He did not wait for his men, and none questioned him as his deliberate stride increased in pace until a near run. What he longed for, what he willed with all of his being, was a place out of earshot where he could bellow his rage and despair at the cold white sky above him.

But in the end, Rudolfo, son of Jakob, settled for a quiet stream of curses, carried by gouts of steam into the winter air around him. Then he turned back for camp, for there was much to do. There would be hurried meetings with his commanders and scouts, and packing, and after that, he would gather those of his people that he could to bear witness.

When they stood around him with the rising sun, he would name his second captain, Philemus, Over-sheriff of the Wood, placing his green turban of office and his scout knives into that man's care—something done only three times in the history of his people in the New World.

Then afterward, Rudolfo would ride south to honor a treaty that he'd been shaped both to serve and to loathe, and he would save as many Named Lands' lives as he could with that gesture.

Vlad Li Tam

Vlad Li Tam lost count of the days and nights that he walked, remembering only the four times he paused at the oases that presented themselves to him just as his strength began to flag.

Those nights, he slept with his belly full, folded into leaves that cooled him or warmed him as needed, and awakened refreshed and ready to walk again.

The kin-raven, his constant companion now, continued its back and forth as it sped west and then back to him throughout his pilgrimage.

Finally, one afternoon when the sun burned hot and high, the bird flew forth and did not return. Vlad pondered it as he lifted first one foot and then the other, feeling the heat of the sand despite the thick calluses on his feet. He'd grown used to the kin-raven and had even begun to think of it as a friend of sorts in this desolate place.

Not that it is good for anything. He noted its lack of usefulness with a wry smile. Like every Tam before him, he'd been trained from an early age to identify every resource—animal, mineral or vegetable—and keep it inventoried against the day that it might be needed in his family's work.

Of course, also in keeping with his training, he knew that the most potent, effective weapon or tool any Tam could lay hold of was family, and the thought of them brought both shame and longing to the surface of his heart. He'd borne the loss of most of them; he could bear the loss of this bird.

But at the end of the day, as the sun sank low, Vlad heard the kin-raven's cry echoing along the cliff line, and he saw its dark shadow as it circled ahead.

What have you found for me? Vlad drew in a lungful of hot air and felt strength surge into him from the staff. He set that strength into his feet and shuffled them forward until he stopped at a pile of dark boulders at the base of the cliffs.

The kin-raven landed upon one of the boulders and tipped its head. "Be gone," it said.

Vlad squinted at the black stones until he saw what he assumed the kin-raven intended him to see. When he did, he chuckled. "Yes," he said. "You have purpose after all."

Stretching up behind the kin-raven, obscured in twilight shadows, a narrow stairway had been cut into the cliff.

Vlad looked to the strip of beach behind him and before, then out to sea, before circling around to the back of the boulders and the base of the cliff to get a better look at the stairs.

He suspected they were nearly invisible from any real distance and that even in daylight they would be a tricky ascent. But something tickled at him, moving under the surface of his skin and his skull, drawing him upward.

Maybe you crave something other than sand and sea? He pondered this and released the thought. No, it was more. It was not unlike the compulsion that drew him along the beach. As if to test it, he stepped back and thrust the staff into the sand. Then, he released it.

He was not surprised at all when it tipped toward the stairway. But he jumped when the kin-raven once more shrieked its solitary words. "Be gone!"

As if no other route were conceivable, the bird launched itself from the stone, pounding its wings as it rose along the cliff to vanish into the night.

Taking the staff up once again, Vlad Li Tam kilted up his robes and tied them to his belt to keep the tattered hem from tripping him. Then, he slowly began to climb in the dark.

He moved with great care, testing each step tentatively and pressing his body against stone still warm from the day. The moon rose to offer its dim light, but Vlad closed his eyes to it and let his feet carry him upward. Below him, the sound of the surf faded from a roar to a whisper, and when he finally stopped and opened his eyes, he gazed out over an ocean alive with the light of the moon. Craning his neck to look above, he tried to gauge just how far he had left to climb, but the night withheld that information from him.

Twice, he stumbled and caught himself against the wall, and once, he nearly lost the staff in an effort to regain his balance. Each time, he pressed on, slowing his pace to accommodate the sudden ache in his legs and lungs.

The sky lightened to gray and the moon hung low when Vlad crested the cliff to fall panting and sweating into the shade of a large tree that awaited him there. He slept through the day, arose, drank the water that pooled in its large, low-hanging leaves, and nibbled at the fruit that had fallen in its shadow. And he didn't need to look back to know that it evaporated back into the waste when he set out again, following the staff and kin-raven inland in the cool of the evening. But he did marvel at how unsurprised he was now when the staff provided for him in this place.

Still, the village that he stumbled upon the next morning *did* surprise him.

It was dug into a hollow in the dark, barren landscape. When he stumbled upon it, he blinked and rubbed his eyes, unsure of what he saw.

A cluster of buildings lay scattered along a brackish pond, and central to them stood a round building made of stone that Vlad knew all too well.

A Blood Temple.

His stomach knotted at the sudden anger. And with that emotion, something shifted in him, and once more he was a Tam, looking for information and advantage in this newest find. There was a pump house of some kind behind the temple, and pipes from it ran over the ground to buildings he assumed must have some significance, and he noted that the same buildings had what appeared to be boilers pumping steam into the morning sky.

He followed the steam, and movement caught his eye—birds, kin-ravens by the size of them. They circled above the village, diving down and then lifting up. Vlad heard a solitary voice, though he was too far away to hear the words it uttered.

Still, the sound of it compelled him for reasons he did not fathom. The kin-raven he had followed here regarded him with one dead eye, then surged into the air to join the others.

It intends me to follow. He did not know how entering this village would bring him to the spellbook he sought, but after so much had passed, questioning now made little sense.

Sighing, Vlad clutched the staff tightly and slowly made his way down the slope, picking his way among patches of scrub that now speckled the landscape. He moved along the edge of the water, his eyes scanning the village ahead as he went. He could pick up the sound of pigs and chickens somewhere to his west now, and the voice ahead became clearer.

"—bear witness to the death of our sins, poured into your Vessel of Grace," a woman's voice intoned, "that we may be made whole and in turn make whole our world."

Vlad paused, realizing suddenly that the voice spoke no language he was familiar with, yet he understood perfectly. And something in the words compelled him further, his feet picking up their pace as he advanced. He could see a small crowd now, all hanging back from robed, crouched figures there in the square outside the temple. A robed woman stood over them, her hands outstretched in benediction. Her long white hair cascaded over her shoulders, and though he wasn't close enough to see it, he knew her face bore the markings of her faith—words from their gospel spelled out in carefully carved scars.

Vlad willed himself to stop, but his feet did not heed him. He could feel the urgency in the staff now, pulling him toward the village, and as he strode forward, he raised the silver rod into the air.

The audience was a tattered assortment of men, women and children, all dusty despite the early hour. When the first of them saw him coming, he heard the gasp and watched it move from person to person even as they fell back from his advance.

"We thank you for this great gift," the woman said again, noticing Vlad for the first time.

I was right about the scars. He smiled at this, but the smile faded when he saw the twitching, groaning thing that lay sprawled upon the ground.

It had been a woman once, he thought, though he couldn't be certain. The shredded robe she wore revealed skin raw with sores black from the dirt that infected them. Every bit of her that he could see bore the same sores, even the patches of scalp between the thin clumps of her remaining hair. She lay with one cheek in a pool of black vomit, one nostril bubbling in the thick mess. When her eye opened and locked on his, Vlad's urgency became a raging need.

His voice was a roar that surprised him. "This woman needs help and you stand by preaching?"

The other robed women looked up from where they knelt. The one who stood lowered her arms. "Her moment has come at long last, and with it, the passing of sin from the world. Rejoice that you are present to see it, stranger."

Vlad tapped the staff on the ground and felt a ripple of power go out from it that vibrated through the ground. "If her moment has come, why does she lie upon the ground in her own filth? Why is she not stretched out in a borrowed bed or perhaps in your temple?"

The woman regarded him, and now, the crowd was taking him in for the first time. Vlad felt their eyes upon him even as they stepped back. "Our father—*her* father, even—has decreed that her passing be thus or the sins of the world remain," the woman said. "It is written in the Gospel of the Crimson Empress, 'Make straight the passing of the Vessel of Grace in great sorrow, for her sacrifice is for your salvation.'"

Vlad tapped the staff again and still did not understand the compulsion that gripped him. There was anger growing in him as his awareness grew. "I am a father as well," he said. "And I cannot abide salvation at such cost."

But it was a lie and he knew it, twisting in him. He'd sent too many of his own sons and daughters, grandsons and granddaughters into harm's way for his own version of salvation. And he'd paid for it in the Y'Zirite currency of kin-healing himself, watching most of his family cut away beneath Ria's knives.

"I do not know who you are," the woman said, "but I do know that you interfere with the will of Ahm Y'Zir and his daughters."

Vlad raised the staff high now and brought it down, hearing the thunder of it as it smote the ground, showering sparks that bounced and popped over the dry, hard-packed earth. "Who I am is of no importance to you," he said. "But I gladly defy Ahm Y'Zir and his daughters."

Already, the girl was coughing and seizing, wrapped suddenly in a white light as she bucked and twisted. When she finally stopped and the light faded, her sores were gone and her skin shone pink and new. Her eyes were wide as she rolled out of her vomit and rose to her knees. Above, a single kin-raven cried "Be gone," and Vlad looked up in time to see the circling birds disband and scatter, flying straight and low in their separate directions.

Bearing word of what has transpired here, he realized.

He felt hands upon his feet and looked down to see the woman kneeling there, healthy and whole, gazing up at him with tearful eyes. "Lord, how am I restored? Have I borne the sins fully to their grave?"

Vlad Li Tam looked to the evangelist, her face awash with horror and wrath. Then he looked down again. "Yes," he said to the woman.

"Take him," the evangelist said.

When invisible hands seized him, he shook them off easily. When they came for him again, he spun quickly, swinging his staff with two hands. He felt it connect with first one, then another magicked scout, and when the staff touched them, their magicks flashed and popped, guttering out quickly. The two women, clad in dark silks and bearing dark steel knives, lay writhing and twitching on the ground, their lips moving without offering any sound, their eyes wide upon the old man who stood over them.

"You will not *take* me anywhere," Vlad Li Tam said. "But I will come with you."

And then he smiled.

Winters

Winteria bat Mardic drew herself up to full height, though she knew she barely reached the chin of the lieutenant she confronted. "We are not asking your leave, Lieutenant."

Already weary of this assignment, Rudolfo's officer allowed impatience to leak into his voice. "I cannot let you go without consulting with General Rudolfo, Lady Winteria." She watched him look from her to the old man who sat on his saddle pack in the snow. "And certainly, Arch-Engineer Charles, the same applies to you."

Charles's own impatience was also evident. "And how are you going to seek his consultation?"

The man blinked. "We've sent runners to establish a courier route. Surely this matter can wait another day?"

Winters shook her head. "It cannot. Each day we wait is a day lost. And again, Lieutenant, I do not ask. I am a queen. I am not one of Lord Rudolfo's subjects."

"You shelter beneath his trees, Lady." He nodded to Charles. "And you, you serve the general's library."

The old man's eyes grew hard at that. "I serve the light, Forester, and have since your father was a pup."

The man grew red in the face, and Winters suspected that though he was a seasoned veteran, he had many leagues to travel when it came to statecraft and diplomacy—something in which the southern officers tended to have more training.

"It is a simple matter," she told him, offering up the kindest smile she could. "Brother Charles and I must go and investigate this new development. We ask for nothing but horses and supplies for two. You are three days out of Rachyle's Rest. You need only see them to the library; Elder Seamus can handle the rest from there."

She'd already written the letter to the last of her elders and tucked it inside her parka. It outlined Seamus's work getting her small remnant the housing, work and supplies they would need. But there was more. It also included her admonition to him to prepare her people for settling their new home, setting aside a tithe of their supplies in a storehouse against the day that they would somehow reach their promised sanctuary. She drew the letter out and passed it to him. And Winters knew when he took it that she would have her way after all.

"General Rudolfo will not be pleased by this," the man said.

Winters met his stare. "His displeasure will be with me."

"And with me," Charles added.

Shoving the letter angrily into his belt pouch, the lieutenant said nothing as he strode off in the direction of his quartermaster.

Winters grinned at Charles. "I think that went well," she said.

Charles grunted. "We'll know if we have homes to return to." He hefted his saddle pack, and she saw him teetering beneath the weight of it. She quickly stepped over to him and helped, lifting the weight of it until he found his balance. The determination on his face struck her, and realization sparked.

"You've dreamed again," she said.

Until now, in the confrontation with the Gypsy Scout, his face had been a mask of stubborn resolve. But now, it melted away to reveal a man out of his element. "All day," he said in a quiet voice. "I think the kallacaine enhanced it."

That made sense to her. It would lessen any inhibitions even as it eased pain and encouraged sleep. Any walls he might put up around his dreams would be eroded by the drug's efficacy. "Did you learn anything?"

"The girl was back. I . . . it took her and ran. There was a river—the Third River, I think, west of Windwir. And cave walls with paintings in blood." He paused and rubbed his temples. "I think we were being pursued."

Paintings in blood. Winters shivered against the words and patted his shoulder. "We'll leave in an hour and ride through the night," she said. "If you'll see to the horses and supplies, I'll speak to my people. Find me when you're ready."

He nodded and shuffled off toward a cluster of tents. She watched him go, and wondered at the fondness she had for this old Androfrancine. Maybe, she thought, it was that he reminded her of Tertius, the renegade scholar who'd tutored her at her father's insistence. They bore striking similarities in thought and speech, but truly, all Androfrancines seemed alike to her. She turned away from him, lifted her own pack, and went to the large circle of fires where her people awaited.

She'd wondered what she would tell them, having so recently called them out to follow her. She'd imagined making a speech, giving them words that would comfort them, encourage them, in her absence. Or perhaps giving them instruction.

But in the end, she moved through the clusters of Marshfolk, sitting quietly with their resolve in the smeared dirt and ash of their faith. She went from group to group, crouching with them at their fires, inquiring after their well-being, quietly sharing with them her plans to leave. There were some tears among the children. And there were far more offers to accompany her among the men and women than she had expected. Still, two could travel with some discretion. More than that was a company on horseback—not a good idea during what must now be a time of war.

It took longer than an hour—closer to two—but she managed to sit briefly at each campfire and share her plans, her hopes. "I will find the Final Dream," she told each. "And I will pass it to the Homeseeker that he might prepare a place for us."

None asked how or why, and for that Winters was grateful.

Somewhere in the midst of it all, she saw Charles appear at the edge of camp with two horses in tow. He no longer wore the robes of an Androfrancine scholar. Instead, he wore a heavy coat, a fur cap, and dungarees tucked into sturdy boots. Saying nothing, he waited for her to finish, and when she finally approached, he handed her the reins of a dappled mare.

She mounted the horse and looked out over her people. Slowly, silently, they rose to their feet. They raised their hands to her, and she raised hers to them.

Then, she turned the mare and whistled her forward.

They rode out from camp and kept the silence until they were well beyond the firelight. Once the darkness had settled in upon them, the starshine leaked through and the moon caught her eye for the first time that night.

"I don't know how it's possible," she whispered. "And I don't know what to do."

Beside her, Charles cleared his voice. She glanced to him and saw that he, too, watched the sky. "I do not know either," he said, "but it seems far, far more is possible than I'd ever imagined before now."

Yes. Winters fixed her eyes upon the home that awaited her and her people and gave herself to hope.

Chapter
8

Lysias

Lysias lay in the snow beneath a camouflaged tarp and watched the archers do their best work. It had taken two arrows to drop the kin-raven, and when it finally plummeted to the ground, more soldiers leapt to it with spears raised.

When the bird finally went still, he pulled the tarp away and stood, brushing the snow from his winter uniform. "Good work."

It was the second kin-raven they'd brought down since Rudolfo had left for his southwestern borders, but there was no way to know for sure that they'd closed all prying eyes. Keeping the forest's new army a secret was never a realistic expectation. The best they could do, he knew, was control as much as possible just what was and wasn't seen. Between the birds and the blood shrine, there was no way to gauge the eyes and ears they dealt with. Still, until yesterday, it was enough to simply close those ears and eyes they could.

But everything had changed.

The birder's eyes were wide and white in the lamplight when he'd awakened Lysias with the news the night before. And after burying the corpses deep in the forest, the only birds they'd seen were the kin-ravens they'd managed to bring down.

Lysias approached the dead bird now and prodded it with his boot, tipping it over. It was mottled and scarred, with a wider wingspan than a tall man with arms extended. Its single eye was open and glassy, and it taunted the Entrolusian general. "Bury it," he said. "And summon the captains to my cabin."

He left the snow tarp for his aide and exited the clearing, moving back under the cover of evergreens where they'd built their training camp. As he moved through the scattering of makeshift cabins and tents, he nodded to the men as they acknowledged him. On the Delta, where Lysias had spent the majority of his military career, they would have saluted him. But in the field, and in the forest, it made little sense. Each soldier knew him and gave him the respect due his rank with the slightest inclination of their head. And as they did, Lysias measured them.

Farmers, loggers, fishermen and children. Some had served in Rudolfo's Wandering Army during the War for Windwir, and others had continued their service into the Marshland skirmishes that followed. But most of them had little experience with military protocol or combat. Still, Lysias felt a pride rising in him at the army he'd created for the Gypsy King. They were strong men and would fight well when called upon.

Rudolfo and his predecessors had resisted the idea of a standing army for centuries in their relatively safe corner of the world; but the library bombing had compelled the king, and now Lysias was confident that this army would indeed see the war that no doubt raged to the south of them.

The question of whether or not they would prevail was another matter. The enemy used blood magicks, of the sort to make one man as strong as five and as fleet as a horse, and a brutality that lived beyond his Academy-trained sense of just, honorable warfare. Among the last messages he'd received was verified intelligence on Pylos. An entire nation cut surgically from the Named Lands by a plague that did not cross beyond Meirov's borders. Overwhelming violence in response to her attack on Rudolfo's family, the Y'Zirites' Great Mother and Child of Promise.

Thoughts of Lady Tam and Lord Jakob turned his mind to his own family, and Lysias sighed as he pushed open the door of his cabin. He'd rebuilt his relationship with Lynnae as best he could, knowing that not even time could remove the scars a thoughtless, sometimes cruel father might leave upon a daughter. And now, if Rudolfo's last note was true, Lynnae sailed into the heart of Y'Zir with the Gypsy King's bride and heir. Anger and fear vied for the reins of his heart, but Lysias understood his heart well enough and had learned over the years that any emotion could easily be distilled into anger if he bent his will to it.

Moving into the single room, he pulled off his coat and tossed it onto the bed. Then, he lifted his pack onto the room's single table and began gathering those items he would take and that he would send south. When his captains arrived at the door, he pointed to the narrow bed and the handful of chairs.

"Gentlemen," he said, "please take a seat. I'll be brief."

They did, their eyes intent upon him. *Where to begin?*

He studied them. They'd all been sergeants or better in Rudolfo's elite Gypsy Scouts—the most experienced of his men and until recently, the closest thing the Forester's had to a permanent military. Now, they each commanded companies and were competent though uncomfortable with the sudden shift from scout warfare to more traditional infantry tactics. "First," he said slowly, "our suspicions, I fear, are correct. The Named Lands have no doubt been invaded, and by a superior force." Some of them nodded, some of them blinked, but none flinched and none looked afraid. "Second, our communications have been effectively silenced, and it is safest to assume that this is not a local phenomenon but rather a carefully orchestrated event on a much larger scale. Without messenger birds, we're reliant upon couriers, but without such a system in place, it would take a week, maybe more, to establish." He paused, letting them keep pace with him. "Third, from the day that Windwir fell, this Y'Zirite foe has maneuvered the Ninefold Forest and its ruling family into a compromised position in relationship to the other nations, excluding our western neighbors and their new queen."

There were more nods now, more dark glances exchanged.

"We are not poised to win this game of Queen's War," Lysias said. "We are not even on the board. The only two standing armies of any merit are the City States and Turam. Pylos is gone—every man, woman and child. The Emerald Coast's militias are largely inconsequential, and the Divided Isle's peacekeeping sheriffs will have little in the way of men and arms to raise. Years of civil war and months of bloodshed over Windwir have robbed the Named Lands of its ability to respond."

Of course, that had always been the Y'Zirite strategy, and the care with which they'd sown these seeds of conquest astounded the aging general. They'd brought the patience of farmers to this field of war, setting into place schemes meticulously calculated with means beyond any Lysias had seen. Windwir was gone along with the Androfrancine shepherds, their Gray Guard and the war-making magicks and mechanicals they'd kept in secret behind their walls. The Marshfolk had been tamed and turned into a zealous, organized, well-armed foe at the flank of the southern nations. The bonds of kin-clave had been eroded by machination and violence to the point where no one could trust their neighbor. And now, the birds were dead.

It was an impressive and terrifying strategy in its effectiveness, established decades earlier and implemented with great care.

One of the older captains spoke first, breaking the room's silence. "Do you suggest that we cannot prevail, General?"

Lysias smiled a grim smile. "I suggest nothing of the sort, though I do not presume to know exactly how to bring about victory. But I do know how to stave off defeat for the time and put us on the board. Though what I intend to undertake may require as much patience as our enemy has demonstrated in laying out the snares of their invasion."

Another captain's voice rose in the room, made bold no doubt by his colleague. "And what has General Rudolfo in mind for us?"

There it is. Lysias had known it would come eventually in this conversation, and he welcomed it. "General Rudolfo has entrusted this army into my care, and I have sworn allegiance to him, his house and his kin. I will not render this army we've built ineffective by waiting for his runners to tell me what I know must be done. We are at war, Captain, and time is of the essence."

The man inclined his head at the firmness in Lysias's voice, and when the two men's eyes met, he saw that his message was heard. "With all of this laid out before you, here are my orders. We are striking camp this very day. I am dividing the army. The best third of our men will accompany me in two companies—along with those of the Gypsy Scouts still remaining among us and Captains Tybard and Royce. I want my two companies ready to march and completely outfitted. All scout magicks. All medico supplies. All lanterns and fuel. And all rations. Every arrow and knife and sword that can be spared. But gather these items with discretion."

The surprise on their faces was genuine, and he watched mouths begin to open and then close. "Those of you coming with me will need every scrap we can afford. Those of you who aren't will be moving south, to the watchtowers, to protect the Ninefold Forest's borders. You will hunt along the way or forage from the manors en route."

"And what will you do, General?"

Lysias shook his head. "What I do is best kept to as few ears as possible."

He made eye contact with each of them and waited until each had nodded their understanding. "Carry these orders to your first sergeants and set the men to packing." They stood as one and moved for the

door. "You two stay behind for a moment," he told the captains he'd
singled out.

Lysias waited until the others had left, then lowered his voice. "I want
your men well fed and well watered, in dry gear and ready to march at
nightfall."

Royce's eyes betrayed a question, and Lysias gestured to him. "You
made no mention of horses, General," he said.

"Yes," Lysias agreed. "That is correct. I will brief you fully when your
men are ready. We do this all at once. I want any eyes that may be prying
to see one army marching south." Then, he turned to Tybard. "I want
that miner, Barstrum, and his mechoservitor in my cabin within the
hour. Magick a scout and send him after them."

A realization dawned on the man's face, and Lysias hoped the firmness of his gaze conveyed his full meaning. "Wonder what you wish, but
breathe not a word of it to anyone, Captains."

Both men nodded and left.

Lysias was alone again with his thoughts. He had much to do. He
needed to pack. He needed to lay out one of his spare uniforms and designate someone to wear it—probably the captain who had challenged
him—and arrange for those things that he could not carry to be taken
back to the Seventh Forest Manor. Then, he would carefully script and
code his note to Rudolfo and entrust it to the care of a runner.

After, he would meet with the miner and mechoservitor he intended
to guide them when he took the best of Rudolfo's army into the Beneath
Places and eventually into the war.

Neb

Seagulls lifted and scattered, crying at the sky, and Neb felt the slightest
tickle of their alarm in his skin. He stood now, though on trembling
legs, and took in the lagoon and its solitary vessel. Though the shore was
largely overgrown, he could see the remains of the dead city even here:
Bits of white pavement peeking out from the green, a twisted mass of
vines and brush that enwrapped a fallen statue or tumbled spire. And the
jagged, mossy teeth of those glass buildings shining in the sun.

He wondered who had lived here and how long ago.

As an Androfrancine orphan, Neb had enjoyed the finest education in
the heart of Windwir's Great Library. But little was known of the moon
beyond folklore, and most of that had been lost. Digging through the ru-

ins of the Old World, archaeologists had found fragments and scraps of mythology. The best known, of course, were the tales of Felip Carnelyin and his journey to the moon, where he fell in love with the Moon Wizard's daughter and stole her away from her father. Centuries later, that wrathful wizard arrived upon the earth to establish his rule in the Year of the Falling Moon, the beginning of a war that destroyed much of the world. Many of the stories were thought to be fabricated to keep humanity compliant and fearful during that Age of the Wizard Kings.

But now I stand in the shadow of a city on the moon. His heart raced at the reality of it.

He heard laughter and looked up to watch Rafe and his remaining crewman as they walked the length of the ship, examining its hull from the old stone dock. The pirate's smile darkened when he met Neb's eyes. "She's a fine vessel," he said, "though I've never seen anything like it."

Neither had Neb, other than in his dream. It was smaller than most of the ships he'd seen—narrow and long, low in the water with a pilothouse that stood elevated over the deck. It was the color of milk, with a texture that felt more like crystal or stone than wood.

The gangplank was down—made from the same type of material— and the sails, now lowered, were a kind of silk he'd not seen before, bright white and brand-new. He looked from the ship to Petronus. Somewhere behind them, the hounds closed in.

Petronus's face was sober, and it wasn't hard for Neb to sense the man's trepidation. "Where do you propose we sail?"

You sail for D'Anjite's daughter. The voice was clear, and he jumped at it. And he thought only he could hear it, but the widening of Petronus's eyes and the sudden silence that fell over the others told him otherwise. The men looked to him, and the mechoservitors studied them all.

A wave of emotion rushed Neb. *Calm. No fear.* The wave washed him, settled him.

Neb bit his lip and concentrated. *Who are you?*

You may speak audibly, Lord Whym. I know you are new beneath your father's mantle. There was a stir of movement on the ship, and Neb looked up. *I am Aver-Tal-Ka, last of the Keeper's Hatch and last of the People's Builder Warriors.*

The sense of calm was pervasive and seemed to saturate the dock. Though the scouts had weapons drawn, they stood relaxed, their faces transfixed with awe. The mechoservitors were silent but for the hum of their gears and the whistle of released steam. But despite the calm, there was a collective gasp when Aver-Tal-Ka stepped out from the shadows of the forecastle and into the light.

It was tall—at least a span higher than the mechoservitors—and it towered above them from its position on the deck of the ship. Its bone-white body was round but elongated, supported on eight long, slender legs. Both the legs and body were covered in a fine sheen of silver hair. In some ways, Neb realized, it was similar to the mechanical spider that housed his father's ghost, but this was no creature of metal. It was roughly the same shape and size, it moved with measured grace upon those eight legs, and it spoke into his mind. But the similarities ended there. This spider was flesh and blood. And even its similarity to the spiders he'd studied in the natural sciences wing of the library was limited. This particular breed of arachnid had mandibles situated near a single fang, and tiny antennae wriggled above two eyes that shone dark as wet ink. And it was vastly larger.

Calm, it projected. *No fear.*

The body pulsated and rippled as it took another step forward. Then, Aver-Tal-Ka lifted one of its legs. The leg unfolded upward until its spiked tip stretched out over them; then the tip itself unfolded even farther, and a long, slender hand slipped out. It moved its four fingers against its opposable thumb and then spread all out in a gesture Neb instantly recognized as both a greeting and a hand that was empty of weapons. A mouth worked its way open just off-center of the mandible—its lips pink against the white of the spider's flesh. "Greetings, son of Whym," it said. "The terms of Frederico's Bargain are nearly complete. The Continuity Engine of the Elder Gods slowly grinds to life, and the time of sowing is at hand."

He'd asked the question once before, and the spider had answered, but Neb couldn't get his mind around the answer. He had to ask again. "Who are you?"

"I am Aver-Tal-Ka," the spider said again. It lowered its hand. "Last of the Keeper's Hatch and last of the People's Builder Warriors. I am hatched to serve you and Lady D'Anjite in the sowing."

This time, the words were accompanied by an image. Neb saw a cave dimly lit by lichen and moss, its floor scattered with eggs that pulsed beneath thick strands of webbing that hung from the high ceilings. He saw a single spider, easily twice the size of the one before him now, moving among the eggs, pausing here and there for its mandibles to gently move over the surface of this or that pulsing, white orb, with a mother's care and attention.

The Keeper's Hatch. All his life, he'd heard of the Keeper's Wall and the Keeper's Gate, the partition that kept the Named Lands segregated from

the Old World that had been left desolate by Xhum Y'Zir's Seven Cacophonic Deaths. Those place names had survived millennia, though
their meaning had been lost long before the days of P'Andro Whym.
Even as he pondered the connection, the spider spoke again.

"Everything made," it said, "was made for the People." It moved closer
to the rail now, two more of its arms lifting and unfolding to reveal hidden hands. As it spoke, those hands pointed. The one already upraised
now pointed to the world that rose above them, the others to the jungle
and to the city. "All of the People's needs, known and unknown to them,
built into their home for their use." Overhead, Neb saw a dark and barren continent moving slowly past. And as the world turned, he saw the
mountain ranges that segregated that continent, and between those
seemingly natural walls, a swath of green that at first he assumed must
be his former home only seen from a point of view that he'd never imagined possible.

But there is no horn to sail around. He blinked at it and saw other differ-
ences. More rivers, some even that cut through the mountains and into
the barren wastes. He glanced at Petronus, whose eyes were also wide
now. "There are other places that support life," he said. "Like the Named
Lands."

Aver-Tal-Ka inclined its head. "Each continent was made with its
Keeper's Crèche set apart, fed by the blood of the earth against the day
of sowing in the last days of Lasthome."

New images pushed at his awareness now. A planet-sized garden
scattered with bright cities of glass beneath a blazing sun. Birds—silver
and gold and copper—flitting across a blue sky. And fire, twisted and
carried by wind, moving slowly over that garden as black smoke choked
out the sun.

Something in Neb stirred and moved toward comprehension, but the
vastness of the realization staggered him. *Lasthome.*

"These are the last days of Lasthome," he heard himself saying.

Yes. "Yes." The word was both in his mind and in his ears. "And I've
prepared this vessel to bear you to D'Anjite's daughter." The spider lowered its arms and turned its face toward Neb and then Petronus. "You've
seen her in the aether. She waits for you to wake her from her slumber
that the People may not perish."

A mechoservitor's eye shutters clicked open and closed as it released
a gout of steam. It nudged Neb's attention. "I know nothing of this. The
dream that called us is for the tower."

He saw it now, proud and white, where it towered above the moon's jungles. "Yes," Aver-Tal-Ka said. "The Firsthome Temple awaits, but its time is not at hand for you; and the tower was never meant for you alone. Two by two go the People. I hear the song that calls you in the aether but have not yet heard Shadrus's Dream of Unsealing."

Because I lost the dream. He felt his face go red with the thought and hoped that the spider could not read it. Still, if it could, it said nothing. Instead, it turned and scuttled back away from the gangplank.

The hounds draw near, it said. *And the kin-dragons will soon take wing again.* "It is time for us sail, Lord Whym."

A thousand questions pressed him, but Neb knew there would be time enough for them once they were aboard and en route. And he did not know if it was the pervasive sense of calm emanating from Aver-Tal-Ka or if it was the quiet and reassuring voice deep inside of him, but Neb trusted the spider and felt a kinship with that being that he'd not felt before—a bond that assured him that his inexplicable trust was well placed.

When he looked to Petronus and the others, he saw they all watched him now. And he heard the tone of command in his voice as he gave the order to board the ship.

None of them blinked and none of them spoke. Instead, they scrambled up the gangplank and Neb followed. Aver-Tal-Ka moved around them quickly, raising the sails and taking the helm, and Rafe Merrique and his men cast them off.

As the crystalline vessel slipped out of the lagoon, the howling suddenly stopped. Behind them, dark forms broke from cover and paced the beach in brooding silence.

Ahead, a clear green sea beckoned and a warm wind rose to carry them over it.

Petronus

Petronus stretched out upon the sponge-like bed, feeling it conform to his weight as he settled in. He sighed and pulled at his blanket, the rough wool fabric out of place in these surroundings.

The lunar vessel was a wonder the likes of which no Androfrancine had seen. He'd read references from the earliest times about seagoing lords in those Elder Days who ruled from ships like these only larger. And he could see how possible that might be.

The exterior was nearly opaque, though he understood now from their spider guide that it simply bent light around it. And the interior boasted cabins and a galley made of a substance much like a shell, pink in color and carpeted with a lime-colored sea moss. And Petronus wasn't certain what lay in the aft hold, but Aver-Tal-Ka had descended into it and ascended with buckets of fresh water, large shellfish and some kind of medley of sea vegetables still dripping.

After a feast supplemented with pulls from Merrique's flask of firespice, followed by a hot shower, Petronus felt relaxed enough to notice every ache in his bones. But he didn't notice it for long. He fell into sleep quick and hard.

She met him there.

He felt her hands upon him before his eyes were open, and she was strong enough to lift him easily. "I've been waiting for you, Downunder," she said.

Petronus struggled against her. "What do you want with me?"

She smiled, drew his face close to hers. He could smell rotten teeth on the wind of her breath. "I want to know how many of you there are. I want to know about the one you called Nebios . . . Whym's son. I want to know who else is with you." This close, Petronus saw a point of clarity in the madness of the old woman's eyes. "I sense another, but I cannot find their echoes in the aether."

She doesn't know about the spider.

"That," she said. "Right there. What was that?"

He pushed the thought as far from himself as he could. "I have nothing to say to you," he said. The words were barely out of his mouth before she hurled him away from her.

He landed in a patch of dried brambles and rolled to his back as she neared him again. A foot found his ribs, and he heard one crack. "You have plenty," she said. "And I'll have it if we must go the entire night." She leaned over him, reached down, and pulled him up by his beard. "You sail for me, Downunder, and I'll know what is coming my way. My father gave his life—misguided fool—to hide me. I'll not wake up without knowing who comes to wake me."

She dropped him again and brought her feet to bear. Petronus crawled to his hands and knees, grasping at her lashing foot but missing as she danced nimbly aside. "Tell me the story of Nebios Whym," she said.

Petronus closed his eyes and willed himself awake, but to no avail. Finally, he opened his eyes and took in his surroundings for the first time. They were in a clearing in the midst of a dying jungle. Overhead, the world hung like dead fruit in the cold of space. His nose was full of the smell of rotting fish and foliage. "I have nothing—"

A flash of light cut him off, sudden and hot.

Petronus felt his body convulse and he fought it, suddenly pinned by at least four sets of hands.

Peace. No fear. She cannot hurt you again.

He opened his eyes and gasped at the spider's proximity. Its black eye regarded him, its fang slipping from its sheath, its very tip the size of a sewing needle. "Who is she?"

But he knew. It had to be D'Anjite's daughter. Though she was nothing like the girl Neb had described.

The spider nodded. *Yes.*

"Something is wrong with her."

She has been broken by grief too heavy to bear. It has . . . damaged her. But I can make her whole.

The fang moved again, and Petronus felt it slide into his neck. "What are you doing?"

I am treating you. She will not be able to harm you again. Something warm enfolded him, and Petronus wrestled against it. Already, the pain was leaking away and slumber was an inviting well that he teetered over, trying to keep his balance.

His voice was slowing. "She wanted to know about you. About us. About Neb."

The spider nodded again. This time, its lips worked themselves open and a whisper leaked out. "Do not concern yourself with these matters, Petronus. You will sleep now, and you will not remember these dreams or my presence here with you. You will awaken rested. You will gather your strength for the days ahead, for surely you will need it."

Then, the spider embraced him and settled him back into the bed, tucking the blanket beneath his chin as if he were a child.

"Yes," Petronus whispered.

And when he slept, he dreamed of fishing with his father, and when he awakened, he had some vague memory of his mother tucking him in but shook it away as the fog of sleep faded.

Then, Petronus found steaming chai that Rafe Merrique had somehow brewed in the ship's alien galley and watched a world rise once more over the lunar sea he sailed.

Chapter 9

Rudolfo

A cool wind blew in off the sea, and Rudolfo inhaled the salt from it as he stood at the rail. With the Delta finally behind them, he'd been allowed on deck after several days kept locked away in the galley or in his stateroom.

All he'd seen of the invasion were the swamped hulls of gutted Entrolusian ships and the glow of fires where ports burned.

It was the second fastest trip south he could remember making in his lifetime. They rode magicked horses into the ground to rendezvous with the Y'Zirite frigate at Windwir. The magicked vessel caught the last of winter's northeastern winds, the Second River's current adding even more speed to their journey.

He'd tried to learn what he could, but with the portholes shuttered from outside and the language of the sparse crew some guttural tongue he was unfamiliar with, Rudolfo found himself pacing his stateroom for days, coding messages he could not send or poring over a treaty he'd now memorized. On the worst days, he wondered about his son.

He had no doubt the boy was well. But over the course of this separation, Rudolfo found his mind wandering toward what he'd missed. First words and steps. That glint of intelligence in his eye when he learned a new trick. The sound of his laughter ringing down the hallways . . . and the sound of his tears as well.

Of course, it was a road that led him to close to despair, and on those days, his eye went to the bottle of firespice he now carried with him. Something tangible to remind him who he both was and wasn't.

One day I may drink it, he told himself. Just not today.

Today had not been one of those days. This was one of those days when he thought instead of what he'd left behind. He thought of Lysias in the north and the army he built. They'd discussed the likelihood of an invasion before Rudolfo had ridden south to banish Kember's traitorous bunch and meet the Y'Zirite emissary. And Lysias was a skilled general, trained in the Academy and sharpened during the War for Windwir, though on the wrong side of that conflict as one of Sethbert's officers. Now pledged to Rudolfo's service, the old fox had put together an impressive first army in short order. Rudolfo had no doubt that whatever his general got up to, it would serve his Ninefold Forest well indeed.

And Philemus would as well, though his rage was apparent when Rudolfo announced his appointment as Over-sheriff of the Wood, unweaving his turban and laying it with his knives into hands that were reluctantly held open. Rudolfo leaned close and spoke in a quiet voice that betrayed none of his own anger. "These you shall hold in trust for me or my heir," he said. "And know that on the day that he or I take them up from you, you shall owe an accounting for how you've sheriffed your people." He put his hand on the man's shoulder and pressed other words there. *Stand firm, Philemus. Protect the mechoservitors at all costs.*

The man's gray eyes bore into him, and Rudolfo met the stare and held it. "General, reconsider. At least take—"

Rudolfo interrupted him. "No, Sheriff. As you yourself told me—resources are thin. The scout ranks are already far too sparse. I'll be well cared for by the Blood Guard."

El Anyr had stood by, and Rudolfo remembered noting the pleased look upon his face. *Because I behaved as if I trusted him.*

But he didn't trust the man nearly as much as he trusted the man's faith. With each of these Y'Zirites he met, he began to see the one blind spot that they all had.

"They believe these things as writ with no doubt whatsoever." He didn't realize he said it aloud until he heard a soft cough behind him. "I'm sorry," he said.

He felt the hands press into his sides. They were gentle, and he did not jump. *It is because they are utterly convinced it is true, Lord.* The hands stopped but did not leave him. They waited, firm and unmoving, then started again slowly. *And they are not lacking in evidence.* They moved in and up his spine now, faster this time. *They are watching you here. Return to your stateroom; I have information for you.*

The code was that of his house, but the lingering of the hands told him clearly it was not one of his men. They were hands he'd felt upon him not so long ago, and the sudden discomfort of that memory bemused him. Straightening at the rail, he moved slowly for the door, glancing one last time aft at the fires on the Delta.

He let himself in the stateroom and left the door open behind him to the count of three before closing it. He opened his mouth to speak, and an invisible hand blocked it while another pressed words into his shoulder. *Not yet.*

He closed his mouth and let her lead him to the bed, tensing momentarily as she pushed him onto it, her hands on his shoulders.

He'd long ago lost count of the number of women who'd had him. There was a time when he'd even kept a few of the Forest's prostitutes on his rotation. Yet the feeling of strange hands upon him now, guiding him to bed, left him suddenly befuddled. "This can't—"

Her face moved in close to his, and he saw the faintest green of her eye and felt her mouth at his ear. "This is not what you presume it is, Lord." Her voice was more breath than whisper. "You are watched by my sisters, the Blood Guard of the Crimson Empress. One in the hall outside. One on the deck. One in reserve and three others at rest." Her hands continued. *They must not find me here.*

His own hands found her shoulders. *Why are you here?*

"For you, Lord," she whispered. "I have pledged myself to you. I boarded when we took on the officers at Port Carnem." Rudolfo remembered stopping, but it was before he'd been allowed access to the deck. He held his breath as her fingers pressed more words into his flesh. *We are both required at Yazmeera's camp.*

She shifted her weight, and he felt more of her pressing against him as she stretched out. Beneath his own hands he felt lithe muscles stretched over a more petite frame than her sister's, and as much as he wished he couldn't, he felt her small breasts pushing against his own chest. "This," he whispered as quietly as he could, "is a most unusual conversation." Then, with his fingers. *What information do you bring?*

The Named Lands are a headless rooster on the run. Erlund is dead, assassinated by Y'Zirite intelligence. Esarov and his scattered revolutionaries have control of what little remains of the Entrolusian army. Rudolfo felt a shudder pass through her, and she pushed her mouth into his shoulder to suppress a sudden cough that racked her body.

You are ill?

Her breath was warm on his ear. "I've been under the magicks for far too long, Lord." Then, she continued. *Turam's king is up from his sick bed and in hiding. His troops have burned their uniforms and formed insurgency pockets. The free states of the Emerald Coasts are rallying men, but Yazmeera has landed two brigades upon the inner coast, using the former House Li Tam properties as a staging area. Pylos is . . .*

Her words stopped, and Rudolfo found his own. *I know of Pylos.* And he felt the stab of that loss. Meirov had sacrificed her own life and that of her nation's in her rage over the assassination of her young son. She'd funded the attack upon his library, the act that had brought about his family's need to seek sanctuary with the Machtvolk in the north, which in turn had led to their departure from the Named Lands.

"What you do not know," she said, "is that the first ships of settlers have already arrived there to begin the clean-up."

The word surprised him. *Settlers?*

Yes. Surely you do not think this is merely a military venture?

Rudolfo wasn't sure what he'd thought, but he also knew that the events of the last two years had kept him sufficiently off balance. *Y'Zir is bloated, and the barrens around it have lain lifeless too long. The Named Lands are rich with resources and near enough to easily supply the reclamation of the Churning Wastes.*

He blinked. There had been ample references to healing the world throughout the gospel he'd read, but he'd not dared believe they were mad enough to believe life could again be brought forth from the wasteland that Xhum Y'Zir had made when he broke the back of the world in retribution for the murder of his seven sons. Questions lined up for answers behind his eyes, but he shifted topics. "What else can you tell me?"

She yawned. "Your enemy has been beaten on two fronts already." *First,* her hands said, *the Watcher that has been so instrumental in calculating and adjusting this plot is missing and presumed destroyed. And second, the Third Desert Brigade reports that the mechoservitors and their Homeseeker were successful in their launch. The last Pope, Petronus, was believed to be with them.*

Rudolfo's eyes narrowed. He'd seen and heard nothing from Neb since he'd resigned his commission to Aedric in the Churning Wastes and left in the care of Renard the Waste Guide. But he knew the boy had been hunted in the Waste; Petronus had petitioned for scouts to aid him but had not been heard from since. "What launch?"

"The antiphon," she said. "The dream contained the specifications for its construction and instructions for the Homeseeker's mission."

He brushed his fingers over a shoulder, gripping and then pressing with his fingers. *I do not understand.*

"My sisters saw it launch and reported it in the aether. By now, Neb has surely reached the moon."

The words stunned him, draining off his words like tepid bathwater. The moon? Certainly he'd grown up with the legends but had never seriously considered such a possibility. Something sparked for him now, and a piece of the puzzle made sudden sense. *The Marshfolk home.* Even as his hands made the words, he found himself doubting them. It just wasn't possible.

Yes. She coughed again. "And last," she whispered, "your family should be arriving in Y'Zir within days. Lord Jakob will be safe there."

He noted the absence of reassurance regarding Jin Li Tam; he tried to force himself to ask, but in the end, he couldn't. There had been a great deal of anger when he'd first heard of her decision, but now that anger was hollowed out, an empty place that accepted her absence. She had told him long ago, when she'd first conceived, that she had rejected her father's machinations in favor of a family with him, even though the very son she carried was a product of those manipulations. And he'd believed her for a time, but in the end, the script of being the forty-second daughter of Vlad Li Tam had trumped the newer script of being the Forest Queen, his bride and the mother of his heir.

He closed his eyes against the memory of her.

Ire Li Tam moved against him again, this time crawling over him to disentangle herself. In the dim light of the room, she began to take form as her magicks guttered out. He saw close-cropped red hair and a face scarred carefully with the words of Y'Zir. "I must sleep now, my lord," she whispered.

Taking one of his blankets, she slipped to the floor and rolled beneath his narrow bed before he could say a word. Her breathing changed, still barely perceptible.

Rudolfo envied her the sleep she took, but nothing of the sort awaited him. Instead, he lay upon his back and pondered. Windwir was a grave. The Named Lands were invaded and would soon be settled by Y'Zirites. His young son was an ocean away in the care of a woman he could not possibly understand, in the possession of a faith that until recently had been thought gratefully extinct. Rudolfo himself sailed south to take the reins of chancellorship from their conqueror and forge a new life the likes of which he'd never imagined for himself or his people.

And Neb and Petronus are on the moon.

Rudolfo lay awake and let the past, the present and the future have its way with his memory and his imagination. He did not know how many hours passed before he finally slept fitfully. And when he finally dreamed, he could not remember the images themselves, only the emotion they carried. A son's sorrow over the world his father left him and a father's sorrow for the world that he, in turn, passed on.

Jin Li Tam

Jin Li Tam watched the palm trees slipping past on the canal's shoreline as their engines carried them east and upriver in the absence of wind. Two days ago, they'd sighted land—a dark scar of horizon that grew in her porthole until it became a desolate coastline. They'd entered a wide-mouthed river there in a nondescript bay, and the ship began its slow climb, moving up a series of locks. Slowly she could tell by the crew's good humor that they neared home, and she'd capitalized on it to learn as much as she could under the guise of practicing her language skills. She'd already learned the names of most of the crew, had identified the ship's armory and medico supply locker as well as its armorer and medico, and had picked up references to place names that she did not recognize.

She'd also used her sessions with Sister Elsbet to broaden her knowl-edge of Y'Zirite belief and custom. It was an intricate system that inte-grated their faith with life—ritual scarrings during high holy days and monthly bloodlettings into a community still, combined with gospels that were preached and taught on a weekly schedule by a priesthood that consisted mostly of women, and daily prayer led in small clusters. Com-ing from the Named Lands, where religious belief was largely eschewed, she had little frame of reference for such a pervasive form of belief, and she found that it both fascinated and horrified her.

Because ultimately, these people can justify anything if they can find even the slightest support for it within their beliefs. She shuddered and turned away from the porthole.

The door rattled and Lynnae pushed it open. Jakob stood with her, his fist tightly clutching her finger and his eyes alive with excitement. The young woman smiled. "He only fell twice," she said.

They'd been walking the deck several times a day now, giving the boy time to learn his way.

Jin Li Tam smiled and extended her hands. Jakob laughed and ran to her. As she scooped him up, she met Lynnae's eyes and waited for her to close the door before she spoke in a whisper. "Did you find him?"

A hoarse voice nearby answered. "Aye. I'm here." She could still hear the anger in his voice.

She'd only encountered the man twice previously on the ship after their conversation on the deck. He'd hidden himself, foraging for food and water, and somehow managed to keep his presence secret so far. "Good. We near our destination, and it is time for us to hold council."

Aedric's cough was muffled by magicks and by his scarf. "I see no council needed beyond that which places my lord's son into my care and sends us homeward. What you get up to is your own affair."

She bit her tongue, feeling her own anger spike. Jin knew from years of training that every feeling—including and especially anger—was a useful tool. But timing was everything. She pushed past the emotion. "You're not well, Aedric. How long have you been under the powders?"

"I'll be fine." His voice was on the other side of the room now.

"Pig shite," she said. "First, you've over-magicked yourself, going all this time under the powders. And second, when you run out, you're sure to be captured—especially if you're in a weakened state." It wasn't as if he could just resupply himself with the Y'Zirites' scout magicks. Theirs were distilled from forbidden blood magicks and came with a three-day life expectancy, at least for the Marshfolk who'd used them—and her sister, Rae Li Tam. She'd heard rumors that the Y'Zirite Blood Guard did not have that issue, but she'd yet to understand why.

"I'll be fine," Aedric said again.

She felt the anger again and once more pushed it down. "We are in a unique position to gather intelligence, and I am going to need all of our assets functioning at their very best. Whatever anger you bear me, I suggest you put it aside. The sooner we complete our work here, the sooner we return home. And I intend for us to return home."

She walked to the bed and put Jakob down upon it, giving him a carved wooden duck that one of the sailors had made. "The dreamstone has made language acquisition far simpler than I imagined it would be. I'm gathering what information I can. But I'm going to need all of the eyes I can muster when we land. I need to know their defenses, their military protocols, guard rosters and shifts. No different than during our stay with Ria in the north."

Lynnae nodded. "I'll keep my eyes open, Lady."

Aedric grunted his assent in the midst of more quiet coughing, and Jin winced at it. He should have been a resource, but between his rage, his stubbornness and his illness, he was a liability she wasn't sure she could afford. She bid her voice to soften and directed her next words toward him. "You must understand, First Captain Aedric, that we would not be here, having this conversation, if the work were not critical. You saw the ships. You've seen what their magicks are capable of in Pylos and in Windwir—" she gestured to Jakob where he lay on the bed, "—and even at the Firstborn Feast. The armies of the Named Lands will not stand long. This is now a war that can only be won with stealth and cunning."

"If that's the truth," Aedric said, "I don't know what work you and a toddler and a girl and a wrung-out forest scout could possibly do here that could win a war unless . . ." His words died, and she heard him suck in his breath.

He knows. She closed her eyes and waited.

Incredulity shaped his voice as the ciphers of the Rufello lock opened for him as he tested the dials. "Does Rudolfo know?"

She shook her head. "No." She opened her mouth to say more, then closed it. There was no reason for Aedric to know that she herself hadn't known until she was aboard.

"It makes sense," he finally said. The anger was gone now, replaced by something that sounded like a very tentative respect. "One of your father's careful snares, no doubt."

She didn't correct him. The affairs of House Li Tam were just those— and only shared beyond the close bonds of family on a need-to-know basis. It wasn't important for him to know all of the details; it was only important that he saw that it might work, that an empire without its Crimson Empress—especially one so carefully established through gospel and prophecy—had no cohesion without its figurehead.

Now, it was her turn to repeat herself. "I need all assets functioning at their very best," she said. "I will need information—every scrap of it that you find. And I will likely need items . . . procured . . . for the work."

"Aye, Lady."

He addressed me properly. She had no doubt that there would still be a reckoning down the road of some kind. His loyalty to Rudolfo would require it, and even if she succeeded and somehow made her way back to the Ninefold Forest, she had no doubt that Rudolfo would hold her accountable for not honoring their partnership with the truth. And his history with her family would make that dishonor much worse a betrayal for a man who'd lost so much already.

Still, she also had no doubt that if this worked and all was safe and sound at home, Rudolfo would reach a place of acceptance in the matter. And she knew that when he did, so too would his best friend's son.

Until then, if she at least had his respect, she would make do.

Jin Li Tam stood from the bed and saw Jakob was slowing down, his eyes drooping. That meant it neared lunchtime in the galley, and she'd made a point of eavesdropping on the sailors over long, leisurely lunches. "I need to leave," she said. "Will you watch over Jakob?"

Lynnae nodded. "Of course, Lady."

Then, she turned in the direction where she thought she'd last heard Aedric. "I want you to stay here, Captain. Get off the powders and sleep for a spell. You're unwell, and I cannot afford for you to be unwell."

She heard his sigh. "Yes, Lady."

She shot Lynnae a glance. "Keep him here. Lock the door behind me. I'll bring back food."

She slipped out into the hallway and made her way to the galley. Out in the open, her father's training took hold and her eyes moved over everything, taking inventory and measuring value. This sailor's posture. That sailor's smile. The keys that dangled from the armorer's belt as he passed her. And her ears caught the words that they could and the names that she recognized.

An uncharacteristic optimism seized her—a rare and nearly euphoric experience given how much of her life was lived in the shadow of doubt and hypervigilance.

We may just be able to do this.

But even as she thought it, she knew that if they were successful her own likelihood of seeing hearth and home again was slim. And as she thought it, Jin Li Tam was surprised at how acceptable that was to her if it meant her son could grow up in a better world than the one she presently saw on their horizon.

Vlad Li Tam

Vlad Li Tam dozed in the saddle and lurched with the large beast's every step, aware of the small hands that clutched at him. He'd seen pictures of the dromedaries of the Oldest World—the Tam library was renowned throughout the Named Lands, second only to a handful of bookhouses and the Great Androfrancine Library itself. They'd fascinated him as a child.

But I never imagined I would ride one.

Of course, nothing in his life now was something he could have imagined.

They'd ridden for days, the robed women taking up positions behind and before him as they plodded along single-file. Their Blood Guard ran the wastes unmagicked, chewing a root that he suspected was similar to what the guides in the Churning Wastes used for stamina, speed and hydration.

Behind him, the young woman—the Vessel of Grace—clung to him in silence.

After his confrontation with them and her healing there in the shadow of their shrine, they'd ushered him inside the small temple and tried their hand at questioning him. Vlad had waved them off. "I will speak to your superiors."

To their credit, they'd not continued, but he was very aware of their eyes upon his staff, and when he rolled into a borrowed blanket to sleep, he tucked it carefully beneath him.

The next evening, they'd brought out their dromedaries and set out to the southwest. When he'd seen that they had no mount for the young woman, he stopped them.

"Surely," he said, "you do not intend for her to walk?"

The woman who had been preaching the day before shrugged. "She is whole. The walking will go easier for her." Her face was a placid mask, but her eyes carried something in them—fear, he thought, though it was not him that she feared. He held those eyes until she spoke again. "The scripture is clear on this matter: 'And in that day you shall offer her neither food nor water nor shelter, for it is right that the sins of many be borne by the back of one and that the unrighteousness of all be cleansed by her passing.'"

Even Vlad was surprised by his response to the words. Because even as he felt anger over them, he felt an uncontrollable compulsion and suddenly laughed loud and long. Then, he reached down and extended a hand to the woman.

She regarded him with large eyes that flitted from him to the priestess. "It would not be right, my lord," she said.

"Nonsense," he said. "Take my hand." When she hesitated, he looked again to the priestess. "I'm certain you'd like to pass me quickly into the care of your superiors. I've violated your so-called scriptures once. Surely doing so again cannot make matters worse for me in the eyes of your god."

The woman bit her lip and looked away. "Your sin is your sin," she said.

When the Vessel of Grace took hold of his hand, he felt renewed strength pass into him from the staff, and he swung her easily up into the saddle behind him.

That had been nearly a week ago. In that time, he'd not only carried her behind him, but he'd also fed her from his own share of the hardtack, jerky and water his captors provided, and during the day, when they slept, she nestled up against him.

It struck a paternal chord within him, bringing back memories of children and grandchildren he would never see again, whose last words whispered in his ears, barely discernible beneath their screams of agony.

When they crested the rise and saw the wide canal below, Vlad paused to take it in. The waters shone in moonlight, and a warm breeze rustled the palm trees and grass that lined its banks. There, a few leagues south, lay a collection of stone buildings surrounded by a gated wall lit with lanterns.

The sun rose behind them as they made their way to a gate that swung open with their approach. The woman who led them stood in her stirrups and raised her voice as they crossed the threshold. "Behold the Vessel of our Lord's Grace, bearer of sin and salvation. Aid her not nor offer her comfort, for her passing is the hope of this world."

Vlad smiled at the hollow tone of her words, but it faded when he felt the woman shift uncomfortably behind him.

A man and a woman awaited them. The man wore a dark uniform accented by a saber tucked into a wide red sash and highly polished leather boots. The woman wore robes much like the priestess, but her hems bore silver trim and tassels and her long dark hair was piled up beneath a silver scarf.

The woman spoke first. "Sister Agnes, your visit is a pleasant surprise." Nothing in her voice suggested any kind of pleasure, only surprise.

The priestess climbed down from her mount and handed the reins to a boy who appeared from the shadows. She curtsied to the woman. "Deepest apologies, Sister-Mother Drusilla. There have been . . . unforeseen and unfortunate developments."

The woman studied Vlad now, her lips pursed. When she saw the Vessel of Grace riding behind him, a shadow clouded her face, and he thought she might actually gasp. Still, she restrained herself. "I see."

Vlad twisted in the saddle and helped the girl down. Then, he slid down himself. The man in uniform whistled low, and a half-dozen soldiers appeared, thorn rifles ready in their hands. "Stand where you are," the officer said.

Vlad made sure the girl was safely tucked behind him. "I have no intention of doing otherwise," he said. Then, he offered a smile that was
not returned.

Sister Agnes and Sister-Mother Drusilla stepped aside, their voices
low and their hands moving in some kind of code he could not read as
they conferred quickly. When they finished, Drusilla turned to the captain. "This man is in the custody of the Daughters," she said, "for violation of holy writ and interfering with the redemptive work of House
Y'Zir."

Vlad's smile widened. "I am my own custodian," he said. Then, he
nodded to the girl behind him. "And I am her custodian as well."

Now it was the woman's turn to smile; it started as a chuckle. "She
was spoken for millennia before her birth, stranger. Who are you to
steal from Y'Zir's sheepfold?"

"I am the one who made her whole."

The woman shook her head. "You may think you have, but it is not
true." There were more words exchanged between her and Sister Agnes;
then she glanced at the staff before meeting his eyes. "You bear a curious artifact," she said. "How did you come by it? And how do you come
to be here?"

"Love led me to the staff, and murder placed it in my hands," he said,
unsure of where these words suddenly came from as they rang out from
him. "And within the belly of a beast, I came to your shores in search of
the Barrens of Espira."

"You are a long way past the Barrens now, stranger." Her brow furrowed, and it made the scars upon her forehead all the more menacing.
"And why exactly have you interfered in the redemption of this woman
and our world?"

Vlad stared at her. "Because she suffered and I could." Even he did
not understand the why of it. It was as if some deeper instinct moved
in him now, uncoiling a part of his own heart that until now he'd not
comprehended.

"Not all suffering should be healed," the woman said. "I bid you return her to us now that she might complete her work."

Vlad shook his head. "I'll not return her," he said. "But perhaps I can
offer you something better."

The woman raised her eyebrows. "And what could you offer us?"

The staff came up within his hand as if it had a will of its own. Three
times, he stuck it upon the ground, and on the third time, there was a
collective gasp as Drusilla, Agnes and the others that surrounded him

fell to the ground. Vlad reached behind him and took the girl's hand. "Look away," he whispered.

Now they writhed in the dust as sores broke out upon those bits of skin that were exposed. Clawing hands tore out loose fistfuls of hair as their tongues swelled up from dehydration, choking off their cries of agony. Vlad watched them and felt the tension in the girl's hand as she squeezed his.

Others, hearing the commotion, raced into the courtyard and fell, themselves, to writhe and scream.

Vlad counted slowly, intending to go for a full five minutes. But a quiet voice behind him interrupted.

"Please, Lord," the Vessel of Grace said. "No more."

He released held breath and raised his own voice. "You now suffer the afflictions she once bore. Tell me about its saving work in you. Tell me that you wish it to continue, that somehow it benefits you or this world."

The cries were whimpers now.

"What I give you," he said in a quieter voice, "is understanding."

Then Vlad Li Tam tapped the staff thrice more and waited for his new hosts and hostesses to rise from the dust of their past suffering and arrange the next leg of a journey he still could not fully comprehend.

Chapter 10

Charles

Hunched over his saddle, Charles blessed the cold winter wind and begged it to keep him awake.

They'd ridden west for days and had started running into Machtvolk patrols soon after. They'd even seen at least a battalion's-worth of cavalry riding south toward a horizon smudged with a hazy wall of distant smoke. Twice, the patrols had stopped them, demanding their names, where they were from, where they were going. But they seemed to be intent about other business, and Charles's story about a grandfather escorting his displaced granddaughter home wasn't questioned. Charles suspected it was actually a fairly common occurrence with recent events and the massive influx of refugees he'd seen during his stay in the Ninefold Forest.

And so they'd continued on.

The rocking of the horse soothed him, and he nodded again. Even in that split second, he found himself spinning away.

He moved through an evergreen forest now, the girl walking beside him, her shorter legs pumping furiously to keep up his long metal stride. "Where are we going?"

Charles didn't answer. He was scanning the forest, and he'd felt the tickle of something in his skull. "I am uncertain of *my* destination, little human. Your destination is not my concern. You should return home to your family. I do not need—" He stopped, saw the movement ahead and knew in an instant it was three Machtvolk on horseback—half of a squad.

And he did not know why, but the first thing Charles did was grab up the girl into his strong metal arms before sprinting north and away.

Light swallowed him, and on the heels of that light he felt the pain of his back hitting the ground. Charles lay still in the muddy snow and blinked.

Winters turned her horse and started to dismount.

"Don't," Charles said, holding up a hand. Then, he forced himself onto his hands and knees and climbed slowly to his feet.

The girl paused, worry clouding her face. "It's happening a lot," she said.

He grabbed the bridle of his mare and huffed one foot into a stirrup. Pulling himself up, he melted into the saddle. "Every time I fall asleep. I'm either with it or with its dreams. Only . . ."

Only the Watcher was a ruthless, brutal machine. And this one—despite its similarities—was different. It seemed burdened, even sad, as it fled east. And it protected the girl as it did. When it waited for the girl to sleep, its dreams were riddled with violence and haunted by a melody that Charles recognized.

These seemed nothing like the Watcher. He'd only known one other mechoservitor anything like the one he experienced in his dreams, and Charles dared not let himself hope for a moment that it was him.

Those we lose are lost.

But his heart pulled toward it like a wagon wheel to a rut.

Winters watched him, her brow furrowed. "And you're certain you don't want the kallacaine?"

He shook his head. "No. It muddles me."

They nudged their horses forward, and Charles realized that he was taking the lead, adjusting their course instinctively. *It is as if I'm being led.*

They rode on in silence, the landscape becoming more and more wooded as they did. Windwir was near now—but Charles intended to skirt it. The Machtvolk—possibly the Y'Zirites, too—were excavating it. He'd seen items from his own workshop in the Watcher's cave and suspected that the plague spiders that had destroyed Pylos had somehow been resurrected from ancient eggs he'd stored in a Rufello vault with other dangerous leftovers of the Old World and the Wizard Kings who ruled it.

Something silver flashed by, low and near the ground. Turning in the saddle, Charles tried to follow it, but it was already twisting, turning and changing course. Still, he knew what it was and what to do.

Reining his horse in, he lifted his right hand and extended a finger. Winters pulled alongside of him, watching.

The moon sparrow landed easily, its gears whirring as its tiny metal feet clutched at his finger. It chirped twice, and then its mouth opened. Charles expected a metallic voice to whisper out and was surprised when it wasn't. "Arch-engineer Charles," the voice said, "the light requires your service. I am Arch-behaviorist Hebda of the Office for the Preservation of the Light. I must meet with you. I bear urgent information regarding the mechoservitors of Sanctorum Lux and the Y'Zirite mechoservitor designated Watcher. I require your assistance." Then, the man's voice was gone and the metal voice Charles had expected now spoke, whispering a string of numbers. When it finished, the bird ruffled its tiny silver feathers, closed its beak, then cocked its head and opened its beak again, waiting for Charles to speak.

"Message acknowledged," he said. He closed his eyes for a moment, visualizing a map of the region and placing the coordinates he'd been given. "I will be there tomorrow morning."

Closing its beak, the small bird leaped from his finger and sped away, low to the ground. He watched it until he could see it no longer, then became aware of Winters staring at him. He turned to her. "Moon sparrow," he said. "They are an ancient mechanical. The Order kept a small flock on hand—they are the only birds we know of that are effective in the Churning Wastes."

She nodded. "And the man who spoke to you . . . He said his name was Hebda. I know that name."

Charles didn't. He'd known there were secret offices and suspected that much of his work had been in service to them without his knowledge. He'd accepted it as part of his calling to serve the light, and even now, he did not question for a moment the present call. He would certainly go. "I am not familiar with an Arch-behaviorist Hebda," he said.

"Neb's Marshfolk name is Nebios ben Hebda," she said. "His father was Hebda, and I cannot imagine it is a common name."

"No," Charles agreed, "it is not."

Now her face darkened. "But Neb's father was killed at Windwir. He left Neb to tend their wagon so he could fetch letters that had been left behind. He was in the city when it fell."

Of course, Orius and his Gray Guard were supposedly in Windwir as well, but Charles and Isaak had stumbled upon a scouting party of Androfrancine Gray Guard in the Beneath Places. A remnant remained, though he had no way of knowing just how strong their numbers were or how exactly they'd managed to escape Windwir's desolation.

I will know soon enough, he suspected. He nudged the horse forward. "Well, it seems this Hebda's somehow cheated death."

Winters said nothing, but her eyes danced with the same hope that Charles struggled to crush in the cradle of his heart. Still, with each league that they rode, he found that struggle more and more a losing battle, and when the sun finally set at the end of another day in the saddle, he found himself longing for sleep and the dreams it would bring.

Because in those dreams, somehow Isaak lived and searched for his father even as Charles searched for his lost metal son.

Neb

The sound of his breathing and pulse slowed around the steady slap of water against the hull, and Neb savored the landscape of his opening mind as he settled deeper and deeper into himself.

He could taste the salt of the warm breeze on his lips and could smell the spider's musky scent where it knelt nearby, but he could also smell the others—the sweat of the sailors and the grease and metal of the mechoservitors mingled with the odor of Petronus's fish.

"Good," Aver-Tal-Ka said. "You are achieving calm faster. What do you feel?"

Neb kept his eyes closed. "I feel my breath and pulse slowing. As they slow, I'm sensing more. Mostly smells." He cocked his head and listened. He heard the whisper of turning gears and spinning scrolls. And the spider's heart, also beating slowly. "I can hear, too."

Yes. You are finding your way toward who you are.

They'd spent much of their time aboard the ship together, and Neb's head hurt from much of it. Still, the Builder Warrior had held back, doling out information with the care of an Androfrancine. "In time," he told the boy, "you'll know everything."

He'd pushed at first, but the spider was an unmovable wall. Still, he'd learned a great deal, and it boggled him. Everything, Aver-Tal-Ka said, had indeed been made to serve Neb and the People he belonged to, those Neb had grown up regarding as gods. The Younger Gods, they called them—an entire people and their civilization now lost to mythology. But at one time, the spider told him, they'd made their home both here upon the moon and on the world that it orbited. Their cities and gardens and forests and farms had covered both. This much Neb had already known based on the scraps of writings left over from the Oldest World, stories that were legends in the Age of the Weeping Czars, several millennia before the Age of the Wizard Kings.

But the Downunder War—this was new. There had been conflict between the Younger Gods and their children, and the parents were eventually forced to retreat to the moon or hide themselves in the Beneath Places where they slept—much as his father Whym and Amylé's father, D'Anjite, had done. And they would've stayed hidden upon the moon but for that first Y'Zir, the Downunder thief who'd tricked them out of their Firsthome Temple and made their extinction his life's ambition.

You are losing focus. The spider's voice startled him.

"There's . . . so much to understand."

"Yes. And so much more than you realize." The spider chuckled, and it was a chilling sound. "Once you've unsealed the temple, you'll also have the Library of Elder Days to incorporate into your learning."

An image came with the words—a vast white cavern scattered with trees bearing gems that hung like fruit, shining out a rainbow of colors that stung Neb's eye.

Millions of years of knowledge. It staggered him, dwarfing what until now had been the largest repository of knowledge he could conceive of—the Great Library that had fallen with Windwir. He wondered what Petronus would think of it, and the moment the old man's face crossed his mind, he sensed the spider's hesitation.

What is your . . . Neb stretched for the word but couldn't find it.

I am concerned only for your well-being, Lord Whym.

Neb scowled, mindful of the old man who worked his fishing net aft of them. *Why does Petronus concern you?*

Aver-Tal-Ka paused, its mandibles chittering. *Perhaps "concern" is too strong a word. But these things I share with you—and those things that will come later—they are for you. They are for the People and none other. The children of the People have cast aside their birthright. They chased their parents to the moon and chose the Downunder for themselves. They cheered when Y'Zir made himself strong on the blood of their parents and took the temple for himself.*

Neb could sense the distaste and disregard now in the spider's careful words and was surprised that he hadn't sensed it before. *Still, they are not all so. These men have risked their lives to accompany me here.*

Yes, Aver-Tal-Ka said, *but do not mistake that for love. And do not for a moment let down your guard. The children fear the parents and yet long for their baubles.*

He wanted to protest this, but the sudden image of Winters's eyes upon him as he stood over her in his translated form, wrapped in light and infused with the blood of the earth, stopped him. He'd seen the fear in her eyes—in the eyes of everyone in that room but the regent. He had changed, he knew, and that change had terrified the girl he loved. Was it such a stretch to believe it might ultimately have that effect on everyone he'd once counted his friend?

Comfort. No despair. Now, the spider used his mouth. "I'm sorry to upset you with this talk, Lord Whym. These sessions are meant to help you find peace, not conflict. Perhaps my own biases interfere. Forgive me."

Neb inclined his head. The spider moved now, climbing slowly to its feet, and as he did, Neb tasted something new upon the wind. He drew in a great breath and separated out the flowers from the trees and grass and sand he smelled. Turning his head in the direction it came from, he saw the smudge of green on their horizon.

"There," Aver-Tal-Ka pointed. "We will find her there."

Neb thought about the girl they sailed after. She'd shown up in his thoughts regularly since their encounter, but she'd not appeared in his dreams since that first night. He'd even tried, stretching out for her with his carved kin-raven clutched tightly in his fist, but had not found her. All he'd found was the howling of hounds frustrated by his escape to sea and something else that he could not place—something old that watched him from someplace deep within the aether but did not announce itself.

The island took form ahead of them as Rafe and his men sailed them closer. They circled it once with Aver-Tal-Ka and the others standing at the rails to watch. It was a larger island with a hill rising from the center of it, blanketed by thick jungle that erupted into the cries of birds and the chattering of monkeys as they approached. Neb could hear each distinct voice in the jungle's choir, and it was like no other music he had ever heard. There was life in it and in the smells that he drank in. The rich jungle loam, the blossoms and the ripening fruit, mingled with the musky, heavy scent of its inhabitants.

Aver-Tal-Ka's voice slid into his head. *How many monkeys do you hear?*

Eleven. No . . . fourteen.

He felt the spider's pleasure rolling over him, washing him, and he flushed. *Very good.*

Then, the spider scuttled off to ready the anchor and longboat.

It was earthrise when they landed ashore. They'd brought the scout sergeant, Olynder, along with Rafe and Petronus. The two old men carried thorn rifles, and the Gypsy Scout carried a pickaxe and shovel, his bow slung. Aver-Tal-Ka went ahead of them, using three of its arms to clear a path, and Neb followed close behind, the kin-raven clenched tightly in his fist.

Amylé.

When they reached the top of the hill, the spider tore out a swath of ground cover. Then, the scout broke the ground and started shoveling earth away until he struck metal.

Neb recognized the hatch the forester uncovered and knew exactly what the cipher was to unlock it. Kneeling before it, he spun the dials and moved the levers until he'd entered the date of his birth based on the forgotten calendar of the Younger Gods.

Then he swung the hatch open and felt the true presence of her for the first time despite the leagues that still separated them. And, for the first time in his life, despite having been an orphan of the Order, Neb understood just how truly alone he'd been.

Winters

Late-morning sun softened the snow into muddy slush as Winters and Charles rode into Kendrick's Town. Winters had never been this far south—Windwir had been the farthest she'd visited. It was a quiet town, but it was obvious by the condition of the road that a large army had passed through recently.

She let Charles take the lead, bringing her horse in behind his and hoping that the shadows of her hood would hide her scars. They skirted the edge of the town, and she watched the old man as he paused to measure the sun before steering them away from the cluster of buildings and onto a narrow path that ran through the woods.

The farmhouse and its solitary barn stood in a clearing, half a league deep into the pine forest that surrounded the town. Charles pulled up, then climbed down from the saddle before entering the clearing to approach the house.

Winters dismounted as well, leading her horse as she followed after. The scout knife at her hip whispered for her hand to pull it, but she resisted.

Charles looked over his shoulder and caught her eye. "There are eyes upon us," he said.

Even as he said it, Winters felt the slightest breeze and heard the muffled cough of magicked feet on snow. She turned in the direction of the noise, but as soon as she did, it stopped.

She stopped as well and waited while Charles stepped up to the door and knocked. The man who opened it wore the clothing of a farmer, but his eyes told Winters another story. He was tall, his salt-and-pepper hair cut close.

"Come in, Brother Charles," he said. "Gustav will take your horse."

The door opened wider, and a young man stepped out, tugging on a coat. His eyes, she noted, were also wrong for the attire he wore, and he walked more like a scout than a farm boy.

Charles handed him the reins. "Are you Hebda?"

The man shook his head. "No," he said. "I am Renard. You met me long ago in the Wastes when I ran them with my father."

She heard surprise in the old man's voice. "Remus's son?"

Renard inclined his head. "The same." He leaned outside and looked to the left and right. "But let's continue this conversation inside." Then, as an afterthought, he smiled. "We have hot chai. And venison stew."

Winters felt her stomach growl and thought she caught the faintest scent of fresh bread leaking from the house's door. Charles stamped the snow from his boots and went inside. Winters stepped forward and held out her reins to Gustav, but he did not take them. Instead, the young man shot a furtive glance to Renard.

His smile apologized before he did. "I'm sorry, Lady Winteria. These are Androfrancine matters."

Winters shook her head. "They are far more than that, now."

Another voice interrupted from deeper inside the house. "Let her in, Renard. Her dreams are bound up in this. Tertius showed us that."

Tertius. The name startled her, flooding her with memories of the old man and his patient smile. He'd been old when her father had brought him to her, and he'd spent his last years teaching her reading, ciphering, and history among other things. And as the dreaming found her in her early years, she talked about them with him and tried to answer his questions.

Gustav took the reins and slipped off to the barn. Winters took it as her cue to climb onto the porch, stomp her own boots free of snow, and follow Charles inside.

Renard closed the door and ushered them down a narrow hallway that opened into a wide room. In one corner, a stove crackled and the kettle upon it hissed. Near it, a gaunt, hollow-eyed man sat at a table. "Come in," he said, gesturing to empty chairs. "Sit."

Renard moved to a chair by a curtained window and sat at it, peeking out over the calico fabric to watch the yard.

Charles pulled off his coat and draped it over the back of the chair. "Arch-behaviorist Hebda, then?"

The man nodded. "Yes, Arch-engineer Charles."

He sat. "Of the Office for the Preservation of the Light?"

Winters pulled her own coat off, hung it in like manner, and sat. Another young man materialized with a platter of bread, two empty mugs, and two steaming bowls.

Hebda nodded. "Yes. Though I doubt you've heard of me."

Charles shook his head. "Not until yesterday."

Winters watched the man. He moved as if beneath great weight, and his eyes were as devoid of life as the Churning Wastes. "I have heard of you," she said in a quiet voice.

The man flinched. "I suppose you have at that. Neb's told you about me."

She nodded. "Not much. But he thinks you were killed in Windwir. I know he dreamed of you, though." When the memory struck her, it was like a blow and she was surprised. She remembered a voice and an image, though it was vague. "I dreamed of you, too, I think."

"Yes," he said. "You did. And Neb now knows that I'm alive. We spoke before he left."

She heard Renard's soft growl from across the room, but Hebda's words kept her focus squarely upon him. "You saw Neb before he left?"

Hebda sighed. "I did. It was a . . . difficult encounter."

She opened her mouth to ask the obvious question, but Charles spoke first. "Then the boy is alive," the old man said. She could hear the incredulousness in his voice. "He survived the explosion."

Hebda nodded. "We do not know all of the details, but we do know that somehow Nebios reached the antiphon despite his diversion north." He looked at Winters when he said it, and their eyes met briefly before he looked away. "Barring the unforeseen, he, Father Petronus and a handful of others—including five of the Sanctorum Lux mechoservitors—have reached the moon and seek the Moon Wizard's Tower."

She felt the breath go out of her even as a shudder passed through her body. *He'd reached the moon.* She knew Hebda hadn't exactly said that, but she had to believe that if Neb indeed survived his encounter with the Watcher then he'd also survive whatever else must be survived and prepare their new home. Because he had to.

Because I need him to.

Charles continued. "How is the Order involved in this? And how many of you have survived Windwir?" He leaned forward with narrow eyes. "I know about Orius. Isaak and I encountered his scouts in the Beneath Places."

Hebda also leaned forward. "Some of us have survived. Knowing more than that jeopardizes our work and our survival—and the survival of the light. But there are enough that we've managed to keep some intelligence assets operational. Not enough to stave off the Y'Zirite invasion. As to how we are involved . . . I'll let Micah explain that."

At the mention of the name, Winters heard the hiss of releasing steam and the grinding of gears as a metal man stirred to life and lumbered into the room.

"Father," it said as it approached. "It is good to see you."

This mechoservitor was older than Isaak—more boxlike in its construction—but like that metal man, it also wore robes. Winters watched it approach, then watched the old engineer's face as he regarded his metal creation. She wished she had the Francine ability to accurately read emotion; in this case, she saw several, though she hesitated to name them.

"You are Mechoservitor Number Four, First Generation," Charles said.

"Yes," it said, its bellows giving the voice a reedy quality. "But my chosen name is Micah."

"Micah," Hebda said in a low voice, "was the first to approach us about the canticle and its antiphon. He and the other mechoservitors of Sanctorum Lux discovered the artifact and deciphered it, though a mandate coded into it prevented them from involving us initially."

"The dream was not intended for your kind," Micah said. "Your exclusion was for the benefit of the light."

Hebda continued. "I became involved when an infant was brought to me by the mechoservitors and placed into the Order's care." He nodded toward Renard. "It was his sister's child, though now we understand that his sister merely served as an incubator."

Winters blinked. "Neb is not your son?"

Hebda lowered his eyes. "I've tried to love him as if he were. But no. He is not."

She looked at Renard. "And your sister *incubated* him." It wasn't a question, but he still nodded. As he did, something in Winters that she'd tried to keep hidden stirred back to life. The image of Neb, blazing in glory, his face twisted in fear and his eyes full of rage as he burst into her room. The feeling of his hands upon her as the pain fled and her wounds healed. She'd been afraid then, and even now that fear chewed at her heart. But now, that fear went deeper.

"What is he?"

Her question hung in the room uncomfortably until the mechoservitor released a gout of steam and worked its eye shutters. "The Homeseeker is the offspring of the Younger God Whym."

Winters's mouth went dry, and when she reached for the mug she realized it was still empty. Hebda saw and stood quickly to fetch the kettle. "He is also somehow a brother of P'Andro and T'Erys Whym, though we do not yet understand it."

Charles's eyes narrowed. "I don't see how that could be possible."

Hebda filled the mugs. "As I said, we don't understand it yet either. Any more than we understand how it is that the Marsher dream and the dream buried in the canticle are interwoven. But they are. And that brings us to the matter at hand." He looked at Winters and then back to the arch-engineer. "We are aware of the dreams you are having, Charles. Glimpses of them are showing up in the aether."

Charles sipped his chai. "The aether?"

"The aether is an artificially constructed environment to contain and affect dreaming—to share it, even, with others. Something left over from the Age of the Younger Gods. A recreational pursuit, we believe, though there may have been therapeutic and educational uses as well." He held up a small stone that Winters recognized. One of the mechoservitors had pressed a similar stone to her head when it had revealed the Marshfolk's new home to her. "This stone allows access."

She saw competing emotions on Charles's face now. Frustration and curiosity both vying for primacy. "I'm surprised," he said, "that I've not heard of such a thing until now." He held out his hand. "May I?"

Hebda shook his head. "The artifact requires a great deal of training to use it properly. And not using it properly could mean betraying our location here."

"Apologies, Father," the mechoservitor said. "There are many things in this endeavor that were necessarily kept from you."

"And yet you tell me now," Charles said, looking from the metal man to Hebda.

"Yes," Hebda said. "Because for some reason, this new mechoservitor is transmitting to you across the aether in some kind of cipher we do not completely comprehend. We are picking it up sporadically, and we believe the Y'Zirites are as well." Now, he looked to Winters. "We've also seen glimpses of other dreams—not enough for us to make sense, but Micah believes it is connected to the Marsh dreams."

"I can assure you," Micah said, "that it is not a belief but a hypothesis based upon available evidence."

Winters looked at the metal man. "What is your hypothesis?"

Scrolls whirred deep in the metal man's chest cavity even as it fixed its jeweled eyes upon her. "That the mechoservitor is indeed the Watcher and that it is somehow deciphering the Final Dream taken from your Book of Dreaming Kings. And Lord Whym needs that dream to gain access to the tower."

Charles sat back, and Winters saw the conflicting emotion upon his face again. There was a light in his eyes that looked suspiciously like hope, but it seemed out of place in the midst of his tired face and his firm jaw. "What is your evidence for this hypothesis?"

"There is a cave near the Third River, northwest of the Desolation of Windwir," Hebda said. "Its walls are covered in images and symbols . . . painted in blood. Our scouts have seen it. A girl from a nearby village was bringing the mechanical livestock before it abducted her and fled when confronted by villagers."

Charles looked up at the mechoservitor. "And your evidence as to why the Watcher is transmitting to me specifically?"

"We have none," Micah said. "But not only does it transmit to you . . . it seeks you."

Hebda drew a map from his pouch and rolled it out upon the table. "Our scouts have picked up its trail here," he said, pointing. "And then here . . . and here. It has changed its course along with you."

Charles studied the map. "Have you attempted to communicate with it?"

"It flees when our scouts approach. And it is also pursued by Machtvolk patrols. We expect Y'Zirite reinforcements to join in with the discovery of the cave paintings. If it is indeed the Watcher, it has been their key asset in bringing about the invasion, and I'm certain they want to re- claim it."

Charles nodded. "They are looking for it, and it is looking for me."

"Yes," Hebda said.

"And how do wish me to serve the light in this matter?"

But Winters knew the answer to Charles's question before he fin- ished asking it, and she suspected he did, too. And she knew that the answer was her answer as well and her best hope of finding the Final Dream.

"You want us to simply let it find us," she said in a quiet voice.

"Yes," Hebda said. "I think the light depends upon it."

And Winters knew, just as she knew the answer to Charles's question, that the hollow-eyed arch-behaviorist was exactly correct in his suspicion.

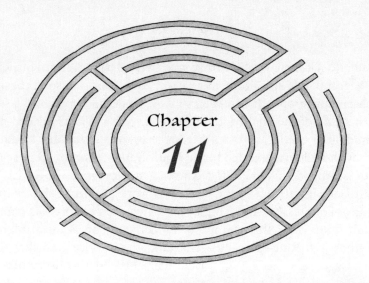

Chapter 11

Rudolfo

It was warm enough to ride coatless on the Divided Isle, and Rudolfo welcomed the sun on his neck. The transition from saddle to sea and then saddle again jarred his bones and muddled his mind.

And my guest did not make it any easier. Ire Li Tam rattled him, and the fact that she could have any impact upon him at all rattled him even more. They'd talked very little after that first night—she'd slept most of the time, tucked away out of sight beneath his bed. And she'd vanished while he was breakfasting the morning that they made landfall.

Now, after two nights spent in inns appropriated by Y'Zirite quartermasters, Rudolfo and his entourage approached the borders of Merrique County. He found himself ready to rest, though he knew that he was far from any real respite.

Still, a bed that didn't sway, one he could use for the better part of a week, would suffice. Of course, it wouldn't matter. He'd still toss and turn, his mind working the Whymer Maze their world had become, trying to find some way to take what victory he could from a situation that had been an unstoppable force in his life going back to the death of his brother and his parents. And he didn't know the details, but this Y'Zirite invasion and Rudolfo's chancellorship had been sanctioned—even arranged—by his own father, a man he'd revered for as long as he had memory.

Rudolfo felt the edges of sorrow and twisted it, added it to his anger.

The farmlands around them gave way to houses, and soon they rode into Merrique proper. It had been well over a decade since he'd last visited this part of the Named Lands. One large island was divided down the middle by a chasm of treacherous seawater. Settled in the earliest years by those less interested in the Androfrancine way of life, a scattering of independent but united counties arose, banded together by a Council of Sheriffs who were elected to work in partnership with the counts or countesses—the families for which each county was named.

He'd first visited this county in the company of its most infamous son—the pirate Rafe Merrique—sneaking into the city in the bottom of a beer wagon and fleeing on stolen, magicked horses. Everything between was a haze of rum and perfume.

Now, as the stallion they'd provided bore him down empty cobblestone streets, he looked for some sign of normalcy and found it only in the occasional chimneys that leaked smoke or the barking of a dog.

It was noon when they reached the center of the county seat and pulled into the courtyard of the sheriff's manor. A tall, angular woman in a red-piped black uniform stood waiting. A ceremonial, curved iron knife adorned her sash alongside a small, silver knife that Rudolfo recognized from the Blood Temples he'd seen. He noted it, seeing the symbol for what it was—the blade of war and the blade of faith both at hand.

Her white hair was pulled back, and her olive skin shone darker for the pale symbols carved into her flesh. As Rudolfo drew closer, she leaned over and whispered something to the younger woman who stood beside her. The young redhead listened and nodded. This one was nearly as tall as the other, her hair close-cropped like a soldier and her face also scarred. Her own dark uniform bore no crimson but the scarf tied to her arm, but she also carried each knife and wore a phylactery at the base of her throat.

El Anyr dismounted first, and Rudolfo followed. "General Yazmeera," the emissary said, bowing. "I present Lord Rudolfo of the Ninefold Forest Houses, father of the Child of Promise and Chancellor of the Named Lands."

She extended her hand to him, and he took hers. The firmness of her grip did not surprise him. "Chancellor," she said. "I hope we can work effectively together to bring the fighting to a swift close." She looked at him, and he knew the look well. She was measuring him, weighing what she could by his appearance and posture and poise. And as quickly as she started, she finished and turned away. "Walk with me."

Rudolfo followed, and the younger woman met his eyes for but a moment, then glanced quickly away as he walked past. He heard her fall in behind them, and even farther back, the emissary El Anyr struggled to keep up.

"I've had quarters prepared for you nearby," Yazmeera said. "I'll leave you to settle into them today and hope you'll join me and my senior staff for dinner this evening. Tomorrow, we'll get started. There is a lot to do."

Rudolfo paced himself so that he walked exactly beside her. There was more activity now—mostly uniformed enlisted men and officers hurrying to and fro. Here in the quarter closest to the sheriff's manor there was no sign whatsoever of anyone *not* in uniform, and it piqued his curiosity. He added it to a growing list. "I will gladly join you for dinner," he said.

"Good," she said. "And I suspect you've not had Y'Zirite fare. It's far livelier than the bland foods you're accustomed to, I'll wager."

He felt a momentary tickle of anger and suppressed it. "I look forward to sampling your cuisine." *And,* he thought, *meeting the senior staff.*

"I'll have the raven-keeper come by so that you can get word home if you wish. And I suspect you might like to get word to the Great Mother as well. This separation can't possibly be easy given everything else." Her relaxed tone caught him off guard, though he wasn't sure why. Perhaps it was how easily she accepted all of this, how normal she made it sound.

But why wouldn't she? She'd likely spent years planning this invasion, knowing all the while what was coming, right down to his own role in it. "I appreciate the gesture," he said, "though I suspect tomorrow will be soon enough."

She nodded and then stopped. They stood at the gate of a small villa. A guard stood post, a long wooden tube cradled in his arms and a long curved sword slung over his shoulder. Rudolfo knew he could not be alone and quickly sighted men stationed on the rooftops across from the villa and a patrol of three women dressed in the light silks and soft boots of scouts who moved past them, their eyes scanning the streets.

"This," she said, "will be your quarters for now. Something more fitting will be acquired once the conflict is brought to a close and we can relocate to the mainland."

Rudolfo nodded. "I'm sure it will be more than sufficient."

Yazmeera regarded him, and Rudolfo waited, knowing that words awaited behind her brief silence. He could see the calculations in her stare. "I know that this must be very difficult for you. The circumstances of your deception—and the betrayal that it must certainly feel like—are most unfortunate. Your father rejoiced in knowing this day would eventually come. I was by his side when he negotiated the treaty with the regent, and Lord Jakob wept tears of gratitude knowing his part—and the part he made for you and for his grandson—in the healing of the world."

The anger was back but no longer a tickling. It was a burning beneath his skin that threatened to redden his face, and the slightest movement of her eye told him that she was watching him even now. Watching and measuring. "It is . . . difficult . . . for many reasons," he finally said. And then the anger was tucked away, hidden beneath the smile he forced to the surface. "But trees that do not bend—"

"Must surely break," she said, finishing his sentence.

Rudolfo inclined his head, and she returned the gesture.

"And with that," Yazmeera said, "I have much to do between now and dinner. So get settled. The house has a modest staff, and Lieutenant Tamyra has been assigned as your personal aide and security." She placed her hand on the young woman's shoulder. "The lieutenant is to be decorated for her actions during her deployment in the Homelands—what the Deicides called the Churning Wastes. She was the sole surviving member of her squad." She smiled as she said this. "That speaks volumes of her competency; I have no doubt she will serve you well."

Rudolfo studied the woman more carefully now and raised his eyebrows. "I'm not certain it's fitting for me to rob you of one of your better assets." Of course, he knew as he said it that it was nothing of the sort. She'd been assigned to him precisely because of being a better asset, and he doubted his need for personal protection was the primary reason for that assignment.

"You'll also find her to be an excellent conversationalist, well versed in Y'Zirite custom, culture and faith."

Rudolfo smiled. "Thank you."

Yazmeera returned the smile, though he could see she'd set guards at the corners of it. "You're most welcome, Lord Rudolfo. And dinner will be at six bells."

Then, abruptly, she was striding back the way they'd come, the emissary still struggling to keep up.

Rudolfo watched her go, then looked to the lieutenant. "Shall we?"

She inclined her head, and the guard opened the gate. They passed through, entered a wide courtyard set with a palm tree and a fountain at its center. Beyond it, a wide veranda welcomed them and glass doors led into the house itself. The small staff waited just inside the doors, and

Rudolfo made a point of introducing himself to each, meeting their eyes and repeating their names back to them. None bore the scars of Y'Zirite faith, and he suspected they may even have been the same staff to whoever had lived here before the invasion. After working through the gauntlet, he and Tamyra were led on a quick tour that ended at his private quarters—a suite of rooms that included a den, bed and bathing chambers and a small bedroom for his aide.

When the house steward left them, Rudolfo looked at the woman again. She stood at a bookcase, her fingers running over the spines. Her posture was suddenly far more relaxed than he would expect of his aide, and there was something familiar about her. *It's her profile,* he realized. And when she spoke, he understood exactly why.

"This," Ire Li Tam said as she took in her surroundings, "will do nicely."

Vlad Li Tam

Kin-wolves bayed beyond the high, barred window of his cell, and Vlad Li Tam sighed as the young woman beside him moved and mumbled in her sleep. The Y'Zirites had tried to separate them, but when the woman's eyes widened at their attempt, Vlad had insisted she stay with him and their hosts had relented.

What choice did they have? They'd already tried to bring him down with one of their thorn rifles. The thorn had lodged in his upper arm and had stung slightly, but nothing more. And his retribution had been swift and complete—five of their soldiers had collapsed into seizures, their own bodies convulsing with the toxins they'd tried to inflict upon him.

Now, they awaited the barge that would take them south along a wide canal and into the city of Ahm's Glory.

Vlad closed his eyes and willed himself back to sleep, but the woman cried out again, her voice rising in fear. He thought he picked words out of her cries and whimpers, but they were incomprehensible.

Still, every night he'd spent with her was filled with the terror she faced in her sleep, though by day she showed no sign at all of that war.

The woman was a Whymer Maze. She still knelt for her prayers each day despite the suffering her faith seemed so set on causing her.

"What war do you fight?" he whispered into the woman's ear.

And closing his eyes, Vlad Li Tam suddenly found himself transported into the midst of it.

It was a dark cave lit by lichen that speckled its high ceiling and the dim light of the silver staff he grasped. The woman crouched there, naked and battered, eyes wide and nostrils flared. Vlad stood near her, easily in her line of sight, but she did not see him. Instead, she watched the cavern, and when she moved, he noticed the chain upon her ankle.

"Come to me, my daughter, my sweet," a singsong voice intoned from the shadows. "Lie with me, my lovely bride."

He heard a whisper in the deeper dark and picked out the faintest glow of something large that shuffled toward them. He heard the woman's breathing catch in a ragged sob and heard the chains clanking as she scrambled to her feet and tried to move away.

"Our night of consummation is only just begun," the voice said again. "Such a strong girl, such a good girl. Do not be afraid." As it moved closer, Vlad thought it was the lichen reflecting off of whatever approached them. But he saw quickly that this was only partially true. Deep inside a large glass orb, a dirty light guttered. And beneath the orb, metal legs moved over the stone, carrying the creature forward.

The girl was scrambling away on her hands and knees when the creature stopped and probed the ground with one of its legs. It lifted the broken end of the chain and yanked it backward. With a scream, the woman fell to be dragged across the ground like a trout on the line, flopping and twisting.

"Light," Vlad cried out, bringing the staff down. It sparked to life, silver light flooding the massive chamber. Only then did the woman seem to see him, though the puzzlement upon her face told him she either did not recognize him or did not comprehend how he could be here with her.

And she wasn't the only one to notice Vlad. With the room now fully lit, the creature that pursued her also saw him. And Vlad took notice now of what stood before him.

It rose up on eight metal legs that joined to a pitted, metal chassis and a dirty glass orb. Wrapped wires rose up from the back of the orb to trail out behind the spider, stretching back along the floor to a dark opening in the wall. Surprised, it dropped the chain, then leaned forward. Bellows beneath the chassis pumped air into a voice box. "And what interloper is this, come wandering with his stick into the fortnight of my nuptials?"

"I am Vlad Li Tam," he said.

"Tam," the spider spat. "Scam, slam, ram, dam, a tasty bit of roasted lamb."

Vlad stepped forward, raising the staff. "What is your business with this woman?"

He could almost hear the incredulousness in the spider's metal voice. "Why, she is my bride. My Vessel of Grace." And then, it too moved forward, bending the glass orb down to just inches from Vlad's face. Some kind of purple mist twisted and writhed beneath the smeared surface, and a solitary pink eye suddenly pressed up against the inside of the orb, blinking yellow ichor onto the glass. "And what is *your* business with her, stick-waver?"

The woman looked up at him, her brown eyes wide with terror and shock, her naked body covered in scabs and filth. Her lower lip trembled, and when he made eye contact with her, she looked away.

"Salvation," Vlad whispered, though he did not understand the compulsion to save her that pervaded every bit of him.

The spider howled laughter and danced backward on seven of its legs and tugged the chain with the eighth. The girl fell again, but she'd stopped whimpering now as it dragged her backward toward the dark doorway.

The staff grew suddenly hot in Vlad's hands, and current coursed the length of his arm, staggering him. *Do not let it leave, my love. Do not let it take her into the dark.*

Vlad strode across the floor, the rod extended before him. He raised his voice, and it bellowed through the cavern. "Release her."

The spider pulled the woman in close to itself with two of its legs, and once she was tucked safely beneath the chassis, it approached Vlad again. This time, the bellows seemed to sniff him and the staff. "Interloper, dance-the-roper, deep-in-dark and sorrow-groper," it sang. "You have no power over me here."

Its name is its power, a woman whispered. *And he must give it if asked; it is the heart of all bargains.* He looked to the girl but knew even as he did that it wasn't her. It was someone closer.

The staff.

Vlad extended it, one-handed, and smote the glass orb. "What is your name, demon?"

"I am the seventh of the seven," the spider said, shuddering from the blow. It scuttled back again, this time faster, and Vlad lunged after it, hitting it again.

"Your name," he demanded.

"I am the last and the lost, the forgotten and forsaken."

It toys with you. Yes, he realized. Because it had to speak the truth, but it didn't have to be direct. Vlad turned his gaze on the woman that dangled in its arms, tucked up beneath the chassis.

"You know its name," he said. "It haunts your nightmares."

She closed her eyes. "I may not speak it."

Vlad closed his own. *Yes, you may.*

And when she mouthed the words, he read them from her lips and spoke them aloud into the cavern. "Ahm Y'Zir," he cried out. "I command you to free this woman."

The spider shrieked and threw the girl aside as if she'd become too hot to carry. Vlad thrust the staff at it and it scrambled away, its legs clacking over the stone floor. He did not pursue it as it ran through the doorway and slipped into shadow. Instead, he turned to the girl, but she was already gone.

Vlad smiled and willed himself awake. She stared at him with eyes more clear than he remembered seeing them before. Her face was more relaxed, and the look upon it made him uncomfortable. It was a strange mixture of joy and wonderment.

"You're free now," he said.

"Yes," she said. "Is it true? What the woman told me?"

Vlad scowled. "What woman?"

"The one in the cave who stood with you."

His eyes narrowed. "What did she tell you?"

The Vessel of Grace stifled a yawn. "That you would also free my daughter."

The staff lay cold beneath him, and Vlad curled his fingers around it, liking the way the metal felt in his grasp. "I'm certain it must be true," he said in a quiet voice.

The woman rolled over and pushed herself against him, her breathing slow and steady. Vlad Li Tam sighed, fell into a light sleep, and dreamed of his grandson's laughter.

Jin Li Tam

The bustle of activity in the stateroom was a near imitation of the same fervor gripping the ship and crew, and Jin Li Tam took to it like an actor to a stage. Aedric slept quietly tucked beneath her bed as she and Lynnae helped each other into formal gowns that had been delivered just after dawn.

Sometime in the night, they'd anchored in the harbor of Ahm's Glory, and she'd watched the sun rise over that vast city from the porthole after finding additional guards at her door.

The city itself was subtle in its difference from any other she'd seen, and Jin could not place that difference. Spires and towers stretched out as far as she could see, and strange beasts of burden—yaks and drome-daries, she suspected—moved up and down the avenues trailing behind the people who led them or walking with ease beneath the people who rode them.

The only thing that seemed clearly unusual to her was the gathering crowd just beyond a well-guarded dock, but Sister Elsbet's arrival with the dresses explained that well enough.

"We'll ride by carriage to the imperial palace," she had said in quiet tones, smiling over a sleeping Jakob. "And take a late lunch there in the gardens with the regent and a few of his closest supporters. But we will not hurry; there are people who slept on the street last night just to glimpse you and your son as you pass by."

Now, Lynnae flushed as she struggled with her dress; and Jakob, stripped down to his diaper, crawled about the floor, pausing to pull him-self up to stand here or there to take tentative steps before returning to his hands and knees. Jin watched them in the mirror and then returned to studying herself.

She could see the events of the last two years in her face—lines at the corners of her mouth and a hardness in her eyes—but for what she'd paid there, her body was a different matter. It was firm, well toned and strong. She adjusted her breasts in the gown and then twisted to see what she could of her bare back.

"You look lovely," Lynnae said.

Jin smiled. "Thank you. It's been a while since I've squeezed into one of these."

Lynnae chuckled. "I don't think I've worn a gown since your wedding."

Jin's mind flashed to the ceremony, held in the gardens of the Sev-enth Forest Manor at Rachyle's Rest. But the image of Rudolfo in his dress uniform and green turban of office—and Jakob dressed in a close approximation of the same—was a knife in her ribs now, and she pushed the memory aside. Instead, she focused on the Entrolusian woman. The light green of her dress complemented her olive complexion, and her dark curly hair was pulled back beneath matching pearl combs. "You look lovely as well, Lynnae."

The woman curtsied. "Thank you, Lady."

A muffled voice cleared behind them both, and Jakob laughed and staggered back as a large hand swiped at him from beneath the bed. Aedric crawled out, growling low like a bear, and Jakob laughed even louder.

Jin's hands moved by instinct. *We've more ears at the door than normal.*

Aedric saw and nodded, his eyes dark. They'd stayed up late, long after Lynnae and Jakob had fallen asleep, shaping the best strategy they could in whispers and words pressed into hands. But the look on his face told her he understood what she now feared. He couldn't stay beneath the powders forever. She'd seen what could happen to scouts who magicked themselves for too long. It was impossible to know any man's threshold for tolerating them, but every scout had his limit. And captured, Aedric would do no one any good.

But what to do? He would not relent in his decision to stay with her and Jakob. She'd even considered turning him in herself but knew that even with her influence as Great Mother, she couldn't be certain that she could sway the regent in that matter. And she couldn't risk failure.

Neither could he. And they both knew the truth now as they lay at harbor. His hours with them were numbered, but Aedric would stay until he absolutely could not any longer. But he would find them again—she had no doubt of it.

A knock at the door sent the scout scuttling back beneath the bed, and Jin Li Tam moved forward quickly to scoop up Jakob. "One moment," she called out.

She shot a glance to Lynnae, and the woman quickly positioned herself in front of the bed. After a final glance confirmed to her that Aedric couldn't be seen, she opened the door a crack.

Eliz Xhum stood, dressed in black robes decorated in silver and crimson, alongside a similarly clothed Sister Elsbet. Both inclined their heads. "It is nearly time, Great Mother. Are you ready?"

Jin smiled. "Very nearly," she said, holding Jakob between her and the door. "We just need to dress him."

Xhum returned her smile. "Certainly," he said. "We'll wait."

Pushing the door closed, she grabbed up Jakob's tiny uniform and dressed him quickly with Lynnae's help. As she finished, she felt hands upon her shoulders. *I am ready, Lady,* Aedric said, pressing the words into her skin.

"Good," she said. Her own hands found his forearm. *Stay close to me.*

Aedric's whisper was barely audible. "Aye."

Then, she nodded Lynnae to the door and gathered Jakob up in her arms. "We're ready," she said.

Lynnae went out first, and Jin allowed a split second for Aedric to slip between them before leaving the stateroom herself. She paused for the regent and the Daughter of Ahm to fall in beside her, and then she counted her steps carefully to give Aedric space to move in. When they reached the deck and climbed out into the sun, she heard a roar that she mistook for thunder before realizing it was a cheer.

The docks were crowded with people, and their scarred, adoring faces felt even more alien than the Machtvolk who had greeted their arrival in the north. A large area had been cleared leading up to several open carriages—and the streets were held clear by a good-sized company of dark-uniformed soldiers. She also saw half-squads of female scouts in black silk with red scarves of rank stationed at the edge of the crowd, their eyes scanning the crowd. Others stood on rooftops, holding short bows.

The gangplank had been adorned with flowers—most of a type familiar to her but some not—and the ship's officers stood at attention at the top. It was when she inclined her head to them that the flash of light caught her eye.

She looked to the bottom of the gangplank and saw it again—sunlight playing upon a mirror.

No, she realized. Not a mirror. Metal.

Two men stood to either side of the carriage with their backs turned, each holding a shield made of Firstfall metal. They watched the reflection, crouching so that the entire area around them could be seen, and nearby Blood Guard, unmagicked themselves, watched as well.

They paused at the top, and the regent raised his hands, bringing up another cheer from the crowd. He drew a phial from his pocket and touched his tongue to a tiny dropper. His voice boomed out into the city. "Behold, the Great Mother and the Child of Promise," he said. "Behold, the Advent of the Crimson Empress is at hand. The healing of the world is upon us."

They were singing now, and the looks upon their faces no longer held the simple adoration of the Machtvolk. The sheer numbers of them—and near hysteria of their aspect—overwhelmed her, flooded her with something she thought must be horror.

Eliz Xhum led them down the gangplank, and Jin forced her attention back to the men and their silver shields. Aedric had to see them. And he had been there that night, when they'd seen the reflections of the blood-magicked assassins who'd murdered Hanric and Ansylus at Rudolfo's Firstborn Feast. Charles had extrapolated upon that discovery, creating a handful of monoscopes that could reveal scout magicks—blood or otherwise.

Beware the shields. It was a message she had no way of sending beyond hope.

Still, even if Aedric saw them, there was little he could do now. He was swept up in the midst of her and the entourage, and breaking free would be problematic without help.

She waited until she was at the bottom of the gangplank and then stumbled against the railing, careful of Jakob, and gasped.

It was enough to startle the others. Lynnae and Sister Elsbet both stopped as Jin took back her balance. In that brief pause, she felt a ghost of movement along the edges of her gown as Aedric slipped beneath the gangplank into shadow.

"I think you should take him," she said to Lynnae as she passed Jakob over. The woman blushed at the sound of the crowd.

Then, they crossed the open area to the waiting carriage and were helped in by waiting drivers. Once inside, Lynnae passed Jakob back to her and Jin held him close. His eyes were wide as he stared at the mob around them, and for a moment, she wasn't sure exactly what he felt.

But she knew soon enough, and when she did, she did not know which frightened her most—the hymn-singing of the faithful, worshiping the arrival of her son or the sound of Jakob's wild laughter.

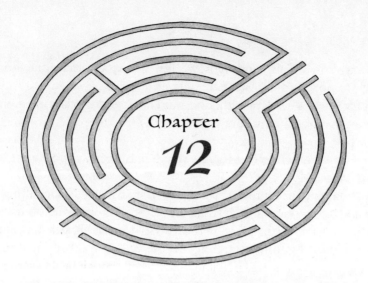

Chapter 12

Neb

Warm air moved over Neb, carrying the scent of Amylé D'Anjite to his flaring nostrils as he raced down passageways that twisted and turned deep beneath the surface of the island. Above him, Petronus and the others waited in a makeshift camp, and behind him, Aver-Tal-Ka followed after.

I can smell her, Neb sent.

Yes, the spider answered. *You have not met your kind before.* It was a statement, but Neb could sense the question that underwrote it.

"No. I didn't know I had a kind other than the ones who raised me." Of course, even then he'd felt alone. But he'd assumed that was how orphans felt, even in an orphanage full of other Androfrancine errors-in-judgment, tucked away in the heart of the world's greatest city. And learning that he was so much more than some supposed moral lapse on Hebda's behalf—that he wasn't even actually kin to the man he'd considered his father—was something he still could not get his mind around. But even now, the quickening he felt at the nearness of another like him was yet more evidence.

He picked up the pace as he went, his fast walk turning to a jog and then to a run. The passageway was metal-lined, and the air did not have the same dead smell as the Beneath Places back home. Overhead, a kind of lichen grew on the ceiling and the upper walls, giving light and, Neb suspected, giving air. And by now, they had to be under the sea, but there was no sign of moisture, no telltale drips of seawater.

Somewhere ahead of him, she waited. Gripping his kin-raven, he sent her name again into the aether. *Amylé D'Anjite.*

Silence.

I've tamped you, Aver-Tal-Ka answered. *It was imprudent for you to wander the aether.*

An image popped into his mind of the hounds. And of something else, large and silver, that watched from above. Neb felt the hairs on his arms stir and understood the emotion that the spider also projected. *Caution.*

He nodded his understanding and slowed as another smell tickled his nostrils. This one was rich and bittersweet, though he'd never known a smell to be so easily experienced as a flavor before. Still, he tasted it and his body craved it, remembered it, and made the connection.

The blood of the earth. "There is a bargaining pool ahead."

Yes.

Neb had used the bargaining pools at home—on Lasthome—to travel thousands of leagues in an instant. He'd also used the thick, quicksilver fluid to clothe himself and infuse himself with strength and power the likes of which he'd never known. And the pool had also healed him, cleansing his flesh of the Y'Zirite scars along with the wounds from their cuttings upon him.

"Will they carry me here on the moon?"

They are not to be trusted. The thief, Y'Zir, poisoned many of them and twisted the connecting lines of many others to set traps for your people.

Neb stretched out a hand and touched the metal wall, feeling the thrum of life that ran through it, then slowed to a walk as the corridor emptied out into a much larger room.

"Light," he shouted into the room, and as his voice echoed out and across the vastness, the glow of the ceiling intensified to illuminate a wide bridge that stretched out over a silver lake. At the center of it, an island rose up to meet the other end of that bridge at least half a league above the quicksilver surface below. Upon that island, a single tree— white and ancient—dominated it, its roots rising and twisting out of the ground and its branches heavy with thorns. The tree stirred as Neb approached his end of the bridge, and he wondered what breeze moved it that he himself could not feel.

Aver-Tal-Ka paused at the edge of the bridge, its legs twitching and mandibles clicking.

Neb stared. "What is it?"

A vague sense of emotion flooded him. *Protection. To slumber within. To rest beneath. To be nourished by.* Aver-Tal-Ka worked his mouth open and spoke with his vocal cords. "It is a Watching Tree."

Neb sniffed at it. "It has no smell."

"No," it agreed. "By design."

But he could smell the girl even stronger now, and he knew she must be nearby. "Can it harm me?"

Yes. "But it will not if you give it what it asks for."

The branches stirred again, and he knew now that no wind moved it. The tree was turning, twisting in the ground, to face Neb. "And it knows I'm here."

Yes. "Now, clothe yourself and approach," the spider said. "And when it gives you the girl, bring her to me. Do not wake her until then. She is very ill, and I must treat her."

Neb hesitated, feeling panic settle onto his neck and into his shoulders. "You're not coming with me?"

Aver-Tal-Ka shuddered. "I am not permitted in this form."

He wanted to ask, but the smell pulled at him and he turned to face the tree. He stretched out a hand over the edge of the chasm. "Clothe me," he commanded.

At first, nothing happened. Then, silver mist drifted up from the lake, swirling around his feet. He felt the mist taking form and heating up as it spread out over the clothes he wore, penetrating them. Light bloomed, and when it faded, he stood draped in a loose-fitting robe that moved over his body with a life of its own.

He gave the spider one final glance, and it tipped its face toward him, the closest approximation it had of inclining its head in respect.

Then Neb moved out onto the bridge, his eyes upon the tree as he approached it. He'd seen some of the old growth in the Ninefold Forest, but this was much larger. Its pale trunk had a circumference at least twice that of the biggest he'd seen there, and it stretched up high enough to scrape the cavern's lichen-covered ceiling. Dark globes of fruit hung from its thorny branches.

At the midpoint, the tree shuddered, and Neb heard a growling noise that he first mistook for wind.

No, he realized. *The tree is growling at me.*

Its sole purpose is to protect the life it shelters, Aver-Tal-Ka sent.

Neb tried to move forward, but his feet were suddenly hesitant as the anxiety moved from his neck and shoulders down into his back and into his stomach.

The spider's words tickled beneath his scalp. *Do not be afraid, Nebios Whym. It, too, is made to serve you.*

Swallowing his fear, he pressed on and did not stop again until he reached the far end of the bridge. The quicksilver sea shifted and shimmered at least a half-league below, and the growling grew. This near, he could see the sap that dripped from the thorns and realized now that what he thought was fruit was something else.

Are they stones?

They were dark and glistened where they hung, moving with the branches. And when they opened in unison to reveal white pupils all trained upon him, Neb blinked.

Stepping off the bridge and onto the island, he flexed his left hand by instinct and felt the robe tighten over him as it shifted into a sheath that covered him in silver light. And the instinct served him well. With a shudder and a roar, a cloud of thorns shot out, and he felt them striking the skin of light that enclosed him.

Neb kept walking, his eyes fixed on a long pink scar on the trunk.

Empty of thorns, the branches lowered, but the eyes continued to regard him. Neb raised both of his hands, spreading the fingers open. "I am here for the girl," he said. "Amylé D'Anjite," he said in a loud voice. "Grant me access to her."

He took another step forward.

Name yourself. The words dropped into his head with enough volume to hurt.

"I am Nebios," he said. "Son of Whym."

A long white root lifted from the floor and slithered toward him, moving from side to side like a snake. *The truth is in your blood.*

Neb resisted the urge to flee as it approached, and when it reached his foot, he saw a single thorn twitched at its tip. It rose up to dance back and forth before him, the thorn approaching and then withdrawing from his hand until Neb understood its intention.

Biting his lip, he concentrated on his hand and imagined peeling the light from it as if it were a glove. Once it was exposed, the thorn slid into the flesh of his wrist, and surprisingly, he felt no pain from it. The vine gulped at his vein for a moment, then pulled away. The wound closed as the light he wore crept back over his hand.

By what song were you carried?

Neb reached into his pouch to draw out the silver crescent, holding it aloft. He could hear the canticle playing from it, and the tree heard as well, its branches shuddering one final time as the eyes closed at once.

He trembled as he approached, stepping over the roots that scattered the dark ground. And when he stood beneath the tree, he ran his hands over the scar and felt it moving beneath his touch. There was a distinct gash in the tree, and he worked his fingers into it to pull the scar open. It gave way, and the smell of her flooded him as he pulled at the fleshy bark.

He caught a glimpse of pale skin tangled in vines and roots, buried in the tree, and his hand brushed the silk of long blond hair. He continued tugging the tree open and blushed when his hand brushed her breast.

"Clothe her," he whispered.

Mist lifted from his own clothing now to twist and turn its way into the tree, and even as it did, Neb's hands found the strength to crack open the last of the trunk that held her. She stood upright, held by the tree, with her eyes closed.

Aver-Tal-Ka's words were a slight whisper in his skull. *Do not wake her, Nebios. Bring her to me so I can heal her.*

Neb couldn't take his eyes off her. *I don't know how to wake her,* he sent back.

But even as he sent it, he realized he *did* know. And before he could stop himself, compulsion overtook him and he leaned in to kiss her softly on the lips.

Agitation. Caution. He could feel the emotions from the spider, but something far stronger captivated him. Neb pulled back, guilt stabbing him.

Her eyes fluttered and opened.

Nebios, I'm coming for you. He could sense fear in Aver-Tal-Ka's message now.

Amylé's mouth worked open. "No," she said. And the tree shivered to life. Neb took a step back, casting a glance at the bridge. Aver-Tal-Ka was midway across the span, scuttling to a stop as the boughs turned in its direction, thorns dripping and ready. "Your companion means me harm, Nebios."

He looked back to her and saw fear in her eyes. "No," he said. "He does not. His name is Aver-Tal-Ka. He brought me to you. But you're not well. He needs to treat you."

"I need no treatment." She climbed from the tree and approached him slowly.

Neb took another step back, feeling the heat rise in his cheeks and ears. He'd not felt anything like this before, and it was starting to frighten him.

Yes. It was Aver-Tal-Ka. *You should be frightened. You are being beguiled.*

Her eyes sharpened. *Enough.*

Her voice was a fist between Neb's temples, and it staggered him. The tree rustled again and began to growl. He glanced to the bridge and saw Aver-Tal-Ka once more approaching. *Nebios, you must return to me.*

She stood before him now and stretched up on her tiptoes to kiss him. This kiss was moist, and Neb felt his heart racing. "We are the last of our kind," she said. "Come swim the light with me."

Then, she ran, and Neb forgot everything but the taste and smell of her, the look and feel of her. It was as if his heart were leashed to her in strands of Firstfall steel, and he found himself running to catch up even as the silver crescent and its pouch tumbled from his hands, discarded.

When she leaped from the cliff, arms flung wide, Nebios Whym gave it no thought whatsoever.

Laughing, he leaped after her.

Marta

Frozen branches slapped at her, and Marta turned her face toward the metal man's shoulder and clung to him. They'd been running for hours now, dodging among the trees, and though she'd seen nothing, she knew they were being harried.

The way the metal man kept changing course was proof enough, but she was fairly certain she'd heard low whistles, slight on the wind, each time they'd changed direction.

The metal man ran at full speed, one hand clutching at her and the other moving what branches it could.

They broke cover, and then suddenly, they weren't running anymore. The metal man was falling, and as it did, it released her and she tumbled off into a snowbank. She scrambled to climb out and felt hands solid upon her chest, pushing her down. "Hold, girl." The woman's voice had a heavy accent.

She saw the metal man thrashing about in a net. "What are you doing?"

"This mechoservitor is in sworn service to House Y'Zir and the Crimson Empress. It is malfunctioning and must be returned to the magister of Y'Zir."

She didn't understand the words, though she'd heard about the Crimson Empress from some of the other girls who'd attended the Y'Zirite school. But the words weren't as important to her as what she saw.

Something about the metal man twisting on the ground made her sad. "Let him go," she said.

But even as she said it, Marta saw the metal man climbing to its feet. It tugged and pulled at invisible captors, fighting in silence. Its metallic voice had a note of panic in it. "Marta?"

"I'm over here," she said.

The metal man shook the last of the nets from itself and moved toward her quickly. Marta felt herself being lifted by invisible hands.

The woman spoke in a harsh language now, then paused as if waiting for a response. When none came, she repeated herself.

"I do not understand you," the mechoservitor said.

"The girl is with me now," the woman said. "Do you know your designation?"

The mechoservitor stepped forward. "I do not know my designation."

Marta felt the scout's hands tighten on her, pulling her back toward the forest. "Your designation is the Watcher. You have been assigned to the Named Lands in preparation for the Advent of the Crimson Empress. You have been damaged and are required to return to the imperial magisters. Your compliance is required."

"No," the mechoservitor said. "Give me the girl."

Before the woman could answer, he surged forward, and Marta heard bones breaking even as the woman cried out. Metal arms scooped her up, and they were running again. From time to time, she felt the slightest of breezes, and now, when it happened, the mechoservitor—the Watcher, they called it—moved toward the noises. At least twice, she'd heard more bones breaking and heard more thrashing in the snow.

Finally, they broke from the trees again, and after hours of no pursuit, the metal man slowed as he approached a ridgeline. When she felt it was safe to speak, she looked up at the metal man. "Did you kill those scouts?"

"No," it said. "I broke their legs."

She felt more relief than she realized she would. And she realized that she truly hadn't known what his answer would be, though she'd hoped against hope. "Is what she said true?"

"I do not know," it said. "It may be."

"Then why didn't you return with her?"

The metal man stopped and looked down at her. "Because I am compelled by my dreams to keep searching."

She stopped as well. "The ones you paint in blood?"

It nodded. "In them, I seek something. I do not know what, but I think it seeks me as well." The metal man straightened and turned back to the slope. "I urge you to discontinue following me."

She shrugged. And when the metal man continued walking, she kept pace with him.

They climbed the ridgeline in the predawn gloom, and when she looked down, Marta's throat knotted up at what she saw.

There was only one place it could be. The snow buried its scar now, but ahead of her a vast plain stretched out, flattened two years ago. Now, it lay full of a hundred watch-fires and a thousand tents. She knew it, and it clenched at her stomach.

Windwir.

She didn't know they would see it, though part of her had longed to as much as another part dreaded the idea.

Marta felt the weight of it and fell to her knees. "She's buried here," she said in a quiet voice.

"Who?"

She couldn't stop the tears, and it angered her. "My mother. The Pope and his army buried her along with the others. My father joined them for a fortnight."

The metal man looked out across the plain, and Marta saw a shudder ripple over its liquid metal skin. Tears coursed its own face as it sank to its knees beside her. "I am sorry, little human."

They knelt and wept together, though she didn't understand what a metal man could ever weep for. When they finished, they stood and moved south along the ridgeline, away from the grave and its grave-robbers.

As they walked, she looked at the Watcher. "Are you damaged?"

"No," it said. "I am not."

And she wanted to, but Marta chose not ask the mechoservitor why it limped.

Petronus

A cool breeze slipped beneath the jungle canopy, adding comfort to the shade where Petronus waited. From his perch, he could see the ship below at anchor and the mechoservitors who waited on its deck.

They'd been reluctant to stay behind, but Neb had insisted upon it, and Petronus suspected it had to do with the spider, Aver-Tal-Ka. It didn't sit right with him, but this was Neb's work; Petronus's part here was

accidental. And none of what he'd experienced since the day he saw the
pillar of smoke on his northern horizon had sat right, so why would he
look for such now? And it wasn't as if anyone else shared his concerns.
Rafe Merrique was fishing while the scouts sharpened their knives and
the solitary sailor napped in the sun.

So Petronus sat and waited, wondering about Neb, wondering about
the spider, and wondering about the girl they'd gone to find. And he
wondered what came next. Surely, the tower.

And the hounds.

He heard a distant rustling deep below, drifting up through the open
hatch, and climbed to his feet. The spider's legs preceded it, and after it
pushed its torso through the hatchway, it turned and swung the metal
hatch shut. It had Neb's pouch—the one that Petronus himself had carried for a time—slung through one of its arms. Within it, Petronus
heard the whispering song and felt fear.

Petronus stepped forward now. "Where's Neb?"

Aver-Tal-Ka shivered, every hair upon its body standing upright as it
did. The pink slit of a mouth whispered open. "I have lost him."

The fear moved to anger quickly. "You *what?*"

Emotions stormed around the spider. Petronus felt them, cold and
sharp. Terror, despair and guilt. His mouth fell open at the force of
them. *I have lost him. I have lost them both.*

Now the anger was a rage, and he saw Aver-Tal-Ka flinch from it.
"How is that possible? Where are they?"

The spider babbled. *I underestimated her. I underestimated the power of the
call.* With each word, Petronus felt the guilt growing into shame, tinged
with anger. *I told him not to wake her, but I just did not realize—*

"Where have they gone?"

"They've fled using the blood of the earth." The spider shuddered
again, and the intensity of the emotion subsided. "I do not know where
they've gone. Her father likely prepared a place for her—someplace safe."
It looked away, then back to Petronus. *I must not speak of these things with
you, Downunder.*

"No," Petronus said, feeling the heat of rage in his tingling scalp.
"You *must* and you *will.*" He tried to find more words but wasn't sure
how to convey the weight of need. His mind flooded with the song even
as his eyes went again to the pouch Aver-Tal-Ka now carried. Buried in
that song, a metal dream had shown the mechoservitors how to build a
vessel he'd always considered more myth than real. Much had gone
wrong—the missing staff, the missing dream, crashing rather than

landing here—but Petronus also knew much had gone right. Neb had survived dark circumstance long enough to meet his true father and receive the blessing in the Beneath Places that transformed him into so much more than the orphaned, bereft boy he'd met in Sethbert's camp so long ago. And the ship had carried them here, to the moon, bringing men and mechoservitors to a place that hadn't been visited in unknown millennia.

Where are the words? He dug more and found the best ones he could. "I need that boy to reach his tower and open it," Petronus said. "I need him to do his part for the light or the dream or whatever the hells it is that drives him." His hands were fists now, and his nails dug into his palms. "I don't know why I need this, but there is no escaping it."

The spider's voice was low. "The call will eventually take them to the Firsthome Temple. It is inevitable that they return there."

Petronus remembered the word from earlier but didn't know what it meant. "What call do you speak of?" Even as he asked it, he suspected it was the canticle, but the spider's answer surprised him.

"The call to mate," Aver-Tal-Ka said. "The People's drive to procreate is in direct proportion to the size of their population. Surely you saw his draw to her?"

He had. The boy's face had lit up when the hatch opened. And in that light, there had been a joy coming off of him in waves combined with a need. He understood. "They are possibly the last of their kind."

Yes. Certainly the only of their kind here in this place.

Petronus felt his eyebrows furrow. "Can they unseal the tower?"

Only the dream that Shadrus swallowed can unseal his temple, the spider answered. *They may still enter through the pool beneath it, if that still lives. But sealed, the temple cannot serve. And without the rod, it will not serve either of them.*

The dream and the staff. Both, according to Neb and his mechoservitors, should have come with them on the ship. But there was nothing to do for it now. "Surely there must be another way to unseal the temple?"

Aver-Tal-Ka looked away. "Only the dream that Shadrus drank." At the mention of it, the spider unslung the pouch and placed it at Petronus's feet.

Only the dream that Shadrus drank. Petronus took up the pouch and tucked the spider's words away for another time. "Then our best course of action is to go there and see for ourselves. If what you say is true, they'll meet us at the tower eventually."

A part of him wanted to resist this. Part of him wanted to climb down into the Beneath Places, take an armed party and search for the boy himself. But he knew that would be fruitless and a waste of time.

Aver-Tal-Ka continued sending off waves of fear and despair, but they subsided now into something less oppressive in their magnitude. *That is sound reasoning.*

Petronus nodded. "And on the way, you will tell me what you know." When he said it, he heard the familiar tone of command in his voice, and it pleased him.

"I will tell what I may," the spider replied. "But when the tower is unsealed, the library herself will tell you whatever you wish if Lord Whym or Lady D'Anjite permit it."

The library herself. The words came with an emotion of wonderment that sent gooseflesh along his arms, and Petronus felt a shiver pass over him. Even Aver-Tal-Ka's fur rose at the mention of it.

Petronus did not wait for the spider. He turned and made his way down the slope, whistling the longboat back to fetch them. Rafe rowed it himself, his face clouded with worry. He looked first to Aver-Tal-Ka and then to Petronus. "Where's our lad and his lady?"

Aver-Tal-Ka steadied the boat as Petronus climbed in but said nothing.

"They've fled," Petronus said. "We're sailing for the tower." He looked at the spider. "We hope that we'll find them waiting there for us."

They rowed back in silence, but as soon as Rafe's feet hit the deck, he started barking orders. Petronus watched the men scramble. Even Aver-Tal-Ka leaped to work.

Petronus wanted to join in, stretch his muscles on the anchor ropes, but he had other work to do. He saw the mechoservitors clustered together, eye shutters opening and closing as they talked among themselves in a code he could not understand.

I have to tell them.

One of them separated from the others as Petronus approached. Steam released from its back as its bellows wheezed air into its voicebox. "Father Petronus," it asked, "where is the Homeseeker Nebios Whym?"

"He's gone with the girl. We're going to meet him at the tower."

He wasn't sure what he expected. Certainly not the anger he'd experienced. But the metal man's jeweled eyes simply went bright and then dim. After a moment, it inclined its head. "Thank you, Father. I will tell the others."

Its response piqued his curiosity. "You are unaffected by this?"

"Yes," it said. "The dream is the dream."

"I don't understand." And he didn't; it sounded like more Marsher mysticism. *But damn me, I'm starting to believe it myself.*

The metal man continued. "The dream has carried us this far. It will carry us through, Father." Then, the mechoservitor turned and walked back to its brothers.

They slipped to sea as the world set and the sky burned the color of dried blood. As they sailed, Petronus wondered how it was that men with no faith could create machines that believed.

And he both marveled and shuddered at the faith that grew within him as a result of it all.

Chapter 13

Rudolfo

Rudolfo sipped chilled pear wine and feigned interest in the dinner conversation.

Yazmeera and her senior staff took their meal in a rooftop garden beneath a lavender sky—a low table surrounded by cushions and spread with dishes he'd never seen in a lifetime of hedonism. Soft music drifted up from a trio of musicians stationed below, at a distance so as not to overpower.

Rudolfo used his chopsticks to lift a steamed oyster to his mouth and savored the spicy lime sauce that mingled with the oyster's juice when he bit into it. He'd been sampling various dishes and wines for the last two hours, and if it had been under different circumstances, he would have considered it one of the better meals of his life.

But instead I sup with my enemy. And so he ate with careful ear and careful tongue, saying only what he needed to say in order to learn what he needed to know. And so far, he knew that Erlund had vanished and was presumed dead by his own hand, leaving a leadership vacuum on the Entrolusian Delta that Esarov had stepped in to fill. There were still skirmishes, but over half of the city-states had fallen, and once they fell, there was little resistance offered. The bodies were still burning in what used to be Pylos, stacked by laborers who had arrived after the first wave of soldiers and scouts. Turam's sickly king was in hiding even as his army crumbled before the onslaught of Y'Zirites. And the Emerald Coasts were falling into place as well, with northern Machtvolk forces keeping them pinned to their peninsula while Yazmeera's armies flooded its independent city-states. No one cheered, but one by one the powers of the Named Land quietly surrendered to the superior force that confronted them.

Of course. After nearly two years of war, the people of the Named Lands were weary and ready for peace even if it meant a change of flags and thrones. Most had no idea what dark and bloody beast lumbered in to settle among them, but even with that knowledge, Rudolfo caught himself wondering what this life could be. A life where his wife and child were revered in an elaborate blood cult and where he was established as the chancellor of a united Named Lands beneath the rule of the Crimson Empress. The life his father wanted for him.

But then, the wrongness of it all reasserted itself and he thought of everything that had been taken away, every drop of blood spilled from Windwir to House Li Tam to Pylos. Hundreds of thousands of lives.

And then, he thought of his own son and pondered how a father could want that for a child. No, he realized, not just any father. *My father.*

He heard his name and forced his attention back to the conversation. "I'm sorry?"

One of Yazmeera's captains—a young man resplendent in a dark silk uniform decorated with silver piping—smiled. "I was asking if you found the oysters satisfactory, Chancellor."

Rudolfo nodded. "Quite. Thank you." He raised his glass to the officer and sipped from it, letting the sweet wine cool the heat in his mouth. "Are you responsible for them?"

He smiled. "I am. Also, the pork and mushroom rice."

"Also quite satisfactory." He turned to Yazmeera. "Are all of your officers so skilled in the kitchen?"

She laughed, and he noted that her cheeks were flushed from the wine. "Most are. Others are quite adept at music." She leaned forward. "I think a strong officer is a well-rounded officer. Tactics and poetry, strategy and steamed oysters go hand-in-hand in my mind. Men who love life fully will fight harder to keep that life."

He inclined his head, hoping it hid his surprise at agreeing with her. "And it is clear that you have formidable officers, General."

It was strange to dine so informally among uniformed men. He was the only one dressed in civilian clothing, though they'd laid a fresh uniform out for him in his dressing room. His head felt naked without his turban of office, and he'd dismissed their offered clothing without even giving it a thought. Instead, he'd gone through the clothing that still filled the villa's closet, eventually settling on cotton trousers and a silk shirt that fit him near enough. He'd sent Ire out to find the walking slippers he now wore, and with his hair oiled and tied back behind, he looked more like the pirate this county was famous for than a Gypsy King or a chancellor.

A bell rang, and the music below stopped abruptly. "Ah," she said, clapping her hands. "We will pause for vespers prayer." She looked to Rudolfo. "Would you care to join us?"

The thought of it repulsed him, and he hoped his body's sudden response to her invitation didn't show on his face. "Thank you," he said, "but I am still unfamiliar and unprepared in these matters."

Yazmeera stood. "Yes. But I'm sure you'll find your way. Meanwhile, if you will excuse us?"

He also stood. "Certainly."

"Please be comfortable. If you need anything, just ring the bell."

"I think," Rudolfo said, "I will take this opportunity to meditate and reflect."

She smiled; then, with a glance to her men, they filed off to the stairs. When they'd gone, he went to the edge of the roof and looked out over the city.

The sky moved from lavender to a deep purple, darkened here and there by clouds on the horizon. And the flat lands of the Divided Isle stretched out in all directions, gray now in twilight, though occasional lights speckled the landscape where houses stood. The city itself was quiet, and most of the buildings were darkened. Patrols of scouts and infantry moved about, but a curfew kept the few citizens who remained indoors. He felt a hand upon his shoulder and understood the words pressed into him.

Are you well, Lord?

He turned. Ire Li Tam stood before him. He saw his wife in her face more and more as he grew accustomed to her unmagicked presence and even saw aspects of his own son Jakob and her father, Vlad Li Tam. It startled him. His own hands moved quickly. *I am as well as I can be.*

She fell in beside him. "They will return in thirty minutes."

"You don't pray with them?"

She shook her head. "I am assigned to you, Chancellor, and may not leave your side. The hours of prayer are not compulsory, and my work with you is considered a satisfactory act of worship according to the Daughters of Ahm Y'Zir."

Her hands moved now, too. *And I do not share their faith.*

He'd suspected as much, and he wondered at what kind of fierce, formidable nature it would take to go beneath the knife of a faith he did not believe in order to accomplish a higher good. Because if her story was true, she'd left House Li Tam when she was but a young girl, placed carefully within the Daughters to work her way to one of their highest honors—service in the Blood Guard, Y'Zir's elite, all-woman scout brigade. All for the purpose of one day bearing word to her sister at the appointed time.

The manipulations and machinations bewildered him, but more than that, her resolve did the same.

They stood quietly and waited until a bell chimed and the others returned. Then, she slipped back to her corner of the roof with the other scouts, and he returned to the table.

General Yazmeera sat first, and the others followed. "Before I left," she said, "I think we were discussing the benefits of a well-rounded officer. I think you used the word 'formidable,' Rudolfo."

Their eyes met. Hers were gray but somewhat glassy from the kallaberries, and they were softer in repose than when she'd met him earlier in the day. "Yes," he said. "I did. The success of your invasion certainly proves that out."

Her eyebrows raised. "Invasion?"

Rudolfo heard the discomfort of bodies shifting upon cushions and held breath. "I'm sorry," he said. "Your . . . *occupation* of the Named Lands."

She smiled. "No apology required. You are not of the faith; you couldn't possibly see it from our perspective."

He leaned forward, returning the smile. "Enlighten me."

She looked to one of her officers—this captain a woman with dark, close-cropped hair. "Captain Mera," she said, "why are we here?"

"By the grace of Y'Zir and the Crimson Empress," she answered. "To heal kinship and earth by blood and by faith."

She looked to another—this one an older man, at least ten years Rudolfo's senior. "And what is the true spirit of the knives we carry, Captain Niva?"

"That some cuts heal and some cuts harm, some cuts save and some cuts slay. It is the hand that guides the blade and the intent that guides the hand."

Yazmeera looked back to Rudolfo. "The only life you have ever known has been changed irrevocably in violence and fear. It stands to reason that you would see our work as an invasion force set to occupy. But we are family, bound by blood, and we have come to liberate you and yours that you might join us in the healing of the world."

He felt his eyes narrow but tried to keep his tone lighter. "And from whom do you liberate us?"

She snorted. "From that Deicide, P'Andro Whym, and his flock of sheep for one. How long have they ruled you, controlled you, cowed you with their magicks and machines, hidden away in their safe city doling out scraps to hungry dogs at the gate?"

He could hear the hate in her voice, though he suspected she thought of it as love. He opened his mouth to say something, but she continued. "And don't for a moment believe that the kin-clave you all lived under somehow put you on equal footing with your former masters. It, like everything else they did, served their purposes. They kept the ruins of the Homelands apart for themselves. The wastes are scattered with the shallow graves of any who ventured there without their sanction. And have you not wondered how it is that in two millennia, your population continues to fit nicely within the careful borders of your Named Lands?"

Rudolfo sat back. "It was a product of the Age of Laughing Madness— leftovers of your Wizard King's devastation. Surely you don't suggest that the Androfrancines somehow regulated our population?"

"No, I suggest that they had the power *not* to and chose otherwise."

Rudolfo scowled. "I find that hard to believe."

"Can you explain how it is that my people outnumber yours six to one?" She leaned forward as he shook his head. "I can. And I will show you myself once we find it. There is a world beneath us, Rudolfo, and it is filled with many wonders. Our excavation at Windwir has proven that your gray-robed diggers knew it well enough, and I'm willing to bet my knife that they knew the truth about this place."

He took a moment to lift his wineglass to his lips, his eyes moving to the other faces around the table. The others watched, some with amusement and others with discomfort. "And what truth would that be?" He said it with a smile, trying to lighten the mood.

"That these places—these Keeper's Crèches—were made to keep us alive. Lifeboats, if you will, for the sinking ship."

Keeper's Crèche. He'd not heard that term before. But that wasn't the part that dropped his jaw. The Androfrancines had maintained vigorously that this small corner of the world and a scattering of islands were the only truly habitable places remaining. The Churning Waste to the east boasted a handful of people who preferred subsistence and Waste-illness to the confines of kin-clave and what until recently had been the Order's strong influence in the Named Lands. But between the Ghosting Crests to the south and east and the Stormwaters to the west, they'd accepted long ago that even if their ships could weather those seas, there was nothing worth finding beyond their own continent. He blinked at her widening smile and could find no words.

"Yes, Rudolfo," she said slowly. "The world is larger than you have been led to believe."

Certainly he'd wondered. They had to come from someplace. His wife and child had to have gone somewhere. But until now, it had been guesswork he'd tucked away. Now, it was real. "How many crèches are there?"

"Five total, we believe. We know of three." She raised her own glass and sipped. "And finding the last two are certainly important, but with the three we know of, we have enough of a start for our work to begin. And at some point—perhaps in another millennia or so—the crèches will become irrelevant."

He ran his fingers along the side of his glass, feeling the beads of condensation. He'd heard enough, had even read their gospels, to know what that work was, but until now, he wasn't sure he fully grasped it. He'd assumed it was more metaphorical. "The healing of the world," he said.

If they could do that—if it were true—what would that mean? A wasteland restored to the garden it once was? A broken continent returned to life?

Her laughter brought his eyes back to hers. "Yes. The healing of the world. And your son—your little boy—and even you, Rudolfo, are an important part of that healing."

When one of the captains proposed a toast to that work, Rudolfo raised his glass with the others, but his heart was not in it. Instead, it tangled in a Whymer Maze where the lines between good and evil blurred to near invisibility, and he realized with sinking heart that despite their madness and their brutal beliefs, these Y'Zirites might have underpinnings of truth guiding their hands.

And, Rudolfo realized, even if they did not have a scrap of truth it would not matter. The greatest, most useful gift victory brought any army was the power to record history in the way that it wished to.

He wondered how his role in that history would be written, though present circumstances definitely gave him some idea. And as he drank to the healing of the world, the sweetness of his wine became bitter and its chill was lost in the heat of anger that flushed his face.

Charles

They rode out into a gray morning and the cold chewed Charles all the more because of one warm night spent indoors. Of course, the night had been near sleepless, between everything he'd learned and the dreams that continued to haunt him.

Still, it was good to set out this morning with a belly full of spiced chai and peppered bacon. And it was good that they no longer rode alone. Renard joined them now, riding point, and though he couldn't confirm it, Charles suspected a full squad of magicked Gray Guard ran silently, invisible around them.

They rode north into a light snowfall, circling west around the lower borders of the Desolation and the excavation of the city. Most items that had been hauled from the ruins during Petronus's grave-digging had ended up on the Delta, and Charles had seen some of them during his captivity there. Some had even found their way back to the Forest's new library once the treaty was negotiated. But every good Androfrancine knew—as the Y'Zirites did, too—that the best of Windwir's secrets lay beneath her. And though the Seven Cacophonic Deaths would have destroyed much of it, certainly some of its hoard of magickal and mechanical wonder would survive. He'd seen the evidence in the Watcher's cave. And he suspected the plague spiders that destroyed Pylos had been drawn from the petrified egg pouches he'd stored in his workshop's lower vaults. It was one item on a list of many that he'd learned to keep in a different type of vault—one he kept for things he did not want to think about overly much. He'd been responsible for the spell's security and for the mechoservitor that was ultimately rescripted to activate the spell. And based on everything he'd learned yesterday from Hebda, it was his very first generation of mechoservitors that had first brought down the dream, had awakened Whym in the Beneath Places and ultimately delivered Neb—the offspring of a Younger God—into the care of the Androfrancine Order and its secret Office for the Preservation of the Light. The office that had allowed Windwir to fall unevacuated because of some dark bargain made to assure Neb of his birthright. He did not fully understand it; but between Hebda and Micah, he'd learned much, and it staggered him.

And my fingerprints are everywhere on it. Certainly, he had no idea at the time, but so much of his work had been co-opted by the schemes of others—the Office, the Y'Zirites, Whym—and it angered him.

The slightest chirping sound brought his attention back to the present, and he watched as a moon swallow settled onto Renard's shoulder, its message a burst of whistled notes. The Waste guide pulled up and shifted the long rod he held across his knees. "We're getting close," he said over his shoulder.

Charles drew up alongside of the man. "And what if he doesn't wish to come with us?"

Renard scanned the forest around them. "I don't think we can force it."

No. They certainly couldn't. He'd seen the Watcher in action—its speed and strength were unparalleled. And if they were wrong about its motives and intentions—if somehow this was an elaborate Y'Zirite ruse—they would know soon enough. But Y'Zirite scouts had been attacked last night, left with their legs broken cleanly, and he suspected the mechoservitor was responsible. "I'll go ahead on foot from here," he said.

Bracing his aching muscles, he slid from the saddle and grunted when his booted feet hit the ground. Beside his mare, he dug into the saddlebags and drew out a folded robe. Then, he looked up and over his shoulder to Winters.

The girl had ridden in silence, but now their eyes met and he could see a calm acceptance there that he wished for his own. Of course, she'd had a lifetime of living by faith, and her faith, so far, had been proved if what Hebda said was true: Neb and Petronus were on the moon, seeking to gain entrance to a structure he'd seen on its surface with telescopes all his life and wondered about. Her faith in her Book of Dreaming Kings—and Isaak's faith in his metal dream—had found legs that had carried men farther than they'd been carried in thousands of years.

"Good luck," Winters said, her voice low, as she inclined her head.

He returned the gesture, then turned away from them and moved off into the snow-drifted trees. He walked quickly at first, until he'd gone deep enough into the forest to carry him out of sight; then he slowed. The air was cold to his lungs and touched with the slightest scent of pine, but even now, it was warmer than it had been just days ago. Winter would turn from snow to rain soon enough before heralding the return of spring. If reports were true, spring would find the Named Lands firmly occupied under its new empress.

He shuddered at the thought—or perhaps the cold—and pushed ahead. Suddenly, just ahead of him, he heard a thrashing in the underbrush and a loud grunt followed by what sounded like a branch breaking. He picked up his pace, uncertain of what was happening until it happened again—this time off to his left.

He is disabling the magicked scouts.

"Hold," Charles said. "They will not harm you." He spun, following the sound of movement, and caught sight of something silver moving fast.

"Don't worry," a girl's voice said nearby. "He won't kill them." He looked to the left and right for some sign of the speaker, and then, at her chuckle, he looked up. She was tucked safely away on the high limb of a nearby evergreen. Her face peeked out, partially hidden by a ratty wool knit cap. "You're very old for a soldier."

He heard more thrashing and turned in its direction. "Stop," he said. "They mean no harm—they're for my protection."

The thrashing stopped, and a new voice spoke—one he recognized from his dreams and from his brief time in the north. "What is your designation and your destination?"

"I am Charles," he said. "And *you* are my destination."

He heard the slightest of hums and watched as the mechoservitor brushed branches aside to stand before him. It regarded him through jeweled eyes that burned red, and in that moment, Charles knew it was not the Watcher that regarded him. The girl cleared her voice, and the metal man turned and reached up to easily pluck her from the pine tree and place her on the ground.

"I'm Martyna," she said. "Marta for short. I'm glad to meet you, Charles."

She was ten, maybe eleven, and dressed in a tattered winter coat stained with mud and grime. She held a sling in her hand. He nodded to the weapon. "I don't think you'll need that. I'm glad to meet you, too, Marta."

Then, he turned back to the metal man. It stood taller than the ones he'd made, though not by much, and it was more slender in design, with joints that were less obvious and a metal skin that rippled and moved with it. And that skin was nothing like the Watcher's dark and pitted skin—this shone so silver that it reflected back the surroundings.

"Why do you seek me?" the metal man asked.

"I do not know," Charles replied. "But it seems we seek each other."

"Our dreams," the mechoservitor said slowly, "compel us."

"Yes."

It looked away, scanning the forest. "There are others with you."

Charles nodded. "A woman named Winters and a man named Renard. And some scouts."

"Renard, son of Remus," it intoned, "and Winteria the Younger, former Queen of the Machtvolk."

Charles blinked. "You know them?"

"I do not remember if I know them."

"But you know their names?"

It nodded. "I do."

"And what about your name?" Charles paused, reframing the question. "What is your designation?"

"I am told that I am designated the Watcher and that I am the property of the Empire of Y'Zir."

Charles felt his brow furrow. "And do you believe this to be true?"

The mechoservitor paused, its eyes brightening and then dimming. "I do not know. It is possible."

He chose his next question with care, guarding his heart against the answer he dared not hope for. "Do you know who I am?"

"You have said that you are Charles."

He nodded. "Yes."

It paused. "I do not know you," it said. And even as he said it, even as Charles's heart sank into his stomach, a shudder worked its way over the mechanical. "But I do know that you are who I seek."

"Then come with me," Charles said. "We will go someplace safe and talk more about our dreams." He remembered the robe now and held it out before him. "I brought you this."

It took the robe and considered it. "My body has no need for protection from the elements."

"You are correct," Charles said. "But it may also help conceal you."

The metal man shrugged and then pulled on the robe. It was too short and gave it a comical look that stabbed at Charles with a knife forged of grief. *You dress him in a robe and hope to see your son.*

Only, he didn't. What stood before him looked nothing like Isaak, and though it knew the others, it did not know him. "We should go," he said. "Our proximity to Windwir does not bode well."

The girl stepped close to the metal man, her small hand reaching out to take its large metal hand. He wasn't sure what to do with her other than bring her along, and he suspected that no other answer would be sufficient for the mechoservitor that had brought her this far.

He turned and saw the others approaching slowly, leading the horses. "We should have brought more horses," he said.

"It is more expedient for me to run."

Charles nodded. When they arrived, he climbed back up into his saddle and pulled the girl up behind him. Then, they turned south, and just as the mechoservitor lurched into an awkward, loping run, he thought he saw, for just an instant, what appeared to be a limp.

It was enough of a foothold for his heart, and Charles blessed it even as he doubted what it meant. Hope, he decided, hangs on with its finger-nails to whatever purchase it can find in its slow climb out of loss.

Vlad Li Tam

A new officer came for him during his second day on the barge, and Vlad went with him, the girl trailing behind. The officer led them out of their quarters and into the hall, climbing the narrow ladder above deck.

Overhead, the sky was a piercing blue, and around them, heat radiated off the rock cliffs and made the trees along the canal's lower shore shimmer. He brought them to a table on the aft deck beneath silk canopies that rustled with the wind as they moved downstream. Sister-Mother Drusilla waited for them there, as did a table spread with various fruits, breads, and cheeses. Vlad waited for his companion to sit and then settled into his own cushion, hooking his leg around the staff as he rested the length of it in his lap.

The officer sat last. Once he was seated, he looked to the priestess and then met Vlad's eyes. "Thank you for joining us. I hoped that we could eat together and perhaps you could answer some questions."

This one's uniform was different than the others he'd seen, but it wasn't the uniform as much as the man's bearing that told Vlad what he needed to know. *He works in intelligence. Probably at a high level.*

Vlad sniffed the food, feeling the staff twitch as he used it. He knew the smell instantly and saw which plates reeked of it. "You should know," he said with a smile, "that cannimn powder won't work on me."

The officer leaned forward to pluck a fig from a silver bowl. "Noted." Then, he returned the smile. "Please eat."

Vlad took a plate and handed it to the girl. Then he took one for himself and helped himself to a few bits of cheese, a slice of raisin wal-nut bread smeared in butter, and three slices of a type of fruit he'd not seen before. While they served themselves, the officer poured them glasses of a chilled mint tea.

Vlad tried the fruit first—a sweet and sour plum-like something that he chased with a bit of the cheese and a sip of the tea.

"Sister-Mother Drusilla has briefed me on your encounter with her, and I spent this morning reading Sister Agnes's report," the officer said. Then, his brow furrowed. "Forgive me. Introductions should come first. My name is Tarviz. I am a colonel attached to the imperial regent's office. The regent himself assigned me to you and bids you welcome to the lands of Y'Zir."

Vlad inclined his head. "Thank you, Colonel Tarviz."

The colonel returned the gesture. "And you are . . . ?"

He sipped more tea and replaced his glass before answering. Then, he met the man's blue eyes with his own. *What do I tell him?* He took the first words that came to mind. "I am a voice from the wilderness."

The man looked bemused, and Vlad glanced to the Daughter of Ahm. She sat, her face a placid mask. The officer continued. "You told Sister-Mother Drusilla that you came by the staff by love and murder . . . that you were seeking the Barrens of Espira?"

Vlad nodded. "I did and I was. But it seems what I seek has changed."

Tarviz's eyes narrowed. "The barrens are forbidden. Even the unscarred avoid them. Is Espira where you acquired the staff?"

He shook his head. "I brought it with me from the sea."

The man sat back, and Vlad had no difficulty reading the emotions upon his face. Curiosity and exasperation vied for control, though he was an obvious expert at keeping his emotions tucked safely away from view. "And you interfered with the Vessel of Grace's saving work because 'she was suffering and I could'?"

Vlad reached over a hand and touched the girl's shoulder briefly. She looked at him and smiled, but he saw anger in her eyes. "Yes. Exactly."

"That alone," the man said, "is a serious offense in our faith."

"Then it is good that I do not share your faith," Vlad answered. "I will not submit to any doctrine that believes the suffering of this woman or anyone else—and the shedding of the blood and the scarring of the flesh—is somehow pleasing to a god or useful for any purpose upon this earth."

Now Drusilla spoke, and he could hear the hate in her voice, though he knew beneath that hate was something far more damning for her—fear. "Your submission to what is right and good is not required for you to be held accountable."

Vlad touched the staff. "In this case, I think it is."

The officer shot her a withering look, then smiled at Vlad. "Certainly we're not interested in any unnecessary confrontation. You've already shown us what this artifact is capable of." He looked back to the sister-mother. "I don't think we need to see more."

She lowered her eyes, and Vlad studied the dynamic between the two. It was obvious that though she held high station, the colonel was the decision-maker at this table. "I'm afraid my answers will not be satisfactory for you," he said. "But perhaps you would be willing to answer some of mine?"

The man's eyes told him that he certainly wasn't, but Vlad was unconcerned. He brushed the staff and felt its warm hum beneath his hand. "What can I *really* expect upon my arrival at Ahm's Glory?"

Tarviz opened his mouth and started to speak, but his words wouldn't come. His lips twisted around them, and his eyes went wide. He stammered for a few moments; then his shoulders slumped. "A military force has gathered at the docks. They will separate you from the staff and take you into custody. The Daughters' best kin-healers have been secured to assist in your interrogation, and the magisters intend to verify if the staff is what they think it is. If so, it will be placed in the regent's care."

Vlad smiled at the man's contorted face. "What do they think it is?"

"The staff of Y'Zir. They've sought it for some time."

His eyes narrowed. "Do they know who I am?"

"They believe you are Vlad Li Tam."

He studied the colonel's face for another minute, then turned to the Daughter of Ahm. "Who do you believe that I am?"

She turned her face away, pursing her lips. A fine sheen of sweat coated her forehead. "I think the magisters' theory is sound if indeed you bear the staff. And your body bears the marks of an unfinished kin-healing."

He nodded, remembering those knives. "It does. But your knives have cut all they will cut from me." He leaned forward, his eyes still meeting the sister-mother's. "Tell me," he said, "about the spider demon in the Beneath Places—the one you gave this woman over to? Have you any idea what your so-called Vessel of Grace experienced during the fortnight you left her with it?"

The woman started to shake her head, and Vlad felt the slightest twitch of anger stirring to life in him. He closed his eyes for a moment, conjuring up the nightmare and shoving it into her. Her eyes bulged, and she would have screamed if he'd not leaned close to her. "You will bear it in silence," he whispered.

Drusilla's lower lip quivered, and Vlad felt a hand on his leg. This time, when he met the Vessel's eyes, they were clear and angry and satisfied. *She will not ask for mercy now.*

He looked back to the colonel, who watched in horror. "Is it Ahm Y'Zir?"

Now, the man's eyes were wide with panic. But he had no choice—the staff drained it from him—and Tarviz answered. "It is what remains of him."

Vlad sat back in the cushions. "Then he truly is the author of his gospels?" He glanced to Drusilla. Her mouth foamed, and the whites of her eyes flickered as they rolled back in her head. She was writhing now, sliding down into the cushions. He tapped the staff, and her body went limp. Then, he looked back to the colonel.

"Yes. Though some of his earlier disciples also contributed their stories and teachings."

Now the answers come easier. Vlad picked up a grape, chewed it slowly, then swallowed. "My people have always been taught that he was killed along with his brothers during P'Andro Whym's night of purging. And that his father's last spell was in retaliation for the death of his seven sons. I want to know what happened."

"P'Andro Whym spared his life, and Rudolfo, Y'Zir's desert thief, smuggled him out of the Homelands," the colonel said. His own forehead was wet now with sweat, and even Vlad felt his own strength ebbing. He'd used the staff a great deal of late, and he'd learned two important things: First, using it exhilarated him more than any kallaberry smoke ever could. And second, using it left him exhausted.

I need to rest soon.

"These events you speak of," he said. "They were over two thousand years ago. How can Ahm Y'Zir still live?" He looked to Drusilla, and her mouth worked open easily now. Her eyes held the brokenness that the Vessel's had when he'd first met her, and it pleased him.

"He is sustained by blood magick, and much of his body is gone now. The magisters preserved him as best they could with what they could scavenge from the Beneath Places."

Vlad blinked. For two millennia, Xhum Y'Zir's seventh son had lived and somehow built an empire by fanning the flames of holy zeal. And he'd done it while the Androfrancines and the first settlers built the Named Lands, a society of survivors governed by the careful code of kin-clave.

His head ached now—a jabbing pain behind his right eye. "I am looking for the spellbook of Y'Zir. I was told it was hidden in the Barrens of Espira. Do you know anything of it?"

Vlad watched both faces. The colonel's was twisted into a grimace. "It was found by the Imperial Archaeology Society over a thousand years ago."

He looked to Drusilla now. "And where is it?"

Her eyes went wide as her voice betrayed her. "It is kept in trust by the Daughters of Ahm Y'Zir."

One last question. He nodded to the Vessel of Grace. "And where is her baby?"

Sister-Mother Drusilla's face went white. "You can't—"

"Yes," Vlad Li Tam said, "I can." But he felt a hand on his arm and looked.

"I know where she is," the Vessel said.

Nodding, he glanced to the sun. It was past noon now, and by his best guess, they were two days' walk from Ahm's Glory. He leaned forward. "I want you to listen to me very carefully. In a minute, you are going to call the captain over and direct him to stop the barge and put us ashore. You will not remember doing so; neither will you remember this conversation. Do you understand?"

They nodded as one.

Ten minutes later, Vlad watched the barge sail south, and when it was gone, he set out along a well-worn path. He glanced at the girl beside him and pondered which of his daughters she reminded him most of. His brow furrowed.

"What is your name?" Vlad asked.

She stopped walking. "I was called Chandra before I went to the Daughters. But my name was taken away as my first step toward Vessel-hood."

He inclined his head to her. "It is a good name."

Then, he turned south and chose a measured pace. The weariness rode him hard, but he knew far more than he'd known before his capture. And as powerful as the staff was, he did not want to lean so heavily upon it as he'd needed to with the Y'Zirites.

And yet I feel twenty years younger when I do. The surge of energy that moved through him was staggering. But so also was the exhaustion. Even now, his muscles and head ached.

But he walked until the sun set, and as it did, they took shelter in an open-faced fruit shed that overlooked the water. And though the day closed in peace, that night his dreams were dark.

Something large and eight-legged snuffled for him in the Beneath Places like a hound on the hunt while Vlad Li Tam struggled to lift a heavy staff that he was too tired to wield.

Neb

The pounding in his head kept time with the song that flooded his senses, and Neb struggled to orient himself as he sat up.

He sat upon a bed of soft moss that smelled vaguely of mint. It was dark, and his first thought was that he was alone. He struggled to his feet, hearing his muscles crack and his joints creak as he did.

The song played all around him now, and in those first moments of wakefulness, he thought somehow it was the crescent, but it wasn't—the song vibrated through the floor and hung upon the air.

"It's deafening, isn't it?"

Neb looked in the direction of the voice and squinted into the dark. "Amylé?"

"Light," she whispered, and a dull glow above drew his eyes to the ceiling of the cavern as light spread across the lichen.

It was a small cavern compared to the one he last remembered, but it was still easily a quarter-league in circumference, with its bargaining pool set in the center. But this pool was different from the others he'd seen. A dark sheen covered its surface, and he could smell something besides the blood of the earth there. A briny smell. And unlike the other pools he'd seen, this one had a series of pipes that disappeared into it and stretched away across the room to climb the wall and disappear into the ceiling.

The girl sat on the floor, not far from him, her arms curled around her knees as she rocked back and forth.

A wave of vertigo moved over him, and he sat down heavily.

He tried to find his memory but couldn't. He remembered Aver-Tal-Ka's shout of surprise and warning. He remembered leaping behind the girl, drunk on her smell and sound and taste, to plunge deep into the thick quicksilver beside her. Then, her arms and legs had intertwined with his and they'd been translated into light to race along the veins of blood that ran through the moon. He remembered laughter and a longing so strong that it became a need that ached. "Where are we?"

"We are where you wished to go," she said. She still rocked back and forth, and Neb climbed back to his feet, despite the dizziness, to walk to her and crouch by her side. He put a tentative hand on her shoulder.

She shrugged it away violently, her head coming up. Rage and madness filled her eyes, and she snarled. "Do not touch me. You will not *ever* touch me."

Neb blinked and sat down again, dropping his hand into his lap. "I'm sorry."

"You reek of them, you know," she said. "It disgusts me. Not even the pool could wash the stink of Downunder off of you."

The vehemence in her words brought his eyes down with a feeling of shame that quickly bloomed into an anger of his own. But he swallowed it and forced his eyes back to the girl. He remembered the spider's words. *She is not well.*

He could see that now, especially juxtaposed against the girl he'd kissed awake inside the tree. The girl who'd kissed him back and bid him swim the light with her. There was nothing of that girl here. He watched her for a moment, head down and rocking, her lips murmuring words he could not understand. Finally, he stood again, and this time, the room spun less.

He left her seated by the bed and walked to the edge of the pool. The smell there turned his stomach, and he knew something had been done to the pool. "Clothe me," he whispered to it.

Nothing happened.

"It will not serve you here," she said. "Not with the temple sealed."

The temple. He looked around them. "We're beneath the tower?"

"We are." She nodded to an opening in the far wall. "There are stairs there that lead up into it."

"We can access it?"

She laughed, but there was something cold and bitter in her laughter. "Of course. And now that you're awake, I fully intend to."

Amylé stood.

"But if the tower is sealed, then—"

"Then it will not serve us. But I do not need it to serve me."

She started for the opening, and Neb paused, looking at the pool again. "I have friends who should know where I am," he said.

She passed through the opening now, her voice echoing behind her. "I'm sure your spider will tell them. But it doesn't matter. With the tower sealed, there is no other entrance but the pool, and she salted it behind her when she fled."

Neb hurried after her. "I don't understand," he said.

The opening led to a circular staircase that she'd already started climbing quickly. Her voice was exasperated. "You do not need to understand."

Neb's confusion blurred into a sharp anger, and Aver-Tal-Ka's words came back to him. "You beguiled me and brought me here," he said as he followed her up the stairs. "I *do* need to understand."

She snorted. "Your body beguiled you, Nebios. I just helped it along."

No, he realized, she'd used it. She'd separated him from the others and brought him here. And though ultimately this was his intended destination, something told him that this was not the way it was supposed to happen. Of course, with the staff and the Final Dream absent, this might be the only way. "Why have you brought me here?"

"We are the last of the People of Firsthome," she said. "It is in our blood to return here."

But even as she said it, he sensed falseness in her answer, though the words themselves were true. "You're not telling me everything."

She chuckled again. "No, Nebios. I'm not."

"Why?"

"Because none of it matters. I do not need you to understand, and I have no interest in explaining it to you."

"Then why did you bring me here?"

"Because," she said, "I cannot let you unseal the temple."

Neb stopped on the stairs. "How will you stop me?"

She kept climbing. "I already have, Nebios."

Sudden fear struck him, and he turned back, taking the stairs three at a time as he descended back to the cavern and the pool. When he reached the quicksilver, he waded out into it. *Carry me,* he willed.

Nothing happened.

It will not serve you, her voice whispered into his mind. And the emotions that rode upon her voice were a mix of rage and despair and conviction that had been twisted and sharpened by an incomprehensible amount of time trapped in sleep yet awake in the aether. The force of those feelings sent a shiver through him.

He stood still, listening to the distant sound of her footfalls upon the stairs as he pondered the pool. "I do not believe you," he whispered. "There has to be a way."

Her laughter drifted down from far above now. There were no words or emotions that came with it, but Neb didn't need either. The madness in it was as clear as the song that thundered through this place.

Swallowing the fear, Nebios Whym turned back to the stairs and began his ascent into the Moon Wizard's Tower.

Winters

They rode through the night with horses and scouts magicked, and the metal man kept pace beside them, its eyes glowing like twin pools of blood smeared occasionally by the banks of fog they encountered. Renard led them, low in his saddle, and Winters took up the rear. Charles took the middle with the girl, Marta, clinging to his back.

Now they stopped for nothing, pushing on for the farmhouse with the scouts spread out on all sides by a half-league in any direction. And as they rode, Winters thought about the mechoservitor that ran with them and about the dream he carried.

How will I dream it? And how would it reach Neb? She had no understanding of how the Final Dream worked. All she knew was that the seeds of it had been coded into the Book of Dreaming Kings—one segment from each king—and she would somehow find within those pages one last dream to unlock whatever it was Neb needed for his work. The culmination of over two millennia of the Homeseeking Dream— something that would carry her people to the moon.

But how?

That was the part, she suspected, where faith came into play.

The softest of whistles reached her ears from behind, and she turned in the saddle as a ghost moved past. The voice was muffled—nearly a whisper—but she heard it clearly. "We are pursued," the Gray Guard said. "Blood Scouts, I'll wager, by their speed."

She turned back to the front and reached for one of her long, curved scout knives.

Renard's voice was clear as well. "Bring in the running watch."

She heard the tinny ruffle of metal wings on the wind, and something small and silver flashed by her face. She'd seen them using the moon sparrows on the run by daylight—the tiny mechanicals were four times faster than a magicked messenger bird and could be directed to multiple destinations.

The Waste guide looked over his shoulder, his face grim in the moonlight. "Forewarn the house," he said. Then, he spurred his horse faster.

She did the same, and they broke from the forest into a snowy meadow. They crossed it quickly, and as they slipped back under cover, she heard a storm behind them as magicked scouts collided, knives clashing, at the far edge of the meadow.

Winters fought the urge to look back. Instead, she kept her eyes on Renard's back.

But he looked back, and shouted when he did. "We keep going," he said, "no matter what."

Gritting her teeth, she leaned down and felt again for the hilt of her knife.

When it happened, it was fast and there was nothing she could do. The mechoservitor pitched suddenly to the left, falling into Charles's horse. The horse stumbled even as unseen assailants pulled the metal man away from it. She saw Marta tumble off, striking a tree before she hit the ground and rolled away. And even as she watched, she tugged her own horse to the left.

Charles's horse regained its footing even as Renard spun around in the saddle, opening his mouth to shout something.

He's going to tell me to leave her. And it made sense. She was a girl. They wouldn't harm her. But she couldn't leave her, and if the metal man was who she thought he might be, he couldn't either.

"I'll get her," Winters shouted.

She reined her horse in, slipping from the saddle as she did. And even as she did, an invisible wall struck her horse, knocking it aside. She saw the metal man now, lifting and tossing another magicked scout with ease.

As it did, it roared out a name. "Marta!"

Winters drew her knives and moved in the direction that she'd seen the girl fall. Something moved past her, brushing her back as it did, and she spun. The footfalls around her now were quiet coughs in the snow, but the clink and clang of steel blade on steel blade betrayed what happened around her. The metal man was moving now, too, and it overtook her to race for a dark, still form half buried in the snow.

Just as it was in reach, the metal man toppled beneath the weight of something that struck it hard in the side. And even as the mechoservitor tumbled to the ground to be dragged through the snow, she saw the limp body of the girl lifted from the snow by invisible hands.

Winters had not used her new skills with the blades. She'd actually witnessed very little combat, let alone participated. Taking a deep breath, she moved for the girl, running low and fast across the snowscape.

"This girl is under the protection of the Blood Guard of the Crimson Empress," a voice whispered from the dark. "Stand down."

Winters gritted her teeth. She could see Marta now, dim in the moonlight. Her eyes were closed, and her hair was wet with blood. "I will not stand down," she said. "Release the girl."

The Blood Scout chuckled. "Take her from me."

Winters kicked snow up in the direction of the voice and then launched herself at the form it betrayed. She felt her knife strike steel and then felt the scout's other blade tear through her coat sleeve. Winters fell back, finding her footing and moving into the dance Jin had taught her. Twice more, she was close enough to be parried, and her side was nicked by a blade that slashed through her coat.

Then, she dodged and came in low, feeling the blade strike cloth and then flesh. It was a jarring sensation that nearly cost her the knife. She heard the scout gasp and came in with her right only to be parried aside.

The strength behind the parry moved her back across the snow, and she lost her footing for a moment. Just as she regained it, she felt the scout's blade slice into her shoulder, near the neck. Twisting, she rolled away and onto her back, kicking more snow up onto the scout. Then, she threw her left knife and heard the scout grunt as it glanced off her and into the snow. Winters braced herself, and even still, the wind went out of her when the Blood Scout fell upon her. She felt the scout's blade cutting through her coat and tried to get her own knife hand free to no avail.

Then suddenly, the metal man loomed over her, and its hands came down to seize the Blood Scout and slam the woman against a tree. Then, it scooped up the little girl.

A hand touched Winters's shoulder, and she sat up. "Take this," a voice whispered. "Chew it." Rough hands pushed a small bit of root into her hand.

"What is it?"

"You run with us now," the voice said. Then, the hand pulled her up to her feet.

She placed the root in her mouth and chewed it, wincing at its bitterness. But she felt warmth suffuse her, and her exhaustion and anxiety melted away even as she felt her legs beginning to twitch.

The mechoservitor now ran toward Charles and Renard with the girl cradled in his arms. "This human requires medical attention."

"There's a medico at the house," Renard said. Then he turned his horse and whistled it forward.

She wanted to look for her knife but knew better. There were more behind them, certainly, and they were at least two hours from the house. So instead, she ran, falling in behind the metal man, who ran alongside Charles.

They changed course twice over the next hour, and as they drew closer to Kendrick's Town, they started encountering the occasional house or farm. Most lay abandoned, but at least two were well lit with smoking chimneys.

Surely we'll be seen. But they kept their pace and ran until they entered the clearing and saw the house and its barn awaiting. The barn door was open, and a solitary lamp lit the front porch of the house.

Renard led them to the barn and dismounted, handing his reins to a young man dressed similarly to him. The man climbed into the saddle and spurred the horse out of the clearing. Another did the same with Charles's horse, and a handful of gray-dressed men took Marta from the mechoservitor.

As Winters approached, a horrible smell assaulted her, and she covered her mouth. "What is that?"

"Dead cattle," Hebda said. "Come inside."

Inside, the smell was stronger, and now, she saw a faint light ahead, but it came from the floor. No, she realized.

A hole in the floor.

There, set into the middle of the barn, was a round steel hatch that stood open. Renard knelt at it, helping Charles down. Behind him, the medicos examined Marta quickly, and a small gang of young men stood by with pitchforks and shovels. Hebda took her by the elbow and guided her toward a medico.

"Lady Winteria has also been hurt," he told the young Androfrancine, who nodded and gestured for her to sit. She flinched when the medico pulled back her coat and shirt to find her wounds, and she winced as his hands poked and prodded. While he cleaned the wounds and bandaged them, Winters watched Hebda and Renard where they stood apart talking in low tones.

When the medico was finished, she stood and walked to them.

"After the site is secured," Hebda told Renard, "get word to Rudolfo of what's transpired here. Tell him he has help." Then, Hebda leaned in and kissed Renard, and it lingered long enough that Winters looked away and blushed. "Don't be gone so long this time," he said.

Renard squeezed his shoulder. "I won't."

Then, Hebda climbed down into the well. She could see now that it stretched down quite a distance, and a lantern far below leaked the light she'd seen.

The medicos carried down Marta next. They were followed by the mechoservitor, and then the surviving magicked scouts slipped past. Finally, Winters lowered herself down, surprised at the warmth of the metal rungs. Already, whatever the medico had rubbed into her wounds was taking the ache away, and she was grateful for it.

Renard smiled down on her. "You drew blood on a Blood Scout," he said. She heard bemused respect in his voice and waited for him to say more, but he didn't.

So she inclined her head to him and then descended into the Beneath Places as the hatch above her closed. She could not hear it, but she knew that already, dirt and moldy hay were being shoveled and forked onto the hatch. And after, the barn would be sealed up with its dead cattle. And the farmhouse would be left abandoned.

As she climbed down, she saw wires and bags that were fastened to some of the rungs. And when she reached the bottom, a middle-aged man, his hairline receding, scampered up the rungs with more wire and more bags.

She looked to Hebda, who must've seen the curiosity on her face. "We've set all our access points to the Named Lands with blast powder charges," he said. "We can't afford for the Beneath Places to fall into Y'Zirite hands."

She nodded, then went to Charles. He stood beside the metal man as the medicos checked Marta again. Now her eyes were open, though both were bruised heavily. "How is she?"

"She'll be fine," he said.

Then Winters nodded to the metal man. "And how is he?"

Charles looked at her with tears in his eyes and smiled. "He's . . . alive," he said.

And she felt the same tears rise in her own eyes and hoped that the old man was right.

Lysias

It was easy to lose track of time without the benefit of the sun, but the lack of cold made it a fair trade. In his few ventures into the Beneath Places this winter, Lysias had always been surprised by the warmth. Now, it was saving lives, he suspected, and that was worth having to rely upon a mechoservitor to know the time of day.

He stretched and stood, then rolled his bedroll. He'd considered a quick wash and shave, followed by a fresh uniform, but if today followed after the last several, it would be futile. He was bound to be wet or muddy before lunch.

Lysias pulled the metal cup from his mess kit and followed his nose to the portable stove his cooks used and the strong chai they had ready there. Crouching, he helped himself and then straightened.

He heard the clanking and clacking of the metal man approaching. "Good morning, General," it said.

He inclined his head to it, though he did not know why. "Good morning." Then, he sipped his chai and moved to the corner of the large cavern that they'd established as the command center.

There, several blankets had been spread out, and the mine chief, Turik, sat on one of them with parchment maps laid out all around him. Lysias noted the dark circles under the man's eyes when he looked up at the general.

Lysias hunkered down and looked at the maps, his eyes finding the red marks that showed passages now either underwater or collapsed. Some had been there already, but more damage had been done by the earthquake in the north. "When was the last time you slept, Chief?"

The man shrugged. "I'm not sure."

Lysias opened his mouth to dismiss the man to his bedroll, but as he did, a wet and muddy lieutenant appeared. "We've found another hatch. This one is wired, too."

His eyes went back to the map. *Those would be the blue markings.* There were two on the map, one to the east—not far actually from the Keeper's Gate—and another farther south.

Turik dug the blue pencil from his kit. "Show me."

The lieutenant pointed to a section of the map and the chief marked it, looking up to catch Lysias's eye. "Someone is definitely interested in restricting access. That's three hatches total now, each wired with enough blast powder to collapse a square league of tunnels."

Lysias nodded. They'd known for some time that they were not alone down here. Even in the early stages of mapping the Beneath Places, they'd come across boot prints and other evidence that someone else was active down here. And these more recent discoveries showed that those people were intent upon keeping others from gaining access.

But who are they? With Y'Zirites excavating Windwir and the recent passage of mechoservitors en route to the northern Marshlands, the Beneath Places weren't the great secret they'd hoped to keep them. But these charges were set for anyone accessing the hatches from above, and that made little sense to him. If everything had transpired as he suspected it had, the Machtvolk already controlled the lands north and west of Windwir, and by now, the Y'Zirites surely had a foothold in the southern nations. It was someone, he suspected, who already occupied the subterranean passages and did not want others joining them.

Lysias looked to the map. "We're going to need food soon," he said. "How easy would it be to defuse one of these hatches?"

Turik shrugged. "I can't imagine it would be too difficult. They're wired from below. I'd just need to get a look at it."

Lysias nodded. "First though," he said, "you'll need some sleep, Chief."

The chief chuckled. "I did sleep, sir. I'll get some chai and head out right—"

Third alarm sounded at the far edges of the cavern, and Lysias turned toward it. Three nearby scouts vanished on the run as they magicked themselves, and others rose up from their bedrolls, spears and swords at hand. Lysias drew his own blade—a saber he'd carried since his days in the Academy on the Delta—and set out at a run for the commotion.

He heard the ring of steel on steel and saw a storm of bedrolls and blankets and mess kits being tossed and kicked aside as magicked scouts fought.

As Lysias drew nearer he heard a voice bellow. "Hold, Gypsies." It was familiar, but not a voice he could recognize out of context. And he saw a small group of men standing in the shadowy entrance to the southern passageway. "Is that you, Lysias?"

He drew closer as the man stepped from the shadows. He wore a simple gray uniform, but the eye patch was all Lysias needed to see. "Stand down," he said to his men. "Orius?"

It wasn't possible. Orius had perished at Windwir with the others. Only about a thousand Androfrancines—those who'd been outside the city busily about the Order's business—had survived that desolation.

The general of the Gray Guard smiled. "When my scouts told me it was you, I had to come myself. What in the hells are you doing down here with a Gypsy army?"

"What are the Gray Guard doing here? How did you survive Windwir?"

Orius shook his head. "A long story, friend. But it is good to see you."

"You as well," Lysias said. Then he realized he'd not yet called the camp back to first alarm. He gave the whistle, and as the men dispersed, he gestured Orius and his entourage toward the chai kettle. As they walked there, he fell in beside Orius. "How did you know I was here?"

Orius chuckled. "We knew someone was down here in large numbers and started gathering data nearly a week ago. Solo scouts, magicked, in and out quickly to learn what they could. But I didn't know until yesterday that it was you."

They'd gone to the Academy together, and of course for years they'd interacted in their respective capacities as generals of neighboring armies. They'd forged a respectful relationship through dozens of affairs of state, though it was of a variety that recognized its limitations. Lysias, when shown evidence that the Androfrancines planned to deploy mechoservitors throughout the Named Lands to deliver the Seven Cacophonic Deaths, had backed Sethbert's plan. He'd been on the side that brought down Windwir before he saw the actual enemy that pulled Sethbert's strings.

And now, a man he thought killed by his nation's preemptive attack on Windwir stood with him in the Beneath Places, holding parley.

He handed Orius a tin of chai and led the man to his command center. They hunkered down against the wall and sipped their drinks. Lysias's had gone cold, but he barely remembered a time when he'd been able to get through an entire cup while it was still hot. "So what are the Androfrancines doing down here, and how are you faring?"

"We've established a camp on a sublayer about a day south and down," Orius said. "We have two others tucked away as well. We are conducting intelligence operations both above- and belowground and have stayed out of sight . . . until recently. But the Y'Zirites have no idea of our numbers, and so far, they've not let themselves into our little basement Whymer Maze."

Lysias blinked. "Exactly what are your numbers?"

Orius shook his head. "Best not to talk in specifics. But I have a sizeable force and some of the Order's best armament."

Lysias glanced to the man, took a sip of the chai, and swallowed. "And what are you learning?"

"Lord Rudolfo is on the Divided Isle and has been installed as chancellor. Supposedly there is a treaty between the Ninefold Forest Houses and Y'Zir, negotiated by Jakob, but I've not seen it yet."

Then it is true. He'd hoped it wasn't for Rudolfo's sake, but he'd heard the kin-raven alongside the Gypsy King and he'd seen the Y'Zirite blood shrine in the forest. "That is unfortunate," he said.

"Perhaps not," Orius said. "We have an operative approaching him now. We may be able to use his position to our advantage, though nothing we learned at the Academy is going to serve us well down here."

No, Lysias realized. But he'd known when he brought his army underground that it was not going to be like any other war he'd fought. "How is the Delta faring?"

Orius shook his head. "City-states are falling—they're worn down by too many years of loss and need. There are still scattered remnants of the army and those damnable Democrats in play, but they're mostly dead, imprisoned, or in hiding. The Isle counties fell without much fight. Turam's ruling house and government are on the move and its army has fallen back with them, but they're being pressed from the north by the Machtvolk." He sighed. "It's bleak, Lysias, but not hopeless. Rudolfo will be a help, I'm certain. And we've some other recent developments that I think are fortuitous." He smiled and nodded toward the camp around them. "The arrival of another seasoned strategist with his own army counts highly on that list. I came to personally invite you and your men to join me."

Lysias's eyes narrowed. "I serve Rudolfo now, and this is ultimately *his* army. I would need to consult with him." Of course, even as he said it, he knew he didn't. He'd not consulted Rudolfo before bringing his army belowground; he'd made the decision for his king because a decision was needed. And he could make this decision as well.

"If my operative is successful, we can get word to him." Orius stood. "But meanwhile, kin-clave does not prevent us working together. If you'll send men back with me, I'll return them with supplies. We've a good supply of fresh game and water. We may even have some apples left."

Lysias stood. "Thank you."

As Orius moved into the cavern, his men fell in around him. "We'll establish a courier line between camps," he said. "The moon sparrows don't fly as well down here. We can also help you find a more permanent camp that is closer, if you like. One with access to water."

Lysias nodded. "We've been looking."

"It truly is a Whymer Maze like no other. And it keeps going down—we've yet to find bottom." Orius stood at the opening to the southern passage now and extended a hand to Lysias.

He took it and shook it once. "It is good to see you, Orius."

The one-eyed general winked. "I'm not sure how we'll do it, but somehow we'll set things right, Lysias."

Lysias stood and watched the man disappear back into the shadows. After he was gone, the general went back to the blankets and the maps they held. There was also a stack of reports now waiting for him, and he went first to the scouts who'd allowed his perimeter to be breached by magicked Gray Guard and the men they escorted. They'd have to be dressed-down in some public manner, he knew, to instill the right sense of urgency among the others. But not until he had all the facts.

An aide brought him a fresh tin of steaming chai as he read. But like the one before it, the chai was cold by the time Lysias finished.

Chapter 15

Rudolfo

Rudolfo moved through an afternoon heat that confounded his body after so long in winter to the north. He felt the sweat running down his sides and stifled a yawn with the back of his hand.

Beside him, Ire Li Tam kept easy pace, and from the corner of his eye, he watched her as she watched their surroundings. The city was quiet even at the peak of its day, with Y'Zirite soldiers and officers still making up the vast majority of the people out and about. But after his morning with General Yazmeera he understood things better. Most of Merrique's citizens had been relocated to outlying counties, but a few had been kept back, impressed into service to support the steady influx of Y'Zirite soldiers, officers, and officials.

He'd learned more than that from the hours spent with their general. He'd also been briefed on the status of the fighting elsewhere and the excavation at Windwir—both of which appeared to be progressing according to the Y'Zirites' timeline. Then, Yazmeera had shown him to his office and he'd brooded over his first assignment—a message to the leaders of the Named Lands. It had taken him two hours to write it, the fits and starts of it evidenced by the pile of crumpled paper that grew in his waste bin.

And now, after Yazmeera's review and approval of the message during a hurried lunch—a spicy shrimp-and-noodle dish served with cold lemon beer—he now made his way to the general's personal birder.

Ire had suggested that they ride, but after weeks in a saddle or at a desk, Rudolfo wanted to stretch his legs under a sun he barely remembered after so long in the snow. As they walked, the buildings thinned and gave way to tree-lined cobblestone avenues and large walled villas that took up entire blocks.

The Y'Zirite communications officers had taken over a villa and its adjacent barn just on the edge of the city. Bored soldiers stood watch at the gate, snapping to attention and saluting briskly at the sight of Ire Li Tam. She returned the salute, and Rudolfo inclined his head as he followed her through the open gate.

Yazmeera's birder was an old man, his face white with the scars of his Y'Zirite faith. He took the general's note from Ire Li Tam and read it. He said something to Ire in the Y'Zirite language, and she nodded, repeating back some of the words. She leaned toward Rudolfo. "He says that forty-five birds is a lot."

"Yes," Rudolfo said. "It is." Though it was likely half the number it would've been before the Y'Zirites invaded.

The old man shuffled off to the barn. As he went, he motioned for them to follow.

When the birder opened the barn door, the smell of decaying meat ambushed Rudolfo's nose, and the force of it nearly made him gag. He met Ire's bemused smile with a glare and then blinked into the slanting rays of sunlight that illuminated the open barn.

Heavy rope had been run to and fro throughout the structure, tied off from the various support beams and posts, and these ropes were crowded with still, black forms. The rafters above were also crowded with the silent birds.

The birder emitted a series of whistles, and Rudolfo watched as kin-ravens stirred to life, dropping from the rafters and ropes to gather around him on the straw-littered floor. The old man pointed to him and spoke to Ire, and the woman turned to him.

"When they cock their heads and open their beaks, recite your message," she said.

Rudolfo nodded, and the old man whistled again. In unison, the birds' beaks dropped open as their heads cocked to the left. These were nothing like the birds he'd used all his life—doves, swallows, even ravens or hawks on occasion. Magicked and trained from their first flights, the messenger birds of the Named Lands took whispered instructions and bore notes carried under the various colors designated by kin-clave to all points in the Named Lands, though they lost much of their effectiveness too far to sea or too far east in the Churning Wastes.

Not the kin-raven. These birds had a stamina that paralleled their stench, and from what Rudolfo had seen, they could bear the exact words of their message—in the voice of the messenger—over vast distances.

Rudolfo cleared his voice and forced his eyes from the kin-ravens to the paper in his hands. Between the smell and the weight of the deed before him, his stomach ached. And already, he edited as he recited, dropping Yazmeera's inserted opening *by the grace of Y'Zir and the Crimson Empress.* Instead, he picked up where his own words began. "To the kin-bound houses of the Named Lands, from Rudolfo, Lord of the Ninefold Forest Houses and Chancellor Designate of the Y'Zirite Empire: Greetings."

He swallowed a deeper breath. "The Androfrancines taught us that change is the path life takes, and we have experienced much change these past two years. Indeed, more change lies ahead—and much work—as we learn a new way of life. As Lord of the Ninefold Forest Houses, I invoke kin-clave and call for Council to discuss the Y'Zirite terms of surrender. Upon acceptance of said terms, Council will be expected to exercise its Option of Dissolution. A new document of governance will be presented and discussed for adoption."

He paused and took another breath, surprised that his anger obeyed him and did not leak into his voice. "Council is called in two weeks' time, in the county seat of Merrique on the Divided Isle. All providences and protections of kin-clave apply, and you are sworn to attend."

He paused, his eyes stumbling over the final line. But he already knew he couldn't escape it a second time. He looked away, though, as he said it. "By the grace of Y'Zir and the Crimson Empress."

Then, Rudolfo looked to the birder and nodded.

The old man whistled, and the kin-ravens' beaks snapped shut even as their necks straightened. He exchanged words with Ire and took the slip of paper she handed him.

The list. It was shorter than it should be. He watched the birder as the man bent and whispered the first destination to the first kin-raven. Then, Rudolfo turned and followed Ire Li Tam back across the cobblestones to the gate.

They walked in silence, and Rudolfo felt the heaviness of the day upon his shoulders. For two years, he and his people had been viewed with suspicion. Sethbert had accused him of the destruction of Windwir, and then the Ninefold Forest Houses had benefited tremendously by that city's fall with both the library and all of the other Androfrancine holdings. Now, he'd actually confirmed their suspicions and presented himself to them as their new chancellor, calling for his own peoples' surrender. In two weeks, he would demand their cooperation in dismantling a way of life and incorporating a new one.

Rudolfo sighed and pretended not to notice Ire's glance or the look of concern on her face. Instead, he kept his eyes on the road ahead.

A woman waited for him at the gate to his own villa, and something about her struck him as familiar though he could not place it. She was tall and more elegant than the silk pants and shirt she wore, her white hair pulled back into a pony tail. Her dark eyes took him in, and he tried to read the look on her face.

She stepped closer. "Rudolfo?"

"Yes?" He stopped. Beside him, Ire picked up her pace, a hand sliding to the knife at her belt.

The force of the woman's spittle struck him full in the face, and Rudolfo flinched backward. He hesitated for a moment, then realized that Ire's knife was out now as she advanced on the woman.

"No," Rudolfo said, and the Blood Scout stopped, though her hand stayed at the hilt of her knife. He wiped his face with his sleeve and furrowed his eyebrows. "You are . . . ?"

"I am Drea Merrique."

He blinked, placing her now. When he was young, he and Gregoric had broken into her father's house in the company of her brother, Rafe. That was their first meeting. Eventually, because of her older brother's penchant for trouble and piracy, she'd become the Countess Merrique, but it had been years since Rudolfo had seen her.

He nodded. "I remember. And have I wronged you in some way?"

Drea Merrique shook her head. "No, Rudolfo," she said, her voice bitter. "You have wronged us all, and you know exactly in what way."

Then, she turned her back to him and walked away, the straightness of her spine more clear than any Writ of Shunning.

I have, Rudolfo thought, *and I do.*

Then, he went inside and spent another evening alone, holding—but not opening—his bottle of firespice until sleep finally carried him into dreams he was glad he could not remember in the morning.

Jin Li Tam

A warm wind pulled at a silk softer than she had ever worn, and Jin Li Tam closed her eyes against it.

The singing had finally settled down, but when it did, it was in fits and starts of spontaneous songs after stretches of quiet. But now, the crowds were dispersing after a day of worship in the city.

Worship of my son. She shuddered and glanced over her shoulder. Jakob slept in a crib beside her own bed, dressed in a light silk nightshirt. He moved as she watched; then Jin Li Tam turned back to the city.

Directly below, the Imperial Gardens filled a walled enclosure. Directly across from the garden, the plain pyramid of the Temple of the Daughters of Ahm Y'Zir stood, its statue of the Wizard King lit from within by some magic she did not comprehend. It shimmered beneficently over the city, one hand outstretched to the palace and the other outstretched to the south to encompass the city.

She heard the faintest cough to her left, and her eyes instantly tracked the noise. A woman in the black-and-red silks of the Blood Guard shifted easily on her feet on the balcony next door. The guard inclined her head, and Jin Li Tam returned the gesture. Then, she went back to watching the city, this time mindful of the roofs and shadows and the secret watchers that waited there.

Guarding us because of our part in their gospel. It horrified her and it humbled her all at once. And the complexity of it baffled her, though she imagined that to an outsider, the ways of kin-clave and the order imposed by the Androfrancines might seem complex as well.

As well watched as they were, she wasn't sure how they'd be reunited with Aedric, though just establishing a line of communication would be helpful. Eyes, ears, feet, and hands outside. She'd not yet seen her target, but she already knew that her own survival was unlikely.

But Jin was also even more convinced now of the sensibility behind her grandfather's decision. The greatest weakness of this people was their faith. And the Crimson Empress was much more than an empress to this people. She was a god, promised by prophecy. Taking her out of the equation would strike a blow at the heart of that faith. She wasn't sure if it would turn the tides of war—she suspected that rage and wrath were just as likely responses—but it would take a massive toll.

And end the madness my grandfather saw here.

She stretched, then left the balcony to return to bed. Jin pushed back the light blankets and stretched out, trying once again to sleep. She tossed and turned for an hour, replaying the parade and then the lunch with the regent and his staff. The day had been a blur as they were settled into their quarters. There had been measurements and then parcels of clothing arriving throughout the day, a whirlwind tour of their wing followed by another lavish meal—this time in formal dress. But beyond all of that, it had been a day of cataloging data. Where entrances and exits were. How many guards worked the wall and gates.

And now, when she should've slept, Jin Li Tam played it all back and could not stop. When the softest chimes rang in the halls beyond her room, she sat up.

Padding to the door, she opened it slowly. Outside, a guard stood in the corner with a clear view of the double doors leading into the wing and each room's door along that short hallway. The double doors were open now, and beyond them, she saw first one and then another robed figure slip past.

Jin stepped into the hall, leaving the door cracked behind her. The guard inclined her head, and she returned the gesture with a smile. "I heard a bell," she said, forming the words carefully in V'Ral.

"First prayer, Mother." The woman's voice was younger than her eyes.

"Ah," Jin said. She looked beyond the double doors. "I think I'm going to walk a bit. Will you send someone for me if Jakob awakens?"

The guard nodded. "Yes, Mother."

She glanced behind her to the partly open door. Lynnae also slept nearby, her own chambers separated from Jin and Jakob's by way of a lavish bathing room. Still, she was hesitant to leave.

He is safer here than anywhere else in the world.

She looked to the guard once more, then slipped down the hallway. Her bare feet were silent in the thick carpet, though she made no effort to conceal her footfalls. She moved out from the wing, into the greater living quarters of the palace. Robed figures moved quickly and quietly down a central staircase, and she was so focused on them that she didn't see the chief mother until the woman was in front of her.

"Lady Tam," Elsbet said. "Are your quarters satisfactory?"

"Quite," she said. "I just couldn't sleep. I heard the chime and came out."

The older woman nodded. "Of course. Strange surroundings and sleep don't often go well together. I'm sure we can find you something in the apothecary's pantry if you wish."

Jin shook her head. "Thank you. No. I prefer to walk. But don't let me keep you from your prayers."

Elsbet smiled. "Nonsense. Prayer takes many forms; certainly walking with our Great Mother is one of them." She paused and raised her eyebrows. "Unless, of course, you prefer to be alone?"

The lie was easy. "I'd be happy for the company."

"Good," the Chief Mother said.

As they walked, they chatted in quiet tones, and Jin Li Tam noted every guard, every door, every window, pausing to ask questions as they went. And when they slipped out into the warm night into gardens scented by lemons, limes, and oranges, she took note of each outbuilding and cobblestone path.

An hour later, Jin found herself once more by the entrance to her wing. "Thank you," she said, inclining her head to the older woman.

"Thank *you*, Great Mother."

Jin's eyes strayed to a closed and ornate set of doors leading into the single wing she'd not yet seen. Two of the Blood Guard stood to either side of the entrance. "Is that where the Crimson Empress resides?"

Elsbet followed her eyes and nodded. "It is."

Jin chose her next words with care, keeping her tone curious and light. "I was surprised that she did not participate in today's celebrations."

Elsbet smiled. "She's been ill. But regardless, she rarely appears in public." She looked at Jin, her eyes softening. "I'm sure formal introductions will be arranged soon. But . . . would you like to see her?"

"I . . ." Jin's voice faltered. "Certainly. But only if it's . . . appropriate."

"You've travelled a long way. I think it's very appropriate."

Elsbet turned to the guards, and Jin watched as her hands moved in some coded sign language she did not comprehend. One of the women unlocked and opened the door.

On the other side, at the end of a hall lined with doors, a servant in red robes sat in a single chair with a leather-bound book open in her lap. When she saw Elsbet and Jin approach she blushed and started to rise. "Chief Mother, I—"

"Please stay seated," Elsbet said with a gentle smile. "How is she tonight?"

"Her cough persists, but she sleeps."

Elsbet nodded. "We'll just look in on her."

Elsbet opened the door a crack just as a fit of coughing started up behind it. The sound of it froze Jin's blood before she even comprehended it, and as the door swung open, a shaft of light spilled into the darkened room.

Jin felt a hand at her elbow, guiding her through the door, but it was a distant touch she barely felt. Instead, her focus was centered on the large, round bed that dominated the room.

Lying in the middle of that bed, sleeping sprawled on her stomach, was a little girl of roughly Jakob's age. Her dark curly hair spilled out on the sheet like ink on clean paper, and she clutched a cloth-made dromedary in one of her hands.

"Behold," Chief Mother Elsbet whispered, "the Crimson Empress . . . Amara Y'Zir . . . the hope of our world."

And in that moment, Jin Li Tam knew that she could never do what her grandfather had sent her here to do, and she felt the hope leaking out from her like so much held breath.

Vlad Li Tam

Awaken, my love.

Vlad Li Tam heard the voice—the slightest whisper—and his eyes flew open. The staff trembled in his hand, and he untangled himself from the woman whose limbs entwined him. He stood and stepped out of the shed and into the warm night.

They'd walked for a day, he and Chandra, and he'd tried to use the staff less and less.

The tools of the parents, he thought. After the interrogation on the boat, his weariness had moved from a dull and pervasive ache to a sharper, clearer pain. His bones hurt now, and he had moments of vertigo that made the ground rush at him like a magicked scout. When he *could* urinate, he pissed red, and he was always thirsty. The staff, he knew, was taking from him for everything that it seemed to give.

And now it whispers to me in the night. No, he realized. *She* whispers.

Vlad stepped out of their latest shelter—an abandoned lean-to on the edge of an orchard that overlooked the river canyon—and stretched. The water below moved slowly, shimmering back the starlight. To the southwest, at the river's end, the lights of Ahm's Glory washed the sky a lighter shade of gray. They would reach that vast city tomorrow if they kept their pace.

And then what?

He wasn't sure, but Vlad had something—faith, he thought—that assured him the right path would be clear just as it always had been before.

He heard the faintest rustle to his right, and he turned quickly, raising the staff. The kin-raven hopped back, its beak open.

"Knives," the kin-raven said.

Vlad blinked. "Knives?"

It chortled and lifted itself into the air, wings stirring up wind. Vlad took a step toward the bird. "Knives?"

"Yes, Uncle," a voice said behind him. "Knives." Vlad turned, feeling the staff vibrate to life in his hands. The man was slight of build, dressed in loose-fitting desert robes that concealed all but the hilts of his scout knives.

It was instinctive now, and he held the man in place with the staff, commanded truth with the staff. "Who are you?"

"We are the Knives of Tam," the man said. "Hidden away for time of need. Our kin-raven brought us to you."

No resistance. But Vlad didn't need the staff to see that the man was being truthful. And neither the dimness of the starlight nor the scars upon his face could conceal the features of a Tam—not from another Tam.

Now he saw there were others with him—two young men and a girl of maybe twelve. They wore simple garb—shades of brown to match the desert—and they carried scout knives. The girl had a blowgun tucked into her belt. He looked back to the man in robes. "Which nephew are you?"

"I am Al Shadryk of Terick's Fall now," he said. "But I was Som Li Tam before my grandfather sent me here."

Som Li Tam. He struggled to make the connection. His brother Tarn's boy? Killed at sea . . . or was it moonpox? There was a time when he would have remembered. It was two decades ago or longer. "My father sent you?"

Som Li Tam nodded, and the others did, too. "We are your knives, set aside and hidden should you need them."

Vlad opened his mouth to speak and closed it as Chandra emerged from the shelter. He could see the fear on her face. "We have guests," he told her.

His nephew inclined his head to her. "You are the Vessel of Grace," he said. It was more a statement than a question.

"Yes," she answered. "I was . . . am."

The man nodded and returned his attention to Vlad. "I bear word to you from Grandfather," he said. He dug into his robes and drew out a folded, sealed envelope.

Vlad felt the age of it as he took it, and he resisted the urge to open it. He tucked it into his own pocket. "And what is your assignment?"

"I serve House Li Tam however you direct me, Uncle. I am your knife."

They all are. He saw their faces, bathed in the light of the city behind him and the stars above. There was determination on them.

And my father hid them here for me. The idea of it staggered him—and though the boy was telling the truth and the note was sure to explain why, Vlad could not fathom his father doing such a thing. Ben Li Tam had been at the heart of the conspiracy that destroyed Windwir and its Androfrancines. And ultimately, his actions had put most of House Li Tam onto the Y'Zirites' cutting tables in a temple he himself had designed.

But Som Li Tam is telling the truth. And that told Vlad he could trust him. "For now, I will need quiet access to Ahm's Glory and lodging for myself and the woman."

The man nodded. "It will be arranged. I'll send the bird with details." He turned and flashed hand-signs to the others that Vlad didn't recognize. A pack and two canteens materialized, and Som placed them on the ground near the lean-to. "Food and water," he said.

Vlad inclined his head. "Thank you."

His nephew returned the gesture. Then he turned and ran into the night, the others falling in around him. The sound of their retreat was a whisper that slowly faded.

When they were gone, he looked to Chandra. "We should sleep. We'll have more walking tomorrow."

They crawled back into their makeshift bed, and Vlad stroked her hair until she fell asleep, her arms and legs once more wrapped around him. As she slept, he lay awake and thought.

I could be wrong to trust him. He didn't think he was, but Vlad had to allow for it. And if he was wrong, he could call upon the staff to help him. But that slightest use earlier left his stomach cramping now as he came down from the euphoria of using it.

Vlad touched the scrap of paper in his pocket. He'd found notes from his father before over the years—it was a custom in the House. And some had been found long after his death, hidden for just the right time. But this was the first since Vlad had learned—and experienced—his father's plans for House Li Tam as an intricate part of this Y'Zirite cult.

It surprised him how badly he wanted the note to explain his father's choices and actions. But Vlad had learned it well and from the very man himself: Tams do not explain their choices and always have a reason for them.

He waited until first light and slipped out beneath a quiet sky to sit on the cliff over the river. Vlad carefully opened the envelope with fingers that betrayed him by shaking, and he pulled out the single sheet of parchment to unfold it.

He held it open before him until the gray of morning was such that he could make out the letters. He read it once, and then he read it again.

There were no coded messages, and the handwriting was his father's—from his later years, after the first stroke.

I was wrong, the note read.

And after those words, a poem in a style familiar to him. About a father who longed for his son's forgiveness but knew he could never attain it.

Vlad tried to feel something for the man who had made him, shaped him, but couldn't. In the end, he tucked the paper away, stood up on aching legs, and went to awaken Chandra for the road ahead.

Chapter 16

Neb

Neb moved up and forward in darkness, his feet careful to find their footing and his hands outstretched before him as he went. He was forced to move slowly, unsure of his step and of what obstacles might block his path, and as he climbed the endlessly spiraling staircase he lost all sense of time. It felt like he'd climbed for days in pursuit of the girl.

She'd not waited for him to return when he had turned back, and his shouts for her to wait had gone unanswered. All he heard was the muffled sound of occasional footfalls someplace above him as she, too, climbed the stairs.

If she intended to leave me behind, why did she wait for me to awaken? Why not just abandon him where he slept? It made little sense, but so far the girl was a contradiction he could not comprehend. One minute innocent, another alluring, and the next enraged.

He didn't know the nature of her illness, but Aver-Tal-Ka was right in his assessment: Amylé D'Anjite was not well.

Neb paused, thinking perhaps he'd heard something. Somewhere above, a new sound tickled at his ears. Metal groaning and creaking. And then the slightest drop in temperature, the faintest scent of something old and dusty, closed off, on the downward-drifting breeze.

He felt the emotions first. *Terror. Panic.* Then he heard the gasp of surprise above him, and it started him climbing again, moving faster through the dark with one hand trailing against the smooth, warm metallic wall. "Amylé?"

He heard fear in the girl's voice, too, but it was nothing compared to the waves of emotion she pulsated with. "Who is it?"

"Nebios," he said. "Nebios Whym."

"Did my father send—?" A sob swallowed the rest of her words and became a snuffled gasp. "You're the boy from the garden at the top of the temple."

"Yes," he said. "Wait for me. I'm coming to you."

Neb increased his pace, aware now that not only had the air changed, but the light—or lack thereof—had changed as well. It wasn't by much, but enough to raise his feet's confidence on the stairs he climbed. And as he drew closer, he saw the source of the light. At the top of the stairs a large, round metal door stood open a crack, and the dimmest light leaked in from it. More than that, the faintest sound of music also leaked into the dark and deep stairwell. Amylé sat in that gray pool of illumination, the white oval of her face turned toward Neb as he approached.

She scrambled back from him, her eyes widening. The questions spilled out of her in a mad rush. "Where are our clothes? Where have you brought me? How did you wake me?"

Neb stopped and dropped to a crouch, holding up his hands. He closed his eyes and tried to push his own emotions toward her. *Peace. Calm.* "Don't be afraid."

But his own fear was too present in the moment. The bitter, angry woman who'd brought him here and had assured him that she'd already stopped him from unsealing the temple now didn't know where she was or how she had come to be there. He couldn't trust her. And he was still coming to grips with just how badly things had gone. Isaak destroyed. Stranded on the moon—in the very tower he was sent to unseal—with no sense of how to do what needed doing.

Her back was to the wall now, beside the door she'd opened. They were on a landing, and he picked out a section of wall as far from her as he could get without staying on the stairs. He moved to it slowly and sat down, feeling the warmth of the metal against his back.

She sobbed again, and now her voice rose. "Tell me where you've brought me. Does my father know?"

Neb swallowed. "I think we're in the Firsthome Temple. And your father . . ." No, he couldn't tell her now that he suspected that the man had been dead for two millennia. He found the closest compromise he could with truth. "I don't think he sent me," he said, "but I think maybe *my* father did." He waited for the words to set in and caught the faint trace of music on the air. Its notes were constant companions to him now. "Do you hear the song?"

Her nod was the faintest outline in the gloom. "I do. It's the Homeseeker's Song."

The Homeseeker's Song. He knew it as the Canticle for the Fallen Moon—a song attributed to the Last Weeping Czar Frederico, though Neb now suspected it originated somewhere above them. A song heard in the Wastes by metal ears, from a crescent buried deep beneath the ruins of the Old World. "Yes. It brought me here to unseal the tower." He paused again. "There is a dream coded into it."

"And it brought you to me as well?"

Neb hesitated. "I think so. I met you in my dreams right after arriving." He paused. "And you said our fathers knew each other."

"Yes," she said. "I remember. You were in the garden at the top of the temple. We watched home-rise together, and I flew away when you woke the hounds."

"Yes."

"You had more hair then." Her voice was matter-of-fact.

Neb blushed, his hand absently moving to his head. The hair was already losing its bristle and softening—growing back after it had burned away far faster than normal. "Yes," he said.

"And after the dream you found me and brought me here?"

Neb shook his head. "I did find you and wake you. But . . ." He wasn't sure he should say more. She was already precariously poised on the brink of something he couldn't comprehend. Finally, he chose his path. "But I didn't bring you here."

"Then who brought us?"

Neb opened his mouth and closed it. *You did.* But he couldn't say it. "I don't know."

She looked around. "And you say it's the Firsthome Temple?"

"I think so." His eyes were adjusting even more now to the dark. "Or maybe we're beneath it. Maybe it's beyond that door."

She was calming down now. He could feel the panic moving into a quieter fear. Amylé looked up at him, and their eyes met. "I don't see how it's possible. I've been to the temple hundreds of times. This place is dark and desolate. The temple is full of life."

Neb shrugged, and her eyes narrowed.

"So why are we here, Nebios?"

"I don't know exactly," he said. It wasn't a lie, though it wasn't the complete truth, either. He nodded to the door. "But I think we should go in."

Neb stood slowly, his eyes on the girl. Everything about her was different now, even her posture. It was hard to believe this was the same woman he had awakened with earlier. He took a step toward her and held out his hand.

She hesitated before taking it and letting him help her to her feet. When their skin touched, Neb felt it like heat moving through his body, and he flushed. Once she was steady, he released her hand quickly and reached forward to push the large metal door open wider. Then, they stepped through together.

The smell of something old and musty mingled with the faintest aroma of spices and ozone. The scents were subtle, but the odd assortment made them somehow overpowering, and he coughed against it. He felt a hand slipping into his own, and that heat stirred again, threatening his balance with an intoxication he did not comprehend.

Her scent is here, too. Neb swallowed and willed his hand to release hers again. But this time, it would not obey him and he closed his eyes against the vertigo of her touch.

It is a mirage, he realized. Because whatever he saw now, there was more to Amylé D'Anjite than the frightened woman he stood with. Neb tried to see the enraged, bitter woman who had lured him here intending to stop him from unsealing the tower, but she seemed gone now. Everything about Amylé was different—her posture, the tone of her voice, the way she looked at him.

Desire. Hope. He felt the emotions rising off of her, and when he met her eyes, she looked away.

"I'm sorry," she said. "I've . . . I've been asleep for a long time. You're the first person I've seen in . . ." The words trailed off into silence. "Well, I don't know how long," she finally said. "Surely you feel it, too?"

"Feel what?"

"The call," she said.

Neb blushed. He didn't have to ask what she meant. The more her anxiety settled, and the more time they spent near each other, the stronger it became. He felt it from her in waves, and he knew she must feel it too. And beyond that, if it went on much longer, he'd not be able to hide the evidence of its physical effect on him. "We should walk while we talk."

She nodded, and they set out hand in hand, naked and unashamed though the idea of it baffled Neb. They moved out into an open space, and the farther they walked, the more Neb's eyes adjusted to the gloom. The floor beneath their feet was soft and pliable, the light emanating from scattered patches of lichen and fungi that glowed faintly around them. Whatever walls or ceiling this large room had were beyond the little light they saw by.

"I don't understand what's happened to the temple," Amylé said in a quiet voice. "Why was it sealed? How long ago?"

Neb shrugged. "I don't know for certain. But I think the Moon Wizard did it before he fell."

Confusion. He sensed it even as he changed direction with his words. "Y'Zir, I mean."

She stopped walking, and he felt the fear returning. "Then he won."

Neb stopped, too, and took a deep breath. "I think he did. But I think maybe I'm here to undo that."

He started to walk, but her grip on his hand tightened and held him back. Her face was sober, and the fear had all but swallowed the desire that had been radiating from her moments before. "How long have I been asleep, Nebios Whym? Where are our fathers? What has become of the People?"

Her voice rose with her panic, and the terror chilled him and forced his eyes away from her.

Tell me. He felt the strength of her words as they struck his mind and he released his held breath.

"I think Y'Zir won a long time ago," he said. "My father was a ghost in a cave deep underground when I met him." He didn't know how to tell her that he'd not even known he was of her kind until recently. And the knowledge still terrified him. So instead, he fell back to a comfortable answer. "And I don't know what became of the People." He paused and felt his own fear rising again. "All I know is to follow the song."

She squeezed his hand. "Okay."

And as they set out across the room, Neb wondered exactly what he would do when he did find the source of the song. And more importantly, he wondered what Amylé D'Anjite would do.

He knew better than to believe that the bitter woman who brought him here was gone. But she was gone for now, and the woman who replaced her left him with a feeling he had never felt before.

It feels, Nebios Whym realized, *like home.*

Winters

Winters paused, her pencil poised above the empty page, and closed her eyes against the noise of the camp beyond her tent.

The taste of sleep still filled her mouth, and the faint scent of boiling chai pulled at her, tempting her away from her morning's work.

I need to remember. Putting down the pencil, she rubbed her eyes. She was dreaming again, but laying hold of the words and images was like swimming in mud. She knew they were there, just beyond the reach of her memory. She felt the presence of the night's dreams in her sweat-damp hair and her sore muscles.

She wasn't exactly sure how long she'd been underground at this point. They'd traveled the Beneath Places on a seemingly endless route of twists and turns and unexpected descents before arriving at the small camp they now occupied. And somewhere along the way, her dreams had returned. Only muted now, veiled and far away and impossible to remember. But they'd become more and more regular the farther down they went.

Winters heard a stirring behind her and looked over her shoulder. Marta sat up in her cot, the blankets pooling around her. "Good morning," the girl said, her voice muffled by sleep.

"Good morning," Winters replied. "How are you feeling?"

The girl's injuries had been relatively minor, though her black eyes made it appear much worse. "I'm fine. Can I see the Watcher now?"

When they'd arrived the day before, the mechoservitor had been hurried off with Hebda, Charles, and the others. Marta had been left in Winters's care, and despite the wonders of an Androfrancine camp buried deep beneath the surface, all the girl could think about—or ask about—had been her metal companion.

Winters scowled. "I don't think that's really his name." But she didn't elaborate; she wasn't sure it was her place.

Marta shrugged. "I don't care what his name is. I just want to see him."

She looked back to the page. All she had were vague recollections of emotions and images lost in shadow. Winters turned her chair so that she faced the girl. "I think that can be arranged," she said. "Did you sleep well?"

The girl shrugged, then yawned. "I think I had bad dreams."

Me too. Winters stood and went to her pack. "What kind of dreams?"

The girl shrugged again. "I can't remember."

Winters dug through her pack, pulling out clean trousers and a shirt. She passed them to the girl. "These will be too big," she said. "But they'll serve better than anything else around here until we can find better."

They both dressed quickly, their backs to one another, and slipped out into a large chamber lined with bedrolls and broken into campsites by company. Winters led them away from their own campsite among the other senior officers, marking its place, and followed a metal pipe suspended above them until they reached the cistern it poured into. There, she dipped them a bucket to wash from, and with faces wet from ice-cold water, they followed the smells of frying bacon and chai to the mess tables.

Charles was already there, sitting alone at a table with a bowl of oats. Winters led Marta through the line, watching the girl stack her tin plate with bacon and a sweetened bread made with corn. Winters took a slice of bacon and an apple, focusing on the chai and ignoring the eyes that took in the latticework of scars that covered her face and arms.

The old arch-engineer looked up as they approached. When she met his eyes, she saw the circles under them and knew he hadn't slept well. Still, he smiled. "How are you feeling?"

Marta touched the stitched gash on her scalp as she set her plate down. "My head hurts."

Winters gingerly moved her shoulder, feeling the bite of her own cut. "I'm okay," she said. Then, she furrowed her brows. "Did you get any sleep?"

Charles shook his head. "I don't know how you ever slept with the dreams going on all night."

Of course, the dreams rarely went all night even at their peak. But whatever Charles experienced was different. Her dreams had been a part of her heritage, in the bones and blood of her family. The old man's dreams came from the mechoservitor, and if Micah and Hebda were correct, they were the stirrings of the Final Dream.

"I think I dreamed about the moon," Marta said as she nibbled a slice of bacon. "It's all . . . fuzzy. I can't remember."

Winters and Charles looked to her at the same time, then to one another. Winters opened her mouth to say something, but another voice interrupted.

"Ah, you're here." Hebda approached their table. "I was just coming to fetch you. General Orius has arrived."

Marta craned her neck, trying to see the man over Winters's shoulder. "Does that mean I can see my friend now?"

Hebda smiled, but his sunken eyes and gaunt features made it a grim, humorless expression. "Yes. I'm sorry it's taken so long."

The girl was already scrambling to her feet, cramming a fistful of bacon into her mouth as she stood. Winters watched the change in her demeanor and found herself smiling at it.

Hebda whistled, and a young man in a gray uniform stepped forward. "Danver will take you to him."

She mumbled her good-byes around her mouthful of food, and Hebda waited until she'd left the tent before continuing. Then, he looked at Winters. "How is she doing?"

"She's fine," Winters said. "But it doesn't seem any of us slept well."

Hebda's smile widened, and she saw giddiness in it. "Yes," he said. "The dreams." He nodded. "Isn't it wonderful?"

"Not," a gruff voice said behind Hebda, "if it brings the Y'Zirites down upon us."

The arch-behaviorist stepped aside, and Winters recognized Orius instantly from the descriptions her scouts had brought her over the years. A broad-shouldered, muscular older man, his hair white and short-cropped. Her own people had taken his eye in some skirmish during her father's reign, and the scar from that taking was visible despite the patch he wore.

"Arch-engineer Charles," Orius said.

Charles stood and inclined his head. "General."

Winters climbed to her feet and extended her hand to the officer. "General Orius," she said.

He took the hand and squeezed. "Winteria bat Mardic," he said. Then, he glanced to Hebda. "Did I say it right?" At his quick nod, the general continued. "Let's walk together. Hebda's convinced me that it's time to show you what has him so excited." He winked at Charles. "And I have much to discuss with you, Arch-engineer."

They set out from the tent, and a half-squad of Gray Guard scouts fell in around them as they went. They went quietly until they were out of earshot of the camp.

Once they were, Orius slowed their pace, and Winters fell in behind Charles. Hebda walked beside her. "It's really quite extraordinary," he said. "There have been dozens of reports of heightened dream activity in the last two nights. It started once the mechoservitor was within a league of it."

Winters glanced to him. "Within a league of what?"

Hebda smiled. "You'll see. I think combined with the mechoservitor as a conduit, the dream should reach them."

The dream should reach them. Neb was alive. And not only was he alive, he was on the moon. Every time her mind turned that corner, it flooded her with relief. Certainly, something had changed in him, and the memory of their last encounter still frightened her. But he was also the boy she had kissed in the forest near the grave of Windwir so long ago. And he was the Homeseeker.

Winters settled into her silence, pondering what lay ahead and listening to Charles and the general.

"I want you to talk to it," Orius said. "Whatever it is, it isn't the same mechanical you built. If it *is* the Watcher, it is an invaluable intelligence asset at a time of great need. I want to know everything it knows."

Hebda cleared his voice, and Winters saw a look on his face that gave her pause. "Of course, the general understands that the mechoservitor's highest priority is the Final Dream."

Orius growled. "Aye. I do. But when it's not dreaming, I want it talking."

Winters saw Charles's back stiffen. *He's angry,* she realized. Of course, his anger made sense. Orius was treating Isaak like property or a prisoner. It even angered her when she thought about it.

Finally, Charles spoke. "I will certainly talk with him."

Orius nodded and they continued on, descending through passageways that twisted and turned before spilling them into another massive cavern. Overhead, a pale light radiated from patches of phosphorescent lichen to illuminate a sea of silver.

Far out in the center, Winters saw a black island of the same stone as the tiny carved kin-raven the metal man had touched her with in the Cave of the Book of Dreaming Kings. And midway between the island and the shore, a rowboat moved slowly toward them, its sole occupant slouched at the oars.

They all gathered at the shore to watch the boat. "This is it," Hebda said. "It's how we've communicated with you, with Neb, and even Petronus for a time."

Winters couldn't take her eyes off the rowing figure. It was frail, small and familiar. "And you think it could reach the moon?"

Hebda nodded. "We do."

The boat was in the shallows now, and soldiers reached out carefully with gaffs to bring it in. The old man cast back the hood of his robe and fixed his eyes upon her, and Winters knew him but didn't all in the same moment. There was no context for seeing the dead unexpectedly alive, and she took a step back, uncertain.

"Oh my child, Winteria," the Arch-scholar Tertius said as tears coursed his cheeks into his beard. "Shadrus's dream has nearly run its course."

She wasn't certain if it was the tone in his voice or the joy in his eyes or if it was just the welcome reminder of home, but whatever it was laid hold of her. Laughing and crying, Winteria bat Mardic fell into her Androfrancine tutor's waiting arms.

Petronus

The scarred world cast twilight over the sea, and Petronus stood in the bow, watching it fill the sky as the warm wind pulled at his hair and beard.

He'd watched it for hours each night since he'd first seen it, and he'd even sketched maps into his journal. Because what he'd seen there had flabbergasted him. Not just one pocket of verdant life nestled between mountain ranges and oceans, the familiar landscape of the Named Lands. No, there was another pocket far to the south. And two more—one in the east, and another in the far north beyond the Dragon's Spine.

"They are called crèches." Petronus jumped at the spider's soft voice beside him. *Apologies for startling you.*

He looked at the spider. Aver-Tal-Ka had been scarce the last three days, disappearing just after they set sail for the tower. The one time Petronus had sought him out, he'd found that the cargo hold the spider frequented had become a jungle of thick silk webbing with Aver-Tal-Ka sleeping in the midst of it. So he'd busied himself as best he could and settled in to wait for their promised conversation. "You're awake."

"Yes. I needed . . . significant restoration and reflection."

Petronus looked back to the sky. "Why are they called crèches?"

"It is a word from an ancient Firsthome tongue. It means 'cradle.' My kind built them as a safeguard for the People."

Petronus turned to face the spider, the first of many questions framing itself. "And what about the dream that Shadrus drank?"

"It was his last work in the temple before sealing it for his master and accompanying Raj Y'Zir Downunder."

The spider's forthrightness caught him off guard. Until now, Aver-Tal-Ka had shared very little—even with Neb—beyond what needed to be shared. "I take it," Petronus said, "that you are ready to talk to me?"

I am. He paused. "But not here. Not . . . this way."

When the large white arachnid moved away toward the hatch leading belowdeck, Petronus followed. He waited for Aver-Tal-Ka to descend, glancing once more at the world that already started its slow drop over the edge of their horizon.

Pausing there, he felt the heaviness in his limbs and the fog between his ears—too long running on fumes, his mind tangled in the Whymer Maze of their present circumstances and his body robbed of sleep from nights spent tossing.

He forced his hands to the rails and lowered himself down. Then, he followed Aver-Tal-Ka into the cargo hold at the end of the narrow passage.

When they entered, the spider pointed to the forest of silk strands with three of his hands. *Climb into my web.*

Petronus hesitated. "I do not—"

Aver-Tal-Ka scuttled past him and climbed into the web. "It is easier explained by showing you."

Petronus took hold of the thick, white ropes, amazed at their softness and strength. He grunted as he climbed up into the web and felt the slightest panic when other hands took hold of him to place him securely within its center. Then, he felt the warm release of more silk against the bare skin of his hands and feet as Aver-Tal-Ka fastened him into place. But before he could open his mouth to protest, words formed in his mind. *Peace. What I do is for your safety.*

Petronus felt a stab of something—he wanted to say it was a memory. But the most tangible thought he could attach to it was the vague sense of being told something similar by this spider. He couldn't place when or why, but he felt the truth of it; and with it, the rise of doubts about the creature's true intentions.

Calm. Petronus felt the spider moving behind him, felt its arms encircling him and pulling him closer. Held tightly in place, he felt a wetness on his neck that lasted all of a second before it passed. Then, he felt something pushing against the skin on the side of his neck.

He wasn't certain which he experienced first—the explosion of spinning color or the burning fire in the veins beneath his skin and the heart and brain they fed.

He opened his mouth, but the pain was gone before the scream was formed. Instead, it collapsed into a gasp, and Petronus felt his body go limp even as the colors all slipped away into darkness.

When everything spun back into focus, Petronus sat at a long table in a room that was instantly familiar. It was the ancient history and mythology wing of the Great Library—a corner where he'd frequently hidden during his years in the Order. It was quiet and out-of-the-way enough that few would notice even a Pope sitting quietly with a book open on the table before him.

The library was empty, and despite the lamps, it felt gloomy. From where he sat, he couldn't see a window, but it had the feel of a midwinter evening.

Petronus inhaled the deep scent of paper and held that breath. He'd not visited the library in over thirty years—unless he counted wandering its burned-out craters as a visit—and returning felt like home. He touched the book in front of him, his fingers nearly afraid of the old paper. It was a book on the Lunarism movement from the time of the Czars written by the Arch-scholar Tertius.

The slightest clearing of voice brought Petronus's head up from the book slowly. The man before him was tall, dressed in a silver robe that looked out of place here. But the man himself looked out of place as well, his skin too white and his eyes too black and penetrating. His hair hung in slender strands that more approximately matched the fine fur of his arachnid form.

"I thought," the man said, "that you might find this less . . . distracting."

Petronus nodded and looked from the man to the room around them. "The venue is comfortable, too."

Aver-Tal-Ka shrugged. "You provided that for me. This must be a place you care about."

"Yes. I used to come here often. To think."

"Then it is fitting." The man took in the endless rows of books that surrounded them and smiled. "So these paper walls contain your understanding of the light?"

Petronus chuckled. "Only a part of it. We've lost more of it than we've found, I fear." The scarred visage of his home planet wandered across his imagination. How many civilizations had risen and fallen there now? At least three, he suspected.

Even as he thought it, he was flooded with emotion from Aver-Tal-Ka. A sense of deeper, greater loss. A spark of hope. And now, the real fear that it might indeed be snuffed out. Petronus blinked into the storm, and it subsided.

Apologies. "The light is much older than you realize—and much more." The man shifted uncomfortably. "But your understanding of it should be sufficient." He pulled out a chair and sat across from Petronus. Then, he reached across the table and took Petronus's warm, dry hands into his own. The coolness of his skin and the deliberate touch left Petronus suddenly uncomfortable. There was something intense and ancient in the man's dark eyes as he gripped Petronus's hands and leaned in to speak in a whisper. "What would you do to save the light, Petronus?"

He thought of Grymlis in that moment, remembering the old captain's question of the young orphans. Dying for the light, he'd told them, was easy. Would they kill for it?

And Petronus knew his answer from experience. He had killed for the light. And he had died for the light. It was the same answer that had brought him here, following Neb. "I would do anything," he said.

Yes. The man leaned forward. "You *have* both killed and died for the light." And now, his voice dropped to nearly a whisper, though it was loud in the empty wing. "Would you again?"

Petronus met the dark eyes. "Which?"

The stare was penetrating. *Either.* "The People believe free will is the first gift given, and love is the second. If you love the light, would you choose to save it if it meant taking life again? Even giving up your own?"

He felt no hesitation. "I would."

Aver-Tal-Ka sat back and regarded him. "I have promised you information. I will offer you more. During my restoration, I felt a stirring in the aether while I searched for Lord Whym and Lady D'Anjite."

Petronus sensed the images more than saw them. They were shadowy, far away, but the feelings that the spider associated with those distant flickers were a mix of hope and sorrow. He waited for Aver-Tal-Ka to continue.

I believe the Final Dream is coming. An image formed of the broken world Petronus had just been studying. "Its dreamer channels in the aether with great strength."

Petronus's eyebrows arched. "This is good news, I would think."

Aver-Tal-Ka nodded slowly. "It is. But with a cost. I found no sign of Lord Whym or Lady D'Anjite—that tells me they are sealed within the temple now. They cannot reach the aether to receive the dream when it comes."

Petronus thought for a moment. "But when they leave the tower—the temple—they'll be able to, right?"

The spider shook his head. "I have not been forthright with you. If they are indeed in the temple, then they are sealed in and cannot leave it. Y'Zir set traps behind him when he left."

Their eyes met again, and Petronus found that the darkness in them chilled his skin. *But there is another way.*

"How?"

"I can make *you* able to receive the dream." And as he said it, Petronus felt that sorrow and hope again and understood the magnitude of the choice.

It will cost me my life.

Yes. "And mine as well," Aver-Tal-Ka said. "But the temple will be unsealed for the sowing. And Lord Whym and Lady D'Anjite will be released."

The light will be saved. Petronus sat with the information and wondered why it was so easy to commit to this. He had no reason to trust Aver-Tal-Ka—moreover, he suspected he had reason *not* to trust him. Something tickled at his sensibilities. Yet here, in this familiar place, he felt conviction rising from the spider to blend with his own resolve.

But more than that, Neb had trusted this creature. And the boy had trusted the song that brought them here. Petronus remembered the mechoservitor's words and knew his trust or mistrust in the spider was irrelevant because Aver-Tal-Ka was not the object of this particular faith. "The dream is the dream," he whispered.

Yes. And the spider now whispered as well. "You must tell me you choose it."

Petronus swallowed. "I do. I choose it."

"And I choose as well." Aver-Tal-Ka stood. Even as he did, the room began to tilt and shift, and Petronus found himself suddenly in two places at once. He was here, in the wing of the library watching Aver-Tal-Ka's back as he walked away. And he was in the cargo hold of the ship, held tight by the spider as it spun its webbing over him, twisting and turning him as the cocoon took shape.

Closing his eyes and hearing only the song, Petronus laid down his life for a second time. He laid it down with ease, and reaching out beyond his wildest imaginings, took hold of another.

Chapter 17

Charles

Charles stood at the edge of the quicksilver lake and watched its waves lap the shore. It did not move like water but something thicker, and the way it slid over the stone shore pulled at his curiosity.

He bent to study it closer, and a hand fell upon his shoulder.

"Careful," Orius said. "We've lost a lot of men here."

Charles straightened. "What does it do to them?"

"It . . ." The general paused, looking for the right words. "They disintegrate."

But the boat is safe. He looked from the surface to the boat, then out to the island beyond. "Fascinating."

Orius chuckled. "There's a lot to fascinate down here."

That made sense to Charles. Such a vast network of caves and rooms was bound to yield treasures far beyond his imagination. He'd spent most of his life studying the magicks and machines of a lost past, but most of those were from the ruins east in the Churning Wastes. The Beneath Places represented an even older time. He looked at the general, his eyes narrowing. "How long has the Order been down here?"

Orius met his eyes. "A long time," he said.

Charles looked away. "And yet as arch-engineer, I knew nothing of it."

Orius shrugged. "Not even the popes knew in most instances." He nodded to Hebda and Tertius, where they stood talking excitedly with

Winters. "You may have noticed that the Office operates largely without oversight." Orius didn't wait until Charles answered. He moved back to where the others stood, said a few quick words, and then looked to the old arch-engineer. "I need to get back," he said. "Walk with me, Charles."

They left the chamber, and immediately, scouts materialized behind and before them. Orius moved at a faster pace now, and Charles worked hard to keep up even as he strained to keep up with the general's words.

"I'd like regular reports on your work with the mechoservitor," Orius said. "I want to know anything it knows about Y'Zirite and Machtvolk military strength. I want to know about intelligence assets, supply chain, and any other schemes they may be up to." He glanced to Charles. "I want to know what they're looking for at Windwir. I meant what I said earlier. When it isn't dreaming, I want it talking."

Charles felt the anger again that had poked at him earlier during their walk out and found the word that raised those feelings: "it." To Orius, the mechoservitor was a thing—certainly not a person. And not too long ago, Charles had felt the same way. But now, it was more than a machine.

He is my son. Even as he thought it, he suspected it was true. "It is possible," he said, "that this is somehow Isaak we're dealing with. Not the Watcher."

Orius stopped abruptly, and Charles did the same. The general regarded him with his single eye for a moment. "Mechoservitor Number Three," he said. "The one they used to bring down the city."

"Yes," Charles said. "Also designated Isaak."

Orius paused, and Charles could tell that he was choosing his words with care. "If that is the case," he said, "then it goes without saying that I want that spell."

He felt his stomach lurch with the general's words. Charles had suspected as much, though he'd hoped otherwise. "The Seven Cacophonic Deaths is perhaps the most dangerous—"

Orius raised a hand, cutting Charles off. "Yes," he said. "It is." They locked eyes again, and the general lowered his voice. "And if that mechoservitor has it, I want it. Whatever comes of Hebda's dreaming doesn't change the reality that we are at war, Charles. The Y'Zirites represent a way of life that is antithetical to everything that P'Andro Whym stood for, everything the Order's stood for, for thousands of years. You either serve the light or you don't." The scouts around them shifted uncomfortably on their feet while Orius's single eye burned into Charles's. "Do you serve the light, Charles?"

Flustered, Charles broke eye contact. "Of course I do."

Orius studied him for a moment before nodding. Then, he set off again, and Charles struggled to keep up. "Good. Because the light you serve is at risk of being snuffed out by an enemy who loves darkness and bloodshed. And by the bones of Windwir, I'll not turn away any advantage that can keep it burning."

They made the rest of the trip without words, and when they reached a guarded metal hatch, Orius stopped. "We're keeping it here—under guard at all times," he said. "When you're finished today, find Hebda. He has set up a table for you in his command tent. I'm returning to headquarters within the next hour."

Charles nodded, his mind still turning over the general's words and the fears that hid beneath them. He hoped that the war he felt inside wasn't showing on his face.

Orius clapped him on the shoulder. "These are hard times, Charles, and the Order needs its best and brightest if we're to dig our way out of the hole we're buried in." Then the old general winked. "And we have a few tricks tucked away still that we'll be talking about as soon as we've gotten this dream business sorted out."

Charles inclined his head, uncomfortable with the heavy hand on his shoulder. Still, he forced his eyes back to Orius's. "I'll do what I can for the light," he said.

Orius gave him one last, hard look and then moved on with his scouts. Charles watched his back, watched his deliberate stride as he moved away, and forced himself to breathe. Then, he glanced to the guards at either side of the door and pushed it open.

The mechoservitor sat on a stool in the corner of the room, and the girl, Marta, sat on another that had been pushed closer. They sat quietly, the metal man's huge hand covering the girl's, and they both looked up as Charles entered.

Charles saw the look of worry on the girl's face and watched as the mechoservitor's red jeweled eyes flashed open and closed. "I have some questions for you," he said.

Marta spoke up. "He doesn't remember anything," she said.

Charles nodded. "I know he doesn't. But sometimes talking can help us remember." He tried to smile but knew it had to look more like a grimace. "Would you excuse us?"

She studied Charles. "You're not going to hurt him, are you?"

He shook his head, surprised by the vehemence and confidence in her voice. "No," he said. "Of course not. I'm his . . ." *Father.* He swallowed the word before he said it, suddenly unsure of it as he took in the tall mechoservitor slouching upon its stool. It was bare of its robe now, and despite its size it seemed small within this context. "I'm his friend," Charles finally finished.

Marta stood, regarding him with a sober expression. "I'd like to come back when you're finished."

"I'll see what I can do."

She nodded and made for the door. As she left, Charles took her stool and moved it so that it was in front of the metal man. He waited until she was gone, and the door closed behind her before he sat. "Do you know who I am?"

The head came up, and the red eyes regarded him. "You are Brother Charles, arch-engineer of the School of Mechanical Science."

"Yes. Are you authorized to converse with me?"

The metal man shifted. "I do not know."

Charles smiled. "If you are not, you will know. Let's start with some simple questions, and we'll see what we can learn." He paused. "What is your designation?"

"I am called the Watcher by the Y'Zirite Imperial Blood Guard."

Charles nodded. "Is this your only designation?"

The metal man shook its head. "I'm uncertain if it is my designation, only or otherwise."

He knew he shouldn't ask, that it was leading the mechanical where he wanted him to go. But he couldn't help himself. "Is your designation also Isaak?"

The metal man said nothing.

Charles continued. "Or are you designated Mechoservitor Number Three?"

The metal man still remained silent, but now, its hands twitched slightly and it looked away.

Charles forced calm into his voice. "What is your first memory?"

"I awakened in a cave three days after my construction."

Charles leaned forward. "How long ago was this?"

"Two weeks, four days, six hours, and forty-three minutes ago," the mechoservitor said.

He sat back. "So you were constructed approximately three weeks ago?"

"Yes," the mechoservitor said.

"Where?"

The metal man's voice shifted to a series of high-pitched beeps and chirps that Charles recognized as coordinates, and he cursed himself for not having a pencil and paper brought to him. Still, they were some-place north—far enough north to be in the Machtvolk Territories.

"Do you remember who constructed you?"

The eyes dimmed, then brightened as the mechoservitor started to shake. "I do not remember."

"Do you remember anything about that day? Do you—" But Charles's words were cut off when the metal man suddenly seized and fell to the side, its arms and legs drumming out on the stone floor of the cave as its voice gave vent to murmurings and cries that Charles could not compre-hend. He reached out, but even as he stretched out his hands, he was overcome himself and also fell over. He heard another voice rising in the enclosed room and knew it was his own, equally incoherent, as it matched the metal man's. And somewhere behind him, he was dimly aware of the door opening and soldiers entering the room.

But even that spun away as something hot and liquid washed him, wrapped him, seared him. He felt everything that he was burn away from him, and in the midst of that cleansing, creative fire, he heard the voice full of command that spoke him into existence and saw a hand outstretched from somewhere above. It was a voice he knew, though he couldn't place it, and it summoned him into being by calling him by name.

And Charles knew the name that echoed through the silver fire of his birth as the cave around him came down and as his creator was trans-lated into light, swept away to seek the antiphon and the lunar dream that built it.

Isaak.

Rudolfo

A warm breeze stirred the curtains of Rudolfo's makeshift office and he sniffed at it, pulling the smell of salt and fresh-cut grass from the air. He rubbed his eyes and glanced to the half-empty wine carafe and the plat-ter of assorted fruits and cheeses. How long had it been since he'd taken lunch, picking his way through it as he worked? It had been hours.

"Are you hungry, Lord Chancellor?" Ire Li Tam sat by the door, and though her posture was relaxed, Rudolfo had no doubt that she could be on her feet, knives drawn and magicked, before he could push back his chair. A leather-bound book rested open in her lap.

"No," he said. "Though I suppose we should join Yazmeera and her officers."

Her eyes met his. "We do have a standing invitation."

He'd dined there most nights, using that time to ask questions about the men and women who served the Y'Zirite general. He asked about their families and about their faith, listening between their words for any useful scrap of information. He noted the cities they were from, filing that data away as well. And he praised their cooking—sincerely, most of the time because it merited such. Still, tonight he felt like dining alone. It had been three days now since the Lady Merrique had spit upon him in the streets, and he still carried the memory of it close to him.

Because she was not wrong. His family had betrayed them all, and his present course of action did nothing to convince otherwise.

He opened his mouth to suggest dining in when there was a loud crash downstairs. "Ire?"

She was on her feet and moving for the door, her knives whispering into her hands. And even as she left the room, he sensed a slight shift in the wind from his window. He felt the breeze against his cheek and heard the slightest buzz on the air. Then, the light vibration of something landing upon his desk. Ire's footfalls were lost to him now, and the buzz was replaced by a chirruping sound. He opened his mouth to call for her and was interrupted.

A man's voice, tinny and faraway, whispered into the room. "Rudolfo, son of Jakob, Lord of the Ninefold Forest Houses and General of the Wandering Army, the light requires service of you." Rudolfo squinted at the place on his desk where it originated and cupped his hands around it.

He felt the tiny metal claws fasten into the back of his hand as the tiny, magicked bird hopped onto it. "I am Renard, son of Remus. If you still serve the light say 'aye' to this bird and send it on its way before your keeper returns."

Renard. He knew that name. He'd met the Waste Guide's father when he was a young man, during his only trip around the horn and into the Churning Wastes. And he knew Renard had been hired by Aedric when the first captain and Neb had gone east in search of the fleeing metal man.

Rudolfo heard muffled cursing below. Then, feet upon the stairs. When the magicked bird chirruped again, he released his held breath, shaping it into a quickly whispered word. "Aye."

The invisible bird leaped from his hand and through the open window even as Ire strode into the room. She held a brick up, her face red with anger.

"You're becoming less popular," she said as she took her seat. "The guards are trying to chase down the culprit, but they should never have gotten this close to a window. I'll speak with the watch officer about increasing the villa's complement."

Rudolfo stroked his beard. "Let's wait on that for now," he said. "This may have been an isolated incident."

Her eyes narrowed, and he shifted into the sign language of House Y'Zir. *I've received a message.*

Ire's hands now moved as well. *From?*

Renard, he signed. And the look on her face told him that she knew exactly who he spoke of. He started to inquire, then stopped himself. That was information for another time. *He wanted to know if I still served the light,* he signed.

Ire nodded. "Regardless of the complement, we still must report this." And beneath the words she spoke, the rest: *If we do not, one of the guards will and that will raise suspicions better left unraised.*

"I concur," Rudolfo said. *Meanwhile,* he signed, *I will wait for further contact. We may have some friends left after all.*

She met his eyes and offered the slightest smile. Then, she placed the brick at her feet and took up the gospel she'd been reading.

They sat quietly together as he pushed himself through more and more reports. The engineers had taken over Merrique County's local gathering hub—an outdoor theater used for plays and choruses until recently—and were expanding it to meet the Council's meeting needs. So far, he'd only received confirmation from a half-dozen houses, but reports from Y'Zirite intelligence indicated that open hostility was transitioning gradually into pockets of resistance from armies in retreat or in hiding throughout the Delta and Turam. Fighting on the Emerald Coasts was still in full force, but half of its independent city-states had fallen. The remaining cities would not be far behind, and Rudolfo had to believe that they all knew what he did now—there was no way to win this war. At least not in the traditional manner. They had to see, as he did, that even trying meant thinning out the ranks of those who'd already survived so much in all of the wars and skirmishes that had transpired since Windwir's fall.

Finally, he pushed the pile of paper back and climbed to his feet. The light was fading now, and when the vespers bell rang, he realized just how many hours had slipped by. "I guess we will not be joining the general for dinner," Rudolfo said.

Ire stood, too, and stretched. "Shall I have the cook prepare something?"

Rudolfo glanced to the half-eaten platter. He should be hungry, he realized, but his appetite had been more and more fleeting these last few days. "I think just chai will suffice."

She nodded and stood. "I will let him know."

He inclined his head as she left, and once she was gone, he started wandering the bookshelves that went from floor to ceiling along the walls of the room. He'd tried to read on some of the evenings that sleep eluded him, but he found his eyes and mind already weary from a day of blurred words upon the page. He could find no focus. Still, he tried.

Rudolfo reached for a book and heard something behind him. He turned slowly, a movement catching his eye in the shadowed corner near the door. His hand went for knives he no longer wore, and his body moved into a crouch.

What was different? The door was partially closed now; Ire had left it open when she left. Rudolfo's eyes narrowed.

The whisper was barely audible, there in the corner. "I need to see your eyes," it said. "Look to me, Rudolfo."

Rudolfo stared. "Renard, I'll wager?"

"Aye." The voice was closer now. "Now tell me you serve the light in spite of your father's best work otherwise."

He felt the shame first, but his rage swallowed it. "I serve the light, though gods know how it matters at this point."

"It matters," Renard whispered. "Now listen closely. Countess Merrique marked you for our birds. She is a friend of the Order and will be our contact with you going forward. She will provide you whatever aid you require. You will provide her with information. She will send the moon swallow nightly to you."

Rudolfo opened his mouth to interrupt but closed it at the sound of footsteps on the stairs.

Renard's voice had moved closer, and now Rudolfo felt something pressed into his hand. He looked at it quickly, noting the plain iron key. "This house and Merrique's—along with several others here on the Isles—were designed with discretion in mind by certain carpenters of the Ninefold Forest. I'm told you'll know what to look for."

Rudolfo slipped the key into his pocket and nodded. He'd spent his childhood learning the multitude of secret passages and doors scattered throughout his father's manors. "I do."

"Do not use them unless the need is dire," Renard whispered. "Use the bird. And do not despair—the Order is not beaten yet. Lysias has hidden an army for you, and Orius has the Y'Zirites' metal man. Charles and Winters are with them, and Nebios Whym is on the moon to unseal the Moon Wizard's Tower."

Rudolfo blinked and found too many questions begging answers from all of this new information. "What of my family?"

There was no answer but the slightest click. Then, the door swung open and Ire pushed her way through the door. "He'll bring the chai up when . . ." Her words trailed off when their eyes met. Then, her hands moved. *You've been contacted; it is written on your face.*

Rudolfo looked away. There was a time when he could've masked it, but it had gotten harder and harder of late. And if what Renard said was true, then Rudolfo had much to ponder and to plan.

He offered nothing and she asked the same. They sat together and drank their chai in silence as the room grew dark around them.

When he was finished, Rudolfo stood without a word and retreated to a bed that he knew would not grant him sleep with these new corners and twists now woven into the Whymer Maze before him.

Jin Li Tam

The sound of children laughing carried through the garden, and Jin Li Tam closed her eyes against it, setting her son's voice apart from that of his new playmate.

Jakob had spent most of his life away from other children, on the move or tucked away from view in this or that manor. So the idea of him playing with others was alien to her already. Add to that exactly who he played with now and it moved beyond the alien and into something that kept her on edge.

Amara Y'Zir. The Crimson Empress.

They had made the introductions once the little empress was well. And since then, the two children had been largely inseparable.

"It bodes well that they get along," Sister Elsbet said.

Jin Li Tam blinked her thoughts away and looked to the woman. They both sat at a table set for a light lunch. A half-dozen young aco-lytes of the Daughters of Ahm ran and played with the children while over a dozen of the elite Blood Guard stood watch nearby. She tried to make a connection with the woman's words but couldn't. "I'm sorry?"

"The children," Elsbet said. "It is good that they get on so well."

Jin nodded. "It is. He's not had an opportunity to make friends."

The older woman offered a sympathetic smile. "Yes. They were born into difficult times. But amazing lives stretch out before them because of those times."

Elsbet's smile bothered her nearly as much as the woman's smug confidence. Still, she swallowed those feelings and forced a smile. "I hope so," she said.

"Hope is found with small steps of trust," Elsbet said, winking.

Jin Li Tam offered a slight nod. "Yes. Small steps."

But these days, her hope was flagging. Discovering that her target was a small child had shaken her. Her grandfather had sent her here to do something that she could never do now that she'd brought a child into this world. Jakob had changed the landscape of her morality, raising the price on life's value even among the few adults she'd killed or seen killed since becoming a mother. Even those who deserved it, like Gervais, the lord who'd hired men to murder her and her son.

"You look troubled."

Jin met the woman's eyes and blushed. She'd not intended Elsbet to see beyond her mask. "I'm sorry. I think I'm homesick."

The woman nodded. "That is understandable. You've been gone a long while. If it helps, I'm told that a cessation of hostilities is close at hand. Your husband is bringing the kin-clave together under new terms and conditions. Once we know it's safe, you'll have an opportunity to return."

She wasn't going to ask but couldn't help herself. "With Jakob?"

The woman laughed. "Of course with Jakob. And at some point, the empress will also visit. It is important that our people—yours and mine—see them together. Which brings up an important matter for us to talk about."

Jin arched an eyebrow. "Yes?"

"The regent and I have been discussing a public betrothal ceremony—one here in Ahm's Glory and then another in the Named Lands once we know it is safe to return."

Betrothal. Of course, all of the scriptures she'd read seemed obvious now. All of the talk of bridegrooms and brides and making straight paths. They'd not been figurative as she'd believed before seeing that the Crimson Empress was a little girl of Jakob's age. They truly intended her son to marry Amara Y'Zir and somehow, from that marriage, bring healing to the world. She hoped the surprise wasn't showing on her face. "A public ceremony?"

Elsbet smiled and nodded. "Yes. Something to inspire a bit of hope after so much sorrow."

Hope for whom? Jin returned the smile. "I can see the value of it. I would certainly want to confer with Lord Rudolfo about the matter."

"Certainly," she said. "I'll have the birder come around. I'm sure the chancellor's waited long enough to hear from your own voice that you and his son are well here."

Jin heard the intentions beneath the words and knew that the woman thought like a Tam, looking for every advantage that she could garner from offering or withholding communication from her husband. And a part of her wanted to resist becoming a part of it, but another part knew that she'd been a part of this strange game of Queen's War since her earliest days. Her very marriage to the Gypsy King was a part of that manipulation. So was the birth of their son. She forced more warmth into her smile. "I am sure he would appreciate that. As would Jakob and I."

The older woman opened her mouth to speak but closed it as a half-squad of Blood Guard approached, escorting the regent in their midst.

Eliz Xhum wore a black uniform now, decorated with a crimson cloak. His boots were a highly polished leather, and he wore a single scout knife offset with the cutting knife of their Y'Zirite faith upon his opposite hip. Over the last few days, Jin had caught glimpses of him and had even dined with him twice, but she'd grown accustomed to seeing little of the man. But when she did, she took inventory.

He did not smile as he approached, and when his eyes met Jin's they lingered only briefly before seeking out the chief mother. "Forgive me," he said. Then, he leaned over and whispered quickly in the woman's ear.

Her eyes narrowed. "You're certain?"

The regent nodded. "Yes."

Elsbet smiled. "Well, I think we should ask her. Why don't you join us?"

The regent nodded. "Very well."

Another chair was brought to the table and Xhum sat. A servant poured cold mint tea into a glass, and the regent took a sip before leaning forward. "I'm sorry, Great Mother, but I have a few questions I would like to ask of you."

Jin smiled. "I'm happy to answer them, Regent Xhum."

"I know that you and your father have been estranged in the last few years. I'm wondering when the last time was that you heard from him or saw him?"

The question caught her off guard, but it was the sort of question that would. So she let the surprise show upon her face. "I think perhaps we had birds from him in the Forest before I left with Jakob for the

Machtvolk Territories." And when *was* the last time she'd seen him? She stretched her memory back. It was before he'd sailed—after he and Baryk had buried her sister, Rae Li Tam, amid the other graves of Windwir. The cuts were still fresh upon his skin, as was the unspeakable loss in his eyes. "It was on the day that Ria healed Jakob," she said. "Why do you ask?"

The regent and the Chief Mother exchanged glances, and the woman spoke up once more. "At this point, we are far beyond the need for secrecy," she said.

"Yes," he agreed, then looked to Jin. "Your father, Vlad Li Tam, is here."

Jin Li Tam once more let her surprise show. "Here? In Y'Zir?"

"In Ahm's Glory, we suspect. And he carries a staff that makes him quite dangerous."

A staff? She knew nothing about this. But she also had no idea why he would be here. The last she'd heard from him, he was scouring the Blood Temple and searching for clues about what they all knew now as the Empire of Y'Zir. "Why would he come here?"

Xhum met her eyes this time and held them. "We were hoping you might have some idea. I have to assume it has something to do with you or Jakob." Now he leaned forward, and Jin read in his posture the gravity of his next question. And she was glad for it, because knowing gave her a moment to steel herself. "Do you know anything at all about a Tam presence here in Y'Zir?"

He knows of Ire. That was her first thought. That somehow, he'd learned about her half-sister, planted here decades ago to work her way into the Blood Guard and play her part in all of this. And Jin's second thought was that somehow the man knew about her grandfather's plot, the true work she'd been honed for—to assassinate the Crimson Empress and end the madness of this faith. But her face did not betray her, and her eyes met his without evidence of guile. "The only Tam presence I am aware of here, Lord Regent, is my own—and I left that family behind when I created my own."

He studied her for a moment longer, then nodded. "Very well. But you can certainly understand why I would want to hear it from your very lips?" At the inclination of her head, he continued. "And you'll understand why I think it most prudent to increase security here in the palace?"

She nodded again. "Certainly, Lord Regent."

He stood now. "And if you do hear from him, you'll let me or Sister Elsbet know?"

"Of course," she said.

Now, he inclined his head and then glanced to Elsbet. "I'm sorry again for the interuption. I know the two of you have much planning ahead."

Then, he moved off with his guards falling in around him.

Jin Li Tam watched him go, and after he'd gone, she settled back into the chair to listen to her son's laughter mixing with that of the girl these people intended him to marry. *My future daughter-by-law, if they have their way.*

Depending, of course, on what her father had planned. Because regardless of this staff they considered so dangerous, she knew something they could not. She knew that if her father wanted to see her, guards or no, staff or no, there was nothing on this earth that would stop Vlad Li Tam from being by the side of his children when he chose to be there.

And, she equally knew, there was nothing that would move him to their side when he did not choose it.

Father, what are you up to?

But she suspected that she knew. And she also knew that she wanted her son far from this place when the wrath of her grief-crazed father fell upon the blood cult of Ahm Y'Zir.

Chapter
18

Neb

Winters moaned into his ear as Neb's mouth found her neck. Her hands were moving over him now, and he was lost in the heat of it. He couldn't remember their last night of shared dreams—at least before the dreams turned dark. Back when they were the playful explorations of teens made possible by their inexplicable link.

His own hands traveled her, the smoothness of her skin surprising him. *I don't even notice the scars of her cutting.*

"Nebios," she whispered. Her hand slid lower, and she smiled at him in the dim light. "The call is upon us."

The call. He opened his mouth to answer and then froze. The eyes that met his were blue, not brown. "Amylé?"

When the change struck her, it was ferocious and instant. Her face contorted, and her voice rose into a shriek of rage and loss that Neb knew too well. Amylé's fist slammed into his nose with surprising strength even as her knee found his softer regions.

White light blurred his vision as the pain bent him into himself. He felt the hot rush of blood wash through his half-open mouth. And he felt the solid blows that she continued to land with her fists and feet and knees and elbows until she'd scrambled to her feet. Her breath was ragged, each pant a small scream of its own.

"You do not touch *me*," she said. Neb tried to move back and away, but he was not fast enough. He was still disoriented from the blow to his nose when her right foot shot out to connect with his left temple.

The white light was back, and then darkness fell for a time and there was no pain.

In the gray, Neb felt the pain flowing back into him and slowly forced his eyes open. He sat up slowly and touched his nose with careful fingers. It ached, as did his groin and the half-dozen bruises and scratches she'd left on him in her enraged assault.

What happened? They'd wandered the tower, stumbling through chambers the size of small towns, climbing ramps and stairs as they found them. They'd climbed until they were too tired to keep going, and they'd finally stopped to sleep. When they'd lain down, they'd been an appropriate distance apart.

And then he'd dreamed and awoke entangled in Amylé D'Anjite.

He climbed to his feet carefully and touched his nose again. Then, he limped in the direction that she had run in.

Neb had no idea how long he walked. But as he went, he noted the openings to smaller chambers and the labyrinthine flow of the tower's narrow corridors and wide avenues. A template emerged for the average, vast floor of the Firsthome Temple—a large central space surrounded by a series of smaller chambers and rooms connected by passages. He counted the stairs and ramps as he went and had ascended three floors when he heard the music.

It was distant, but he knew the song. The sound of it washed him with hope, though he did not know why exactly. Finding the source of the dream would not necessarily change his circumstances. He was still sealed within a tower without the tools necessary to unseal it, trapped with a dangerous woman he could not trust but also could not abandon.

Neb moved through the dimly lit rooms, steering in the direction of the music. As he drew nearer, the notes upon the harp became more rich and full, and he found himself moving faster.

When the song stopped abruptly, followed by the sound of something breaking against a hard surface, Neb broke into a run.

Ahead, the light began to change. It took on a whiter, brighter glow, and he found his eyes hurting from it. He moved through interconnected chambers until the rooms spilled into a wider passage lined with darkened hallways . . . but for one. At the far end of the passage and to the left, light spilled from a corridor. Neb approached it and slowly leaned his head around the corner. The hall ended upon an open door. And in that light, Neb could see the tracks clearly in the dust. It looked like

Amylé had come and gone from this place—and not too long ago, if she was responsible for stopping the song. He watched her tracks vanish farther down the passage, then looked to the open door again.

I have to see. Squinting against the light, he moved down the hallway only to stop halfway when he heard something beyond the door. It sounded like the faintest whisper, a quiet but steady murmur. He took a few tentative steps forward, and when he noticed no change in the noise, he walked to the door.

His eye caught movement, and he jumped at it. In the corner of the room, a silver mechoservitor sat upon a stone stool, its arms and fingers mimicking a harpist. Its red jeweled eyes were dark, and its body whispered with the movements of the arms, hands, and fingers. If it noticed him, it showed no sign of it.

Neb stared at it. It was nothing like Isaak and the other Androfrancine models. Charles had built them from Rufello's *Book of Specifications,* and that old Czarist engineer's approximation of the ancient mechoservitors of the Younger Gods. This, Neb knew, was one of those original metal men. He'd encountered another—the Watcher—though that one had lost its silver, its metal surface dark and pitted.

Neb forced his eyes away to take in the rest of the room. It was lit by several large, egg-shaped stones that burned white-hot. There was a tangle of string and black crystal shards that must have been the harp. He walked to it and saw that it had already been gone through. A section of the harp was missing, and he had no doubt that it was the sharpest shard that she'd taken. He started to do the same and paused.

He had no interest in hurting this girl. But she'd attacked him once, easily overpowering him before she had a weapon. Now that she was armed, he did not know that he would survive another encounter. The only thing in his favor was that she might experience another shift. Finally, he resisted the shards of crystal that had comprised the body of the harp and instead carefully unwound three of the strange silver strings. Then, he turned back to the metal man.

"What is your designation?"

It did not answer. Its dead eyes stared at nothing as its fingers plucked out the song Neb knew as "A Canticle for the Fallen Moon in D Minor." The song that had, buried within it, a dream that led somehow to his birth and to the ship that brought them here.

He looked down at the stone table that sat before the mechoservitor and noticed the bare patch surrounded by dust. It was the shape of a crescent. He looked back to the metal man.

"Can you hear me?" He snapped his fingers in front of its eyes. Nothing moved on the metal man but what was necessary to play its song.

Neb looked back to the table. It made sense that it would be another crescent here, carrying the music to the crescent the mechoservitors of Sanctorum Lux had found buried in the Churning Waste. He did not know how many years the mechoservitor had sat here, playing the song into the crescent. Thousands, he suspected. And she'd ended it. And by taking the crescent it meant that, in addition to being armed, she now also had a means of communicating with Petronus and the others.

And she's climbing for the top now. She'd trapped them here to keep the temple sealed. And now she'd ended the song that had been set up to play from this room. Neb wondered what she intended next.

Whatever it was, it couldn't be good. And his only hope of stopping her was to catch her unaware or to find the less dangerous version of her.

Wrapping the harp strings around his closed fist, Neb turned his back on the room and its single resident and once again took up his pursuit of the girl.

Petronus

Petronus wandered darkened wings of the library that he did not remember existing before, pulling down unfamiliar volumes by unfamiliar authors and hauling them back to his table. He took the solitary lamp with him as he ventured out, each time going farther, until finally he ran the risk of getting lost. When he reached that point, he started using the books themselves, laying them upon the floor to mark his progress and show him the path back to his table.

The windows were dark, and at one point, when he grew curious enough, he tried to open one. It was wedged closed, but Petronus thought it might be a blessing. Beyond its glass, he saw nothing whatsoever. No stars. No dimly lit cityscape of the ghost of a city, tucked away in his own mind beyond the walls of the library he waited in.

Is this what it means to be dead? He didn't think so. He'd been dead before, and it had been pain and light and disorientation followed by the nothingness of sleep . . . until he'd come choking and gasping back to life again. This felt real.

It is the aether, Aver-Tal-Ka whispered into his mind. *It is real and it isn't, the fabric of dreams but in a context that can be manipulated from within and without.*

Petronus turned instinctively back to the table, knowing somehow that the spider now waited for him there. He tucked the three volumes under his arm and shuffled in that direction, the lamp extended before him to cast light for his return.

He wasn't sure how long he'd been alone here, but it had been long enough to read a goodly stack of books. "Where have you been?" he asked.

He heard his voice carry down the hall, then heard Aver-Tal-Ka's reply. "We are approaching the temple canal," he said. "But we are not yet ready, so I needed to instruct the crew. Have you found answers to your questions?"

Some. But each answer opened a floodgate to an ocean of more. The Order had documented evidence of three cataclysms: One that he now knew of as the Downunder War, followed millennia later by the Wizard's War that toppled Frederico's empire. The survivors of that apocalypse had founded a new home under the reign of the Wizard Kings. And then, P'Andro Whym had led the overthrow of the Wizard Kings in a Night of Purging, bringing about the most recent cataclysm—the Seven Cacophonic Deaths of Xhum Y'Zir.

But now, he knew that P'Andro Whym was a reproduction—not quite offspring but more closely a replica—of the Younger God Whym. And he'd learned even more: He knew now that the Younger Gods were gods only by the limits of human imagination to come up with any other explanation in the face of such capability. But they were not gods at all.

They were the People and we are their children.

And they were merely the children of those who'd gone before them, the Elder Gods. Who, Petronus realized, were also the People. It stretched back over vast distances in space and time, and it contained cataclysm after cataclysm, a species rising up to fall again on the blade of its own propensity for self-destruction. But its tenacity to survive, again and again, finally brought about a mechanism to assure their future.

The Continuity Engine of the Elder Gods.

A way of living forever that, as a result of Y'Zir and his Downunder War, had been shut down.

"That is a close approximation," Aver-Tal-Ka said. His voice was closer, and Petronus recognized the books placed on the floor now. He rounded a shelf and saw the pale man seated at his table, waiting.

Petronus placed the lamp upon the table. "It is a lot to fathom," he said as he sat. "So many questions."

The man nodded. "It is a lot. It would take you several lifetimes to know it all."

The statement gave him pause. "But I don't have lifetimes, I suspect."

"No. Neither of us do."

Petronus leaned forward on the table. "How long *do* we have?"

The man's eyes narrowed, and Petronus knew he was calculating how much of an answer to give. "I won't leave this ship," Aver-Tal-Ka said. "You will have weeks. Maybe months."

"But I will be able to hear the dream and unseal the temple?"

He nodded. "Yes. But I can't tell you how it works. It lies beyond my knowledge."

Somehow, Petronus felt the subtext beneath the words, and it raised another question. "These books—they're based on what you *do* know."

Aver-Tal-Ka inclined his head slightly. "They are. I've populated this construct within the aether with modules of information for you. You are ingesting them through a process familiar to you—reading words upon a printed page—but that is merely a perception."

And a way for me to pass the time while we wait, he thought. "For whatever it is you are doing to me."

Yes, the spider answered. "And more details about it are in the volume beneath your left hand."

Petronus looked down and lifted his hand to see the title. "Restoration." The word sounded flat in the room.

"Again, a close approximation," Aver-Tal-Ka said. "You are a descendant of the People; everything that made them who they are exists within you, though aspects have been shunted and tamped, bred away and covered up for many millennia now. Your encounter with the blood of the earth activated some portions of that heritage, but the workers and makers in my own blood will be necessary. They will carry that restoration as far as it can go within you." Aver-Tal-Ka bowed his head. "Still, it is a temporary change. Ultimately, your body will revert, and you will not be able to sustain that reversion."

Petronus looked from the spider to the book. "Will it hurt?"

The spider also looked away. "I do not think so. Does it matter?"

He sighed. "No," he said. "No, it doesn't." He would do what he had to do for the light. More than that, he realized. He would do it for Neb.

For the briefest moment, he was carried away from the library to stand outside Sethbert's tent. It felt like yesterday and yet decades ago, that first day he'd seen Neb there studying the Entrolusian overlord's security and contemplating revenge. He'd taken the boy under his protection that day, then watched him grow and shine in the midst of the darkness of Windwir's grave-digging. That same boy had brought him to the moon and was in trouble again. And since Neb was the closest thing Petronus had to a son . . .

Yes, Aver-Tal-Ka whispered, and Petronus started. "You do what a father must do."

He nodded. "I don't just serve the light; I serve the boy, too."

Understanding. Agreement. He felt the words rising in his mind. "Good," Aver-Tal-Ka said. "It will not be long now. The disturbances in the aether are growing. And you are nearly ready." The man stood, and as he did, Petronus felt that duality again as the cocoon trembled beneath the spider's twitching legs.

"I am tired now," the spider said.

Petronus saw it in the slow-blinking black eyes. He glanced back to the book. "I'm fine here. Go rest."

Aver-Tal-Ka inclined his head and slipped into the shadows.

Petronus was deep into the book, his eyes wide with the wonder of it all, when a loud crash brought him to his feet, heart pounding. It sounded as if some nearby part of the library had collapsed, though Petronus knew that couldn't be true here in the aether. He took up his lamp and prowled the shelves, aware that something was different but uncertain of exactly what that difference was.

Aver-Tal-Ka's voice followed his thought. *The Sowing Song has stopped.*

Petronus strained for it but heard nothing. The song that had been a part of his background no longer played in the aether. Its absence was disorienting, and it caught him off guard. "What does that mean?"

They have reached the temple.

But it meant more than that, too, and Petronus sensed it beneath the spider's words. The song that lay waiting for them deep in the Churning Wastes, hidden away until metal ears could hear it and heed it, was gone now. Whatever had been set into motion so long ago was coming to a close, regardless of whether or not they achieved their desired outcome.

There will not be another dream beyond this.

Petronus sat back down to his table and rummaged through the books upon it. He pulled out the one entitled *Origins of the Firsthome Temple Sowing Song* and opened it to the first page.

Cradled in the spider's embrace and hidden within his cocoon while the workers and makers reshaped him, Petronus read long into his imaginary night.

Winters

Winters moved quickly through the passages, her shorter legs working hard to keep up with the aide who had been sent for her. She'd not slept much—few had with the dreams becoming more intense. But beyond the dreams, her afternoon with Tertius had played its own part in disrupting her sleep.

Tertius lives. By now, she shouldn't be surprised. He certainly wasn't the first to come back from the dead. She'd attended his funeral, burying him in the earth following the rituals of her people. But not only had the old Androfrancine not died in his sleep so many years before—he'd actually never been who she'd thought he was.

"Your father permitted my work in secret kin-clave with the Office for the Preservation of the Light," he had told her as they walked along the silver lake. "He died before that work was done, and when it was time for my departure, I arranged my own demise in much the same manner that Pope Petronus did."

All to study the Book of Dreaming Kings and the lunar prophecies it contained. *And to study me,* she realized. The notion staggered her. Access to the book was forbidden to outsiders, and there were two millennia of conflict and enmity between the Androfrancines and the Marshfolk to make such an allowance unlikely.

But the metal dream of their mechoservitors at Sanctorum Lux had intersected with the dreams of Shadrus's line in some way, and so they'd planted their foremost expert on her people's dreaming in their midst.

"Ultimately," Tertius had told her, "the preservation of the light required it. Even your father agreed."

Now, Winters moved through the Beneath Places following after a member of the Gray Guard, heeding a summons from Hebda and Charles. She rubbed the sleep out of her eyes as she approached a closed metal door and the two soldiers that guarded it.

They opened it for her, and she slipped into a small stone chamber lit with a lamp in the corner despite the soft white light from the lichen that covered the ceiling. Tertius, Hebda, and Charles all sat to one side in plain stools, and in the far corner, the mechoservitor lay stretched out upon a pile of blankets, its jeweled eyes dark.

The three men looked up as she entered, and she took in Charles first. The old man's eyes were dark-circled from lack of sleep, and his face held new lines of worry. Beside him, Hebda also looked sober, though better rested. Tertius, easily a decade older than Charles, was the only one who smiled. He pointed to the only empty stool.

"Sit with us, Lady Winteria," he said.

Winters glanced at the mechoservitor, and Hebda must have seen the question forming in her eyes. "Isaak is dreaming now," the arch-behaviorist said in a quiet voice.

Isaak. At the sound of the name, her eyes met Charles's, and she saw the truth of it in them. She couldn't help the smile that pulled at her lips. "Then he *does* live."

Charles nodded. "They both do, it seems."

Tertius's smile grew wider. "It is amazing," he said. "It seems that your Homeseeker is responsible for it." He chuckled and nudged Charles. "Tell her."

Charles looked at the metal man and then at Hebda before looking back to her. "I still don't fully understand it, but he reconstructed Isaak after the explosion."

Reconstructed. She studied the silver mechoservitor. It was nothing like the others, taller and more slender in its build. And from everything she knew, the mechoservitors she was more familiar with took months to build. Not even the Androfrancines' best could do better than that, nor could they attain the level of craftsmanship this new mechanical exhibited. "How is that possible?"

Hebda answered. "We suspect Neb accessed and manipulated the bargaining pool. It reconstructed Isaak using the Watcher as its template." He looked at the old arch-engineer across from him. "Which means, practically speaking, that both mechoservitors are functional. Isaak is now accessing the Book of Dreaming Kings from the Watcher's memory."

Winters blinked at this. "And he's dreaming it?"

Now Tertius nodded. "He is. Actually, he *has* been from the start. But he has more control now, along with more awareness. And with the dreamstone nearby, we're all experiencing those dreams to some extent."

Winters forced her eyes away from the metal man and back to Tertius. "So he will dream the Final Dream?"

The old man met her gaze. "You both will, Winteria," he said. "When the time comes, we will row you both out to the stone. It is still a dream made for the line of Shadrus to dream."

Her eyebrows rose. "And you believe it will reach Neb on the moon?"

"Yes," Hebda said. "Between the stone and the mechoservitor's obvious affinity for its use, we think there will be sufficient range."

Tertius leaned forward. "More range, probably, than we want," he said. "Isaak has already broken every dream tamp we've brought within three leagues of him, and when he is turned loose to dream into the stone, there's no telling how far the dream will reach." He paused, glancing to the other two before continuing. "It is possible that it will reach every capable dreamer both here and on the moon."

"We had thought," Hebda said, "that only the blood-affected—those exposed to blood magicks—could access the aether. But Isaak seems to be proving us wrong."

"Or proving," Tertius said, "that the aether accesses *us* rather than the reverse."

"Regardless," Hebda said, "it poses considerable risk for us. The Y'Zirite Blood Guard and their priestesses are accustomed to the aether and have learned how to track the dreamers within it. It is still a relatively new phenomenon for us. Orius is prepared to sacrifice the dreamstone if necessary—*after* we've made contact with Neb. Our engineers are already running the wires and setting the blast bags."

Winters remembered the wires at the entrance to the Beneath Places there beneath the barn in Kendrick's Town, and she wondered just how many bags of blast powder it would take to collapse the massive cavern and its solitary black island. "But he will wait until after we've reached Neb?"

Hebda nodded. "He says he will wait until the Y'Zirites are upon us."

For the first time, she heard a bitterness in Tertius's voice. "That old kin-wolf certainly won't wait so long as that," he said.

And as her old tutor spoke, Winters met Charles's eyes and saw agreement in them. And it made sense—if the Androfrancines couldn't keep the dreamstone for their own use, burying it was a better option than giving it over to the Y'Zirites. She saw the logic in it, but she also saw the look in Charles's eyes and heard the tone in Tertius's voice. The men she sat with were not convinced that Orius had their mission's success at the center of his scheming.

As if reading her mind, Charles spoke, and his voice was nearly a whisper. "Orius has ambitions beyond the dream," he said. "He wants the spell."

Winters felt the words like a blow to her stomach and flinched, her mind's eye suddenly filled with the ash and bones of Windwir, her nose choked with the smell of its funeral pyre. She tried to find words but could not.

Hebda was silent, his face grim and his eyes far away.

But Tertius broke the silence. "That is not an option," he said. "Deploying the spell here in the Named Lands would cost us more than it could ever gain."

Charles shrugged. "According to Petronus's research, they brought it back for that very purpose. To protect the Named Lands."

Hebda's eyes went hard for a moment, and Winters watched him choose his words. "You were a part of that work, Charles."

"I was not told that it was for military purposes," Charles said, his own eyes now flashing anger. Then, his shoulders slouched and his head dropped. "But you're right: I should have known."

"Those are matters for another day," Tertius said, a gentle kindness easing into his voice. "Orius has already concurred, albeit reluctantly, that the dream comes first." He turned to Winters. "Which brings us to your part in this."

She looked at the metal man again before looking back to her tutor. "What do you want me to do?"

Hebda drew a small phial from his trouser pocket. "We want you to join Isaak in the dreaming. We don't know exactly how the missing pages from the book will form the Final Dream, but we know it was not meant for him—it was meant for *you*. It was coded into your blood. At least on your father's side." She caught Tertius's sharp glare from the corner of her eye at the mention of her father and watched Hebda falter and recover. "This will put you to sleep and keep you there. We will monitor you in the aether, and at your word, we will wake you both and take you to the dreamstone."

She looked over at Isaak, stretched out upon the floor, and saw now that they'd made room for her beside him. Winters stretched out a hand to take the phial. She turned it over in her hands. A part of her felt eager to find her way back into the dreams—not the disjointed and violent nightmares she caught glimpses of, but the clear, powerful dreams she'd attributed to heaven's reach into her. Gradually, she was realizing that heaven may have had less to do with it than she'd been taught. But the dreams were real, and they waited for her.

And I've missed them.

She looked at the men. "I'll do this," she said, "but not with all of you staring at me."

Tertius nodded and stood first. "Of course."

The others stood as well.

She unstopped the phial and touched her lips to it, tentatively tasting the sweet, thick syrup it contained. Tipping her head back, she swallowed it down.

Tertius leaned over her and kissed her forehead. "Good dreaming, Winteria. I will see you shortly." Then, the old man hurried out of the room.

Hebda and Charles each inclined their heads to her as they also moved through the door, and when she was alone with the metal man, she went over to him and stretched out on the blankets beside him. Already sleep pulled at her eyes, and she felt the heaviness settling into her bones and brain.

Taking Isaak's warm metal hand into her own, Winteria bat Mardic squeezed it tightly, closed her eyes, and let herself tip forward into the river of his dreams.

Chapter
19

Vlad Li Tam

The streets of Ahm's Glory slowly emptied as the sunset painted the sky in purple and mauve, and Vlad Li Tam watched the crowds dwindling from the shadows of an alley near the Courtyard of Imminent Grace. He'd spent several days in the city now, mostly in the basement of a house near the banking district. Their arrival, buried beneath bolts of silk in the back of a merchant's wagon, had been entirely without incident despite the strong military presence.

And until today, Vlad had contented himself with maps and notes and bits of information gathered by his Knives, Som Li Tam and the others bringing him whatever he needed and answering whatever questions he had. All the while, he'd kept the staff nearby but was glad not to need it. Still, he felt the effects of it in the aching of his bones and the blood he passed in his urine and occasionally from his nose. The headaches had subsided, at least, but he felt one coming on now.

The staff tingled in his hand and he closed his eyes, savoring the feel of it. Then, he opened them and looked across the courtyard. It was a wide, paved area with a fountain in the center and palm trees lining it. At the eastern end stood the massive Temple of the Daughters of Ahm, its golden statue of the Wizard King perched above it with arms outstretched to save. North of that, the military headquarters sat somber and dark, plain against the backdrop of the other buildings around it. And to the west, the high-walled Imperial Palace waited, its golden gates closed now, though Vlad had it on good authority that they'd been kept open during daylight hours until recently.

Since my daughter's arrival, he thought. *Or maybe mine.*

Because Vlad had no doubt they knew by now that he was here. He doubted they knew why, though he supposed that their magisters might have found some way to counter the staff's power over Colonel Tarviz and Sister-Mother Drusilla. But it didn't matter. He was here and had no intention of being found until he chose it.

He squeezed the staff again and smiled even as he watched a platoon of soldiers march across the courtyard, thorn rifles held to their shoulders. Beside him, Som Li Tam shifted.

"I think we should return," his nephew said.

Vlad glanced at him before looking back to the soldiers. "Soon."

He'd seen the major points upon his map in the course of a day, the staff masking him as his nephew escorted him about the city. They'd taken lunch near the docks, watching fresh-faced soldiers loading onto transport ships no doubt aimed at the Named Lands. Then, they'd spent the afternoon making their way through the market district and into the outskirts of the city where the Magisters of the Knowledge of the Faithful had situated their quiet, white-marble halls. And now, they closed out the day here, where Vlad knew with certainty his work must begin.

Tonight.

His eyes went to the statue and he measured it, weighing it in his mind. It seemed as good a place to start as anywhere. The massive form of the benevolent Wizard King dominated the cityscape and would certainly catch everyone's attention.

Movement in the courtyard caught his eye—a figure that moved differently than the others—and he tracked it. *Show me,* he willed the staff, and he felt the change in his eyesight with a wave of vertigo and a twisting knife in his temple. It was a robed figure, moving quickly in a measured, careful step that spoke of more comfort in the forest than the city.

That one is out of place here. Vlad watched him make his way across the courtyard, changing course ever so slightly to avoid the handful of soldiers that moved to and fro. More than that, this one avoided everything. And all the while, his head moved from building to building as he reconnoitered. Vlad looked to his nephew. "Is that one of ours?"

Som Li Tam squinted at the distance. "No," he said.

Vlad watched the man look away just as a small group of young women dressed in acolyte's robes moved past him. "I want him followed."

"I will see to it."

He nodded and waited while Som signed to one of the younger Knives who waited nearby to escort them back to their makeshift headquarters. She moved out into the courtyard, a wrapped package in her hands. After a count of twenty, another followed.

"And now," Vlad said, "we go."

They slipped out of the alley and made their way onto the wide avenue that marked the edge of the courtyard. Vlad took the lead, letting Som fall in behind him as they turned east. He held the staff at his side as he went, willing it to bend the eyes of others over and around them. Vlad did not know exactly what they saw—an old man out for a walk with his son, perhaps—but it mattered little to him.

As long as they do not see me until I wish to be seen.

When they reached the edge of the temple, they paused in the shadows beneath the trees, and he craned his neck upward. The last of the light gave the gold a bloody tint, and he smiled at it.

Then, three times, he tapped the staff upon the pavement and shook it out over the avenue. A globe of silver the size of a small egg dripped from the staff's tip to puddle on the paving stone. Vlad looked around, then dropped to his hands and knees. He gently blew upon the puddle, and when his breath touched it, it balled up and started to slowly, erratically, move toward the temple.

He climbed slowly to his feet and watched the silver sphere roll to the wall, flatten against it, and begin its slow climb upward. As it climbed, he felt the power flowing out of him, replaced with a hollow weariness and a sharp pain behind his eyes that made him wince. "We're finished here," he said.

They took the meandering path around the courtyard, and when they reached the far end, he looked back to the statue. As the last of the light shone upon it, he willed distance to his eyesight again and watched the silver lines emerge on the statue's legs, torso, face, and arms. The lines took the shape of scars—the very scars of kin-healing that Vlad himself bore upon his body—and then those scars became wounds.

He turned away from the statue then and let his nephew lead them along the Whymer Maze of alleys and streets that would take him home to a bed he suddenly, desperately craved.

Behind him, the statue of Ahm Y'Zir began to bleed. But he did not need to see the hundred tiny rivers of red that trickled down the legs, over the base they stood upon, or the hundred crimson raindrops that fell upon the temple's roof beneath those outstretched, saving hands. He knew they were there.

And he also knew that soon, the others would know it, too, and so his first message would be delivered to Ahm Y'Zir.

"Now," Vlad Li Tam said in a quiet voice, "it is *my* turn to heal the world."

And with his Knives and his staff at hand, he knew beyond doubting that this particular kin-healing would not go unfinished.

Rudolfo

The morning air felt cool upon his skin as Rudolfo stretched by the door of his villa. The last of the stars pulsed in a sky that moved from dark to gray, and a light breeze ruffled the trees that lined the street.

He stretched, feeling too many days of saddle and desk in the way his joints popped and his muscles pulled. He'd noticed over the last several months—maybe even over the last two years—the bulge at his middle and the ease with which he became winded. He didn't have his own wardrobe to measure against, but he knew he'd gained weight before he left the forest, and try as he might, the duties of a deskbound leader and the stresses of his life had started him down a path that shamed him. Most of his life, he'd eaten as he wanted, but he'd also been active. He'd danced the knives and run the forests with his men, and he'd played at other dances in the darkened rooms of his Nine Forest Manors with the women he'd kept company. He was fit and lean and strong. But the weight of war and the stresses of his new life had taken their toll, and he knew he'd become soft.

When General Yazmeera had suggested the afternoon before that perhaps he might consider joining her for her morning run, he'd heard the subtext beneath her invitation and knew he could not refuse.

So he stretched now in the predawn light, dressed in doeskin moccasins, light cotton trousers, and a loose-fitting short-sleeved shirt. Ire Li Tam watched him, the amusement only slightly visible in her eyes as he cursed and tried to reach his toes.

"Good morning, Rudolfo." The general's voice was almost cheery, and it rang out in the quiet morning.

He looked up as she ran in place, her own aide a respectful distance behind. She was dressed similarly, though she still carried her knives. "I think," he said, "it may still be night."

She chuckled. "Only to those without something to wake up for."

He forced a smile, and when she set off at an easy run, he fell in beside her even as Ire Li Tam fell in behind him.

They ran quietly for a time, their feet slapping the cobblestones as they slipped past houses lit and unlit as the city of Merrique slowly woke around them. At one point, Rudolfo heard the cry of a small child and at another, the barking of a distant, frenzied dog. And at the edge of town, he smelled fresh baking sweet bread that made his stomach growl.

He broke sweat as they left the city and heard the work of his lungs as he gulped the morning air. Yazmeera noticed and slowed her pace, and he resented it but did not resist.

Once they were surrounded by the flat farmlands, she slowed even further. "The Letters of Sister Alouise tell us that our bodies are the knives of the gods," she said, her voice even and her breath steady. "That we must keep them sharp and ready that we might make our marks—*their* marks, even—upon the world."

"I've read that in one of the gospels." Rudolfo's own voice was more of a pant. "I see the wisdom of it." But it was half of an honest answer. More accurately, he saw the foolishness of not taking better care of himself at a time when he needed every resource possible to determine his best path.

She slowed even further and looked at him. "You've continued in your studies?"

"Of course," he said. He'd made a point of adding an hour or two of reading to his days. The general had provided him with five slender volumes, crisp and new. And those same five books were finding their way into more and more hands throughout the Named Lands. He'd seen crates of them in the quartermaster's warehouse while checking in on how the supply chain was preparing for the upcoming Council. "I've read some of them three times now."

Her smile was wide and genuine. "It pleases me to hear this, Rudolfo."

He met her eyes only briefly, looking back to the road they ran. Rudolfo brought his own smile forward. "I've been taught all my years that change is the path life takes," he said. "I will not pretend to say this change is easy or that I fully understand it." He paused, drawing in a deep breath. "But it is inevitable."

She stopped, and he stopped, too. Ahead of them, a wooden bridge spanned a flat, wide river that marked the border of Merrique County. "You truly are your father's son," she said.

Rudolfo felt the words like a knife twisted in his lung and hoped that the despair did not show on his face. He had no reply for her words, and it was all he could do not to flinch when her hand fell upon his shoulder, firm and warm.

"I have something to discuss with you," she said. "I think perhaps this is a good time for it." At his nod, she turned to the Blood Guard who escorted them. "Give us some space," she said. "We're going to rest for a bit. And talk."

He welcomed the break, his clothes wet from sweat and his legs sore from the few leagues they'd covered. He followed her as she left the road along a narrow path through the tall grass.

"I often pause here to meditate and pray," she told him as they approached the riverbank. When she sat in the grass, he did the same. "It centers me. And you have beautiful country here."

Rudolfo nodded and watched the river. The sun was barely up, the pink still in the sky. And already, the temperature climbed. "I prefer the forest," he said.

She smiled. "You'll be able to live wherever you wish once we've settled the peace. Your office does not require a central location. And you will have ministries to support you throughout the region—constabulary and internal intelligence—regardless of where you reside." Her smile faded. "But we *do* expect resistance, Rudolfo, regardless of next week's Council. There are those in the Named Lands who hate everything we stand for. So if you do choose to leave the Isle, you will be expected to accept a Blood Guard escort to assist your Gypsy Scouts in protecting our chancellor and his family."

Rudolfo glanced at her. "My scouts are formidable."

She inclined her head. "As are *mine,* Lord Chancellor."

He offered a weak smile and looked past her, to where the two women stood at a distance, their heads constantly turning to take in the surroundings even as their hands lingered near the knives they wore on their belts. He'd seen the Blood Guard fight. And the single prisoner he'd taken had resisted even their darkest tactics, giving them nothing useful before he executed her. "They are indeed formidable," he said, returning her nod.

Her eyes lingered upon his own, and he met her gaze until she looked away. "These have been difficult times for you and for your people."

Yes. Hearing her say it in such a calm, measured voice made the anger stir in his gut. "They have. Yes."

"So much change. And so much violence to acquire that change. Your people are tired of fighting. Their Androfrancine shepherds are gone. They are ready to learn the truth, I think, about the darkness they've lived in that's masqueraded so long as light." She paused. "They are ready for something new to believe in."

He felt that anger now moving out from his stomach. He felt it moving into his shoulders. He took a deep breath and forced his tone and words to cooperate even as his eyes shifted to the river. "That may be so," he said, "but belief cannot be forced."

She laughed. "No, it absolutely cannot. We'd never compel anyone to accept our faith. But we can help them find their way to it by showing them. Provide them with schools for their children to learn in and services—food, shelter, work—for those who have sustained loss during these years of conflict."

He thought of the evangelists that had come out of the Machtvolk Territories and about the school Jin and Jakob had visited there in the north. She'd written him about it in one of her messages. It was a brilliant strategy to teach these things to children—they were young and impressionable, their minds eager to be filled with knowledge. In one or two generations, it would be as normal to quote the Y'Zirite gospel as it would have been to quote the Precepts of P'Andro Whym just three years ago.

He said nothing and hoped that the horror he felt was not visible in his posture or his eyes.

"There is a way that you can help as well, Rudolfo."

He forced his eyes back to hers. "How?"

She took a deep breath. "I do not expect you to believe. Not yet. But your house is bound with House Y'Zir and always has been. Your son will soon be betrothed to the Crimson Empress, and when their union bears fruit—years from now—their child will heal the world. Your father knew that he was a part of something greater than himself, and in time, saw the truth of our faith and practices. But not at first. It was a process—a journey, if you will."

Betrothed? It fostered a hundred questions that he could not afford to ask in this moment, so he forced them aside. This moment was about faith, and he had to keep his focus.

Rudolfo carefully fashioned a half-lie. "I do not yet believe," he said. "But I am trying to."

She leaned forward and put a hand on his. "I know you are," Yazmeera said. "And I am certain that you will find it because you are *seeking* it. And I would like you to do something in trust of that coming day. Something that will help matters here in the Named Lands, I believe."

He stared at her hand where it clasped his own, and he felt the sincerity of her words and her care in this moment. His mouth was suddenly dry, but he asked the question anyway. "What would you have me do?"

She said nothing for a moment, and he looked to her, surprised to meet her stare but unable to look away. "At the conclusion of the Council of Kin-Clave, I would like you to take the mark of Y'Zir."

He could not mask the look that must've passed over his face. He could only hope that she misinterpreted it as something other than the hatred he felt. "You want me to take the mark despite my lack of belief?"

She nodded. "It would be good for your people. But I also think it would be good for *you*, Rudolfo, personally. Sometimes we need to meet faith half of the way in order to find it." She drew back her hand and then stood. "But please do not misunderstand me; it is entirely your choice."

He continued to sit. "And if I choose not to?"

She shrugged. "Then you choose not to. I only ask that you entertain the notion and consider its benefits in the transition we are in the midst of."

Rudolfo drew in a deep breath and held it. He felt the hate now moving underneath his skin, breeding with his rage. And in that breeding, he knew that violence would ultimately be their offspring. Standing above him, Yazmeera offered him a hand.

"I will certainly consider it," he said.

And smiling at that coming violence, Rudolfo, Lord of the Ninefold Forest, General of the Wandering Army and Chancellor of the Named Lands, took his enemy's hand and let her pull him to his feet.

Lysias

Lysias moved along the tunnels at a brisk pace, the thread looped around his wrist allowing him to run in the dark, close behind the Gray Guard scouts who led him. Behind, his own scouts followed. Occasionally, they passed through patches of dim light, twisting and turning as they made their way deeper down to the main Androfrancine camp. And from time to time, he caught a chill breeze to counter the warm air around them.

The Gray Guard had arrived a day earlier with Orius's request that Lysias join them. His own men were settling into their new camp beside an underground stream, and morale was holding. But weeks of living underground was starting to take its toll. They were an army of refugees and foresters, not seasoned veterans, and the lack of knowledge about what was happening aboveground combined with the lack of sunlight below wore on them. The infusion of rations and fresh game from the Androfrancines had helped, as had the fresh running water, but Lysias knew better than to believe that they could stay sharp for long hidden in the Beneath Places like sewer rats. So he'd packed a three-day kit and left with Orius's scouts, leaving his first captain in charge.

Now, a day and a half later, he saw signs of life in the tunnels. They'd run across a returning hunting party shortly after crawling from their bedrolls, and they'd passed two checkpoints.

He saw the lights of the camp before they turned the corner and spilled into it. The sudden sight of it made him blink and squint. It was a massive chamber, its vaulted ceiling lit not by lichen but by gems set into the stone. It was warm as sunlight on his skin, and he raised his hand to shield his eyes from it. "Gods," he whispered.

"Lysias," a familiar voice bellowed. "Good to see you."

He saw the general moving toward him quickly, his hand extended. Lysias met him and took the hand, squeezing it firmly. "Orius."

"How is the new camp?"

Already, they were on the move as the Gray Guard fell in around them. "It's perfect. But I'm pretty confident we won't be there long."

Orius chuckled, and it was a dark sound. "You're right about that, I fear."

They moved quickly through a bustling camp. As Lysias's eyes adjusted to the light, he saw row upon row of tents of varying sizes. As they passed the mess tables, he could smell frying bacon and onions mingled with the scent of baking bread and boiled chai. It made his stomach growl after too many days of dried rations. Orius couldn't have heard it but somehow knew nonetheless. He clapped a hand on Lysias's shoulder and shot him a sideways glance as they stopped. "I'll have some breakfast brought to us," he said. "Stand your scouts down now so they can eat. We've got bunks for them, too, when they finish."

Lysias looked over his shoulder and caught his lieutenant's eye. "You heard the general. Get some food and get some sleep."

One of Orius's men stayed back with the scouts while Lysias and his Androfrancine counterpart continued to make their way through camp. They moved quickly and silently across the wide cavern, stopping at a central tent where Orius left quiet instructions with a captain before motioning Lysias to follow him. Then, they made their way to the back wall of the chamber, slipping into a narrow passage barely wide enough for their shoulders to clear the walls as they followed it.

They arrived to a guarded metal door that one of the soldiers opened for them. The room within was small, lit by a single gem that sat on a table in the far corner. The walls were covered in maps of both above and below ground, and the room was furnished with the small table, two chairs and a cot. The blanket on the cot was folded with military precision, and a rucksack sat, closed, at the foot of the bed with a pair of freshly shined boots nearby. Orius gestured to one of the chairs as he took the other.

Lysias sat as the guards closed the door behind him, his eyes drawn to the maps. Orius followed his gaze and pointed. "The red," he said, "is the Y'Zirite advance. The black is the Machtvolk at the flank."

And the colors in between are the few in the Named Lands still standing. "How recent is your intelligence?"

Orius shrugged. "Two days, give or take."

He turned to the maps of the Beneath Places and saw similar red and black marks. "And they've been below as well."

The Androfrancine general nodded. "They have. Machtvolk initially, but we've also spotted Y'Zirites in the tunnels. They've found two access points in the north, and their diggers have broken through in the craters of Windwir. We're running out of time. At some point, they'll make their way lower—or access one of the hatches that we've wired. And once we start collapsing tunnels, they'll certainly know we're here." Orius leaned forward. "We're running out of time," he said again, "but we may not need much."

Lysias looked into Orius's single eye and tried to read the man. His posture was straight, his jaw firm. That spoke of a confidence he did not have at their last meeting. "There have been new developments?"

Orius nodded. "Rudolfo is with us. We've established contact, and we expect a significant flow of intelligence from his position." He sat back in the chair. "We've also acquired the mechoservitor—and the former Queen of the Marsh. The behaviorist assures me that this dream of theirs is the salvation of the light. And we've a Pope and a boy on the moon to prove it. I'm under papal unction to see them through this dream. But more than that, my service to the light is an unction of its own." When his fist came down, it jumped the table, and the noise of it made Lysias blink. "And that unction requires me to rid the Androfrancine Order—and the Named Lands—of its enemies. And I can do that. But I need your help."

He has a plan. The confidence was there again in the way his eye didn't blink. Lysias leaned forward. "How?"

Orius smiled and stood. "I'll show you." He moved to a map of the Named Lands and pointed to a mark in the far north.

Lysias recognized it. "The papal summer palace?"

Orius nodded. "Yes. Now . . . here." He pointed to a map of the Beneath Places. "This is the area below the ruins of the papal summer palace."

Lysias knew the palace, though he'd only seen it from afar. For centuries it had been the Androfrancine fort that kept watch over the Marshers and their madness, pretending to be a retreat for the Pope and his closest advisors. It had been destroyed by the Y'Zirites hidden within the Marshfolk not long after Windwir's fall. He nodded. "How far beneath?"

"Far," Orius said. "I want you and your army to escort three of my officers there and keep them alive at all costs."

Lysias blinked and stood himself, moving in to get a closer look at the map. "The entire army?"

Orius nodded. "Yes. I want you to establish outposts and a chain of couriers along the way, and I want you to hold that location until you hear otherwise."

"Why?"

The Androfrancine general shook his head. "I can't tell you that, Lysias. I need your trust."

Lysias's eyebrows went up. "You're asking me to risk an army without knowing the desired outcome. And not my army—Rudolfo's. Have you orders from him regarding this? I think I need *your* trust, General."

Orius considered him for moment and finally nodded. "Fair enough. Come with me. But not a word of what I show you."

"Understood," Lysias said.

They slipped out of the room, and two guards fell in behind as Orius led them farther up the narrow passage. It twisted and turned, then climbed a bit before leveling off into a flat, wide space. At the far side of it, Lysias saw light from beneath a closed door.

Scouts materialized from the gloom around them, and Orius whistled them off as he approached the door. He spun it open himself, and once more, bright light caused Lysias to squint.

They stepped into a chamber that had been converted into a workshop—counters covered in packets of powders and phials of fluid. Two young men in robes were hunched over those counters. They stood to attention when Orius entered, the surprise of Lysias's presence obvious on their faces.

"Is the next one ready?" Orius asked.

One of the men stammered and then spoke. "We were waiting another few hours, but I'm certain she is ready."

Orius nodded. "I want General Lysias to see what you showed me." He grabbed up a canteen and tossed it to the other man.

Lysias watched as the man poured water from a pitcher into the canteen. Then, he went to a Rufello lockbox in the corner of the room, spun the cipher, and drew out a small phial. He opened it carefully and touched the tip of a length of thread to the dark liquid in the glass before putting the phial back into the lockbox. Next, he dipped the thread into the canteen. And after, he carefully coiled the thread into a small box.

Then, he shook the canteen and passed it to Orius.

The general opened it and took a long drink. "Try it," he said, handing the canteen over.

Lysias hesitated. "What is it?"

Orius chuckled. "Water."

He took a tentative drink, then took a longer one. The water was cold and sweet. He passed the canteen back. "I don't understand."

"You will," Orius said as he hooked the canteen into his belt.

At a nod, the men led them from the room and down another passage. At the end of the hall, another room opened—this one occupied by three guards. There were several doors in the room and Orius stepped aside, taking Lysias by the arm while they opened one of the doors.

Behind it, chained to a bolt in the floor, was a woman. Her face and arms were laced with scars. She wore plain gray Androfrancine trousers and shirt, and her eyes were dead from whatever Orius's men had done to extract any useful knowledge she had. She looked up from where she sat on the floor.

Orius stepped forward slowly and crouched before her, unhooking the canteen from his belt. "The war is over," he told her. "We've surrendered, and your release is a term of that surrender. Do you understand?"

She looked at him, and Lysias read the hope as it settled over her. She nodded.

Orius uncapped the canteen and took a drink. "Unchain her," he told one of the guards.

As the guard bent with his key, Orius passed the canteen to her.

Then, he stood slowly and backed away.

Her hands shook as she raised the canteen and took a drink.

The results were instantaneous. She collapsed, wheezing, as her body began to seize. She threw herself over onto her side and then onto her back, her hands tearing at her skin as her eyes went wide. Lysias turned away as her tongue began to swell, suddenly sick to his stomach.

We drank the same water. The realization struck him, and when he looked to Orius the old general nodded. "Yes."

"I don't understand." Lysias looked at the girl. Her eyes had rolled back into her head and already she gasped her last. "Blood magick?"

"Not exactly," Orius said. "But you've just seen how it interacts with blood magicks." He nodded to the woman. "She was one of their Blood Guard."

Lysias looked at the woman and then at Orius. "You've found a way to kill the Y'Zirites."

"Some of them," Orius said. "We estimate most of their officers and priestesses and all of their scouts."

Her eyes were glazing over in death. Lysias couldn't look away. "How many have you tested it on?"

"Two scouts. One kin-raven."

He nodded. "And what's beneath the papal palace?"

"Access to the water tables of the Named Lands," he said.

And Lysias didn't know exactly what that meant—or how the Androfrancines knew this—but he did know that he'd seen enough to give Orius his trust. He would take Rudolfo's army north and keep them underground like rats for as long as it took if it might turn the tide in a war that had been one-sided for far too long.

Chapter 20

Jin Li Tam

Jin Li Tam awoke to a light tap at the door and forced herself from her sheet-tangled bed to answer. Jakob lay spread-eagle on his stomach in the middle of the plush mattress, though she couldn't remember just when she'd fetched him from his crib.

She unbolted the lock and cracked the door open, rubbing her eyes. "Yes?"

"Regent Xhum and Mother Elsbet wish to speak with you about a matter of some urgency," the young Blood Guard said. Behind her, Lynnae yawned and rubbed her own eyes, also pulled too soon from bed.

Jin pulled the door open. "Very well. I'll be with you shortly."

Lynnae slipped past the guard, and Jin closed the door behind her. "Damnation," the younger woman said. "It's barely light out."

Jin glanced to the window on her way to the dressing room. Beyond the gauzy curtains, a gray sky slowly moved toward pink. "I wonder what's afoot?"

Lynnae walked to the bed, a smile pulling at her mouth as she saw the little Gypsy Prince sprawled out. "He's well on his way to kingship," she said. "Look at the territory he's learned to conquer."

Jin chuckled and pulled on a pair of silk pants before shrugging out of her sleep shift. "He takes every bit he can." She'd lost count of the times his tiny feet had found her in the night, kicking her farther and farther to the edge of the bed.

Lynnae sat heavily in the armchair beside the bed and slouched down into it, closing her eyes. "I may sleep more."

Jin looked up from the shirts she considered, glancing from the woman to her sleeping son. "He'll sleep another hour or two, I suspect. Get whatever sleep you can." She picked a green short-sleeved top and slipped into it.

Lynnae yawned again and settled deeper into the chair. Jin put on a pair of sandals and opened the door. The Blood Guard awaited. Moreover, she saw that others had joined her. A half-squad of lithe, dark-clad women took up various positions in the hall beyond her quarters. She looked at the guard who'd awakened her and no doubt Lynnae as well. "What is happening?"

"Regent Xhum has increased your security detail, Great Mother," she said. "I'm confident he and Mother Elsbet will answer any questions you have."

Jin inclined her head and fell in behind the woman as she led the way. As they moved from the guest wing and into the central halls and wide open spaces of the main palace, she saw soldiers everywhere, both the men of the regular army and the elite women of the Blood Guard of the Crimson Empress. When she passed the large double doors leading to the wing that housed Empress Amara's living quarters, Jin saw that they were closed and heavily guarded as well.

And she did not know exactly what had had happened, but she knew it was significant, and she had a strong suspicion as to who exactly was responsible.

Father, what have you done?

Her escort led Jin quickly through the building, skirting the central throne room and through another guarded door, to the regent's conference room. Elsbet, Xhum, and a robed man she did not recognize waited for her there around a large round table.

They stood as she entered, and Regent Xhum approached first, his hand extended. "I'm sorry to wake you, Great Mother."

She took the hand and grasped it. Then, took Elsbet's.

The man she did not recognize approached last. His own hand was cool but dry. "Great Mother," he said. "It is an honor to meet you. I am Magister General Ahmir."

She inclined her head. She'd heard of the magisters but had yet to meet one. They kept to themselves in their white marble compound on the edge of the city. "The honor is mine, Magister General."

At a nod, the guards left the room. Jin started to sit but stopped when Xhum and the others did not. Instead, Xhum gestured to the wide balcony. Its curtains rustled in the morning breeze. Beyond it, the sky was moving from purple to pink now. "Something . . . *unexpected* . . . has happened," Xhum said as he looked beyond the balcony.

The others did not move. Instead, they watched her and she felt the discomfort of their stares. She joined him and followed his eyes out beyond the central courtyard and its fountain to the Daughter's temple beyond.

The courtyard was crowded now with at least a battalion of soldiers, officers and noncommissioned officers moving up and down the ranks, sending platoons out into the city. The temple itself was surrounded by a gathering crowd, a line of soldiers holding them back. She followed the craned necks of the men and women who stood around the temple and saw men moving carefully across the roof, scrambling around the base of the statue of Ahm Y'Zir. And as the first of the sun's light touched the gold of the statue, she saw what had brought the palace and city to such a state of heightened alarm.

The statue and the sides of the building were streaked in red as blood dripped from a hundred different gashes upon the gold. It puddled in the street below, thick and dark in the morning gloom.

Jin realized she held her breath and released it slowly.

She was still staring at the pooling blood when Eliz Xhum spoke. "We believe your father is responsible for this," he said.

Jin nodded. *Yes.*

She felt a hand upon her upper arm and looked over to see Elsbet's concerned face. "The magisters tell us that the statue bears the marks of a kin-healing. The same used upon your father . . . though his was not completed." The woman looked away, but before she did, Jin saw something in her eyes that she recognized. The incomplete kin-healing had significance of some kind. And the woman did not want Jin to know what it was. She noted it for another time. "These marks are complete."

The magister spoke up. "The marks themselves are irrelevant beyond their symbolism and the impact that will have upon the people. But the blood—flowing from a statue made of solid gold—is *very* relevant. He is mastering use of the staff."

The regent turned from the balcony and returned to the table. "Yes," he said as he gestured for everyone to sit. "That appears to be our situation." He paused as they took their seats. Then, he looked at Jin Li Tam, and she saw a hardness in his eyes that she had not seen there before. "What I want to know," he said slowly, "is *why*. What does your father want, Lady Tam?"

He did not call me Great Mother. She looked at him and let him see the surprise on her face. Still, she managed to slip a subtle message into her reply. "I have no idea what he wants, *Lord* Xhum."

Elsbet spoke now, and Jin instantly recognized the ploy and wondered if they'd agreed to their parts before waking her. The older woman's hand slid across the table to cover Jin's. "If you do know something, Great Mother, this is the time to tell it."

She met the woman's eyes and let her surprise become anger. "As I've said before, I do not know why he is here. I've not seen him since he sailed for your island Blood Temple."

"But surely," the magister said, "you've heard from him."

"No," she said. "I have not." But she *had* heard from a sister thought long dead, and she'd heard her grandfather's voice whispering to her in a message left decades ago for whichever daughter landed this particular role in his scheme to end the Y'Zirite madness.

Regent Eliz Xhum cleared his throat, and Jin looked at him, measuring the line of his jaw. "Mother Elsbet is correct. Now is the time to speak up if you are holding anything back."

Jin said nothing but did not break eye contact.

The regent slowly nodded. "Very well," he said. "But I want to assure you that you and your son are only as safe as our empress. Any threat to her is a threat to us all—and to you and the Child of Promise. We know that your father travels with the Vessel of Grace."

A subtle threat. Still, she kept her focus and felt her eyebrows furrow. "The Vessel of Grace?" It was familiar to her—referenced in passing in the gospel she'd nearly memorized now.

Elsbet's voice was low. "Through her, Lord Y'Zir gave us the Crimson Empress, and upon her he then laid the sins of the world to usher in a new age."

Jin tried to make sense of it but couldn't. Instead, she turned to Xhum. "Lord Regent," she said, "I fully realize that my safety and my son's safety are at risk here as well. I assure you that I am unaware of my father's motivations, but I am aware of just how dangerous—how utterly ruthless—he can be." She paused to give her words time to settle into him. And in that pause, Jin wished she were wrong about him. But the man had sent too many of his sons and daughters, nephews and nieces to die in his thousand schemes and manipulations. She glanced to the balcony and then back to the regent. "I did not know of his presence here until our last conversation about this matter."

Xhum took a deep breath, held it, and then released it. "I will accept your word on it. I apologize for my lack of trust."

She forced concern into her voice, willing it to lend a soothing quality. "As you've told me, Lord Regent, these are hard times."

He opened his mouth to answer but closed it when the door opened and a colonel hurried into the room.

The officer bent over the regent, whispering quickly into his ear. Jin saw the regent's face pale as his eyes went wide. He whispered a reply, then stood.

"There has been another development," the regent said looking to the magister and then the priestess of Ahm, "and we are needed elsewhere." Then he looked to Jin, and she saw fear in his eyes that he could not hide. "The soldiers and acolytes who first discovered the blood have fallen ill," he said. "Some kind of fever."

Jin felt the fear now herself, fed by the awe in the regent's voice. What was her father up to? And was her son safe here?

She had no illusions. She knew the Y'Zirites would not harm even a hair on her son's head as long as their faith continued to be in force and knew equally that the same was not true of her father. He used his children as weapons and tools to build and break the world into what House Li Tam felt it should be. He'd twisted Rudolfo's life, her own life, in ways inconceivable to leverage change. And he himself had been used by his own father as a tool, ultimately seeing most of his family die beneath Y'Zirite cutting knives.

In this moment, Jin Li Tam realized, her father seemed to have the upper hand. And she saw her kinship with him in that, as the others stood to file out of the room, her first thought was how to use this moment to her own advantage.

Jin Li Tam, forty-second daughter of Vlad Li Tam, stood and slipped out of the room as well. She followed her guard in silence, her eyes noting every soldier, every scout, every door, and every window.

Something hurtled her way now, and she did not know what it was. She could not quantify how she knew it, but the truth felt solid within her. Darkness gathered in this place with her father's advent here, and a reckoning was soon coming for Y'Zir. And she knew that she must take her son and flee before that happened.

Winters

Winters stood upon shattered land breathing the reek of sulfur and burnt meat, ozone and smoke. She was alone in vast, pockmarked territory and still reeling from the sudden change of venue.

She'd swum, weightless, in dark before this, with whispering all around her that she could not understand. It took her hours to realize that it was the glossolalia that she'd heard and uttered as a result of the dream's work within her family.

And nowhere in the midst of it had she seen Isaak.

She turned to take her surroundings in once again. The charred horizon stretched out all around her, lost eventually to a charcoal haze of distant smoke.

The world is burning.

"Isaak?"

There was no response.

She set out at a slow walk, mindful of the blackened bones that crunched beneath her feet. The sun, hot upon her skin, gave Winters the only compass she needed, and she walked west. To her left, she saw distant mountains, though they were burned as black as the ground she covered. Keeping those mountains to the south, she walked for hours. And despite the heat and exertion, she found that in the aether, she had no need of water or rest.

The sun was setting ahead of her when she saw something that interrupted the landscape. At first, it was an indistinguishable mass shimmering on the horizon. But as she drew closer she realized it was a tall, dark, and thorn-covered tree. The last of the setting sun shone off of something metal that waited beneath it, and she moved to a run. "Isaak?"

But as she drew nearer, she saw that it was not Isaak but another of the robed mechoservitors. "Lady Winteria," Micah said, "I've been waiting for you. Come with me." He rapped the tree twice with a shepherd's staff he carried, and a large gash opened in the side of it. The metal man slipped through first, and after looking around, Winters followed.

The tree closed behind them, and suddenly she found herself in a dim-lit subterranean workroom crowded with other mechoservitors who stood around them in a circle, their eye shutters opening and closing, their pulsing jeweled eyes giving light to the room as they held hands.

"We can speak safely here," Micah said. "Away from the listening ears and prying eyes of Isaak and Brother Tertius."

And any Blood Guard nearby, she thought. She looked at the metal man and his companions. "How do you come to be here?"

"We monitor the aether as well. The metal dream gave us access to it, and it bore us to Whym. But our range is more limited than our cousin's." The mechoservitor pointed to a schematic of Isaak that hung upon the wall. "He is a much earlier model, designed with the capacity to manipulate the dreamstone in ways we never would have imagined."

Hearing an automaton use the word "imagined" was an odd experience, but no more odd than suddenly being led into a room of metal men hidden within a tree in a desolate land. "And he is dreaming," she said.

Micah inclined his head. "Yes, he dreams, and the Final Dream is near. But we fear for his safety—and our own—once he finishes the dream. We do not trust General Orius. He serves more than the light."

It is truth, she thought. "He serves his desire for revenge."

"Yes," Micah agreed. "And his hatred of the Y'Zirite faith."

But she could understand that. They had reduced his city—his people—to craters and bones. They'd pitted the nations of the Named Lands against each other in two wars and a handful of other conflicts. And they'd turned her people against her, turning them from the Homeward Dream. "He wants the spell," she said.

"Yes," Micah said. "And he knows we are the only vessels that can bear it for him. But we will not be used in such a way. Our cousins from the Forest even now make preparations for us. We intend to flee with Isaak once the dream is dreamed."

She looked around the room and saw the maps upon its walls. "Where will you go?"

"We'll sail for the Moon Wizard's Ladder," he said. "And after, we sail the moon."

She felt the words settle upon her. *We sail the moon.* And even as she thought it, the others opened their eyes so that the light in the room grew. Micah raised his hands into the air, and his voice lowered, even as the bellows pumped air to feed it. "Winteria bat Mardic," he said, "the Homeseeking is upon you. The homeward dreaming is nearly fulfilled. It is time to gather your people and lead them to their new home. And by our own dream, we are pledged to see you there."

"We will need ships," she said. "And supplies."

Micah nodded. "We will have them. My cousins are . . . *resourceful.* At your word, they will gather your people in the Forest."

Winters pondered this. "Yes. Send your cousins to Seamus. Tell him to gather the people and their tithe."

"Yes," he said. His eyes opened and closed as he tilted his head. "And now we must return you. Your absence has been noted."

The tree opened, spilling heat and the smell of burnt stone into the room. She pushed herself through, climbing up and into the barren landscape. Winters fell climbing from the tree, striking the ground with her hands and knees. When she pulled herself to her feet, she realized the tree was gone.

"Winteria!"

She turned in the direction of the voice and saw the old man, Tertius, moving toward her at a fast pace. She brushed the ash from her knees. "I'm here," she said.

"Where were you?"

Did he see the tree? She had no way of knowing. She ventured into a lie that went with the surprise upon her face. "I . . . I've been here."

"You left the aether," he said. "I was tracking you, and then you vanished."

She shrugged. "I don't know. I was floating. And then I was here." The lie felt foreign in her mouth, especially with Tertius, but then again, he'd feigned death for how many years? And the truth of it was, she did not know how much she could trust him—or any of the other Androfrancines beyond Charles.

His brow furrowed. "I suppose it could be a fluctuation in your sleep."

Winters met his gaze. "I suppose it could." Then, she turned to take in the shattered landscape again. "Do we have any idea where Isaak is?"

Tertius pointed west. "Your instincts were correct."

They set out westward at an easy pace, and as they went, the sky took on the color of a yellowing bruise. At first, she enjoyed the quiet, but she found after a while that the silence bred more questions, setting her mind to spinning the lock dials to find the right cipher. Finally, she turned to Tertius. "So you have been with the Androfrancines this entire time?"

He cleared his voice with a soft swallow. "Yes. I returned through the Beneath Places a few days after my funeral."

"Did Hanric know?"

Tertius shook his head. "No. No one knew outside the Order."

She kept her eyes on the blackened ground ahead of her feet, uncomfortable with the anger she felt over his faked death. "And all this time you've been monitoring the dreams?"

"Yes," he said.

She stopped walking, and he continued on a few steps before stopping himself and turning to face her. "You realize," she said, "that I cried myself to sleep for days?"

He stared at her, and she thought she saw the dark hint of sorrow in his eyes and in the line of his jaw. "I did what was necessary for the light. But I never intended to harm you, Winteria."

She believed him, but she also believed he knew more than he told, and after years of deception and subterfuge, it felt suddenly freeing to take the more direct path. "I'm confident of that," she told him. "But I don't think you've told me everything."

She watched the surprise register on his face before it resolved again to the placid mask she was accustomed to. "I have not told you everything," he agreed.

Now, she started walking again and let him work to catch up. Her frustration fueled her feet. "And when do you suppose you will?"

He sighed. "Soon, Winteria. When the Final Dream is dreamed I will tell you everything I know."

Even as he said it, she felt the ground buck and shift beneath her. It dropped her to one knee and knocked the old man to the ground.

"The dream is changing," he said. And before he'd finished, the ground had bucked again and everything exploded into light.

When it passed, she lay in a field of tall, green grass studying a massive dead world that filled the sky above them. Stretching up against the backdrop of that planet, she saw a massive, bone-white tower thrust like a pointing finger. She turned her head and saw Tertius stretched out beside her, his eyes blinking at the sudden change of venue.

"This dream," she whispered, "is of my home."

And then something large and winged and silver blotted out the sun even as it shrieked something that might have been rage or surprise at their sudden presence in this place.

The name for it flashed across her mind even as she closed her eyes against its sudden dive.

The kin-dragons, Winters thought, *are flying.*

Though she did not know exactly what a kin-dragon was. Or what their flight meant within her homeward dreaming.

Marta

The warmth of the passage wall upon her back fed her drowsiness, and Marta opened her eyes against the sleep that threatened.

For the first few days, she'd wandered the camp in between the few visits with Isaak she'd been allowed. She was always careful to return to the door frequently to check on her metal friend. But once they'd stopped letting her see him, and after Lady Winteria entered the room and did not come out, Marta stopped wandering and stayed near the door.

Isaak. She'd heard the old man—Charles—use that name. It was hard to think of the tall mechoservitor as an Isaak. But she'd never been able to think of him as a Watcher, either. Instead, she thought of him as some-one lost.

Someone like her, though she'd not seen it until she'd met the metal man. And in a way, Marta thought she might be fortunate in that she'd not only found the metal man, but had been found by him *before* she'd realized her own lostness.

Marta sat in the shadows and watched the men who guarded the door. There were comings and goings every few hours, and each day the captain of the watch had come and warned her off. He'd done it twice the first day and once on the second. Each time, she'd slouched away only to return when he'd gone. No one had arrested her yet, and she suspected she could outrun most of them if they tried.

She could not leave this place. Not until Isaak was released. She knew it in a deep-down way that was unlike most knowing. Because Marta knew something beyond being lost, beyond being found. And beyond finding Isaak.

I know my part, she realized. And as her father had said, everyone must do their part.

The door opened, and she willed the light spilling from it not to find her. Charles came through and initially turned in the direction of the camp, but as he did, his eyes searched the opposite direction.

Marta cringed when he paused. She tensed her muscles for flight and slowly shifted her weight against the wall as she readied herself to stand.

He nodded to her, and her face and ears burned when he spoke to her. "There's fresh ham at the officer's mess," he said. "You've not left those shadows since I went in six hours ago, I'll wager. You need to eat, girl."

"I'm not hungry," she said. Even as she told the lie, she felt her stom-ach growling at the promise of food. "And I'm not leaving without Isaak."

Charles chuckled. "He isn't going anywhere. You'll be fine for an hour or so, I'm sure." He nodded to the two guards. "They'll see to it he's safe."

She knew the old man was right. And her mouth watered at the thought of hot food. She stood and moved slowly toward him. As she passed the door, she noticed a slight smile on one of the guard's faces and forced her eyes away from it, the heat rising again in her ears.

Charles waited for her to reach his side; then he chuckled again and set off in the direction of the camp. He moved slowly, and she had to force herself to stay behind him, resisting the urge to move ahead and force him to keep up.

She wanted to wait until they reached the tent and had their trays of food before she asked. But she couldn't hold the question in her mouth. "How is he?"

"He's fine," Charles said. "He's sleeping."

"He's still having nightmares," she said. The little sleep she'd allowed herself had been peppered with them, and she knew he was the cause of it—she'd seen the paintings he'd made with blood and remembered the tears he'd shed over the violence of his dreams. Now, she shared those dreams, and some of them were so horrific that she couldn't remember the details after waking. But they'd left her soaking wet in cold sweat despite the warmth of the Beneath Places.

Charles nodded. "He is still having nightmares. Many of us are experiencing them, too." His voice lowered. "Including me."

The next question came easily. "Why are we sharing his dreams?"

Charles looked at her, his brows furrowed. "There are some things I can't talk about. That's one of them."

She scowled. "What else can't you tell me about?"

He laughed and walked faster. She could smell the mess tables now. The scent of ham and fried potatoes permeated the air and lured them toward a tent set deep in the command center of the camp. He gestured her ahead of him, and the guard at the tent nodded at Charles's raised eyebrows.

They took their metal trays through the line, and she marveled at the feast as it was laid out. Thick slices of ham served over a bed of fried potatoes and onions, canned pears in thick syrup, and a sugar-crusted slice of sweet bread, all to be chased with fresh, hot chai and sweet cream.

Charles guided them to a small table for two in the back, and she shoved her first forkful of meat into her mouth, chewing quickly before she asked her next question. "Did you name him Isaak, or did he choose the name himself?"

Charles paused to swallow before answering. "I did not name him; he had a numeric designation. Lord Rudolfo named him when he found him in Windwir."

Marta blinked. "*I* found him . . . in the woods near the river."

The old man chuckled. "You did. But so did Rudolfo. Two years ago." He sipped his chai.

"In Windwir, you said?" She felt the blood draining from her face. She didn't like to think about the city. It made her stomach hurt. Remembering it now as a snow-swept plain somehow made it better, but in her nightmares, she'd seen it smoldering and pockmarked with craters where deep basements had once been.

"Yes," he said. "Rudolfo's scouts . . ." She saw him studying her face and watched his own face change. He closed his mouth as he thought for a moment. "Also something I cannot talk about with you."

They ate quietly—not because her questions had settled, but because she was not sure which to ask next—and the hot food, perfectly cooked, demanded her attention. Besides, Marta suspected that most of her questions lay in the realm of "I cannot talk about that" for the old Androfrancine.

But finally, her tray was empty, and the silence, with nothing to occupy her, was too much. "So what happens after Isaak's dream is finished?"

She saw the cloud pass over his face and the subtle way that his eyes left hers and wandered to the door of the tent. "I do not know," he finally said. He pointed to his sweet bread with a loosely clenched fork. "Do you want this?"

Even as she nodded, he pushed the tray toward her, and she scooped the bread up with her hands. She nibbled it and watched the old man. "Will they let him go?"

He met her eyes. "Where would he go?"

She shrugged at his question. "Wherever he wants to."

He chuckled, but it was humorless. And there was something there in his dark eyes that told her this was more than something he could not talk about. "I don't think they could stop him."

"No," she said, "but I think *you* could. You're his father, after all."

He leaned forward. "Here you are, hidden underground with a bunch of soldiers and mechoservitors and tired old men. Could your father have stopped you from following Isaak here?"

Marta smiled. "No, he couldn't. But he wouldn't stop me now that I know my part." She saw the cloud pass into curiosity, and she continued. "He's very insistent that everyone know their part and do it. It's the most important thing to him, I think." She paused. "Maybe to me, too," she said.

Charles sipped his chai. "And what is your part?"

She raised her eyebrows. "Same as you. To look after Isaak."

"Why?"

It amazed her how slow some adults could be when it came to matters of obvious truth. "Same as you," she said, trying not to be condescending. "Because I love him and he needs looking after."

Charles sat back, and she saw another look pass over his face, though she did not comprehend what it meant. He watched her for a full minute until she became uncomfortable and looked away, fidgeting in her chair.

"I do love him," Charles said.

"Of course you do."

He looked at her. "You love him, too."

She nodded. "Of course I do."

He picked at his tray and finally placed his fork on the table beside it. He stared at it for a moment; then he leaned forward and his voice became a whisper. "When they take him from the room, be ready to flee this place," he said. "I will help you if I can."

She stared at him. "Why? What's going to happen?"

But the old Androfrancine was already standing. "You'll know when the dream is finished," he said. Then, he repeated himself. "Be ready."

Marta nodded. And after he'd left, because no one asked her to leave with him, she grabbed another tray and went back through the line again.

This time, she wolfed her food down and stuffed the extra bread into her pocket, folded into a cloth napkin. Then, Marta made her way back into the tunnels and took up her post again in the shadows near the door.

As she sat, she wondered what doing her part would ultimately mean for her. For her father, it meant raising two children—one now with her gone—without a wife or mother, keeping food on their table and a roof above their heads. For her mother, it had meant taking the produce she'd grown to Windwir like she had so many times before and then, one day, not coming back.

Still, Marta knew that the outcome did not matter. Because she'd learned the greatest secret, she suspected, of all. Knowing and doing one's part was the most important bit. The cost was much less important.

Chapter

21

Petronus

The spider no longer visited, and Petronus no longer read. His mind reeled from the weight of a history he'd never imagined—a species that crawled out of oceans and into the stars, carrying its cycle of self-destruction and survival for millions of years. He'd read about Firsthome and how it had been lost after the Cousin Wars and then found again at the end of its star's life.

He'd seen the end of that cycle here on Lasthome with the final war that had silenced the Continuity Engine of the Elder Gods—a war waged upon the last of the Younger Gods who hid on the moon and watched their offspring down below. Petronus experienced layer upon layer of his mythologies explained.

And it was the slightest drop in a vast ocean of knowledge that awaited within the Firsthome Temple.

He spent most of his time now pacing and thinking about that.

Petronus looked to the windows less, now, too. He'd given up on trying to somehow track the time. For a while, he measured it by the spider's visits. But he had no other measurement without those.

Petronus.

It was a quiet whisper. An old voice. He answered it. "Yes?"

Petronus turned in the direction he thought it came from, then paused. He felt the slightest tingling in his fingers and toes. And it was moving up his body, slowly. He felt his heart rate rise, and he heard it, along with the increased intake of air.

I'm waking up. He felt it and sensed light at his closed eyelids. He heard the distant sound of waves and the labored sound of someone else breathing nearby.

He felt his hands and feet now and moved his arms, surprised at how easily his fingers ripped into the cocoon. He could taste the dry, papery air in the cocoon now, and it choked him as he drew it in. As he pushed through, his feet found the cool surface of the ship and he stood, stretching, as he forced his eyes open.

The light hurt, and he squinted through it. Aver-Tal-Ka clung to the web, its body shriveled and gray, its eyes gray as well. "The tools of the parents are not toys for their children," the spider whispered slowly. Then, it dropped its words into Petronus's mind. *The blood of the earth will serve you now, but do not let it carry you—the veins are trapped. Go to the temple gate. Receive the Final Dream of Shadrus.*

Petronus felt off balance, oddly lighter, and he was amazed at how crisp and clear everything in his field of vision was despite the blinding light just moments ago. And he could smell frying fish and saltwater and sweat on the air, along with the sweet smell of the dying spider. He leaned close to it now. "I don't know how to unseal the temple," he said. "What do I do?"

The dream will tell you. But you are far from the tower, and you do not have much time. The dream is building.

"Can I do anything for you?"

The spider said nothing; it sagged in its web, and Petronus felt a stab of sorrow he had not expected. He stood for a moment, then turned and saw Neb's pouch where it hung on a peg by the door. The song was gone now, but he lifted the pouch by habit as he slipped through the door. He was in the hall, halfway up the stairs, when he realized he was naked.

And in the same moment, he also realized that the hair on his arms and knuckles was dark brown. He raised his hand to his head to touch the bald spot he'd carried for nearly twenty years now and found a thick tangle of hair that didn't have the unruly nature that came with gray.

And my scar no longer itches. He swallowed and touched his fingers to it as he had a thousand times since Ria had given it to him. Only now, his skin was unmarred, and a thick beard covered most of it.

The door to the upper deck swung open, and one of Merrique's men jumped back when the light fell on Petronus. He whistled third alarm and Petronus found himself blushing as two Gypsy Scouts approached the hatch with knives drawn.

"Gods," Petronus said. "Stand down. It's me."

He heard Rafe Merrique's voice rise up from behind the men. "Come up here."

Petronus sighed and shuffled forward. Then, he paused and placed a hand on the side of ship. He didn't fully know why, but something he thought he remembered from a dream—or maybe something he'd heard Neb say—compelled him. "Clothe me," he whispered.

The wall shuddered, and he felt it move into his fingertips and spread over his body, flowing out into loose-fitting silver robes. And with those robes, Petronus felt strength surging through him. He stepped forward and slowly climbed the ladder.

The men parted as he emerged, and Rafe Merrique regarded him. "Petronus?"

He chuckled. "Yes. Of course."

The old pirate whistled his awe. When he saw that Petronus didn't comprehend, he pointed to the burnished surface of one of the metal men. "Look at yourself."

Petronus leaned in and studied his reflection in the metal. It was a face he had not seen since his thirtieth year. Maybe earlier, even. He tried to force his eyes away, but the image confirmed what he felt within his body—muscles and bones that no longer ached and eyes that no longer squinted at distances.

I am young again. He touched the place where the scar should have been, his fingers gentle over the smooth skin.

Rafe Merrique lowered his voice. "What did it do to you?"

Petronus said nothing. Finally, he looked away from his reflection and took in the rest of his surroundings. The ship moved up a wide canal now, its wake the only disturbance on the flat surface of the water. They traveled in shade, though there were no trees within reach to provide it. The shade was cast by a large, massive column that stretched up into the sky straight off their bow.

His hand found the sleeve of his robe and he toyed with it, rubbing the smooth silver fabric between his thumb and his forefinger. As he did, he felt it undulate and tighten over his body. And with it, he felt greater strength even as his sense of smell and hearing increased. He released the sleeve and the robe loosened.

He looked from the tower to Rafe. "How far away are we?"

The pirate looked to the sun and then the tower. "Three days."

Petronus shook his head. "Not fast enough," he said. Then, he stretched his legs and touched the sleeve again. The robe pulled in, spreading like liquid over his body until he felt entirely encased by it. The air he breathed now tasted richer, and he felt light and strong.

Rafe and his men jumped back at the sudden change. "Gods," the old pirate said.

Petronus ignored him and fastened his eye on the metal men. "The dream requires service of you," he said. When their eyes came to life, their shutters opening and closing quickly, he turned to Rafe. "I need you to put us ashore. We don't have three days."

The old man stared at him, and Petronus wondered what he must see. Finally, he turned away and shouted orders to the sailor at the wheel.

Petronus heard something distant, and he strained out the wind and the birds to focus upon this new sound. It was familiar.

It grew more distinct. The howling of the hounds.

"You should hold back," Petronus said, flexing his feet and feeling strength flood his legs. "I'll send word when it's safe to approach."

Rafe opened his mouth to protest but then closed it as he heard the hounds.

Petronus and the metal men went ashore. He waved Rafe Merrique and the others off and then turned to the tower. "Now," he said, "we run."

They ran the bank of the canal, building speed quickly, and Petronus realized that he kept pace with the mechoservitors and their long, mechanical strides with no difficulty. After several leagues, he pushed himself harder and found he could put distance quickly between them, surging ahead.

He felt a sudden fear rising to ambush him when it struck him just how fast the jungle and canal were blurring past him as he ran. And even as the fear rose, an equally sudden calm flooded his body, and all he felt now was strength and power. He slowed and let the mechoservitors catch up to him, then settled into an even, easy run.

Behind them, the hounds kept howling though the distance had not closed, and Petronus suspected by the sound of them that they were on the opposite side of the wide canal. It gave them time, and Petronus increased his speed slightly to see if the mechoservitors could keep up. They could and he pushed them, his eyes on the tower.

He ran in the light of the sun and the twilight of Lasthome when the sun had set.

Petronus ran and did not stop running until he heard the girl crying in the crescent. And even then, he lurched back into a run even as he held the crescent to his ear.

"Tell Nebios I am coming for him," Petronus whispered to the daughter of D'Anjite.

Vlad Li Tam

Vlad Li Tam stood by the window, the curtain pulled slightly to the side so he could see the gloomy street outside. The room was a quiet, steady buzz around him now as his Knives finished the last of their packing. Som moved from person to person, whispering instructions into their ears and waiting for their nod of understanding. They would not come back to this place. Another house had been acquired on the far edge of the city, and all evidence of their stay in this place had already been seen to.

It is nearly time. The fever was killing now, and his Knives had begun their surgery—bits of gossip here and there, left in the taverns and the markets. Speculations of angry gods who punished pride. It wasn't much, but it wouldn't take much of a lever to move this boulder. Not with the staff to aid him.

He ached all of the time now, and he'd taken to smoking the kallaberries to ease the headaches and help him sleep each night. And he tried to limit his use of the staff, but that no longer helped. Still, it gave him the army he needed to do his work in the world.

Vlad heard something in the hall, and his eyes went from the window to the door. It opened, and two of his Knives slipped inside, a magicked bundle between them that kicked and twisted silently. He smiled and moved to the bundle, crouching beside it. "My apologies for such an impolite introduction, First Captain. If you can keep your wits about you I'll have you untied and ungagged."

He heard assent in the man's grunt and nodded to the Knives who had carried the man in. They stooped to unroll the magicked tarp and then free the person struggling within it. Aedric's dark eyes flashed their anger, and Vlad stepped back as the first captain stood.

Aedric was a young man—not even thirty, his dark, curly hair pulled back and tied with a cord. But youth couldn't hide the truth his eyes spoke so loudly. This was a dangerous man who had taken life and lived with it as a consequence of service to his king, Rudolfo.

And I am responsible for the death of his father. Vlad released held breath and took another step back, watching the recognition dawn in the man's eyes.

"Tam?" The first captain of Rudolfo's Gypsy Scouts took a step forward, eyes darkening. The Tams around him reached for hidden blades.

Vlad raised his voice. "Hold, Aedric. We share desired outcomes that transcend our unfortunate history."

Aedric's voice was venomous. "I knew you were behind this. *You* summoned her here, didn't you?"

Vlad shook his head. "I did not bring my daughter to Y'Zir. My father arranged it for purposes I've yet to learn." His jaw firmed. "But whatever those purposes, I have my own calling to fulfill and limited time in which to fulfill it."

Aedric's eyes narrowed. "I care nothing for your calling, Tam. I want Lord Jakob free of these bloodletting savages and home to his father's care."

"And what care would that be?" Vlad asked. "Surely you are aware of the great Y'Zirite victory in the Named Lands? An entire people enslaved in the darkness of the Deicide's deception now ushered into light, joined with their lost cousins through the Great Mother and her Child of Promise?" He paused to let his voice lower. "Surely you have heard that Lord Chancellor Rudolfo is calling together the last Council of Kin-Clave and calling for an oath of fealty to the Crimson Empress? It's common gossip on the streets here. As long as the Y'Zirites are in power, Jakob has no home to go back to."

"And you intend to take them out of power?"

Vlad nodded slowly. "I've already started."

Aedric's eyes widened. "You are the prophet of the Younger Gods they whisper about. You made the statue bleed and brought the fever."

Vlad nodded again. "Yes. And I intend more. Today." He went back to the window and glanced outside. The sun would be up soon, and it was nearly time to start. "I want you to join me," he said.

Aedric stared at him. "And do what?"

"Strike off the head," Vlad said, "and the serpent will die." He knew those words would get the Gypsy's attention. They were from the Third Hymn of the Wandering Army, something Vlad should not have known but did.

The first captain blinked. "The regent?"

Vlad shook his head. He looked at Chandra, and she met his eyes coolly now, her own anger banked against the people who had betrayed her. "Not just the regent," he said. "Y'Zir himself."

Aedric's mouth fell open, and it took a moment for him to find his words. "Y'Zir still lives?"

"He does," Vlad said. "For now. So what say you?"

Aedric's eyes held conflict in them now. "My sole desire is to see my lord's son homeward."

"This is the only path to any kind of home that makes sense," Vlad said. But he didn't need to say it, because he saw the first captain calculating his odds of success alone, having no idea that there was only one answer that let him leave on his own two feet. His Knives had their orders, depending on what Aedric said next.

The silence stretched long. Finally, Aedric hung his head. "What would you have me do?"

"Help me take Jakob from the palace," Vlad said. "Along with the Crimson Empress."

Their eyes met. "I will help you," Aedric said.

Vlad inclined his head to the man. "Thank you." At a nod, Som Li Tam returned the scout's knives to him. Vlad looked to the others as Aedric sheathed his blades. "It's time," he said.

Two by two they left, and Vlad waited until all but he, Aedric, and Som remained. He counted slowly to a hundred before nodding to his nephew and his latest ally.

They slipped out into the morning, moving quickly through the empty streets. Twice they passed patrolling Blood Guards who turned to them before Vlad squeezed the staff and felt the power leak out of him as they turned away.

When they reached the courtyard, Vlad saw that the Y'Zirite army had cordoned off the growing pools of blood around the temple. And there were more soldiers now than before, but he also saw the beginnings of terror in the few citizens who were out. They moved quickly, their mouths covered with scarves, moving away from anyone who crossed their paths. Their terror would move to panic, and panic would bring movement.

They will fight or they will flee. And either would serve his purpose.

He led his group to the middle of the courtyard and climbed onto a meditation bench near the fountain. He pressed the staff with his thumb and felt the change in this throat and lungs as he drew in his breath. "Hear me," he said, and his voice was the rumbling of many waters.

Vlad closed his eyes and waited. He breathed in slowly and out slowly, willing her ghost to rise and fill him. "It has been written that life is given by the shedding of blood. But I say to you that this is a lie. Death comes by the shedding of blood. It has also been written that wholeness is found beneath the cutting knife. And that also is a lie."

He opened his eyes now and saw the soldiers approaching. Beside him, Som and Aedric both tensed, hands moving to the hidden hilts of sharp and ready blades. "There is life without blood and wholeness without scars," he said. He paused. "But Y'Zir, that coward, thief, and liar, knows nothing of such things. Ask for the gospel about the extermination of the Younger Gods. Will he show you the gardens where his forefather bled them out and fed upon them in his appetite for their power?" Vlad gathered himself up. "A reckoning is at hand for the crimes of your house, Ahm Y'Zir, and I call you forth to answer for them."

The soldiers were close now, but they moved slowly and their weapons were not drawn. Curiosity brought them to him, but the staff kept them at a sufficient distance. He raised his voice again, turning to the temple. "Ahm Y'Zir, do you hear me? I call you forth. I require the spellbook of you, and I require your life."

The gathering crowd collectively released their breath. Vlad looked at them and lowered his voice. "Where is your god now?"

Then, he lifted the staff and brought it down upon the cobblestones once, twice, three times. And upon the third strike, a rumbling went out in the ground away from him, cracking the stones and moving quickly for the temple. It climbed the temple's wall, crumbling and cracking the rock as it did, and when it reached the bloody statue, the massive figure of gold began to rock and sway. Something cracked, and Vlad looked away as the statue tottered. The soldiers no longer saw him—their eyes were fixed upon the statue—and he took that moment to glance at Aedric and Som.

They both nodded and then followed Vlad as they slipped away quickly. They were halfway across the courtyard when the ground shook and a loud crash woke the drowsy city. And they were tucked safely back in the shadows, Vlad sagging in the arms of the two men, when the sirens of alarm broke out across Ahm's Glory.

Rudolfo

Rudolfo stood and stretched, grateful for the afternoon sun that streamed through his office window. His muscles ached from three mornings of running with Yazmeera, and his eyes ached from the reports and correspondence of the day. The facilities for the Council were complete, and the quartermaster was fully stocked and staffed for those attending. Rudolfo had spared no expense, and Yazmeera had concurred with his decision.

He went to the window and inhaled the fresh, warm air. With his more urgent tasks now out of the way, he had a few hours now to pursue the research he'd begun. Yazmeera had gladly provided him the books— a sizeable pile—and Ire had translated the references that the general personally marked for him in the books.

He'd learned that the mark was the first cutting—normally given upon reaching the age of reason. Of course, those who received it were still children, and their choice followed upon a lifetime of exposure to those beliefs. So he doubted that reason actually had much to do with it.

But reason has everything to do with my consideration of it. He knew that well even as he fought the rage it evoked. Because he did not need to share their beliefs to receive this mark, and he believed Yazmeera when she said that this was not required of him. He had no doubt of her sincerity. But there was an excitement in the subtext of her tone and in her eagerness to provide him with the information he requested about the mark's meaning and the ceremony in which it was taken.

Ire was the opposite. She translated the texts without any of the enthusiasm of her general. And when he asked questions, she answered them in a matter-of-fact tone that betrayed her lack of faith. It lent itself well to his objective examination of it and helped him keep his anger in check in ways that the general's smug conviction couldn't.

Somewhere within this Whymer Maze, Rudolfo hoped, was the right path.

He sighed. Behind him, he heard a single knock upon his half-open door. He turned. "Yes?"

Yazmeera leaned in. "You've a raven waiting below," she said.

He felt his eyebrows rise. "It came here and not to the birder?"

She smiled. "It's from Y'Zir."

Y'Zir. He felt his heart in his temples even as his feet carried him forward. "Thank you," he told her as he moved quickly past.

He made his way quickly down the wide hall, barely aware of the general falling in behind him as he went. He knew it was from her—and he warred with feelings on the matter. On the one hand, he longed for some word from her, some word that she and his son were safe and well. Some assurance that they were indeed somehow safer there, away from this war, than they would be here.

But at the same time, he felt that anger stirring. She'd made him a father, giving his line a continuance he'd stopped hoping for in his younger years, finally contented with the notion of taking on a ward in his later years whom he could raise up as his heir. She'd taken him down a path that had surprised him with its joy and its love.

And with its fear. He'd faced fear in more skirmishes and battles than he could count, he and his men pitted against blade and bow with the odds against them, but it had not prepared him in the least for this new fear. He'd first felt it when the library had been bombed, that eternity of terror while he waited for his wife and his son to be found within its wreckage. And then he'd felt it again when he learned that Jin Li Tam had taken his son, without his consultation or consent, into the heart of their enemy's territory—the imperial capital of Ahm's Glory.

These fears were like nothing he'd ever known. They rode his shoulders and kicked at his gut, filled his night with dreams of terror and violence that he could not remember in the morning. And for some reason, the very thought of word from them flooded him with a hope he dared not feel.

Rudolfo took the stairs two at a time and moved out into the sunshine of the open courtyard in the center of the villa. The bird stood upon its perch, fixing a glassy black eye upon Rudolfo as he approached.

"I am here," Rudolfo said.

The kin-raven's beak dropped open as it cocked its head. Even though he was prepared for it, Jin Li Tam's voice made him blink. "Rudolfo my *king* and my love," she said. "I must be brief. First *know* that Jakob and I are well. We have arrived safely in Ahm's Glory and have been greeted with great hospitality." She cleared her voice slightly, and Rudolfo noted it. "Second, I have been asked to *consult* with you regarding a betrothal ceremony for our son."

Betrothal. Rudolfo blinked. "Pause," he said.

The bird's beak snapped closed, and he turned to Yazmeera. Her face was calm. "Perhaps," she said, "you'd prefer to take the message privately?"

Betrothal. He wasn't sure which surprised him more—the idea itself that his son, not even two years old, might be betrothed—or the larger, vaster meaning. The scriptures he'd read about his son and about the Crimson Empress took on a sharper focus now, and there was a simplicity in it that confounded him.

Their union will heal the world. He swallowed. "No," he said. "That will not be necessary." He looked to the bird. "Continue."

Jin Li Tam's voice drifted out as the beak opened. "I am assured that

another ceremony will be conducted in the Named Lands upon our return, but by your grace I will permit them to move forward here for the
general populace of Y'Zir. There is great excitement here at our arrival."
She continued for a time, and as she did, he forced himself to note the
inflections in her voice, the measured pacing of syllables, looking for the
code. But there was nothing coded as of yet, and he wasn't confident
that they had any codes left unbroken by the Y'Zirites.

After a few minutes of news about her journey and reception, Rudolfo heard a toddler's voice in the background and felt his heart rising
at the sound of his son. His eyes stung from the tears that ambushed
him when she called Jakob over to the bird to babble at him. He blinked
as she concluded. "As always, you bear my grace above all others and have
all of my love. I will hope to return to you when the peace is more established."

He drew in a breath and held it. He willed the emotion to drain from
his face along with the sudden stiffness in his neck and shoulders, aware
of Yazmeera's eyes upon him. He glanced to the aide who stood nearby.
"I'd like the message transcribed," he said.

The young woman inclined her head. "Yes, Lord Chancellor."

Then, he turned for the stairs. He felt a hand upon his arm.
"Rudolfo?"

He turned to the general. "Yes?"

"Do you want to send a reply? I can arrange to have the bird brought
to your office."

He furrowed his brow, wondering what exactly he would say to his
wife. His eyes met Yazmeera's, and he quickly looked away. "Perhaps
later," he said. Then, he paused. *This is an opportunity,* he realized. "But
you could provide me with any reference material you have on Y'Zirite
betrothal ceremonies."

Yazmeera smiled. "I will have them to you by morning, Rudolfo."

He inclined his head. "Thank you, Yazmeera."

Then he turned away and took the stairs with deliberate strides, forcing his fists to open. As he walked, he savored the anger, because it was
better than the fear. Still, this latest event whispered at a fear that he'd
felt growing within him as he read Yazmeera's scriptures regarding the
mark of Y'Zir. By tomorrow, he'd be reading her references to the union
of his son and the Crimson Empress, and that event spoke of years, po-
tentially decades that stretched ahead of them. *Me with the mark and my
boy raised up in this madness.*

Nearly losing them at the library had taken him into terror unimagined, and losing them to Y'Zir had done the same. But a greater fear now grew within his heart, breeding with his anger. It grew and twisted itself with every new turn in the Whymer Maze. Until now, he'd thought his son relatively safe in Y'Zir, but that was not the case. Certainly, his body was safe. But his mind was at risk.

If we do not find some way to end this, my son will grow up believing this is true.

And so Rudolfo sat down again to his desk and started through his notes about the mark. He would internalize as much as he could, and over dinner, he would ask questions of Yazmeera and her men about the day they took their own marks. He would fuel the conversation with comments and comparisons wherever he could in order to keep them talking about themselves and their beliefs.

He would note their words and frame questions for the dinners to follow. And somewhere, Rudolfo knew, in the midst of it he would find the path and somehow undo his father's handiwork and spare his son a future he could not abide.

Chapter 22

Jin Li Tam

Jin Li Tam paced while Jakob fussed his way to sleep in the other room. She was vaguely aware of the lullaby Lynnae hummed in the same way she was aware of the scent of lemon blossoms and smoke on the warm night wind.

Portions of the city still burned beyond her balcony. Fires set, the regent assured her, to coincide with the distraction and destruction of her father's challenge and the toppled statue.

"They found tracts," he told her through a clenched jaw. "Burning in a warehouse by the docks. Not many. But enough. Supposedly we are victims of the Younger Gods' wrath." She remembered the hollowness in his eyes and remembered hoping that he could not see her pleasure at his words.

Father, I see your hand in this. Vlad Li Tam was speaking to the Y'Zirites in a language and context they understood, and it was working. People were fleeing the city as the plague ravaged them. Hundreds had been killed when the statue fell, dozens more in the fires. There was a calculated brutality to it that she respected, given what her father had endured, though she did not fathom how he'd come into the power to impose his vengeance so completely.

She saw his agenda clearly, and it tasked her to reach deeper for her own. She was a Tam, and the moment she saw her father's work, she saw in it her own opportunity to make use of the distraction he provided.

But to use it for what?

Security had increased, with more and more of the elite Blood Guard brought in from beyond the city to guard the palace. More and more of the black-robed magisters prowled the halls now, too, as they responded to the growing threat outside. She'd heard very little, but she knew that the plague had spread beyond the city, carried by caravan. And she knew that they were burning bodies on the outskirts of town.

Jin Li Tam stopped pacing and faced the city. The statue lay where it had fallen, cracked and broken across the courtyard. Beneath and around it, the rubble of the walls and buildings it had broken in its fall lay scattered about. They'd tended to the casualties, but beyond that, the army did not have the resources to remove the wreckage. Already thinned significantly by the plague, the army was now overtasked just supplementing security and fighting fires that threatened the docks and the magisters' compound.

She closed her eyes and felt the tired beneath her skin. She'd spent the last two days learning more of the nooks and crannies of the palace, including its armory and the low, squat laundry facility tucked into the back of the massive building. She found herself rehearsing the various routes she'd taken, noting how and where each room and hallway connected, what types of doors and locks she would encounter along the way.

"It is good that you are preparing." The voice made her jump, and she spun, suddenly disoriented and uncertain on her feet. The room was gone now, and instead, she stood in her father's open-air office at the top of his tower overlooking the sea.

Vlad Li Tam sat in the center of the room upon a simple pillow, his low work table empty but for the long silver staff that lay upon it. The old man inclined his head. "Hello, Daughter."

Jin felt her mouth go dry and she licked her lips, habit bringing her chin down in his direction. "Father."

"They are watching for me here," he said. "I will be brief. They will come asking what I've told you." She tried to read the emotion in his eyes and found nothing. "Tell them," he said.

She blinked. "Tell them what?"

He nodded. "The truth," he said. "What your grandfather knew. There is only one way to end this madness. I am coming for the children." He reached out and touched the staff. When he did, it twisted into a snake of silver light, shifting and coiling upon his table with a hiss that chilled her blood. Her father lowered his voice to almost a whisper, and Jin heard sorrow and finality in his voice. "Tell them I am coming for the children, and there is nothing they can do to stop me."

"What do you mean?" Her stomach had turned to ice with his words.

"You know what I mean, Daughter. And you will not be able to stop me any more than they will." He looked up, and beyond her, his eyes fixing upon something she could not see and narrowed slightly as they did. "I must go now."

She opened her mouth to reply and realized she no longer stood. Instead, she lay stretched out upon the floor. Lynnae crouched over her, her hands upon Jin's shoulders as she shook her. "Lady Tam?"

"Call the guards in," she said as she sat up. Vertigo took her as she climbed to her feet. She staggered toward the sudden quiet of Jakob's attached room, feeling the panic rise within her as she moved forward on wobbly legs.

She felt a sob tear from her as she approached his bed, then paused. He slept, his chest moving with each deep breath. Jin Li Tam steadied herself against the doorframe and slowed her own breathing. His words—and the tone of them—rolled over and around her, washing her in certainty. *I am coming for the children, and there is nothing they can do to stop me.*

The guards were in the room now, and Lynnae guided Jin to sit at the edge of the bed, pushing a glass of water into her hand. There was concern in the young woman's voice. "What happened?"

Jin sipped the water and breathed, feeling her heart rate slow with each lungful of air she pulled into herself and pushed out. "A nightmare," she said.

But I was awake when it happened. She'd experienced waking dreams since the last days of her pregnancy with Jakob. Only they had been rare and much less vivid.

"It was my father," she said. And she knew it was the truth, regardless of how she wished it were a nightmare. She took another drink of the water and turned at the commotion behind her.

Sister Elsbet moved quickly into the room, a full squad of Blood Guard moving about her to take up positions near the door and in the hallway around it. Her face was calm, but Jin saw alarm in the woman's eyes as she came to the bed and crouched by her. "We sensed him in the aether, Great Mother."

She nodded. "He told me you would."

A Blood Scout moved a chair for Sister Elsbet, and the woman smoothed her robes as she sat. "What did he want?"

Jin's eyes moved to Jakob, then took in the gathering crowd in the room. Elsbet noticed and snapped her fingers. "Leave us."

Lynnae squeezed Jin's shoulder and moved away, filing through the door with the others. She waited until the door was closed, then took another drink. "He wants the children."

Jin watched the woman grow pale, her lips pursed together and graying from the pressure. Finally, Elsbet released her breath. "Tell me," she said.

She recounted the conversation word for word, leaving nothing out, and when she finished the woman nodded. "And now tell me the rest." Their eyes met. "What your grandfather knew?"

Jin swallowed. "My grandfather knew your faith was madness and that the only way to end it was to kill the Crimson Empress and crush your beliefs in that cradle."

Elsbet nodded slowly. "And he sent you," she added, "to do this dark deed."

Jin stared at the woman. *Tell them the truth.* "Yes," she said.

Elsbet smiled. "Yes."

"How long have you known?"

She shrugged. "We suspected all along. You came easily with us at the regent's request. And we know your family all too well." Her eyes narrowed. "But I suppose I knew it when I finally introduced you to Empress Amara."

Jin let the surprise pass over her face. "Yet you did nothing?"

"There was nothing to do," she said. "I knew you could not harm the girl."

Could not. She swallowed. "How could you know that?"

Now Elsbet laughed, her eyes losing their fear for just a moment. "Because despite whatever else you may be, you are the Great Mother first and foremost, Lady Tam." Then, the fear returned, and she placed a hand upon Jin's shoulder. "The question is whether or not your father could harm the children."

And when Jin answered, she knew she answered not just for the Crimson Empress she'd been sent to assassinate but also for her own son. Her breath caught in her throat as she answered.

"Yes," the forty-second daughter of Vlad Li Tam said with complete certainty, feeling her own fear running cold beneath the skin. "He is *very* capable."

And he is coming.

Neb

Neb measured time by the healing of his wounds with no sense of how accurate the measurement was. He walked until he was too tired to continue, then slept where he fell, aware now keenly of the food and water he needed. Sometimes, he heard the girl moving ahead of him in the distance. But most times, he heard nothing at all but the sound of his own footfalls as he slowly climbed the tower.

He kept the harp strings wrapped tightly around his hand, their biting presence a reminder of how dangerous the girl was. He did not grasp the nature of her illness, but he knew that at least some part of her wanted him dead.

And she has the means to do it, he realized, thinking about the broken crystalline harp. There was no doubt in his mind that she would use the weapon she'd fashioned if he gave her the opportunity. The thought of it slowed his pace as he strained his ears for some sign of her ahead.

He overtook her while she was sleeping and nearly missed it. It was the faintest movement on the far side of the chamber he crept through that caught his attention. Neb paused, then moved slowly in her direction.

Amylé D'Anjite slept nestled into the corner, her sharpened length of crystal clenched tightly to her chest. He paused for a moment, stilled by the sight of her. He certainly felt the call upon him, but beneath it there was simply an extraordinary beauty to her sleeping form. He blinked and slowly unrolled a length of wire.

Neb launched himself at her, kicking the weapon away as he forced her onto her stomach. She fought, but not with the ferocity of their earlier encounter, and he quickly pinned her, bringing a cry of pain from her as he pushed his knee into her back. "Hold still," he said.

She bucked and kicked at him, but he tied her hands. Once he was sure of the knots, he pushed away from her.

Her voice held as much fear as it did anger. "What are you doing?"

He didn't answer. Instead, he climbed to his feet and wished the ache in his stomach would subside. He forced himself to look at her, letting the shame pass over him and through him. He studied her, not sure what to say. He stooped and picked up the shard of crystal. "You nearly killed me the last time I saw you," he said. "I can't let that happen."

Her eyes went wide and her nostrils flared. "I don't see how that's possible."

Neb snorted. "You don't have to see it."

She moved, testing the wire that held her wrists. "What will you do with me?"

Neb wasn't sure how to answer. He couldn't leave her, but he also wasn't convinced that bringing her along was his best choice. Even tied, he suspected fierce resistance if and when the other part of her surged back to life. And he knew that when that darker side to her emerged it would do so with the utmost brutality and no warning whatsoever. He stood over her, finally stumbling into the first words he found. "Do you want to go back to sleep?"

Now she snorted. "I don't think so."

"Then you want to keep going?"

She said nothing, and he took her silence as consent, bending to catch her arm and help her up. He felt the warmth of her body brushing against him, accompanied by another stab of the shame. Once she was on her feet, he stood her to the side, and his eye caught what her sleeping form had been covering. He reached for the crescent and raised it to his ear.

"You found this in the room with the mechoservitor and the harp," he said.

She shook her head. "I don't know where I found it; I woke up with it. But I've met Petronus. He told me to tell you that he is coming."

Neb looked away from her for a moment to the crescent in his hands. Unlike the other, this was slightly larger and had different impressions worn into its surface. He felt the outline of continents and mountain ranges beneath his fingers and tilted an end of the crescent toward his mouth. "Petronus?"

"I've not heard him for a while," the girl said. "They were being pursued."

Neb brought the crescent down from his ear to stare at it. Then, he looked to the girl. "But he's coming?"

She nodded, and he felt something like relief struggling to break loose in him. He'd lost track of the days, but even with the strength of his new body, he could not hold out forever. He woke up after each period of sleep still tired, still thirsty, still hungry. And he still had no sense of how to be free of the tower. He climbed because the girl climbed, and now that he'd found her, he wasn't certain of what to do next. He found himself wishing he could ask Petronus what to do, or even consult with the mechoservitors, though he knew the old man—along with the others in his troop—were looking to *him* for that direction.

And there was the spider.

Of all of them, Aver-Tal-Ka should be able to tell him what to do. The ancient creature had awakened to serve him, to point him to the temple and set him upon his way. Of course, the spider had also led him to the girl. . . .

He looked back to her and sighed. "I don't know what to do with you."

But his body seemed to, and it confounded him. It woke to her presence, the sight and smell of her, unbidden, and it shamed him. But even she felt it. He could see it in the wideness of her eyes and the way she held her mouth. Even after ambushing her in her sleep and binding her with the harp-wire, she would have him. The calling lay between them, their bodies vibrating with a resonance that defied their circumstances.

Their eyes met. *It is strong between us.* He heard the words as they dropped into his mind; her lips did not move to make them.

Neb swallowed. "It is. But that is not why I've come."

Her eyes narrowed. "How do you know this?"

Because I know. But even as he thought it, he had no certainty in his conviction. He forced his mind to Winters as a last resort, though he knew she was lost to him now. The look on her face when she'd last seen him told him that. Still, he conjured up her image from memories he held tightly. Nights spent in hot and giggling dreams together. The memory of the first taste of her mouth on the Plains of Windwir. The bitterness of its taste when he'd said good-bye and left her after Hanric's funeral.

But those memories did nothing to still what he felt for Amylé D'Anjite, and he knew that there was a biological component to it that transcended what he felt for Winters. It was as if he were one of Brother Charles's metal men, running a script he had no control over. Not that any of it mattered if they could not get free of the temple.

He looked again at the girl, then at the weapon he held in one hand and the crescent he held in the other. Drawing back his arm, he threw the crystal shard as far away from him as he could. Then, he took hold of the loose bit of wire that hung behind the girl's back.

"Let's walk," he said.

They moved slowly and climbed until they could climb no more. The last of their path was a wide and winding staircase that ended at a large round door. The light had grown as they climbed, and here at the top, it was clear enough that he could see the door's seam clearly. He ran his fingers over it, poking and prodding as he did. Nothing budged.

"Is this the top?"

Amylé nodded. "The roof gardens should lie beyond," she said.

His thirst was a dull ache. His hunger was a sharp pain that ground in his stomach. He was caught off guard but not completely surprised when the shift overcame the girl and her foot lashed out at him.

She spat and hissed, her eyes narrow and feral in her hate, and he knocked her over with ease, then pinned her legs beneath his weight.

"Enough," he said.

She bucked and pitched against him, and he watched the blood from her wrists smear along the gray floor of the temple as she struggled against her bonds. Finally, she stopped for a moment, her face pressed into the floor and close to his.

"It doesn't matter what you do to me," she whispered. "We die here and end this."

She continued to strain at the wires, and finally, he flipped her onto her stomach and used his own arm to leverage hers in such a way that she couldn't cut herself further. He felt the hot slickness of her blood upon his bare skin and heard her breathing grow quiet though he knew she did not sleep and would not sleep.

He cast a furtive glance at the crescent, discarded in the struggle, and wished that someone or something would tell him what to do. A dream. Or a voice. *Anything.*

But there was nothing. And the longer he lay still and held the broken girl, the more convinced he became that she was likely right: It didn't matter anymore what he did. He had been sent to unseal the temple and open a path homeward for Winters and her people, to save the very light. He'd been beset at every step along the way.

And now Neb knew that here, at the top of this tower, if the girl beneath him did not find some way to bring about his ending, time itself—reliable and relentless—would do it for her.

Charles

Time in the Beneath Places moved forward slowly, and Charles found himself leaving Isaak's and Winters's sleeping bodies less and less as they settled deeper into dreaming. Occasionally, Hebda or one of the other behaviorists brought him food and drink, and those times that they did, Charles found himself eating and drinking little, sending back platters and cups still half-full.

There was an agitation growing in the camp as the dreams grew more and more intense, and he wondered how much longer it could be. More than that, he wondered what would happen once the dreams were channeled through Tertius's dreamstone.

And will it do the work it was intended to do?

Charles looked up as the door opened a crack and found himself staring at Orius's solitary eye. The general glanced to Hebda and then back to the two sleeping figures. "You," the general said to Charles, crooking his finger.

Charles stood from his chair and walked to the door, mindful that his legs and lower back were numb from too long sitting. The general held the door for him and closed it behind as Charles stepped into the passage.

He looked to the shadows where the girl, Marta, had been hiding of late. There was no sign of her now, and he found it odd. Orius guided him by the arm into the hall and then set a brisk pace toward camp. The general's tone was impatient, as was his posture. "How much longer do you think this will be?"

Charles struggled to keep up. "I don't know, General. Hebda says it shouldn't be long now."

"And we've no idea whether or not it will be effective?"

Charles shook his head.

Orius snorted. "If Introspect hadn't been so damned convinced by this, I'd have closed it up by now. As it is, my men are on edge with these infernal nightmares."

Charles glanced to the man but saw from his jaw that he'd not finished what he'd intended to say. Time had taught him to wait, especially for the military types, because they brooked interruption far less gracefully than the politicos of the Order.

The general stopped. "Do you still have authority over the mechoservitors?" he asked. "Both the ones from Sanctorum Lux and from the Forest Library?"

Charles nodded. "I believe I do."

"And Isaak as well?"

This is the moment I've dreaded. He knew it and didn't answer, because the look in Orius's eye told him that the old Gray Guard general knew it, too, and was not going to let it stand in the way of his work. Charles said nothing.

They stood in silence for a moment. "You serve the light, Charles." It was a statement, but he heard a question in it and responded.

"Yes," he said. "I do."

"When this matter of the dream is concluded, I want all of the mechoservitors retasked. Including those at Rudolfo's library. They can return to their bookmaking when we've ended the war."

Charles did not want to speak now, did not want to ask the question but knew he needed to in order to formulate his response. "What would you have them retasked to do, General?"

Orius snorted. "You know very well what. I want them ready in a week."

Charles held his breath, then released it. "By whose authority?"

Orius held up his left hand and ran his thumb across the silver band on his third finger. Only those closest to the Pope were considered his bondsmen, the general of the Gray Guard one of four. "By the authority of the Holy See of the Androfrancine Order."

"The Androfrancine Order," Charles said slowly, "was dissolved nearly two years ago by Pope Petronus in Holy Conference. All of her assets and resources were transferred to Lord Rudolfo of the Ninefold Forest."

Orius laughed, and it was a loud bark in the quiet. "Then whose army am I taking to the fight?" The general started walking again, and his voice softened. "I've no love for what must be done, Charles. But it must be done. The tide turns soon, my friend, but only if we finish turning it. I need that spell to make it happen. Introspect will have his man on the moon; I'll have the Named Lands from the jaws of Y'Zir."

The camp was astir with activity as men struck tents and checked kits. Engineers were busy running wires, and lines of men were already forming up at various exit points. Charles vaguely recalled the orders from earlier in the day—all but a bare minimum were loading up and heading out.

Charles stopped. "And then what?" he finally asked.

Orius stopped as well. "And then what? I'll give them back to Rudolfo for his damned library. Hells, you can personally expunge it from their memory scrolls if you wish it."

It should have never been brought back in the first place.

Orius's face was stern. "A week, Arch-engineer. That's all we have."

Charles said nothing. Behind him, he heard footfalls in the corridor and turned. Hebda was out of breath and motioning for Charles to return.

"It's started," the arch-behaviorist said.

Charles met Orius's single eye. "A week," the general said again.

Then, the general turned and strode into camp.

Charles moved quickly back in the direction he'd just come from,

Orius's hidden question echoing across the singular focus of his mind: Do you serve the light?

More than ever, Charles realized, even as he also knew that General Orius had stopped serving the light and started serving something else too many years ago.

Chapter

23

Rudolfo

Rudolfo crouched in a copse of trees overlooking Merrique's manor, forcing his eyes open against the vertigo and nausea the scout magicks caused.

Three full nights had passed since his last run with Yazmeera—two since his message from Jin Li Tam—and he'd slept little. His mind continued playing over the events again and again, knowing there was a path but not finding it. Now in the middle of his third night, he knew what he must do. And so he had come out, the iron key that would let him into Merrique's home clutched in a hand made cold and clammy by the powders. He used the scout magicks infrequently despite having been trained on them since he was a pup. Kin-clave was clear on the matter—officers, gentlemen, and lords did not use the powders unless severe circumstances dictated otherwise.

The pouch of powders had been left for him in the hidden room adjacent to his library, along with a sharp, curved knife; a plain gray robe; a canteen; and a week's supply of combat rations in packages sealed with the Androfrancine Gray Guard insignia. He'd waited to magick himself until after he'd snuck through the hidden passages of his own house to reach one of its secret doors into the back garden.

It had been simple enough to slip past the guards and over his own low wall. And equally simple to scale Drea Merrique's wall and slip past her even smaller security detachment. Now, he waited and watched her house, trying to conjure up memories of it from his last visit over twenty years ago.

He remembered Drea Merrique, though she'd been much younger when he'd seen her last. Her father was still the Count of Merrique in those days, and her brother had already earned enough of a reputation at sea for the young Gypsy King to have followed his exploits from an early age, eventually joining his crew for a season. Had his father lived, Rudolfo might've found himself in a different situation. It wasn't uncommon for young lords or ladies to spend time away from their houses, usually incognito, as a part of their education and preparation for their later responsibilities, but sailing with renowned pirates was not the typical expression of this value.

Still, Rudolfo and Gregoric had sailed with the pirate, and early in their time with him, they'd helped him break into his father's house.

A patrol moved past, and Rudolfo counted their steps before they rounded the corner of the house. Then, holding his breath, he ran for the house and let his fingers move over the wood surface at about the height of his breastbone until he found the hidden keyhole.

He slid the key into it, twisted it, and then used the key to pull the section of wall outward enough for him to slip inside, withdrawing the key as he went. He pulled it closed behind him and waited in the small, enclosed space for his eyes to adjust. The magicks helped, but so did the intermittent holes the Gypsy craftsman had left to let air and light into these hidden places within the houses he'd designed.

Once his eyes had adjusted, Rudolfo moved slowly through the passage. The absence of dust told him that the spaces were used regularly. He followed a long, narrow corridor tucked between rooms and along the way, saw robes and knives and supplies placed strategically even as they'd been within his own house.

He had made his way through the first level of the house and was paused, mid-climb, on a ladder to the second level when he heard weight shifting above him.

"You're here to see the countess, I'll warrant," a gruff voice whispered.

Rudolfo looked up. A white face materialized above him, squinting down. "I am—"

"Lord Chancellor Rudolfo," the man said. "I know who you are. Anyone else but our own would've been dead by now." The man moved back from the ladder, and Rudolfo finished climbing. Now, in the gloomy light, he saw the man better—he was thirtyish and dressed in simple clothing that didn't match the man's poise and hard, gray eyes. "Let's wake the countess."

The man shuffled off quietly along the passage, twisting and turning here and there, before they came to a somewhat larger room. This one, Rudolfo saw, had a table covered in papers and a series of maps on its wall. He saw markings on the map that were familiar and realized they were the troop movements he'd provided the day before, whispered to the tiny moon swallow in the dead of night.

"This way," the man said. He worked a lever in the wall, and Rudolfo watched it slide out, creating a narrow opening. The man waited until Rudolfo passed through the hidden door and into the foyer beyond. Then, he closed the door and went to another, tapping on it three times. He pointed to a chair. "Sit," he said.

Rudolfo sat.

The door opened, and Drea Merrique came into the room, rubbing sleep from her eyes as she looked around for her guest. "Lord Rudolfo," she muttered, "to what do I owe this nocturnal visit?"

The man who'd led Rudolfo to her retreated from the room as she sat in the chair opposite. She squinted across at him, but Rudolfo knew the magicks and the darkened room gave her nothing to see. "I require assistance," Rudolfo said.

"What kind of assistance?"

Rudolfo wet his lips. The magicks made his mouth dry cotton; the subject matter did as well. "There have been developments," he said. "Yazmeera has asked me to take the mark of Y'Zir at her Council of Kin-Clave. As a demonstration of my soon-arriving faith."

Drea blinked at him. "That is unexpected."

Rudolfo nodded, though she couldn't see it. "Yes," he said. "It is." That conversation with Yazmeera and the message from Jin Li Tam about Jakob's betrothal ceremony had overfilled his waking moments with thoughts that raced too quickly for him to keep up. "And it seems there is a betrothal ceremony planned between my son and the Crimson Empress."

Drea sat back and folded her arms across her chest. "Very unexpected," she said again. She squinted again, trying to catch some sight of him.

She can't read me, he realized. "I believe it is time for a new path," he said. "I intend to leave for Y'Zir, but there is a work I would finish before."

Drea Merrique sat back. "You wish to leave? To what end?"

Rudolfo took a deep breath, then released it. "I've looked for the high road and the long fight to protect my son, but it is not his life that is in danger. I will not let him be used in this way. His is a river that need not be bent."

The countess scowled. "And what brought you to this path?"

Rudolfo closed his eyes. "I realized that I would gladly take the mark for my son's sake. But I could not bear the thought that he might take the mark himself one day." He opened his eyes now, amazed at the clarity the powders gave his vision. "And there is no doubt he'll take that mark if he's raised up as a fixture in their faith."

Now she leaned forward, searching for his eyes, and for a moment, she had them. Her voice lowered. "Don't throw your life at a blade you cannot turn. The landscape will soon be changing, Rudolfo. I cannot tell you more. But we need you here now."

Rudolfo shook his head. "I will not stay. But I can give you something on my way out."

She sighed and sat back. "Continue."

Rudolfo felt for the list in his pocket. "You were an apothecary before you became countess. I recall Rafe swearing by your magicks and powders. It was your magicks that ultimately saw us safely out of Merrique County the last time I was"—he cleared his throat—"a guest here."

She nodded, but the slightest narrowing of her eyes betrayed something hidden there. "I've dabbled a bit. What I can't make myself, I can acquire."

He slid the list out of his pocket and into her hands. As it left contact with his skin and clothing, it became visible, and she unfolded it. "If I take their mark, I am afforded a feast as part of the ritual," Rudolfo said. "I will be expected, like all of Yazmeera's officers, to contribute something to this meal. And naturally I would want to. All of Yazmeera's senior staff will be present as well as officers visiting for the council."

She looked up from the list. "Renard and Orius will not be happy with this."

"Their happiness is not my concern," he said. "I will give them this gift as I go because it pleases me and because we share an enemy. But my son is the only light I serve."

Drea looked back to the list. "I will pass word to them of your proposal." Then, she looked up, and he saw firm lines upon her face. "I never became a mother," she said, "but I suppose if I had I would not have wanted this for my child, either." She reached out a hand, and something in him compelled him to take it and squeeze it. "If they sanction this, I can help you in ways you would not believe."

He released her hand. "Thank you."

"So you will take the mark?"

Rudolfo nodded, though he knew she couldn't see. "I will."

She sighed. "I'm sorry."

Rudolfo chuckled. "I am not. They are only cutting my skin. What I get from it—and who I do it for—is worth another scar."

She nodded. "I'll contact you within the day," she said. Then, she stood. "I'm back to bed. You should be, too."

Rudolfo stood. "Aye."

She'd already left when hands guided him back to the passageway. He moved silently along behind his guide, and when he was released he moved across the lawn at a low run. He did not take the roads but instead, he ran out into the fields and did not stop until he was far from any houses, alone beneath the blue-green moon.

Worth another scar.

Yes, Rudolfo realized, and one of his own choosing for a change.

Winters

Winters resisted the metal hands that lifted her, her eyes heavy and her brain sluggish from sleep. "I can walk," she muttered.

But even as her feet touched the ground, she knew her legs would not carry her. She leaned against Isaak's solid metal chassis and yawned. "Or maybe I can't."

She was vaguely aware of the guards around her. Charles and Hebda both stood by as well. The old arch-engineer looked worried, but there was excitement on the arch-behaviorist's face.

"I will carry you," Isaak said.

Winters relaxed and let the metal man lift her. It was an odd sensation, being carried, and she found herself remembering the last time she'd experienced it. It was Garyt, Seamus's grandson, bearing her from the cutting table on the Mass of the Falling Moon.

They moved out from the room, leaving her bedding behind. Hebda took the lead with his guards, and Isaak followed. Charles walked beside him.

The steady motion of the metal legs rocked her toward more sleep, and she found it impossible to keep her eyes open. She felt a hand on her shoulder and squinted at Charles.

His voice was low—barely a whisper—and she knew it was meant for her and Isaak's ears alone. "When this is finished," he said, "we need to leave."

Winters tried to focus, remembering a conversation from what seemed decades ago now. She tried to speak and found her tongue thick and heavy. "Micah?"

If Charles understood, he said nothing. Isaak continued moving forward, his flashing red eyes the only acknowledgment of the arch-engineer's words.

They moved quickly through the passages, and she found herself drowsing as they moved, the images of her people's long night of dreaming playing out behind her closed eyes. She'd read the Book of Dreaming Kings, certainly, as she grew into her role. But experiencing the dreams themselves, re-created through the mechoservitor's complex memory system, was a different matter. She'd seen the rise and fall and rise and fall so many times, seen so many nightmare landscapes of war followed by the inevitable crawl up from violence into survival, that when the dreams came suddenly to a stop, she was jarred to a false wakefulness in a vast and quiet field of flowers.

Isaak had been there, and when their eyes met, they'd both known. *The Final Dream comes now.*

And so he'd left the aether to tell the others, and now, they hurried through the Beneath Places to the dreamstone.

As they drew closer, she found herself disoriented as the dream began to reassert itself. The meadow of flowers was back now, and Isaak carried her through it even as they took the twists and turns along the way to the wide, high-ceilinged chamber that waited for them.

The rowboat was out at the stone already, but a larger vessel—a low, flat barge—waited now at the shore. Men stood by the barge and also out on the massive floating black stone, and though the light was too dim to see, Winters felt their fear through the dream. Her eyes fluttered open when she realized this. She looked to Charles and sensed fear as well, but something stronger—determination—rose off of him in waves that she could feel.

What is happening?

Isaak's voice was low and lilting. "The stone is drawing us all together into the aether," he said.

They climbed onto the barge, and she inhaled the pungent, ozone smell of the blood of the earth, the silver fluid they moved over. As they approached, she saw Tertius stretched out, both in the field of flowers and upon the stone, though in the field his eyes were open and watching them approach.

Gray Guard pulled at a creaking rope until the barge brushed up against the dreamstone. Then, Isaak carried her to Tertius and gently placed her on the stone beside him. The mechoservitor stretched out as well, and for a moment, Winters wasn't certain she'd be able to fall back into sleep with the small group of onlookers that gathered.

But once Isaak's head softly scraped against the black stone, she found the pull of the dream irresistible, and the meadow of flowers pushed out the stone and everyone gathered upon it. She smelled the sweetness of the blossoms—unfamiliar and purple—felt the wind moving over them, heard the rustle of the blades of grass, and realized that now, she and Isaak and a multitude of others stood upon a plain that stretched out for an impossible distance all about them.

At the center of the meadow stood an ancient white tree, its limbs heavy with seed similar to that of a dandelion. It towered in the sky but cast no shadow as it did despite a blazing summer sun.

Winters looked to her left and saw Isaak beside her. "What do we do?"

Isaak shrugged. "It is your dream, Lady Winteria. I merely gave you the ingredients for it."

A movement caught her eye, and Winters turned. Others were appearing now, too. Tertius. Hebda. Charles. The soldiers who had accompanied them. They stood wide-eyed, open-mouthed, at what they saw. She turned back to Isaak. "What about your dream?"

Isaak shook his head. "Our dreams are separate, though interdependent."

She saw more people appearing now. Most in Gray Guard uniform. But there were men and women and children also standing, all looking incredulously at the tree and one another.

Somewhere in the distance, Winters heard howling and squinted past the tree to the rolling meadow beyond. On the horizon, she saw a speck of silver moving quickly in her direction. Behind it, several dark and loping forms.

Neb. She wasn't sure how she knew, but the knowing made her breath catch. Winters reached for knives that leaped into her hands simply because she expected them to be at her hips, then launched into a run. "Neb!"

She heard a whispering beside her and looked to see Isaak running as well, his limp giving him a strange gait. She brought her eyes forward just in time to dodge an old man suddenly in her path, and she could see more and more figures occupying the field ahead.

Winters wove in and out of the people materializing around her. She noticed dark uniforms—worn by some who seemed surprised at their arrival in this place and others who did not seem surprised at all. These latter moved quietly, steadily among the others, studying everything. Three of them—women—broke from the gathering crowd to run with her.

Blood Guard. But they did not advance upon her, merely ran beside her, matching her pace.

Winters turned her attention back to the silver figure ahead and the beasts that chased him. He was slowing, and the long, dark creatures gained on him. She gripped her knives tightly and begged her legs to carry her faster.

And they did.

She and Isaak pulled ahead of the Blood Guard, and then, as she clenched her teeth and forced more air into her lungs, Winters roared and pulled ahead of even the metal man. Her eyes widened at the speed she continued to build, and she adjusted her course.

It was a man, but it wasn't Neb. This man was shorter, broader and dark of hair. He moved fast, silver mist lifting from him like steam as he ran, his face grim. He saw her, and when their eyes met, she heard his voice though his mouth did not move.

Lady Winteria, beware the hounds. With the voice, she felt his fear and his resolve. And she saw why—the sheen of silver that covered his body was burning off of him, leaving large exposed patches of pale skin.

Behind the man, she saw better what pursued him. They were long and sleek, ebony-skinned with dark teeth lining dog-like snouts as cat-like legs carried them forward. There were five—no six of them.

What manner of hounds are these? And more, she wondered: What were they doing in her dream? Were they something that the dreamstone had drawn here like the others? And like this man she'd mistaken for Neb?

One surged ahead, and its paw lashed out to catch the man's foot and tumble him.

Winters leaped at the beast even as it gathered itself up to pounce. She crashed into its side, her knives and feet both striking it, and watched the force of her blow lift the animal up and drop it in the grass even as she landed on her back and rolled into a crouch.

Another surged past her, and she stretched out a blade even as she launched herself upward, feeling the satisfaction as it tore into the beast's skin just behind its right foreleg and drew a long, white gash along its side and up into its groin. It yowled and fell kicking up flowers and dirt with its claws.

She spun in time to see the man tossing one of the hounds aside even as another leaped for him. She threw herself into the air and brought her knives down into the beast's spine, dragging it down, but not before its claws ripped through the man's arm and side, shredding more of the silver and drawing deep gashes as it knocked him over.

Winters kicked it aside and it slunk away. The others paused as well, sniffing the air. For the first time, they seemed to notice the others that were gathering on the plain.

She turned to the man. He looked nothing like Neb, though he had familiar features. "Stay behind me," she said, and he nodded.

The hounds started moving now, slowly, walking in long circles around the two of them. Beyond, Winters saw more people, though they kept their distance. Isaak and the Blood Guard pulled up, and other mechoservitors ran toward them too.

Two of the hounds moved off toward the metal men. One watched Winters. *Why have you brought us to this place?*

Winters blinked at the words. "You can speak?"

Who are you? You have the smell of Abomination about you. And yet . . . The voice did not finish.

"I am Winteria bat Mardic," she said. "Who are you, and why are you pursuing this man?"

We are the Hounds of Shadrus, and we hunt as our master commanded.

Her eyes narrowed, and she watched them as they prowled a perimeter around them. "Shadrus is your master?"

The lead hound regarded her with curious eyes. *We hunt Abominations on his behalf in service to his master Lord Y'Zir. Who are you to challenge the hunt?*

Abominations. Winters had heard the term before; the regent and Ria had both called Neb the same. Looking at the man behind her, it was clear that they knew their work very well.

She wasn't sure how she knew to do it. Perhaps it was the dream. Or perhaps it just seemed to make the most sense at the time. But Winters sheathed her knives, took a step forward and extended her hands before her. "I am the last heir of Shadrus," she said. "And I have returned bearing his Final Dream. I am your master now, and I command you to cease your hunting."

The man behind her gasped when the hounds, as one, sat and bowed their heads to her.

She turned to the man. "Where is Nebios ben Hebda?" she asked. "And how do you know who I am?"

The man smiled. "I almost didn't without the mud and ash," he said.

His voice was familiar, and the more she studied his face, the more familiar it became as well. Though now his hair was brown instead of gray. It didn't seem possible unless maybe the dream had somehow done this. "Petronus?"

"Aye," he said. He nodded to the tree. "And Neb is in the tower waiting for us to unseal him from it with your dream."

She followed his nod, and for a moment, the tree was dwarfed by a massive bone-white structure. For a moment, the meadow of flowers was replaced by a clearing in the thick jungle. And in that same moment, a large scarred planet hung overhead to cast its shadow over all of them.

Then, only the field and its solitary tree and its multitude of witnesses remained. Isaak stepped forward, the Blood Guard moving beside him.

"Hold," Winters shouted. When she did, she felt the word roll out away from her, carried by something more powerful than any voice magick. Everyone stopped and looked to her.

I do not know what to do. But maybe she did not have to. She'd heard it called the dream that Shadrus drank. Which meant it was inside of her and inside of each who went before. A story written into her bones that had slowly been dreamed over generations to this final moment.

Winters raised her hands and gave herself to the dream, closing her eyes and hearing a distant murmur that grew on the air. When the wind moved over her, she opened her eyes and watched as it rushed out over the field. All turned to follow it as it closed in upon the tree, and when it reached the tree, it swirled around it once, twice, three times before moving up over its surface. As it moved, it pulled the seeds from the branches to form a white billowing snake that spun upward, over the tree, only to dive down and swirl once more three times around it again. Then, it engulfed the tree, and there was a loud cracking sound as the writhing mass of seeds exploded over the tree and began to rain down slowly over the meadow.

Now the tree stood dead and black.

Yet a wave of euphoria washed over her, through her, leaving a profound sense of calm in its wake. There was something beautiful in what she'd seen, though she could find no meaning in it. She looked around at the others and saw a look upon their faces that she knew must now also be upon hers.

It is hope.

When the words took her, she fell, and as she fell so did every other soul who stood upon that field. And this time, though she knew the words she uttered were in the glossolalia of her dream life, she understood them fully, and she knew that everyone around her did as well. She climbed back to her feet and reached out a hand to point to the tree. "That which was closed is open," she cried out. "That which was lost is returned." Winters stretched herself up to her full height and raised her arms into the sky. "The Homeseeker is now Homefinder. I call the children of Shadrus forth to take back their place upon the moon and serve the temple of their forebears."

Collective gasps and shouts rose up among the multitudes, and at first, Winters thought it was at her words. But then, she realized they were all looking down.

And there, where each seed had struck the waiting ground, the white sapling of a newly planted tree sprung up.

Weeping at the sight of it, Winteria awoke.

Petronus

Face wet with tears, Petronus forced himself to his feet, disoriented from the sudden, jarring return to the edge of the jungle. He was naked now, the silver robes burned fully away, and most of his wounds were healed.

He looked around.

The hounds regarded him in silence where they sat, and stretching out behind them, he saw the rolling, grassy plains that led to the base of the massive white tower that dominated his northern horizon, with his broken homeworld as a backdrop that dominated the sky around it. A wide canal moved north through the grasslands, though the water smelled wrong to him, and somewhere leagues behind, Rafe and the others followed. He checked his pouch, felt the silent crescent within it, and then turned at the sound of moving brush. The last of the mechoservitors broke through into the clearing, steam and smoke billowing from tears in its metal skin. One of its eyes was cracked and dark, its shutters twisted and ripped. They'd tried to hold the hounds back, but when Petronus had seen the first of the metal men fall, he'd pushed himself to run faster to draw the hounds off of them. The mechoservitor limped to him and stopped. Its mouth opened and closed, and a rasping, wheezing noise leaked out but formed no words Petronus could understand.

"You are damaged," Petronus said.

The mechoservitor staggered closer, then placed its hands upon his upper arms. Its fingers began to press his skin, and it took him a moment to comprehend the words. *I am functional.*

Barely, at best, Petronus knew. He turned to the hounds. "Are you finished with us?"

They met his words with silence and he sighed, turning again to take in the tower. He wasn't certain what to do with what he'd seen and heard, and he found himself wondering if Aver-Tal-Ka hadn't made a mistake in choosing to give his life, his very essence, to prepare Petronus for something that, here in the moment, he could not begin to comprehend. And there were parts of it, like his arrival in the meadow of flowers and the multitude of ghosts that populated it that seemed hazy and dream-like to him. And there were other parts, like the rising wind and the whirling mass of seeds, the words Winters uttered and the saplings that rose up, that seemed very clear. As if they were seared into his memory.

He tested that hypothesis by repeating her words aloud, surprised that though he recalled the meaning of each, the actual words that he could recall perfectly were in the ecstatic utterance that Winters had spoken them in.

"I call the children of Shadrus forth to take back their place upon the moon," Petronus said, "and serve the temple of their forebears."

The mechoservitor's single eye flashed as Petronus spoke, and when he finished, the metal hands sought his arms once more. *I do not understand,* it said. *My auditory capacity may be damaged.*

Petronus squinted at the metal man. "They are the words that Winters said, in the dream."

The fingers moved again. *I understood the words in the dream,* it said, *but I do not understand these.*

Petronus turned to the hounds. "What about you? Did you understand what I was saying just now?"

They said nothing.

He furrowed his brow and looked back to the metal man. "But you understand everything else I'm saying? And you can recall the other details of the dream?"

The metal man nodded.

"That," Petronus said, "would be a curious type of auditory damage."

It may have occurred during her actual speech, the metal man pressed into his skin.

"Curious." A cool wind arose and reminded him of his nakedness. Petronus shivered and traced his fingers in the air. "Clothe me," he said.

Mist lifted from the ground, and he felt it moving over his skin like liquid until his robes were restored. When he rubbed the hem of the sleeve between his thumb and forefinger, he felt resistance and knew that the blood of the earth would not let him push himself beyond what his body could handle. And he knew just as instinctively that the blood was in him now, working its way over his body to heal tissue and organs damaged in combat, mitigating his pain and hydrating him. *I am not ready to run,* he realized.

And so he set out for the tower at a brisk walk, the mechoservitor falling in beside him and the Hounds of Shadrus padding along behind. He walked while the light gradually faded into a twilight cast by his former home. Overhead, he saw the greens and blues of the Named Lands, his eye naturally pulled to Caldus Bay. He marveled at whatever magick or machine had given Winters's dream enough range to reach him on the moon. By the looks of the crowd, she'd drawn in far more than just Petronus, and he found himself wondering just how many might've experienced her Final Dream along with him. And what impact would that have?

He himself had no idea what it meant, but just the experience of it alone was a profound moment. There was a singularity of purpose about that wind and a clarity in Winters's proclamation perfectly punctuated by cascading seeds that took root and grew. There was deep longing and deeper satisfaction in it, as if something inside of him was completed by the act, and it altered his perceptions in a way that he wished Franci B'Yot were alive to study. He had experienced something larger than himself, something less cerebral than his so-called light. And yet, somehow he knew that even that which gave him this experience was a product of the same light, sparked in aeons past on Firsthome.

As he walked, he found himself whistling, and as he did, it rang out clear on the darkening night. He whistled the canticle that had for so long filled his mind and ears, a song he'd become intimately familiar with in the last year. He whistled it in time to their walk, and it became a cadence that they kept.

Lasthome was setting, and the sun was on the rise when he reached the base of the tower. When its new light fell upon the white surface, he saw shadows that he'd not noticed before. And when he stretched out his hands to touch them, he felt the symbols carved there.

They were more noticeable as the sun rose, and he traced a line of them with fingers and eye.

He walked at least a league with the rough surface passing beneath his outstretched hand before he stopped suddenly and took a step back.

Those symbols held meaning.

Temple, he realized. One of the words that Winters had uttered.

He felt the other symbols around it, and as his fingers found them, those that comprised the individual letters began to take shape. Then, he continued on, pausing as other words and other symbols became familiar.

And at some point, as he walked, Petronus began to read and comprehend the story waiting for him there, weeping and laughing as he went.

Vlad Li Tam

The air was heavy with smoke, and Vlad Li Tam inhaled the taste of his handiwork on the hot wind. His full complement of Knives surrounded him now, and Aedric stood at his right hand. They huddled close to him, hidden by the staff.

He felt a hand on his shoulder and looked over to Som Li Tam, who pushed a small stack of folded notes, bound together with twine, into his hand.

"I was asked to give you these," his nephew said.

Vlad took the bundle and slid it into his robe. He knew what they were without looking at them, and it twisted in his stomach like a knife. *Their last words.*

He looked up and around at these lost children of House Li Tam, and he made a point of meeting each one's eyes. "Let us hope," he said, "that no last words need sharing. I have further work for my Knives beyond tonight." But even as he said it, he knew that tonight could not happen without losing more of his family, and it broke his heart in ways that it never had before.

He looked to Aedric. "Are you ready?"

The first captain nodded. "Aye."

Vlad turned to Som Li Tam. "Okay. Go."

Som and half of his Knives slipped to the edge of the alley, already shadows as their magicks took hold. They were on the run now for the Temple of the Daughters. He counted to thirty and then left the alley himself as the others magicked themselves and stayed near.

The courtyard was empty. Most of the available soldiers were fighting fires or policing the sick and those displaced by fire. And the elite Blood Guard were all now in the very place Vlad planned to go.

He drew in a deep breath and then moved for the gate. Each step ached now, but he willed the pain to fuel him and it obeyed.

And then the world exploded into light even as a vertigo seized him and drove him to his knees. His Knives fell, too, and when he rose, he was no longer in the courtyard.

He stood in a field with a multitude of others surrounding a tall and ancient tree gone white with seed. He saw Y'Zirite soldiers and Blood Guard gathered on the plain along with magisters and Daughters of Ahm. And farther out into the crowd, he saw the men and women and children of Y'Zir.

Vlad felt a jolt of power from the staff that moved up his arm and out into the rest of his body, finally leaving through his feet. He felt it trembling through the ground, and as it did, a wind rose.

He heard a woman's voice booming out about a temple and about Shadrus, but he found the words impossible to focus on. Instead, he savored the sensation that now moved through him. It was a pure joy the likes of which he'd never known—and he knew it was the staff. Something in it rejoiced at the sight of the tree, and Vlad could not help but join it. A sense of euphoria and hope flooded him, and for a brief moment, he lost sight of everything but what he presently experienced.

But when he saw the woman in black staring at him, he found his focus again. All of the others were caught up in what was happening, but she regarded him with some mix of fear and rage. "Are you responsible for this, Vlad Li Tam?"

"No," he said, shaking his head. She looked important—her robes were more ornate than the other Daughters, and she was older than most of them. "This is not my work."

She opened her mouth to say more but closed it when the booming voice rolled out once more across the meadow.

Where did that voice come from? He looked around the field and found its source. The staff brought the young woman clearly into focus, and it took him a moment to recognize Winteria bat Mardic, the deposed Queen of the Marshfolk. Beside her, a tall silver mechoservitor stood, and nearby, a man he recognized from his youth knelt on the ground.

Petronus? Only not the old man he had most recently seen. The young man who'd been the youngest pope to take office. His boyhood friend.

His eyes moved to the mechoservitor. There were others nearby, but this one stood apart. It was taller, newer, and yet he knew somehow it was actually older. Far older. And made from the same mirror-polished metal as the staff in his hand. He felt the kinship between the two even as the metal man's eyes shifted to meet his own.

Lord Tam. He heard the voice in his mind and winced at its force. *The tools of the parents are not toys for the children.*

Vlad blinked. *And who are you?*

But before the mechoservitor could answer, he felt the staff answering for him. The metal peeled away, and his breath caught as a rush of information filled his head. Images and ciphers and music.

He knew who it was, though he did not comprehend it.

Isaak.

And there was more; he felt the weight of it in the pit of his stomach. *He has the spell.*

Vlad Li Tam looked away, suddenly aware of a change in the atmosphere around them. The seeds were falling around them now like snowflakes, and he felt a jolt of energy moving up his arm from the staff, spreading through his body. It moved out around him, and as it spread it seemed as if the seeds fell faster, drawn by whatever energy the staff had infused the ground with.

But he did not wait to see what that meant. Others were gathering around the woman now, and they, too, could see him. He tapped the field gently with the staff and willed himself away from the aether.

The last thing he saw was Isaak's red eyes burning into him.

He climbed to his feet, disoriented from the sudden shift to and from the aether. Then, he tapped the courtyard with the silver rod and woke his Knives from their forced slumber. "We go now while we have the advantage," he said.

Vlad forced strength into his legs, wincing at the sharp pain behind his eyes from commanding the staff. But it complied, and he gave himself to a slow run.

The palace gates were closed, and a full squad of guards lay sprawled about, still caught up in the dream. He and his Knives did not pause—he thrust the staff ahead and watched the massive gate collapse in on itself just as their feet whispered over it. Beyond the gate, the garden stretched out with its citrus orchards and flowers.

"Fires," Vlad whispered.

He did not see his runners spread out, though he could've tasked the staff with aiding his eyes even to the point of seeing beyond their magicks. Tonight would tax him enough, and he knew he could trust them to do their work with or without his eyes upon them. And even as he ran, he smelled the smoke from the fires they set. When he reached the inner gate, he smelled oranges and lemons burning on the wind.

The guards were stirring here, and his Knives moved in over them, returning them to a longer, dreamless sleep, even as Vlad tapped the inner gate with the staff to send it toppling over.

Now they were met by rushing wind, and he held his breath as he squeezed more from the staff. He felt it heating up as it leeched the blood magicks out of the women who approached them. Confounded, they fell back even as his own magicked Knives slipped past him to strike them down. But these, they didn't kill. They left them moaning, hamstrung, in their blood.

The dead use fewer resources, he thought as he ran. And the whimpers of the wounded were one more tool to erode the morale and resolve of his enemy.

"Fires," Vlad whispered again. Then, he stretched out his left hand toward Aedric. He felt the magicked Gypsy's lead line slip over his wrist and tighten, and he tugged it, letting the first captain take point.

They took the central stairway two steps at a time as the sounds of alarm and the smell of smoke rose around them. Above, another squad of Blood Guard spilled down the stairs toward them, and once more, Vlad gritted his teeth and called upon the staff and felt the heat of their magicks as it drew them out of them. These staggered on the stairs, tumbling aside as Vlad and his escort moved past. He heard the sound of blades as they rushed upward and heard the bodies falling, sliding down the stairs as his Knives did their cutting.

Once they reached the top, Aedric guided them down a wide corridor, following the directions Som Li Tam had drilled into them all for most of the last two days. The heat from the fires below followed them, and Vlad felt sweat beading on his forehead.

But it is more than the heat. He was fevered now, shored up by the staff even as that ancient artifact tore down his body. He understood the mechoservitor's words very well now about the tools of the parents. Each new ache within his bones or stabbing pain within his chest reminded him starkly that time was short for him. Shorter still each time he squeezed more power from the Moon Wizard's staff.

They pressed their way down the corridor now, twice more encountering Y'Zirite soldiers as they worked their way deeper into the palace's residential quarters. Vlad had no way of knowing exactly how many of his Knives were lost along the way, but from what his ears could tell him, they held their own well enough.

And we are close.

Despite knowing that, he was surprised when they suddenly burst through a door and into the empress's bedchambers. Once more he pulled the magicks from the Blood Guard, but this time, the staff pulsed in his hand and he staggered from the force of it. His Knives fell upon the Y'Zirites, but these were fiercer. They gathered around a large round bed and stood the longest of all the others as his Knives rushed over them.

A man in dark robes entered the room from a set of double doors that led to the main hallway. He moved toward Vlad, his face set with resolve and his hand held up as if to stop Vlad's advance.

Vlad recognized the silver insignias from his reconnaissance around the city. This was one of the magisters.

You will stop now. The words were sharp behind his temples, and Vlad felt them grabbing at him, slowing him even as he plowed into Aedric's back. The other Knives stopped as well.

No, Vlad replied. *I will not ever stop.*

The staff beat like a heart now, and with each pulse Vlad found his eyes drawn to the silver ring upon the magister's hand. He felt it, his mind moving through it and around it. He tasted the coolness of the metal on his tongue and heard the whispers buried deeply in its small black stone. When he comprehended it, he smiled.

And when he tapped the staff upon the floor he heard a pop and saw a flash of light as the black stone shattered and the metal melted from the magister's finger. The man screamed, and Vlad advanced, swinging the staff like a club. He felt the solid, satisfying jolt along his arms as it connected and heard a loud crack as the magister went down.

Vlad turned to the bed. A little girl stirred there and whimpered. He approached her slowly. "Amara," he said. "I'm here to take you to your mother." She couldn't possibly understand what he meant, but it wasn't the words that were important. It was the tone of his voice as he willed all threat or menace from it. He paused. "Aedric?"

"I'm here, Tam."

"Are you ready?" He felt a tug at the lead line as the first captain shifted.

"I am."

Vlad nodded. He slipped the lead line from his wrist and took the heavy sack that Aedric pushed into his hands, wincing at the memory of what was inside. Then, he looked down at the Crimson Empress in her bed. She had her mother's eyes, and they were fixed on his now as her lower lip quivered.

"Sleep," he said. The girl's eyes closed, and her body went still.

And after Aedric gently slipped her into a magicked sack, they left by the way they came and turned their eyes toward his grandson's quarters so he could once more break his daughter's heart.

Rudolfo

The late-morning sun was hot upon his neck as Rudolfo ran, eyes forward and scanning the nearby pastures and the line of trees on his horizon. He'd run the same route initially, but as his legs and lungs adapted, he'd increased the distance. And as his plans took shape, he'd taken to randomly changing his route. On some days Yazmeera joined him; but on most he ran alone.

No, not alone. It was easy to forget his shadow, Ire Li Tam, running silently to the left and rear of him. He glanced back at her now and caught her watching him.

She met his eyes. "You're not as soft as you were. But are you ready for what's coming?"

He nodded. "I am."

When he'd confided in her, her initial reaction had been incredulous, but once he'd lain out the basics of his plan and she'd seen his resolve, the Blood Guard had added her own insights to the planning. And now, with the Council—and his banquet—just days away, there was little left to do but watch and wait.

The briefest flash of silver caught his eye, and he saw the tiny bird moving low over the ground, disappearing into the tree line ahead. He forced his feet to carry him faster.

When he slipped into the shadows of the trees that lined the river, he slowed to a walk.

He heard the quiet whistle and turned toward it.

A man dressed in the nondescript clothing of an orchard worker crouched against a tree overlooking the slow-moving water; Rudolfo and Ire joined him.

Rudolfo had met Renard years earlier as a younger man, but time had largely erased his recollections of the Waste Guide. His memory of the man's father, Remus, was clearer. And to be certain, Renard was certainly his son. He had the height, the salt-and-pepper hair, and intensely blue eyes. Rudolfo crouched beside him while Ire Li Tam took up a position nearby, her eyes prowling for any movement that might indicate they'd been followed.

Renard's eyes measured him, and Rudolfo met them with his jaw set. "We've expedited the wine shipment," the Waste Guide said. "It should arrive later today."

Rudolfo nodded. "Good." There had been a steady stream of messages by the bird since his midnight infiltration of Drea Merrique's estate. To their credit, they'd not tried to talk him out of his decision, only into waiting. And now five barrels of his wine of choice—made from the peaches of Glimmerglam—made their way to him. "It will need time to properly chill," he said.

Renard nodded. "Yes, of course." The Waste Guide smiled. "But otherwise, it is ready for your intended purpose."

Rudolfo raised his eyebrow. "And you're assured of the outcome? It will only affect the Y'Zirites who drink it?"

The Waste Guide opened his mouth to answer, but Rudolfo didn't hear the words. Light burst behind his eyes, and a vertigo gripped him suddenly, pitching him over into the grass. He was vaguely aware of Renard falling as well, and in the distance, he thought he heard Ire Li Tam gasp.

When the blinding light spiderwebbed itself to something more manageable, he sat up and blinked. When Renard extended a hand to him, he took it and let the man pull him to his feet.

The field stretched out before Rudolfo, and even as he watched, he saw ghosts materializing upon it—at first, men and women dressed in the garb of county folk, and later, soldiers and scouts in the familiar black of the Y'Zirite army. Beyond them, people dressed in other clothing, other uniforms, also gathered in a sea of spectators. They gathered around a gigantic white tree that rose up from the center of the plains, and from somewhere distant, he heard a woman's voice rolling out over them, louder than any blood magick he'd ever heard. "Hold!"

I know this voice. He squinted but couldn't find the speaker.

"We're in the aether," Renard whispered. "In the dream."

Rudolfo turned. "The dream?"

Renard's voice was awestruck. "The Final Dream."

Rudolfo's brow furrowed. "My understanding is that the Final Dream was lost with the Watcher."

Renard regarded him thoughtfully before speaking. "Your understanding is . . . incomplete." Then he looked up, and Rudolfo followed his gaze. Black-robed women moved among the crowd, their eyes moving to and fro, setting them apart from the wide-eyed stares of the others who'd found themselves here.

Incomplete? Rudolfo scanned the field again and now saw the flashes of metal where mechoservitors moved among them, and he wondered what Renard meant. But his wondering faltered when the wind rose and carried a different voice—a child's voice—to his ears.

"Papa!"

Rudolfo turned and took in the small boy who toddled toward him. There were black-robes with the child, their faces concerned and their hands stretching out, but their hands passed through him as if he weren't there. The boy fell, laughed, and climbed back to his feet even as the wind gusted and surged toward the tree.

It couldn't be.

He hadn't seen him in months, but there was no mistaking the high Tam cheekbones of his mother or the dark eyes and curly hair that Rudolfo had seen in mirrors since his own childhood. "Jakob?"

Hope ambushed him as he ran for his son. Even as it did, his will betrayed him and tears streamed from his eyes to wet his beard. As the gathering crowd gasped aloud and wind took the tree, Rudolfo fixed his eyes upon his son and felt the euphoria rising up within him.

He knew the voice now, and he heard it clearly as he met his son's eyes and knelt before him to hold his gaze as an equal.

"That which was closed is open," Winters cried out. "That which was lost is returned. The Homeseeker is now Homefinder."

Her other words were lost to him now as his son's eyes drowned her voice. His first instinct was to gather his boy up into his arms, but some part of him resisted. What if it was the dream? Some figment in the aether? Somehow, the idea that he might touch his son and that his son might disappear kept him back. Instead, he crouched and looked his son in the eye as the seeds fell down around them to take root in sacred ground.

Rudolfo awoke to Renard's hand shaking him and sat up quickly, his face still wet from his tears. "I must go," the Waste Guide said. "I was seen in the aether by their casting bitches."

Rudolfo climbed to his feet. "I am overdue as well."

Renard inclined his head. "Hunt well, Rudolfo. Remember: Drink deep. You will not be harmed."

Rudolfo nodded. "I will hunt well indeed," he said.

With murder in his heart and his son's eyes in his memory, Rudolfo turned back to the road and ran with the sound of Winters's voice still echoing in his ears.

That which was closed is open. That which was lost is returned.

And Rudolfo knew now, just as he'd known that day so long ago upon another plain, that the world had changed, had become something different. Only the pillar of smoke was now a great tree. And the ashes raining down were the seeds of hope and home.

Neb

"Nebios?"

The voice was familiar but far away. Neb forced his eyes open. "Father?" His surroundings were taking shape now, and he saw the girl stirring where he'd tied her. He lifted the silver crescent from his lap and held it to his ear.

"Neb!" It was Petronus. "I've figured it out."

Figured what out? He pushed at the fog that disoriented him and tried to remember how long it had been since he'd had water. His mouth was dry and his skin felt hot. He blinked at the words.

He had vague recollections of Petronus's voice now, tinny and far away as he recited the story of the People carved into the surface of the temple. He'd heard bits of the story from Aver-Tal-Ka, but this version was fuller, more polished, and though he couldn't remember all of it, he remembered enough.

We are the People, it began. And it told the long tale of a species both terrible and gifted, mastering the elemental building blocks of the universe for both war and peace, destruction and survival. They'd grown up and managed to live forever despite their propensity for cataclysm. He remembered the words gentling him as he lay against the wall.

"Neb? Are you there?"

He felt the slightest tremble move through the tower and heard the faintest of whispers as something stirred to life. "I am here," he said.

"And the girl? Is she with you still?"

Neb saw her watching him, her eyes dark and empty. She lay on her side, her hands and feet tied. "I am with him," she said, her own voice a croak. He couldn't tell which woman she was at the moment, but he'd learned along the way that he couldn't trust his instincts where that was concerned. Hers was a weather that could change in a moment, storms of wrath or terror alternating without any notice.

"I can help her," Petronus said. "Wait for me on the roof."

Neb watched her face as she heard the words and could read on it which woman currently sat behind those wounded eyes. The fear and uncertainty betrayed her as the lost girl he'd initially met in his dreams.

The whispering grew, and as it did, Neb realized the light also increased. Behind him, the door he leaned against became warm and slightly pliable, and it struck him all at once what was happening.

The tower was awakening.

He didn't know what made Petronus able to unseal the temple, and though the old man had told him about the dream, he'd heard about it in a fog of exhaustion and dehydration.

Neb forced himself to his feet and felt the surface of the door. It responded to his touch, tingling his fingers and the palm of his hand. "Open," he whispered.

And it opened.

At first, the sunlight and sky blinded him, but as he blinked into the light, the roof took shape. The garden and grass was gone now, but he saw the pool and started for it. Then, remembering the girl, he stopped and went back.

Neb leaned over her and helped her up, feeling the spark in his own body the moment their skin touched. He resisted the pull of the call and stood her on her feet. Then, he stooped again and untied her feet, careful to stand in such a way that those same feet couldn't reach him if the other Amylé showed up.

She did not resist, and when he'd finished, he led her out into the light.

The sky was expansive and blue overhead, flecked with high clouds. Around and below them, the canopy of jungle stretched out to meet a clear green sea. He saw these but forced his eyes instead to the patch of roof where the fountain had once stood. Even as he moved toward it, he heard the gurgle of water, and it hastened him forward.

Then, he heard Amylé cry out and turned even as she stopped. He saw the fear and surprise on her face, then followed her eyes. Hanging high in the sky, the dead world he'd come from stared down at them.

When she collapsed, the dead weight of her pulled him down as well. "Oh Neb," she whispered, her eyes never leaving the broken planet. "What have they done to Lasthome?"

She started to cry, and he wanted to stay and hold her but resisted. He could smell the water now, and he looked from the girl to the pool. Finally, he left her and staggered to it, dropping the crescent and falling to his knees.

The water seeped into it slowly, forming a small but growing puddle in the bottom. He scooped it into his mouth, surprised at how cold and sweet it was. Neb forced himself to drink slowly, and when he felt his stomach threatening to revolt, he made himself stop. Then, he stood and returned to the girl.

She lay where she'd fallen, her eyes fixed upon the sky. "What have they done?" she asked again.

Neb crouched beside her. "They did it a long time ago," he said.

Her eyes went from the sky to his face. "Then my father is truly dead?"

Neb shrugged. "I think he is. I don't know." He thought for a moment. "I'm alive. You're alive. It's hard to say if there are others."

Amylé sighed. "I'm thirsty, Nebios Whym."

He climbed slowly to his feet, then reached down to take her by the arms and lift her. Once more, the hot smooth call of her flesh stirred him and he blushed at it. She noticed and bit her lip but said nothing as he led her to the water and lowered her to lie beside it.

"Can you untie me?"

His eyes narrowed as he tried to read some sign of her intentions. He rolled her to her side and started working the harp-string before pausing. Neb took a deep breath. "I don't think—"

The sound—three long blasts—drifted in from somewhere to the south of them. And just on the heels of that deep, loud tone the tower shuddered beneath him and released a similar noise so loud that he felt the waves of sound moving over his skin, saw it rippling the water in the pool.

Her face lit up at the sound. "The seaway is open."

"The seaway?"

She nodded south. "Untie me and I'll show you."

He shook his head. "I don't think so." Instead, he repositioned her so that she could turn her head and drink from the pool's edge. Then, he turned and walked to the southern edge of the temple to study the horizon. Far out in the sea, he saw light reflecting on a sphere of Firstfall metal suspended over a large white object. "What is it?"

She didn't answer. A light wind moved over the tower's surface, and he shivered despite the heat in it. He started to turn back toward her, but movement below caught his eye and he looked down. A tiny crystalline ship made its way up the canal. He saw the bright-colored specks of Gypsy Scouts and pirates moving over the deck. Then, he looked over his shoulder at the girl.

She was on her feet now, and her eyes were fixed on him. He read the hatred in them and knew she'd changed again.

Amylé D'Anjite smiled. "I am finished here," she said.

And when she bolted for the opposite edge of the tower Neb understood her intent and lurched into a run to intercept her. As she ran, a cry rose up from within her that he thought at first was a shriek of rage. But as it grew in volume and pitch, it became something else—something inhuman.

He reached for her, and she eluded him by a finger's breadth before toppling over the side of the temple. She did not struggle as she fell. Instead, she leaned back into it with her mouth open wide and her call upon the wind.

Neb cried out, stretching his hands, and nearly lost his own balance when a shriek from above answered her.

He fell back, scrambling away from the edge, as something massive and metallic flashed by him. It moved too fast for him to comprehend it—long and with paired wings fore and aft. It was sleek and silver, and as its wings shifted to drop it over the falling girl, it stretched out four of its six arms to catch her.

Only, instead of catching her and holding her, it grabbed the woman and pulled her into itself. It paused for a moment, its wings holding it in place. Then, it shot south and built speed until thunder cracked the air.

Neb watched it, and when it had vanished from view, he climbed back to his feet and returned to the pool. He drank and then slept, and when he awakened, he filled himself with water. In the hours he'd slept, the temple had continued to come alive. The pool was full and clear now, and the once bone-white surface smelled of rich earth and ozone.

Neb walked to the door and paused. Somewhere below, Petronus climbed toward him, and they would meet approximately in the middle. Stretching out his hand to the wall, Neb felt the energy rising from it like static on his hand. "Clothe me," he whispered.

The blood of the earth enfolded him, evaporating his hunger and his thirst, easing the ache in his muscles. Robed in silver, Nebios Whym thought about Amylé D'Anjite as he descended the tower and wondered at the beast she'd called forth.

Wherever it carried her, he suspected no good could come of it.

Jin Li Tam

Sleep pulled at the edges of her awareness and Jin Li Tam clawed her way up from it, feeling the sweat in the sheets that tangled her as she did.

Jakob.

She'd been dreaming. There was a tree. And Winters was there. Isaak, too, though she didn't know how that could be. But what she remembered most was that Jakob had been there with her and then suddenly was not. And she'd found herself running across a vast plain of people, searching for her son. She still felt the terror that flooded her even as she reached out in the bed to find him.

He was there, asleep, and she moved closer, feeling the warmth of him and taking comfort from it, she drowsed until the smell of smoke brought her upright in bed. She heard roaring outside, and the orange glow of fire cast shadows on the wall. Jin Li Tam slipped from the bed, her hands moving for knives she did not have. She padded to the balcony and looked out into the burning night. Not just the orchards, but the city burned, too, along with parts of the palace. The alarms were ringing now, and the knot in her stomach told her what came her way. She recognized the tactics of mayhem and precision that marked her father's House, and she went first to her closet to dress quickly.

Once she was dressed, she went to her son and gathered him up into her arms. He shifted and wriggled, pushing himself closer to her as his small arms encircled her neck, and she inhaled the scent of his hair, afraid in a way that she hadn't been in a long, long time.

Jin moved through the room and opened the door that led into the bath chambers, moving beyond the large marble soaking tub to the door leading to Lynnae's room. She entered quietly, closing the door behind her, and went quickly to the bed. "Lynnae?"

The woman mumbled and shifted in the bed, then sat up. "I smell smoke."

"The palace and orchards are burning. You need to get dressed."

Lynnae scrambled from the bed. "Where are we going?"

Jin paused. "I don't know," she said. "Anywhere but here."

The younger woman moved to the closet, pulling out loose silk pants and a matching shirt. She slipped into both quickly, then bent to put on a pair of low-cut boots.

There was a commotion outside—the sounds of shouting and steel against steel—and Jin moved to the door, listening. Jakob stirred and mumbled something. It took her a moment to comprehend the word.

Papa.

She wasn't sure why that single word felt so heavy in her ears, or why it stabbed at her with a wave of guilt precipitated by the memory of Rudolfo's face on the morning that Jakob was born. She swallowed and pressed her ear to the door, waiting until she heard her own door, just down the hall, fly open.

"Now," she whispered.

She opened the door slowly, quietly, and moved into the hallway. There were Blood Guard strewn along the corridor, some dead and some moaning, and she stooped to recover a long, curved knife. With Jakob clutched to her breast and the knife extended, Jin ran and begged her feet to be silent over the floor. Lynnae followed after.

She'd not gone far when a voice behind her called out with quiet authority. "Daughter."

Jin stopped, her legs suddenly unwilling to carry her. She tried to force them, and when they still refused, she tried to turn and couldn't. She heard a cry from behind her and realized it was Lynnae.

"You can't have him," the young woman shouted.

There was a loud thump and the sound of a body falling. Then, her father's breath was on the back of her neck. "Face me, Daughter."

Now she resisted turning, but his words compelled her and she did as he commanded.

Vlad Li Tam stood before her, though he was nothing like the man she'd last seen boarding a ship on the edge of the Desolation of Windwir. His hair and beard had grown long, and he'd lost weight, becoming a shriveled, haggard man with hollow, deep-set eyes. He wore simple robes, and in his hands, a silver staff blazed and hummed.

"Give him to me." She saw something on her father's face that was unfamiliar to her, and she thought for a moment it must be pity or love. Still, she banished that notion quickly.

"I will not," she said.

He sighed. "Who bid you bear Rudolfo an heir?"

She remembered the note from her father, tucked beneath her pillow at a time when she trusted him above all others and took pleasure in serving his purposes. He'd bid it, but for the first time in her life, she'd not done it for him. She'd done it for Rudolfo.

No, she realized. More than that. She'd done it for herself. "Who bid me is irrelevant. He is my son."

She heard the sound of boots upon the stairs behind her and smelled the smoke as it rose up from the fires in the palace below. Jin clung to her son and willed the Y'Zirites to hurry, though she knew that if they could stop her father, they would've done so before he'd gotten this far.

"Give him to me," Vlad said again, and she felt her arms and hands complying.

Jakob stirred as he moved from her arms to her father's, and when his eyes opened and took in his grandfather, Jin saw a look of adoration and love on the old man's face that was in direct contrast to what her heart told her came next.

"Sleep," he whispered to the boy. Jakob's eyes closed, and Jin felt a sob rising up in her that threatened to become a scream.

Her voice was a whisper. "Don't do this, Father."

She saw agony upon his face now and heard the sorrow in his words. "I'm sorry."

When he turned to flee, she tried to follow and couldn't. Powerlessness and rage caused her body to tremble violently, and when the Y'Zirites overtook her, she felt the power of his staff release her and she dropped to her knees from the suddenness of it. They raced the corridor, knives drawn as they magicked themselves and vanished.

She gave it no thought whatsoever. Gripping her knife, she followed and let her fear become a rage that gave strength to her legs. Jin ran, leaping over the wounded and the dead as she pursued her father. She climbed another set of stairs and followed the sounds of combat until she came to yet another staircase—this one narrow and leading to the roof.

It had to be for maintenance—it opened upon a wide, tile roof that sloped down to meet the upward rise of another. Her father now climbed the other side, moving quickly. She could not see any evidence of his escort now, and she did not know if they'd fallen or if they'd been diverted.

Or if they lie in wait for me. She moved onto the roof with the knife extended before her, and when no hands or blades fell on her, she picked up her pace and leaped for the other roof. Her father climbed for the highest point, moving north. From this height, she could see the fires scattered out across the city, and the night air grew hotter from the palace that burned beneath her feet.

"Stop," she cried out.

Her father paused and looked to her. Jin braced herself for the staff to once more stop her feet and hold her. But it didn't. Instead, Vlad turned away and continued his run.

She saw the large sack he carried now, slung haphazardly over his shoulder. It was still, but she knew what it contained, and until he reached the highest point of the roof and paused, she had no idea what he intended.

But when he braced himself with the staff and began to swing the sack, she understood. With unnatural strength, he swung the sack in the air like a sling, and she pushed her feet to carry her faster, measuring the distance between them.

The sack built speed as he swung it round and round, and when he released it, he pointed with his staff at a burning building across the courtyard, and the sack arched up and away like something discarded by a giant.

She fell to her knees even as the sack crashed down through the burning roof at least a half-league away, and she felt the knife of despair twisting in her, gutting and coring her.

I have lost everything.

She heard a long and mournful wail rise up into the night and knew that it was her own voice bearing witness to a loss she could not sustain. She tried to climb back to her feet, to stagger toward the man who'd murdered her son, and she fell again as tears and trembling overtook her.

I have lost . . . everything.

Overpowered and broken, Jin Li Tam closed her eyes and let the abyss of loss have its way with her.

Chapter 25

Winters

The black stone was cold upon her cheek when Winteria bat Mardic awakened. For a moment, she lay there and let her body remember what had happened: the tree and the field and the multitude of people and the wind.

And my words.

Traces of the euphoria she'd experienced with her hands outstretched beneath those falling seeds were still with her, and she sensed at the core of her that something unexpected had happened. The Final Dream had been meant for Neb, and as far as she could tell, he was the only one who hadn't experienced it. But the others had—a vast sea of people. And by their faces, they'd felt the euphoria of that gathering as well. Somehow the stone—and Isaak—had amplified the dream to the point of reaching the moon. And everyone else in between, it seemed.

Winters opened her eyes and let them adjust to the gloom of the cavern.

Beside her, Isaak's eyes flashed open, and the mechoservitor sat up quickly. "Lord Tam has the staff of Y'Zir," he said. "I must retrieve it."

The others stirred now. Charles, Hebda, and Tertius were all sitting up and rubbing their faces. Tears flowed down Tertius's cheeks, and he made no attempt to wipe them.

"It was beautiful," he whispered.

The old Androfrancine had studied her people and their dream most of his life; her own tutelage had been part of that study. And now, it took seeing him moved for her to fully feel what had just happened.

Winters released held breath and felt her own tears rise. "The time of dreaming has passed," she said in a quiet voice.

Hebda nodded. "It has."

Charles looked to the shore across the silver pool and raised his eyebrows. "But what new time is upon us?"

She followed his eyes and saw the gathered soldiers and their general at the center. It was a fair question, and for her she knew it was now the time of gathering. The mechoservitors in the north would bring her people south—the few who had followed her and her dreaming now—and she would lead them home from there.

But how?

The soldiers who had accompanied them to the large black island stood by the barge now and waited. When she looked to Hebda, she saw the beginnings of fear on his face. She watched his glance move from Isaak to the shore, and then she looked at Charles.

The old man's face was stone now, and his eyes never left the general and the men who waited for them. She moved closer to him and lowered her voice. "What is happening?"

His own voice was barely a whisper. "They're not going to let Isaak leave."

She blinked. "What about the rest of us?"

Charles sighed but said nothing. Still, the look on his face answered her question.

"Can we get away?"

The arch-engineer looked away from the shore and met her eyes. "Yes. With help."

Then, he moved away toward the barge. They boarded in silence and let the soldiers pull them back to the other side. Winters was the first to leap ashore. She approached Orius and watched as his men fell back around him.

She inclined her head to the officer. "Thank you, General Orius, for your hospitality. Now that my people's dreaming is at an end, I must go to them and make preparations for our journey."

The firm line of the man's jaw told her all she needed to know before he opened his mouth. His single eye narrowed. "I'm sure you can appreciate why that won't be possible at this time, Lady Winteria."

She met his stare and let the anger creep into her own eyes. "No,"

she said. "I cannot. I am not your prisoner; I am your guest. I came here
for a specific purpose, and that purpose is concluded. I intend to leave."

Orius looked to Hebda and Tertius, but she did not allow herself to
look away from the man and see their response.

Hebda spoke first. "She is correct, General. The Office has no further need of her; she should be permitted to return to her people."

Orius growled. "The Office's work is now concluded as far as I'm
concerned. The dream is dreamed. What remains is a war. And war is
my office." He looked back at Winters. "You are indeed a guest here until you prove yourself otherwise. But leaving now is not an option." He
lowered his voice. "The advantage in this war is about to turn. I do not
think you'll be forced to suffer our hospitality for long, Lady Winteria."

Charles cleared his voice. "Of all people, General, she needs to leave
now."

Something in his tone caused her to look, and when she did, she saw
Hebda's face as well and saw somber agreement there. She looked back
to Orius. "What does he mean?"

The general shook his head. "These are not matters to discuss openly,
Charles. I will—"

The arch-engineer interrupted. "She's been exposed to blood
magicks her entire life, as have many of her people. Tertius maintains
that the dream itself is likely some form of generational blood magick
inherited through Mardic and his line going back to Shadrus."

She looked at Tertius and saw understanding dawn on his face. Even
as it dawned, he went pale. "Orius, what have you done?" The old man
looked to Hebda. "Did you know about this?"

"I did. But I did not know she was staying."

Winters felt anger tickling at her spine and scalp. She turned on
Charles. "What is happening?"

He kept his eyes upon the general. "Orius is introducing a pathogen
into the water tables. It targets those exposed to blood magick."

Pathogen. She wasn't sure of the word, and she wasn't sure exactly how
it could be put into the water, but the somber tone Charles used and Tertius's obvious horror told her it couldn't be good. "What does it do?"

Orius answered, his anger with Charles clearly written on his face.
"It kills them. We can discuss it further on the march. The others are
ready by now, I'm sure." He looked around, taking in the wires and
sacks of blast powder, turning to one of his engineers. "We'll want at
least a day between us and the explosion when you collapse the cavern."

The man saluted. "Yes, General."

Isaak had remained silent until now, but the slightest hum from the mechoservitor brought Winters's attention to him. He stepped forward, his red eyes bathing the Androfrancine general's face the color of blood. "The light requires service of us elsewhere, General Orius. I advise you to let us pass."

Orius did not acknowledge the metal man. Instead, he looked at Charles. "I want the mechoservitors rescripted, Arch-engineer, and I want the spell disseminated to the others."

The spell. She remembered the day she'd seen the spell's handiwork for the first time in the Named Lands—the pillar of smoke and fire on her southern horizon. And she remembered what she'd seen when she and Hanric had ridden to the Desolation that was Windwir's grave. Isaak had borne that spell—guided by Y'Zirite hands using Sethbert as their puppet.

Charles's voice was husky with rage. "I will not do it, Orius."

Orius snorted. Then, he leaned in closer to Isaak. "Tell your *maker* that it is in his best interests to keep in mind just what you were made for. I'm sure your friend Marta would concur."

Winters was completely unprepared for the speed with which Isaak moved. His right hand shot out to grip the Androfrancine general's throat, lifting the man easily from the ground. And as he lifted, the metal man's left hand shot out to knock aside the two soldiers who lunged forward. He limped forward with Orius's feet kicking at air until he could press the general into the wall of the cave. "Where is Marta?"

The general's face moved from pale to purple as the other soldiers drew their swords and advanced. One of them took a swing, and the blade rang out as it struck Isaak's back, turned easily away by the silver steel.

Orius gurgled, and the metal man relaxed his grip. "She's safe." His eyes bulged. "Charles, call your machine off."

Now Charles leaned in, and when he spoke, his voice was low and menacing. "As you can see, Orius, he's not mine. And he's not yours either."

Isaak started squeezing again. "Where is Marta?"

Orius's eyes rolled back into his head, and his body twitched and jerked violently.

"I will bring her to you," one of the other officers said, his face pale with fear.

Isaak regarded the man for a moment, then nodded. "If you do not, I will kill your general." Eyes widening, the man fled on foot. Then, Isaak relaxed his grip on Orius and lowered him to the ground. "I do not wish to harm anyone," the metal man said. "But you should know that I am capable of doing so if it is required of me."

Orius fell to his knees, gasping and coughing, as the metal man released him. Winters watched him, and when he looked up to meet her eyes, she saw wrath in the general's single eye and knew in that moment that harm was something he also was quite capable of.

She shuddered at the hatred, so contrary to the dream they'd all just shared. Then Winters turned away from that to wait quietly with Isaak and the others for Marta's return and wondered exactly what harm Orius had arranged for her and for her people in the midst of making his war.

Marta

Marta paced the room that had become her cell and cursed herself for her lack of resistance when they came for her.

She'd heeded Charles, gathering and stockpiling what she could and staying ready with an eye on the room where they kept Isaak. But she hadn't expected Orius and his guards to pay her any heed after days and days of ignoring her. When they took her, it was quick and painless—for her, at least. She was pretty certain her feet and fists had made it slightly less painless for her captors.

If I'd had a scout knife they'd have never had me. Of course, she knew it was the bravado built over time that made her more courageous in hindsight. When their hands had fallen on her and they'd dragged her to her feet, she'd been terrified.

And not long thereafter, she'd fallen into the dream.

Marta had no frame of reference for it. Tens of thousands—maybe hundreds of thousands—of people gathered on a plain surrounding a massive white tree. A voice she recognized as Winters calling her people home to the moon. And a metal figure standing beside the young Marsh Queen that she recognized very well. She'd even called out to him, but the roaring wind had drowned out her voice, and as that wind blew over her, it had reduced her urgency to a sense of hope that made no sense given her present predicament. It was as if nothing else mattered.

When the seeds sprang to life at her feet and she awakened, Marta leaped up as if nothing happened at all and went back to her pacing.

She heard sharp voices on the other side of the door and moved to the rear wall. The door opened slowly, and a guard looked in.

An officer of some kind stood beside him, his face flushed and wet with sweat. "Bring her."

"We will escort her to Brother Isaak," another voice said from beyond the room.

Now, the officer paled, and Marta soon saw why. Three mechoservitors—similar but different from Isaak—stood in the shadows, their eyes an amber glow in the dim light. They wore robes and carried packs but were unarmed. Still, they loomed over the humans, and the officer and guards fell back before them. One of the metal men stepped forward.

"I am Enoch," he said.

She stared, unsure what to do. Finally, she offered a half-hearted curtsy. "I am Marta."

Enoch turned to the guard. "Where are Lady Marta's belongings?"

The guard moved away quickly, returning with her pack and handing it to a mechoservitor who reached for it. The metal man inclined his head to the soldier and then turned to her. "May I carry you, Lady Marta?"

She nodded and closed her eyes as the metal hands reached out and lifted her and held her close. She could hear the whispering of gears and something that ticked and clacked beneath the hard, warm chest.

Enoch took in the officer and his guards once more, his eye shutters opening and closing as steam released from the exhaust grate in his back, whistling against the leather pack that partially blocked it. "It would not be prudent to follow us," he told them.

Then, they ran.

She'd run with Isaak, but it hadn't prepared her for this later generation. Enoch was not as fast; Isaak was faster. And he was not as fleet of foot, his balance more of an effort. Still, he was effective. He carried her through a series of tunnels that took them up and away from the massive cavern that had once held the Androfrancine camp, the other two metal men ahead of them and running point.

Marta wasn't sure how long they ran—twenty minutes, perhaps—before they burst into another massive chamber. This one stretched out farther than the light would reveal, and it held a lake of silver. A barge was pulled up on the shore, a series of ropes and pulleys running from the wall out to an island of black stone. And near the point where they entered, she saw Isaak and the others standing over a handful of Androfrancines, including the one-eyed general, Orius.

"Isaak!" Marta pushed against Enoch, and the metal man stopped and stood her upon her feet. She threw herself at her friend, overcome suddenly with the urge to cry.

"Hello, little human," Isaak said, his metal arms rising up to embrace her, pulling her in close to him. "Have you been harmed?"

She shook her head. "Have you?"

Isaak stared at Orius. "No. I have not."

Marta blushed when she realized the others were watching her. It was in that moment that she took notice of Winters and Charles. Near them stood the ancient man Tertius and the gaunt man whose eyes looked older than his years—Hebda, she thought his name was. They were different from the other Androfrancines she'd encountered. Like Charles, they looked more the part of scholars than soldiers, and they stood apart from Orius and his guards.

Marta disentangled herself from the mechoservitor. "Are they letting us go now?"

Orius's single eye blazed at her.

Isaak said nothing.

Winters spoke up. "Yes," she said. "They are. Reluctantly."

Now Charles stepped forward. "You should leave," he told the general and his men. "Take your engineers with you. And do not pursue us."

Marta saw the anger rising from Orius. She could tell that he was a man unaccustomed to taking orders from others even as she could tell that Charles was uncomfortable giving those orders. Two of the Gray Guard reached down to help the general to his feet, and the old officer shook them off when he was standing. "You are a traitor to the light, Charles." Then he looked to the mechoservitors. "As are your playthings."

Charles snorted. "You lost the light long ago. And my so-called playthings have saved the best of Windwir." He paused and glanced at Isaak. "And they may save the light as well."

Now Orius laughed, and it was a bitter bark as he nodded toward the tall, silver mechoservitor. "They saved only a fraction of what *he* destroyed. Mark me, Charles. You will regret this day."

Marta looked from Orius to Isaak, something cold and dark suddenly coming to life in her belly. *What he destroyed?* Her inner eye flashed back to the image of him kneeling on the hill overlooking the Desolation of Windwir, and she remembered the overpowering sense of sorrow she'd sensed in him. She'd been told over the last few years that the Androfrancines had somehow brought back the very spell that had created the Churning Wastes, that it was their arrogance and unwillingness to leave the past in the past that had killed her mother. But she'd never really learned exactly how, just that the Entrolusians were somehow involved; Sethbert had been tried and executed for it. Now she thought perhaps she knew more of how Sethbert had brought down the city but didn't want to believe her friend was complicit.

Orius and the others left, and when they'd gone, she turned on Isaak. "What did you do?"

The mechoservitor looked at her and blinked. He turned away, and she sensed his shame even as it worked its way out into his body and his shoulders shook with his grief. When he looked back there were silver tears running down the metal man's cheeks. "I destroyed the city of Windwir, little human."

Marta's world fell away, and she felt her legs grow weak. The anger she'd kept buried since those earliest days when the city had fallen surged suddenly to the surface, and she launched herself at him, her hands balled into fists that bruised themselves on the metal of his torso as she struck him again and again. A guttural, raging cry filled the cavern—the sound of a wounded and cornered beast—and she knew it was her own voice that gave it. Wounded and cornered because despite this terrible revelation, she could not relinquish her love for the metal man.

Isaak remained still before her as she struck him, and the dull ache in her fists told her she should stop, but she couldn't. Large, rough hands settled onto her shoulders.

"Oh child," she heard Charles whisper, "it wasn't his fault. It was mine as much as anyone's. I should have never let them bring back the spell."

She turned on the old arch-engineer now. "And what of Orius? What was his part in it?"

Charles shrugged. "He is Gray Guard. He wanted to use the spell to protect the Named Lands." The old man regarded her for a moment. "Walk with me."

For the second time in a handful of minutes, she remembered the others who stood around her, and she blushed at what she'd let them see. She shot Isaak a glance that she knew carried the full duality of her love and hate for him and held her eyes upon him until he turned away, his metal head hung low. Then, she let the arch-engineer guide her away from the others and along the shore.

After they were out of earshot, Charles looked down at her and lowered his voice. "What I hate most," he said, "is how they used him."

She looked up at him and said nothing.

The Androfrancine sighed. "My apprentice—a gifted man, a devout man—betrayed me and all of the Named Lands. I was taken—drugged and hidden away aboard an Entrolusian merchant galley bound for the Delta. And Isaak was rescripted without his knowledge or his consent. He completed the last of the translation and cataloging of the spell, destroyed the original parchments, and went into the city's central square to sing the Seven Cacophonic Deaths."

The central square. It was near the library and across town from the market district where her mother had gone to sell their second summer harvest. "And he survived it?"

Charles turned, and she turned with him, following his eyes back to the others. "His kind was designed originally to bear the spell. Of course, he was different then. He was more like the others—the closest approximation we could achieve. I did not build him as he is now."

She furrowed her brow, trying to understand. She suspected it was beyond her grasp, but even she could see the vast difference between the tall, slender silver mechanical and the shorter, blockier versions that had carried her here. "What is he now?"

"Something older," Charles said. "Something not even I fully understand. But that is a recent development. When the Gypsy King found him, he was sobbing in a crater over what he'd done. Rudolfo says he immediately requested that he be held accountable for his crimes. Of course, ultimately it was Sethbert who was held accountable. He was the one who paid to make it happen. But even the overseer was just a puppet. We didn't know that until it was too late. And once the Androfrancines were eliminated, the way was paved for the Y'Zirites."

"And the Machtvolk?" she asked, remembering the sudden transformation of the north. "They are a part of this as well?"

The old man nodded. "Yes. The Machtvolk, the assassinations, the civil wars. They were part of a complex plot to soften us for invasion."

She looked at Isaak. "He hates what he did."

When Charles sighed, she heard the beginnings of a sob in it. "We all hate our part in it, Marta. And there were many of us who had parts."

A thought struck her. "How is the dream a part of this?"

Just mentioning the dream resurrected some bit of the hope and euphoria she'd experienced in the midst of it, and she knew it did the same for Charles, because his face softened. "I do not know, child." He nodded to Isaak and the others. "But they do. And I have to believe that whatever part it plays—the seeds, the return of Winters and her people to the moon and its temple—that part must be worth the price we've paid for it." He paused. "At least I hope it is. It is hard for me to fathom."

Marta nodded. It was hard for her to fathom as well. But she hoped the old man was right and that what was coming was worth its cost in blood and sorrow.

She watched Isaak and knew that as much as she hated what he had done, he must hate it more. And she found that alongside her rage, the love she held for him multiplied.

Love, Marta decided, made no sense at all. And yet she knew that because of it, there was nothing that would keep her from following her metal friend wherever he might go. And maybe, if she followed him long enough, her anger would quiet and only the love would remain.

Charles

The blood of the earth licked at the floor of the cave, and Charles watched it, mesmerized, as it advanced and then retreated over the stone surface. It was thick, moving like no liquid he'd ever seen. Certainly earlier generations within the Order had studied it, but the Articles of Kin-Clave forbid its use, and though the Androfrancines rarely followed the articles to the letter, they had largely done so when it came to this particularly dangerous substance. Still, it fascinated him. And his few talks with Isaak had him convinced that somehow, the blood of the earth had something to do with how his metal son was brought back, combined somehow with the Watcher.

Now, something about it soothed him as he sat and thought.

He heard movement behind him and looked up to see Tertius and Hebda standing over him. Near the entrance, Winters sat talking quietly with Marta. Isaak and the other mechanicals were loading the barge. They'd put the packs on first, then had moved along the edges of the cavern, pulling down the wire and bags of blast powder. Two of them stacked the explosives while the others rolled the wire.

The two men crouched beside him, and Charles brought his attention back to the moment at hand. "So what are you going to do now?"

Hebda shrugged. "We can't go back to Orius."

Tertius grunted his agreement. "The man's rage over Windwir and his need to avenge it has taken him far afield, I fear."

Yes. Charles saw that plainly. "And I think he'll have his vengeance. Once the water supply is poisoned, the Y'Zirites will have no advantage here but numbers. And even that will vanish without their spiritual and military leadership. Without their scouts."

He shifted and let his eyes move to Winters again. Tertius followed them and cleared his voice. "We need to get her and those of her people we can out of the Named Lands."

Charles nodded. "Yes," he said. "We do."

Hebda took a deep breath and then released it. "But how do we get them to the moon?"

Charles wondered that very thing. But they'd put Petronus and Neb on the moon. And seeing Petronus, though briefly, in the dream convinced him that anything could happen. The man had been just a few years older than Charles, and yet the man he'd seen being pursued when Winters intervened was at least forty years younger. He wished he could talk to his former Pope and hear about the moon and about what strange wonder had given Petronus back his youth. But then again, Charles had wished a lot of things.

His eyes went to Isaak again and he sighed. "I don't know how we get them to the moon, but I'm sure their dream will continue to lay a path." He met first Tertius's and then Hebda's eyes. "So will you go with her?"

There was no hesitation in Tertius's voice, and that didn't surprise Charles at all. The old scholar had long been fascinated with the Marshers and their mysticism. "Absolutely," he said. "How could I not?"

But Hebda *did* hesitate. "I don't know," he said. "Renard and I have talked about it. He wants to. But . . ." The man's face clouded with sorrow and guilt. "But I'm not sure Neb would appreciate my presence."

Charles's eyes went back to Isaak again. "We've both had interesting fatherhoods. I'm sure by now, the boy sees why you did what you did."

Hebda shrugged. "Regardless. For now, I'll at least see them safely off. What about you?"

The notion of the moon excited the scientist in him. To see a place no one had visited in thousands of years, to experience the wonders he was certain the Moon Wizard's Tower had to contain—these appealed to him. And he suspected that Isaak and the others would go as well, though some selfish part of him hoped they would stay and work the Forest Library.

Because at the end of it all, I've grown tired. He felt his age now with every step. His bones ached and his body was slowing down. If he was completely honest, what he wanted most now was to return to his workshop in the Ninefold Forest and live out his last handful of years tinkering and helping Rudolfo create something wonderful—something untainted by the Androfrancine's backward dream and open for the world to experience and learn from.

Finally, he answered Hebda. "I don't know what I'll do. But we can't stay here." Then, he climbed to his feet, and the others steadied him as he did. He walked slowly toward Winters, letting her and Marta see him approach, giving the young village girl time to wipe her eyes.

He regretted Orius's words and wished he could have kept Isaak's involvement in the destruction of Windwir from her. But when had hiding the truth ever gone well for anyone? Rarely, if ever. More commonly, truth eventually brought understanding and with it, healing.

Winters looked up at him. "Are we ready to go?"

He nodded. "We are. I'm certain Orius's men will be back. He can't afford to let the dreamstone fall into Y'Zirite hands, and their Blood Guard are quite effective at triangulating in the aether. He'll want to bury this cave."

Winters looked out over the silver lake and sighed. "It's an amazing thing to bury."

Charles thought about his old workshop in Windwir and about the items he'd seen dug up from there in the Watcher's cave. Like the plague spider eggs that ultimately led to the eradication of Pylos. "Some amazing things should be buried," he said.

Winters didn't answer. Instead, she stood, and Marta stood with her. "Then we should probably—"

Charles felt the wind before he understood it, and even as he opened his mouth, he heard a high-pitched whistle and realized it was one of the metal men sounding the alarm. But even as the mechoservitor warned the others, there was an explosion and it fell backward, smoke pouring from a fist-sized hole in its chest cavity.

Charles cried out and moved toward the fallen metal man only to find invisible hands falling upon him. "Arch-engineer Charles," a voice rasped, "the light requires your immediate surrender."

He struggled against the scout who held him and saw Winters and Marta each struggling as well. Another explosion echoed across the cavern, and one of the mechanicals—Enoch, he thought—twisted as the hand cannon's lead projectile took its metal arm off at the elbow.

"I will not surrender to you," Charles said, and as he did, he felt the sharp point of a knife pressing at his ribs. He kicked and felt the knife slide into him as something large and silver collided with his attacker, lifting the magicked Gray Guard up into the air. He saw the slightest shimmer on the air as the soldier was tossed against the cave's wall and fell with a thud onto the floor.

Charles reached for the wound only to discover the knife still lodged in his side, then felt the air going out of him as the pain flooded his body and dropped him to his knees.

Nearby, Winters lashed out with feet and fists, and he heard the solid thud of each blow that landed upon her invisible assailant. The pain was so intense now that his vision was graying around the edges, and he tried to scramble back and away to give Winters more room to fight.

She did not need it. Isaak spun, his hands moving in a blur as he grabbed a magicked arm and wrenched it, sending a knife Charles couldn't see clattering across the floor. He heard the cracking of bone and the muffled grunt of another Gray Guard tossed brutally against the stone wall.

Enoch, despite missing an arm, was now pulling magicked scouts away from Tertius and Hebda.

They're not going to let us go. Charles tried to shout and found himself short of breath. And when Marta ran to him and took his hand, he realized that it was tingling. When the pains in his chest started they were sharper and more intense than the knife in his side, and he groaned.

"He's been hurt," Marta shouted.

Isaak spun and approached even as another explosion set Charles's ears to ringing. Isaak rocked backward and then regained his footing, roaring with something Charles thought must be wrath. The metal man surged across the room to grab hold of another magicked scout, and this time, he did not toss him against the wall but instead, hurled him out and into the lake.

The silver moved around the form that landed in it, and half of a scream reverberated across the cavern until there was a flash of blue and green. Then, the blood of the earth rippled and gurgled before returning to its placid state.

Charles found himself once more mesmerized by it even as the world around him started fading.

"We need to leave now," Winters said.

Metal hands moved beneath him, gently lifting him as if he were a child, to place him on the barge. He was vaguely aware of the others joining him and of the metal men casting them off and taking up their wooden oars.

As Charles let the dark take him, he wondered where this silver sea would carry them and hoped there would be light for him in that place.

Chapter 26

Vlad Li Tam

Concealed by the staff and making no attempt to govern his tears, Vlad Li Tam moved through the empty streets of Ahm's Glory. Despite the clamor of soldiers at their bucket brigades and the ringing alarms, the only noise that filled his ears and broke open his heart was the memory of his forty-second daughter's wail of grief.

How many children have I broken? There was a time when he knew the number, just as he'd known the number of how many members of his family he'd sacrificed to bend the river in the direction required. But something had happened to him on Ria's island, beneath her knife, while most of House Li Tam was surgically removed as he watched. She'd called it kin-healing, and the experience had changed him profoundly. More than that, it had prepared him for what came next: The ghost in the water. Amal Y'Zir.

The sight of her and the sound of her song in his ears had changed him even further, introducing a kind of love to his inner landscape the likes of which he'd never known.

And somehow, that confluence of deep loss and deep love had brought him to a new place. He'd always grieved the loss of his children. He'd also always celebrated their sacrifices, and they had done the same, their last words celebrating a father who loved them so much that he would allow them to participate in the betterment of the world.

It was different now. *Because I feel shame now,* he realized.

And yet he'd known he had to do what he'd done. He had considered confiding in his daughter. Even there on the roof, after he'd done what he'd needed to do, he'd wanted to gather her into his arms and assure her that all was not what it seemed, that what he did was for their salvation. But he couldn't. He needed her to believe in order for her hosts to do the same. They were already suspicious—that she would arrive in Y'Zir at the same time as he had was already a coincidence that jeopardized her credibility with the Y'Zirites. If he'd brought her into his confidence, he would've needed to remove her along with the children, and that would have assured their disbelief. Because he knew she could never have fabricated the grief of that kind of loss.

They needed to believe that their Crimson Empress and Child of Promise were dead. And for that to happen, his daughter had to believe it, too.

But his guilt did not stop there. Because to engineer this latest misdirection, he'd needed children. When the Y'Zirites finally made their way into the charred ruins of the building, they had to find the remains of two small children, a boy and a girl, burnt beyond recognition. And his Knives had found those corpses for him in the makeshift morgues that his plague had created. There was a time when he certainly could've killed a child with his own hands to serve the greater purpose he believed in. And he knew there was no real distinction between what he did himself or had others do for him. Because he'd sent the plague, he knew beyond any doubt that he had murdered the two children that he'd later tossed without effort into the fire. Two children out of likely hundreds now and perhaps thousands before he finished. But he would not stop. He could not stop.

And so he sobbed as he made his way to the agreed-upon rendezvous.

Twice he paused, and magicked Blood Guard swept past him, and at least once he stopped to rest though he knew there would be no real respite until he reached someplace safe enough to lay aside the staff. He knew that once he did, the pain would be unbearable. And the bleeding would start again.

We all die for our sins. Vlad Li Tam knew that he was dying. The only thing he didn't know was exactly how long he had. But if he had his way, it would be after he'd finished his work here. Today, he'd taken the most important step. If the illusion held.

He pushed himself to take the last league quickly, and when he reached the docks he skirted them for the row of warehouses that stood above the canal. The sky moved toward gray now as morning approached, and Vlad moved to the warehouse where they'd hidden the wagon. Aedric and the others would've arrived at least an hour ahead of him, and with everything ready to go, he knew they could be outside of the city before the sun rose completely. They would slip out under the guise of refugees and make their way along the canal until Behemoth found them.

If all went according to plan, Behemoth would bring him the tool he needed to complete his work and then bear his grandchild and his betrothed to safety. He knew exactly which island to hide them on and hoped the kin-clave he had helped to forge there would make them welcome for a season, until there was a home that might be safe to return to in the Named Lands.

He eased the door open and slipped inside, surprised that they'd kept the large open area darkened. The silence that met his ears was his second clue that something was amiss.

Tapping the staff lightly on the floor, he summoned light and felt the world sway when he saw the wagon standing alone in the center of the empty warehouse.

He heard his gasp of surprise echoing through the open space and broke into a run. He reached the wagon and found it also empty. Their supplies, carefully gathered, were nowhere to be found, and there was no sign of his Knives, of Aedric, or of the children. The once-dusty floor had been recently swept, and he suspected that he could spend an entire day looking and find no evidence whatsoever of their presence here.

He climbed up into the wagon and searched more carefully, pausing when he reached the driver's bench. There, beneath a single white stone the size of a fig, was a small scrap of paper. He picked up the stone first and squinted at it. It had been worn smooth and was almost round. It was not a type of stone he'd seen before, and it certainly looked out of place here.

He slipped it into the pocket of his robe and picked up the scrap of paper. He recognized it instantly as one of the tracts he'd seen, taken by one of his Knives from one of the warehouses they'd burned. It was to his advantage that the Y'Zirites credited his own reign of terror in their city as a part of the same movement, but for Vlad, it was a happy coincidence. The idea that there might be an opposing faith that struggled in subversion in this place was not so out of reach for him, and he'd even found joy in fulfilling some of their prophecies.

But now, he found no joy. Instead he found anger, though he knew that there was the slightest moment of fear preceding the rage that fell upon him.

Someone had interfered in his work and divided his focus, and whoever it was knew well enough that even this event could not deter him from what he'd set out to accomplish. This net was in the water and nearly full; he could not leave off hauling it into his boat to cast another net.

Which meant he had until Behemoth arrived to find his missing grandson and the others. He suspected strongly that they lived; whoever had orchestrated this had been privy to his plans, and if they had meant the children harm, he would have found their bodies—and the bodies of his Knives—instead of an empty warehouse. It was the same intuition that told him those who'd written the tracts were the very same who'd taken the children, though he did not know why. And they'd been able to overpower his Knives, Aedric, and an angry mother who'd been separated from her daughter for far too long.

He even suspected it was likely that they were trying to assist him in his work, though he'd have preferred to have known about it. *We share an enemy and find odd friendship in the sharing.*

Vlad went to a corner and leaned the staff into it, feeling the spasms of pain rack his body as his hand left the warm metal surface of it. Then, he sat and braced himself for the headache and nosebleed that would inevitably find him.

As he sat, his mind took him back through recent events as he cataloged every face, every sideways glance, every overheard word as he spun the Rufello lock and looked for the ciphers that would open this newest mystery to him. He went back to his first entrance into the city, then to Y'Zir itself, and found nothing. Despite the pounding of his head and the blood that bubbled in his nose, Vlad managed to sleep, and in sleeping, he dreamed.

He saw the tree again, but the field of seedlings had grown up into a jungle, and the tree was now a tower, massive and white against an azure sky. He heard quiet voices from the canopy of trees, the whisper of lovers, and he turned his ear in that direction, reaching for the staff to aid his hearing.

"This dream is of our home," he heard a girl's voice whisper.

He took another step in the direction of the voices and stopped when he heard a commotion from behind him.

Spinning, he saw the kin-raven as it dropped from the pinnacle of the tower to land upon a large white stone that could've been the parent of the stone in his pocket.

"Endicott," the kin-raven croaked.

Neb

The tower he descended bore little resemblance to the one he'd climbed, and Neb found himself moving at a slower pace, his eyes and nose taking in the sights and smells of the temple as it emerged from its long slumber. The light was brighter, and it cast a warm glow over walls and floors that slowly came to life. He found trees bearing unfamiliar fruit and sampled them as he went, his mouth watering from the mix of tart and sweet that intersected with his palate and his growling stomach.

As he walked, Neb thought about the girl and wondered where she'd gone even as he marveled at the beast that had taken her. He knew it was no accident, and he suspected strongly that after calling it and being consumed by it, Amylé had then commanded it to bear her where she wished to go.

Along the way, he conversed in quiet tones with Petronus, describing what he saw and experienced, listening as the man told him the same. When they met in the middle, Neb gasped at what he saw.

The old pope was recognizable, to be sure, but only because Neb had grown up beneath the smile of the younger man's papal portrait in the Great Library of Windwir. Now, Petronus was even younger than that visage.

His hair was thick and brown; and he was less portly now, though stocky, with the muscular build of a man now just a decade Neb's senior in appearance. And as surprising as that was, the biggest surprise was the silver robes the man wore.

The sight of the man overpowered him, and Neb found tears filling his eyes. "I don't understand it," he said. "But it is good to see you." Then, he looked beyond the man. "Where is Aver-Tal-Ka?"

There was sadness in Petronus's eyes even as awe filled his voice. "He's dead." He held up his hands, and Neb saw him studying them. "What he did to me cost him his life, but he gladly gave himself to it."

He felt a stab of grief himself but pushed it aside. "But you were able to receive the dream."

At the mention of the dream, Petronus's face shifted from sorrow to something Neb had not seen in what felt like years. It was joy. Or hope. Or both. "It was . . ." Petronus couldn't find the words, and Neb watched him look for them. "It was like nothing I've ever seen. Rafe and the others experienced it, too. Even the mechoservitors."

Neb sighed. He'd come so far and yet missed so much of what he'd journeyed here to do. Regret and guilt pushed at his heart, and Petronus must have seen it. He settled his large hand onto Neb's shoulder, and their eyes met.

"You've had few choices in all of this, Nebios," Petronus said. "And yet you've risen admirably to everything you've faced. Do not for a moment see this as failure." He offered a gentle smile. "You trusted the dream to bring us here, and now, the temple is unsealed."

Neb nodded, but his words didn't lift the veil of his sadness. "Yes." He looked around, remembering the gloom and must and lifelessness he'd seen along the way. "It's nothing like it was before."

But what now? He lacked the staff necessary to command this place and had no sense of how to retrieve it. Or how to bring about whatever was needed to bring Winters and her people home.

They stood outside an ornate door that breathed, an aroma rising from it that called for his fingers to gently touch it. Even as Neb reached for it, he saw Petronus doing the same, and when their hands met the door's warm surface, it yielded to their touch and spread itself open. Beyond it, a large and high-ceilinged room stretched out before them.

White trees grew up within that room, limbs heavy with unlikely fruit—gems of various size and shape and color that cast rainbow light over the room. And at the center of the room, a ring of white stones that surrounded a smaller tree. A memory that he should not have tickled at the back of his mind, and Neb looked to Petronus as they both whispered the words that formed, unbidden, in their minds.

"The Library of Elder Days," they said in unison.

They moved into the library together, spreading out to cover more ground. The room was far larger than it should've been given the space it occupied in the tower, and already, a lush grass—punctuated here and there with flowers of a dozen colors and scents—grew up to meet their feet and ankles with soothing coolness.

As Neb passed beneath the trees, he felt the slightest tickling of their whispered voices in his ear, though he didn't understand what they said. There were too many of them. He paused beneath a tree bearing emerald-colored stones and touched one with its finger. The color rippled across it at his touch, and a voice became clear, dropping into his head like a stone in a pond.

Authorization for library access is denied. Please see the Firsthome Temple administrator to request library access.

He looked across to Petronus. "Did you hear that?"

The man shook his head, his face curious. Then, he stretched out a finger and touched one of the stones that dangled from a different tree. His eyes went wide. "Oh."

They met at the ring of stones and stepped into it to study the smaller tree that grew there. At first, Neb wasn't sure exactly what he saw hanging from it, but as he drew closer, he saw that most of the branches had been picked clean. He stretched out a finger to touch one of the dozen silver rings remaining upon the tree. This time, there was no voice and no call to visit the administrator.

"What do you think it is?" Petronus asked.

Neb looked over his shoulder, then back to the ring. "I don't know."

He took hold of it, and pulled and as he did, he heard a growl and stopped. A familiar tree shuddered nearby, thorns suddenly springing from its branches as its dark fruit turned on him like eyes. He released the ring and stepped back with his hands held high.

Petronus leaped back. "What in the hells is *that?*"

What had Aver-Tal Ka called it? "A Watching Tree. They are guardians of a sort," Neb said.

"Maybe we should leave," Petronus offered.

They backed out of the library and watched the door fold closed. Once they were alone in the wide hall, Neb released his held breath. "I wonder who the administrator is?"

Petronus smiled. "At this point, I suspect it's you. You heard the story, Neb. These are your people."

He shook his head. "You unsealed the temple. Maybe that makes you the administrator." He took in the younger pope again, noticing the thick brown hair on his arms and the ease of his stride. "They're your people, too."

A momentary cloud crossed Petronus's eyes. "Certainly, we're all descended from them. But I'm so many generations removed from it that the world your people made no longer recognizes me. It only serves me now because of what Aver-Tal-Ka did." He held his hands up again and studied them. "And this is temporary. When it plays out, I'll not be good for much administrating." His laugh was brief and bitter. "Not that I ever enjoyed that work especially."

The darkness was there again in his eyes, and with the bitterness of the laugh, Neb knew there was more Petronus wasn't telling. But then again, he also knew the old pope—no, not old—kept his own counsel and invited others into it in his own time. "I need the staff," he said.

Petronus clapped him on the back. "Yes. And I've no doubt you'll find it."

But how? The pools had been tampered with, and their ship had been destroyed. Neb hoped the mechoservitors that awaited below might have some idea. And if not them, perhaps they'd be able to somehow repair the ancient mechanical that had brought them here with its song and it would know. Or maybe he could find Amylé, wherever she'd fled, and convince her somehow to tell him.

Beyond those things, he did not know what else he could do.

Neb took a deep breath, held it, and released it. Then, once more, he resumed his descent.

Rudolfo

Rudolfo stood at the entrance of the amphitheater flanked with Yazmeera's guards. The general had traded her dress uniform for an ornate robe, and he recognized her rank sewn into the silver piping. He also recognized the silver knife she wore at her belt.

Rudolfo breathed and then jumped when he felt Ire Li Tam's hands straightening the white scarf that accented his own dark clothing. He'd reluctantly worn the uniform befitting his rank as chancellor, refusing the green turban that had appeared with it in his dressing room. He'd found himself more distracted in the days since he'd seen Jakob in his dreams, and yet he'd still managed to assist the cooks as they prepared for his Markday Feast. He'd selected four or five Named Lands dishes with all of the same care he'd put into his betrothal dinner for Jin Li Tam, knowing full well that if all went as it should, it would largely go uneaten.

Yazmeera leaned in to take in the uncrowded rows of benches. She sighed. "I'd hoped more would come."

Why would they? Kin-clave may have required their attendance, but if it was being disbanded anyway, there was little point attending. The minimum number of representatives were present, accounting for very few of the benches, and the rest were locals that had been invited. Rudolfo smiled and waved his hand in a flourish. "Those who need to be here are here," he said.

Yazmeera faced him, placing her hands on his shoulders and leaning back to take him in. "You look splendid, Lord Chancellor," she said. "How do you feel?"

Rudolfo swallowed the truth and let the lie out with ease. "I feel splendid," he said.

The truth would have been that he did not know how he felt exactly.

Seeing Jakob and experiencing the shared dream had reinforced his decision, and something in that dream had raised his hopes in ways that didn't feel commensurate to the times he now lived in. He suspected some kind of magick at work, and the Y'Zirites did as well. Since that day, they'd been flooded with kin-ravens bearing reports of the same thing both here in the Named Lands and from back in Y'Zir.

From what he could gather, everyone had experienced the same dream, and it was introducing an unexpected and unwelcome element to the Y'Zirites' plans. He'd sat in meetings with Yazmeera and her advisors—including the priestesses who oversaw the evangelists and schoolteachers—and listened carefully to their heated conversations on how to best explain this unexplainable event in a way that did not undermine their worldview or their work.

From what he saw, it could only help him with what lay ahead.

"It's time," Yazmeera said.

Rudolfo nodded. Then, he walked out into the amphitheater and braced himself for the chilly reception he expected.

His eyes wandered the seating and found Philemus first, acting now on his behalf as over-sheriff. The second captain sat with a half-squad of Gypsy Scouts, his face without expression even as his eyes met Rudolfo's. Near him, Esarov sat with a handful of Delta Scouts, and he recognized several others. Most, however, were unfamiliar to him, and he knew they were lower-ranking aides sent from houses that could not go so far as to ignore the call of kin-clave but also would not support it fully.

As he entered, the others followed him and took up seats nearby. Blood Guard stood at each of the entrances and took up positions at key points throughout the wide open space, one hand upon their knife hilts and the other upon the phials of blood magick on chains around their necks.

He walked to the podium and forced a smile. "I open this kin-clave in the cause of peace and under the providence of the forebears who established it."

Their reply was muted, lips moving but the words of response impossible to hear. As he looked out over the room, he saw mostly hard stares or averted eyes. Esarov inclined his head and offered a smile. Philemus continued to meet his eyes, and Rudolfo held the man's stare for a moment before continuing.

"We've been told our entire lives that change is the path life takes," Rudolfo said in a slow and measured voice, leaning on the podium. "And there can be no doubt now that our world has changed."

From there, he moved into his opening remarks and watched as his audience shifted uncomfortably on their benches. He kept his voice sober, and when he proposed the dissolution of kin-clave, he waited a full minute for someone among the houses represented to offer back the motion necessary to move them forward. When none did, he looked to Philemus and inclined his head slowly.

The kin-raven had been clear, but despite that, the second captain waited. Then, in a voice heavy with grief or maybe anger, the old Gypsy Scout stood and spoke. "Under protest," he said, "I call for the dissolution of kin-clave on behalf of the Ninefold Forest."

Rudolfo didn't need to wait for Esarov. The man stood quickly and sat quickly. "I concur on behalf of the United City-States of the Entrolusian Delta and call for the vote of those gathered under the providence of kin-clave."

They moved through the remainder of the Council quickly, Rudolfo briefly outlining the oath of fealty that they would soon take. None dared walk out, but he saw the desire to do so upon their faces, and he knew that Yazmeera and her people did as well, marking those they thought could later be problematic.

Rudolfo felt a light sweat gathering on his brow and tickling his armpits as the heat of the day grew. He'd bracketed his own feelings through most of the morning, setting aside his rage and playing the part with all of his heart. When it was finally time, he stepped aside from the podium.

"In deference to our new empress and as a show of good faith for our hopeful future under her care," Rudolfo said, "I have agreed to a demonstration of our commitment to the coming grace and peace of her reign. Reverend General Yazmeera of the Imperial First Legion will explain."

This was Yazmeera's cue, and she stepped out onto the platform now, her smile beneficent in the late-morning sun. She turned to Rudolfo and inclined her head. "Thank you, Lord Chancellor."

Rudolfo returned the gesture and watched the faces around the amphitheater as she began explaining the origin of the mark. There were few gasps, and he suspected it was because few were surprised. His forefathers had maintained Tormentor's Row for millennia in their distant corner of the Named Lands, its Physicians of Penitent Torture known well for their dark work.

The truth was, Rudolfo realized, that his people had never been fully trusted. They'd not even been invited to the first Council of Kin-Clave formed by the Androfrancine settlers.

Blood Guard carried out the table now and set it up even as Yazmeera continued her discourse. At its conclusion, she turned to Rudolfo, and her smile became even sweeter. "Are you ready, Lord Chancellor?"

Rudolfo nodded. "I am." Then, he disrobed completely, folding each garment and laying it into waiting hands. When he stood naked before them all, he saw the discomfort rising on their faces. He swallowed against the shame that threatened and felt a sudden stab of rage for his father.

I named my son for you, he thought, *and would change that now if I could because of the shame you've brought upon us.* It was the worst insult he could imagine for the man, and even that was not strong enough. But even this anger was set aside, tucked away to give him strength later. Instead, he thought about the chilled peach wine.

And when they tied him to the table and tilted it up for the audience to see, he turned his thoughts to the little boy he'd seen so recently in the dream. The memory of him and of those falling seeds soothed and settled him.

Yazmeera drew her knife and held it aloft, offering a prayer that she followed with a hymn sung only by those who knew it—her own people—as the others watched in slack-mouthed horror. As they sang, she stepped to Rudolfo and laid the knife to his chest. She lowered her voice and let the others carry the song as she leaned in. "It is not considered unseemly to scream," she said. "Most do."

He nodded but said nothing.

Their song of praise was a requiem to him now, a dirge to the ending of one life and the beginning of another. But even so, he knew that beyond this moment and this ending, there would be a beginning. Dreams would rise. Seeds would fall. And he would take action to at least spare his son what now happened to him.

His eyes met Philemus's again as the knife cut into him with slow and precise skill. He was surprised to see tears there now and finally noticed the frantically moving hands. *What madness is this?* his second captain asked.

But even as her knife cut the mark of Y'Zir over his heart, Rudolfo knew that he was saner now than he'd felt in a long time. And that this requiem would be recompensed a hundredfold soon enough.

Chapter 27

Jin Li Tam

Jin Li Tam swam in deep places amid the flickering blue-green lights, disoriented and straining to reach a place of clarity. But her mind would not clear; the ocean she swam had tides and undercurrents that pulled her farther beneath the surface, farther out from shore.

Give yourself to it, Great Mother.

She did not recognize the voice and had no assurance that it truly was a voice and not some fragment of dream. But still, she resisted, forcing arms and legs she didn't have to swim against the forces that tugged at her.

What happened? Something terrible, but whatever it was, it lived far beyond her, taunting her from the shore. Daring her to remember.

Even as she broke the surface, Jin became aware of light behind her eyes and of the hand that clutched hers tightly and the voice that whispered gently.

"Can you hear me?"

She knew the voice, and she willed her lips to answer Lynnae's question, but the only reply she could make was a soft croak of acknowledgment. Still, she felt the woman squeezing her hand.

Jin opened her eyes and lay still. She could feel the bed now, though it was unfamiliar to her. And from the corner of her eye, she saw Lynnae's face, brow furrowed with grief and care, looking down on her with tear-filled eyes.

What happened? She knew something was wrong, horrifically wrong. As if something were missing and the crater where it had been was so vast that she could see no end of it.

"Jakob," she whispered.

Lynnae's face collapsed in grief as the woman's control gave out. The tears flowed freely now, and as they did, Jin felt a panic rise up within her.

Another nearby voice spoke up. "Perhaps we need to sedate her again."

It took her a moment to place it. *Sister Elsbet.* She licked her lips. "No sedation," she said.

And then the memory that eluded her made its ambush, and the crushing weight of that mountain of grief fell upon her. She closed her eyes and felt her own tears. She struggled to sit up with Lynnae's help, and at the woman's touch, everything within her crumbled, and she clutched at the woman with the sudden need of someone drowning. Lynnae's arms were strong as she gathered Jin up; and as Jin was pulled in and held, she gave herself to sobs she couldn't contain.

I've lost everything.

The mantra played its loop as the memories of that night returned through the haze of kallacaine. She felt another hand upon her now, strongly gripping her shoulder, and she forced her eyes open to see Sister Elsbet also weeping as she stood over her. She was vaguely aware of others in the room now, too, and heard their sobs mingling with her own. The sound of it made her shoulders heave with even more force as the sobbing built in pitch. She felt it slipping beyond her control, and she felt a wail rising within her. The wail built into a shriek, and before she knew what was happening, Elsbet's other hand quickly slipped a dropper of bittersweet kallacaine into her mouth.

"I'm sorry, Great Mother," the older woman whispered. "I am so, so sorry."

Jin felt the kalla taking hold instantly, her body flooding with warmth even as her shriek faltered. She tried to make her tongue work to protest, but it already felt as if it filled her mouth. Her eyes, burning from her tears, became heavy, and her body relaxed as sleep took her again.

When she awoke again, she felt a warm body beside her, and her thought was that it was Jakob before her muddled brain comprehended that this form that held her close was far too big to be her son. No, it was Lynnae, and the woman had fallen asleep holding Jin close.

The truth of it all reasserted itself. *I've lost everything.*

The tears started again, and as they did, images flashed across her inner eye. Those early days of learning she was with child, the expression on Rudolfo's face when she'd told him his soldiers had swords after all. The terror and exhilaration of watching her body change, and then that day Jakob finally arrived. He'd come into the midst of pandemonium and catastrophe, born on the heels of the world changing in ways no one had foreseen.

Born as a part of that manipulated change.

She felt Lynnae stirring against her and felt those comforting hands upon her. "I know," the woman whispered. Then, she repeated it. "I know."

Jin remembered the circumstances of Lynnae's arrival in their household, fresh on the heels of Lynnae's own child's death. Her son had died of the moonshadow pox not long after birth, and because she still had milk, she'd shared the nursing with Jakob when the powders he'd needed to keep him alive—ingested through the milk—had been too much for one woman to bear.

Somehow, the memory of the young, lost woman settled her, and Jin found some semblance of control. She pushed against Lynnae and then forced herself up in the bed, dizzy suddenly from the effort.

More images of her son washed over her, accompanied by other senses. The smoothness of his skin. The smell of his dark, curly hair. The sound of his laughter.

Things I'll never experience again. The sobs were back, and this time, she turned inward to face them and force them to submit to her. She focused on her breathing and lost track of the minutes before she realized she was staring at nothing.

Lynnae sat up beside her in the bed. "I'm so sorry."

She took another deep breath. "Does Rudolfo know?"

Lynnae shook her head. "No. They're trying to keep it quiet, though they're losing control of that silence. The kin-ravens have been grounded and Ahm's Glory is closed, but the word's out already here and the people are panicking. The city is in collapse."

The next question fell from Jin's lips, and she heard the poisonous rage in the calmness of her voice. "And what of my father?"

"They're turning the city inside out, but they haven't found him yet."

Jin blinked, surprised suddenly at the focus she found in this place. "Have they found . . ." She couldn't finish the question.

Lynnae nodded slowly, and her voice was somber. "They have," she said. "They found them yesterday."

Yesterday. She looked over at the woman. "How long have I been sedated?"

"Off and on for three days," Lynnae answered. "You were . . . out of control. You put three soldiers and a Blood Scout in the infirmary when they approached you on the roof. I think you broke the imperial physician's nose, too."

Jin nodded, the words sliding over her as her mind continued finding a focal point to center her. "I need to see him."

"The physician?"

She shook her head. "No. I need to see Jakob."

Lynnae's hand found her shoulder and squeezed it. Her voice was husky with her own tears. "Morning will be here soon," she said. "We can sort that out then."

Jin nodded. "Good." Then, she repeated herself. "I need to see him."

She sat silent for a moment and tried to stay within the inhales and exhales of her breath. But it wasn't helping. She felt hollowness spreading within her and found her eyes unfocusing again. Finally, she reached over to touch Lynnae's leg. "I think I need to be alone now."

Lynnae inclined her head. "Absolutely."

Jin waited until the woman had left the room before she got out of the bed. She started pacing, moving back and forth across the floor of the unfamiliar room with deliberate strides.

There was only one place of calm in this for her, and she gave herself to it.

Father.

He was the one who'd orchestrated her marriage to Rudolfo and had commanded her to bear the Gypsy King a son. And she'd followed the orders given to her just as any child—son or daughter—would do for the Lord of House Li Tam. They'd known from childhood that their house's work in the Named Lands was vital and that their father's honor was to use his children as tools and weapons to shape the world.

But as she'd grown to love Rudolfo, she'd found herself more and more at odds with her father, and by the time she became pregnant, she knew that what she did was for herself and for her beloved. Seeing what her father had done to the man she loved—then multiplying that against the untold numbers of others her house had sacrificed for her father's plans—had made her transition into the Ninefold Forest the rejection of one family for another.

I've lost everything.

No, she realized. *It's been taken from me.*

She'd come to this place with murder in her heart, sent by her grandfather to assassinate the Crimson Empress. And when she'd learned that the empress was a girl the same age as Jakob, she'd known she could never do such a thing. It staggered her that her grandfather could even conceive of such a thing, but she also remembered a time when she could have followed those orders without regret or remorse.

Because I could never harm a child now that I've had one.

She felt that focus tightening, and as it did, she felt her grief twisting into something else. The idea that her own father could—that he'd ordered dozens of her brothers and sisters to their deaths, murdered or humiliated thousands of innocents, and given no thought or regard to anything beyond his family's plans—pointed to a clear difference between her and the man who'd fathered her. Something that set her apart from him and from his father before him.

And the last of the fog fell away as Jin Li Tam realized that because of what he had done, she would now do what should have been done long ago.

She could not kill a child. But Jin Li Tam knew that she *could* kill her father, and in knowing, the forty-second daughter of Vlad Li Tam found the truest clarity of purpose she'd ever known.

Petronus

The night was gray with the light of Lasthome when Petronus went out into it from their makeshift camp just inside the temple. The wide doors murmured open at his touch and then closed behind him. The air was warm on his naked skin, and for the thousandth time, he looked down at himself to take in his well-toned body.

He gave a soft chuckle. Even when he'd been the age his body now appeared to be, he'd never been particularly fit. Certainly as a child, working the nets with his father, he'd been in shape. But once he'd followed the call to join the Order, he'd traded a life of working with his hands for a life spent behind a desk in the midst of a world of books.

And when he'd been that age, he'd not really considered the other uses of his body. But now, having left his seventies for something akin to thirty, he was suddenly aware of his entire body coming to life. He'd taken his vows of celibacy seriously, for the most part—he'd allowed himself a few indiscretions when he was younger—and for the longest time, his libido had been checked and supplanted by focus on his work with the Order. And then it had become a comfortable habit after he'd faked his death and gone into hiding.

But now, he found himself waking up with a level of arousal that made him uncomfortable both emotionally and physically. He gave himself a final glance, chuckled at his discomfort, and then stretched out a hand on the morning air. "Clothe me," he said.

The mist wrapped him, and he felt it clinging to his flesh as his silver robe took shape. Then, he set out along the canal at a leisurely pace.

He'd finally grown accustomed to the heightened senses he now commanded. He could hear the lunar wildlife stirring as the jungle prepared for morning, and his nose was full of the scent of flowers and fruits still foreign to him. And some of the fruits made his mouth water—evidence as far as he was concerned that those fruits were likely intended for eating.

All of this was made for us. The story of the People had kept his mind full these past several days. The idea that his ancestors had that kind of power baffled him. They had made worlds with everything their children might need built into them, including and especially the blood of the earth he now clothed himself in.

He'd read the best Androfrancine thought on their origins, including the scraps of apocryphal material about the Younger and Elder Gods, but nothing in the Great Library of Windwir had prepared him for this.

He suspected that once the library was open to them, he could spend decades in it and still have only learned a small percentage of what it held.

But I do not have decades.

He wasn't sure how much time he had. Right now, he felt fine. He'd had a few headaches and nosebleeds here and there, but they left as quickly as they arrived. And he'd not yet told Neb and the others what was surely coming at some point in the near future. He didn't want to believe it himself.

Of course, he'd died before. But this time, Petronus knew he wasn't coming back. And though he told himself he was ready, that he'd lived more life than many, he knew he wasn't ready at all.

Life asserts itself where it will. It was something P'Andro Whym had said in his Eighth Precept. And in Petronus's case, his desire for more life—especially with this new body and in this new place—was strong.

He heard a noise behind him and looked over his shoulder to see Neb moving in his direction. The young man had changed so much in the time he'd known him. He walked with more confidence now, his posture upright and his head moving slightly to the left and right, tracking the sounds and the smells around him. His hair was fully grown in now, and his face had lost the softness of boyhood in favor of the sharper angles of adulthood.

"Hail, Petronus," he called out as he approached.

Petronus smiled. "Hail, Nebios. Couldn't sleep?"

Neb shook his head. "No. And I like the early morning."

Petronus nodded. "I do, too. Always have. There's something peaceful about it."

He started walking again, and Neb fell in alongside him. The sky moved toward pink, and the first of the morning chatterers started up in the jungle. As far as he could tell, the entire lunar climate was tropical in nature, and he suspected it was engineered that way. It was something else to check the library for once they could.

Petronus chuckled at the thought. When he realized Neb was waiting for an explanation, he stopped walking. "I've spent most of my life growing old in a library," he said. He held up his hands before Neb. "Now, I'm young again and walking on the moon, and all I can think about is getting back into that library to learn more about this place."

Now Neb chuckled, too. "I feel the same way. But since we can't, there's only one alternative."

Petronus waited for him to finish, and when he didn't, he raised a single eyebrow. "And what alternative is that?"

Neb started walking briskly. "To experience it," he said. And as he said it, he started running, building speed quickly so that when he shouted next, his voice already seemed far away. "Come on, old man."

Petronus lurched into an easy run and caught up to Neb with ease. It felt good to stretch his legs without being chased by something, and he found himself smiling. "Try to keep up," he shouted as he passed the boy.

They ran for hours, until the sun was up and Lasthome tucked away, darting away from the canal to follow trails deep into the jungle that had once been roads, past hills that had once been buildings. They ran, their laughter running ahead of them to scatter birds and send monkeys scrambling into trees. When they stumbled upon a pool, they stopped and swam, then stuffed themselves on the sweet-tart fruit that grew in abundance around it. After, they stretched out in the sun to dry.

I am at peace. Petronus couldn't remember feeling like this in a long time. Maybe it was that last night of limericks in Caldus Bay, the night before the pillar of smoke sent him to see what had happened to his city. He looked over to Neb and saw the brooding look upon his face. *But he is not.* "What are you thinking about?"

Neb looked to him, then looked away. "I don't know what to do next."

Petronus sighed. "I've certainly had a lot of those days myself." He met the boy's eyes. "But you will know. And when you don't, things still have a way of turning out if you just keep your eyes and ears open for the opportunities around you."

Neb nodded. "I know."

Petronus suspected that he did indeed. He'd carried a lot, that one. And he'd seen too much for his years. Suddenly, he felt the need to say something he'd never said before, and the suddenness of his need surprised him nearly as much as the lump that he found growing in his throat. "I never had a son," he said, "but if I had I would've wished him to become a man like you, Nebios. You'd have been a fine Pope someday yourself."

Neb smiled. "You excommunicated me so that I couldn't."

Petronus chuckled even though the memory of it stung. "I did, but not because I didn't think you'd be a fine Pope. I didn't want you to kill Sethbert and carry that scar upon you."

Neb shrugged. "I thought he'd killed my father. In the end, he hadn't. And the man I thought was my father wasn't." Then, he looked at Petronus, and Petronus saw the young man's tears now, too. "But I suppose if I could've picked a father for myself you would have been the man I would have chosen."

They were silent after that for a while, and when they were dry, they climbed to their feet. Petronus stood still in that place, savoring that moment and savoring the words that they had shared with one another on the moon, by a pool, in a meadow beneath the sun. He knew he did not have many days left, but Petronus hoped that more of them would be like this one.

He watched Neb leap into a run and listened to the boy's wild laughter as Neb vanished into the jungle.

He tried on the words quietly. "My son."

Petronus smiled at the sound of it and then let his own laughter and feet carry him forward at breakneck pace as he ran the jungles of the moon.

Charles

It was winter when he faded in and out of awareness—cold and unforgiving—and Charles felt himself buffeted and shaken by a metal wind that whispered when it should have shouted.

What is happening to me?

He forced his eyes open and saw the dimly lit ceiling of the Beneath Places sliding past overhead. It took a moment for him to realize he was being carried, and that information struggled to connect with his most recent memory. They'd been on the barge and had been rowing for what seemed forever. When had they reached shore? He had no recollection of it.

But what did he recollect?

He remembered the knife. And he remembered its removal and how badly it had hurt. He remembered feeling as if his heart—his entire chest—were being crushed to the point he couldn't breathe, the pain shooting down his left arm.

Now, he felt nothing but cold.

His awareness continued to grow, and Charles realized it was Isaak who carried him. The metal man must have noticed him looking, because his red eyes turned downward to take him in. He stopped, and Charles heard others stopping as well. "He's awake," Isaak said.

He felt a hand on his shoulder and tried to crane his head to see who it was. But the voice gave her away. "How do you feel, Charles?"

Cold. He worked his mouth around the word but couldn't find his voice. He tried again. "I'm cold."

She moved, and now he could see her, could also see the sweat that beaded on her forehead. He could also see the look of fear upon her face. "Are you thirsty?"

He realized he was and nodded. She opened a canteen and held it to his mouth. He couldn't taste the water, but he felt it in his mouth and as it trickled down his throat. "Where are we?"

"Somewhere beneath the Entrolusian Delta," Winters said, "if the maps are correct. Moving toward Caldus Bay."

He wanted to ask what was in Caldus Bay, but those few questions he'd asked left him exhausted. And he suspected that he wouldn't live to see Caldus Bay, regardless, though that knowledge felt strangely detached given its gravity. He closed his eyes and drifted off, not opening them again until he did so from a pile of blankets on the ground. The chattering of his teeth awakened him, and when he stirred he felt a form moving beside him as a hand squeezed his.

Charles squinted into the gloom. He felt more alert now, though he still had a sense of disconnect after falling asleep on a barge, waking up while carried and then waking up again in this new place. From what he could tell, it was an intersection. He could not see the mechoservitors, but he saw several blanket-covered forms scattered about, along with various piles of equipment.

"Do you want some water?" a voice whispered. He looked over and down to find Marta cuddled up against him, one hand holding his and the other holding a canteen.

He nodded, and she pressed it to his mouth. He swallowed. "Thank you."

She offered a weak smile. "How are you feeling?"

He suspected his own smile was grim. "Not well."

She squeezed his hand again, then pointed with the canteen to the tunnel ahead of them. "There is an access hatch up ahead and a physician in Caldus Bay. We'll be there in a few days."

Yes, he suspected there was. But he could tell from the look in her eyes that she didn't believe it would help. And she was right not to. He didn't have a few days.

And of course, the mechanicals have basic medico knowledge. "Isaak told you, then?"

Her lower lip quivered. "And Hebda. He's had medico training."

Charles coughed. "Where is Isaak now."

"He and the other mechanicals are . . . hunting."

Hunting. "What are they hunting?"

Marta's voice dropped even lower. "There are Y'Zirites and Gray Guard in the tunnels."

Her words impacted Charles like a fist, and he found himself suddenly trying to stand. He had no strength and sagged back into the blankets. "No," he said. "I can't let them—"

She squeezed his hand again. "It's okay, Charles. They're not *killing* them. They're just breaking their legs."

"Call them back and wake the others," he said. "I need to talk to them."

Charles drowsed while he waited, and when he heard them humming and clacking up the corridor, he let Winters and Marta sit him up.

Isaak limped to him and knelt, his eyes casting the gloom with the color of blood.

"How many have you found?" Charles asked.

"Six. They have been disabled and left with supplies. Two were Y'Zirite Blood Guard."

Charles sighed. "There will be more when they don't return."

"Yes," Isaak agreed.

Charles thought about the magicked scout Isaak had tossed into the blood of the earth. "I don't want you to kill them."

"I will do whatever I must," Isaak said. "But I don't want to kill them either."

Charles nodded. "Good. Then listen to me." He looked up. "All of you, listen."

Then, he quietly and simply laid out the facts and then his solution. There was argument from Marta, questions from Winters. Hebda and Tertius stood silently by. It wasn't until the others had packed and were ready that they each came by to crouch beside him.

Winters hugged him, and her tears were cold on his neck. "Thank you," she said.

"Take your people home," he said. Then he chuckled. "And keep your damned dreams on the moon."

She chuckled, too. "Do you need anything?"

He nodded. "Do you have any root?"

She dug in her pocket and pressed a black strip into his hand. He slipped it into his mouth and started chewing it. Her questioning look prompted an explanation. "It will keep me awake," he said. "Ideally until they're here. Or until I can't stay awake any longer."

She nodded. "I hope I see you in my dreams, Charles."

"I've liked the ones we've already shared," he replied.

He found himself tearing up when it was Marta's turn. He looked from her to where Isaak worked with the others, running wires and setting bags. "You really do love him, don't you?"

She nodded. "I kind of hate him too now, because of Windwir, but there's enough love to handle the hate."

"Take care of him for me," Charles said. "And for what it's worth, I think he loves you, too."

Marta blushed. Then she moved on.

Hebda and Tertius crouched together, and their exchange was brief and to the point. After they'd finished and gripped his hand, they moved off with the others in the direction of the access hatch.

Isaak and the mechoservitors finished setting the charges and brought him the metal detonation trigger that he himself had designed. He checked it by touch with his fingers, surprised at how fast the root was taking hold in him. Everything was brighter, and he felt strength moving through him. Of course, the ache in his chest worsened.

His metal children gathered around him, and he saw that Enoch's missing arm had been reattached, though it hung oddly now and would require more attention. "You will need to take care of each other now," he told them.

Isaak's shoulders began to shake as his eyes filled with silver tears. "One of us could stay back," he said.

Charles laughed. "I scripted you better than that, Isaak. There is no logic in robbing the world of something as amazing as one of you, with so much good that you can do. I've had a long life. And my outcome is likely the same no matter what I do. But your outcome, statistically and tactically speaking, is far superior if I take this action."

Isaak looked away. "Yes, Father."

"Go and find the staff. See Winters to the moon."

Isaak crouched down and pushed his cold metal mouth to Charles's forehead. The tears that struck the bald patch of Charles's head were the first warmth he'd felt in what seemed years of winter, and he reached up a hand to the side of Isaak's face. "You are my son, and I am pleased with you," he said. He looked up to the others. "All of you are."

Isaak inclined his head, and the others did the same. Then, they moved up the corridor to join the others.

Charles listened to them as they left and thought he heard the distant clang of the hatch closing behind them. And after they were gone, he settled into the vast silence of that remarkable underground world and let the hours move past him.

As he sat, he thought about his life—the things he'd longed for and found, the things he'd loved and lost. The people and places and promises he'd seen made and broken.

He'd lived his life in service to the light, and he had no regrets, but at the end of that life, he knew that what he'd learned most and best had come from a metal man he'd made who later made him. And what he'd learned in that making was that the light was far vaster than he'd ever realized before. Far beyond what the Androfrancines thought it might be.

He heard a noise now in the dark. Rhythmic, the sound of feet upon the ground muffled by magicks but noticeable because of the root. He held his breath and waited. He heard more feet and then quiet whispers as those footfalls stopped.

Charles smiled and shared the lesson of his life.

"We're all light," he said in a quiet voice.

And then he pulled the trigger and made it so.

Chapter
28

Winters

The ground rumbled and shook, and though she'd been expecting it for hours, Winters still staggered and then came to a full stop. The others around her did as well.

She'd hoped it would help, knowing he likely wouldn't have survived the rest of the journey. But it hadn't. Some part of her bargained in a different direction, despite the fact that the old arch-engineer had been perfectly clear about his wishes and perfectly logical in his presentation of the facts.

Life is more than facts. But she also knew that love made sacrifices, and he'd done what he'd done not just to hasten them on their way and cover their escape; he'd done it to prevent his children from having to kill—by doing the killing himself if it had gone the way he'd planned. And if not, at the very least he'd closed the way behind them to anyone who might've been tracking them in the Beneath Places.

And left at the time of his own choosing.

She looked to Isaak first where he'd stopped. His back was piled high with their packs and equipment—the three mechoservitors had divided everything between them, leaving the others bearing less. Still, even unencumbered, Winters felt their rapid pace away from the hatch deep in her legs and lower back. She wasn't sure how many leagues they'd covered, but they'd moved quickly over the last six hours.

No one spoke, and Winters scanned the group. Despite Hebda's and Tertius's years and experience, she'd fallen naturally into the role of leading them, and she knew this was a moment to show that leadership. "Charles has bought us some time, but the explosion is bound to attract attention. We need to keep moving."

As they set out again, she watched Marta from the corner of her eye. The girl had walked near Isaak this entire time, but now she slipped closer beside him and took his hand in hers. She heard the girl whisper something to the metal man and saw him incline his head.

Then, Winters moved on ahead to take up her place at the front beside Enoch.

Tertius fell in beside her. Hebda took up a place behind them. The old man's voice was low. "What will you do now?"

She wasn't certain, and the lack of knowing was a rock in her boot that constantly agitated. "I know it's time to gather everyone. But beyond that, I do not know." She paused, Orius's words coming back to her. She turned her head and gave Tertius a hard stare. "What is he doing with the water? What will it do to my people?"

The old man's face went pale. "I'm not certain this is the time to discuss the matter, Lady Winteria."

She felt a spark of anger. "Tertius, the time for secrets is past. It's been past for some time now. Tell me what you know. Tell me what Orius is doing to the water. Tell me what it will do to my people."

The old man sighed and shot a glance over his shoulder to Hebda before continuing. "Not just your people. Anyone in the Named Lands with blood magick exposure."

She wrinkled her brow as she thought about this. Surely many of her people had used blood magicks for various ceremonies and in some instances, for medicinal purposes. But she knew the circle was wider than that. She thought about the crowd of refugees she'd watched Rudolfo banish from his lands. "Including the Y'Zirites?"

He nodded. "They are Orius's intended target. But it is indiscriminate—it will affect anyone exposed to blood magick."

Now her face paled as another realization struck her. The memory of that day in the pavilion came back quickly as she saw Jin Li Tam on her knees, begging Ria for the life of her son after watching Petronus come back from the dead. "And Lord Jakob?"

"Yes," the man said.

Then, the truth of his words sunk even deeper, and it chilled the core of her. "And me as well."

Tertius said nothing, and she glanced at him again. He'd looked away, biting his lip, and the conflict written upon his face said more than his words could have.

She stopped walking and reached a hand to his shoulder, turning him toward her. "And me," she said again. "Right? I've used blood magicks."

There were secrets in his eyes again, and he looked away. When he spoke, his voice was low. "We have reason to believe that you may be immune to this particular pathogen." As he said it, she glanced at Hebda to see his face a gray mask of control.

"Why?"

But neither Androfrancine answered, and she suspected that short of Rudolfo's Physicians of Penitent Torture, they were not going to.

Winters drew in a long, slow breath. Then, she exhaled it. "I am disappointed in you, Tertius." She looked back at Hebda. "And you, Hebda. I suspect your own secrets have earned you Neb's hatred."

And cost hundreds of thousands of lives, she thought.

She gave Tertius a final, hard stare. She understood suddenly Rudolfo's rage at the hidden Y'Zirites in his forest and the betrayal that their secrecy constituted. Now she understood the man upon the hill far better, and her own anger was cold in her voice. "I will have the truth from you before this is done, Tertius, or you will be left behind." She looked at Hebda next. "Neb will make his own decisions regarding you. And I will support them."

Then she turned her back on them and started walking at a pace she knew they could not keep up with. Enoch kept pace with her, and for the longest time, she walked in silence. Finally, when the others were out of earshot, she lowered her voice.

"I do not know what to do next, Enoch," she said.

Enoch's bellows wheezed. "It is time to gather your people, Lady Winteria, and take them home."

Winters thought for a minute. "Not all of my people are within my reach."

"Maybe," Enoch said, "your people have always only been those within your reach. And maybe those beyond it were never really yours after all."

When the metal man said it, she felt a quickening within her that both calmed and excited her. *Yes.*

She regarded the damaged metal man, realizing suddenly how like Isaak he sounded. Their dream was changing them, just as her dream changed her. They were no longer merely mechanicals built by the man who'd so recently given his life for them. They were a people of their own, with thought and feeling and wisdom beyond their scripting.

Maybe those beyond my reach were never mine after all. Maybe my people really are only those within my reach. She looked at the small group she walked with now. And she remembered the dream and the multitudes that gathered around her as she declared her people's home once again open. So many influenced by her dream.

So many, she realized, longing for a home.

Then light fell upon Winteria bat Mardic in that place, and she knew with sudden certainty how she might increase that reach.

Home awaited; she would not keep it waiting for much longer.

Neb

The stars hung low overhead, throbbing in the night, and Nebios Whym lay beneath them at the top of the tower.

He'd spent the morning running with Petronus, finding a sense of abandon in his time with the former Pope. He suspected it was because the man made him feel less alone.

He'd always known he was different. He'd assumed it was because he was an Androfrancine orphan, but he'd no idea how different he really was until he'd met Winters and shared her dreams, then had met the Blood Guard in the Wastes whose hatred of him was clear in the poison of their tone. *Abomination.*

And when he'd seen the terror on Winters's face he knew of a certainty that he had nothing in common even with those he'd felt closest to. Meeting Amylé had changed that, but even that had somehow been twisted into something that left him feeling more lonely than he'd felt before knowing she existed.

Petronus helped. But something in what the man didn't say whispered to Neb that even this couldn't be counted on.

I am alone.

No, he realized. She was out there somewhere. Amylé had fled him, and he suspected the seaway she'd shown him had something to do with it. Rafe had sailed out for it yesterday with a skeleton crew. But that would take time. And as much as he hated being alone, he knew a higher purpose called to him.

I need to go back. I need the staff.

Neb sighed.

A warm breeze blew up and over the tower, carrying the scents up from the jungle to blend with the aroma of flowers and plants that now bloomed in the garden he lay in. He stretched, and as he did, something dark moved high across the sky. He squinted at it, and when the epiphany struck him, it was sudden and evidenced by the hair rising on his arms.

Neb stood and watched it as it flew and opened his mouth. How had it gone? He tried to make the sound from memory, his voice lower than the girl's. His first attempt sounded nothing like hers, but his second was close, and he watched the large object pause before resuming.

Neb increased the volume and poured himself into the call, feeling his throat strain against a noise that it wasn't designed to make easily. The high-pitched shriek rose up, and he felt something snap into place inside of him. It was as if his voice were a line and whatever soared above him were the striking fish. He felt its pull and felt the fullness of its might even as he watched it turn and bear down upon him.

Continuing the cry, Neb ran for the tower's edge. *Bear me,* he willed the beast that now plunged for him. He heard the roar of it upon the wind, louder even than the roar in his ears as he fell. His eardrums threatened to pop from the sound of it even as its metal arms encircled him and pulled him into the beast.

And suddenly, Neb was what bore him. He lost all sense of his body, his hands, his feet. He was massive now and yet lighter than air, his four wings buzzing like a hummingbird and his limbs retracting back into his long, sleek body. He turned his head and twisted his body, his wings shifting to hold him in place, and realized that he was still shrieking into the night, though now it went out for league upon league with a force stronger than any voice magick.

Neb tried to laugh but found he'd forgotten how. Instead, he shifted the shriek into a low howl and turned himself to the sea.

He pushed himself and felt the wind gathering around him as he surged out over the jungle. Two blinks and he was over the water now. Another, and the air cracked around him as he leaped forward.

Lasthome rose now, and by its gray light, he saw the massive white bones rising up from the sea. There were lights in the water around it, blue and green, and he knew without knowing that these were the d'jin he'd heard stories of all his life. Now, he saw them gathering around a series of large white pillars that rose up from the sea like the ribs of some long-dead beast. At the top where they met, a silver orb spun slowly, and he realized by the continents etched in the surface that it was an approximation of Lasthome itself.

Within those towering white bones, the water foamed and churned, and he saw the blue-green lights now as they moved in and out of it.

Neb lowered himself and slowed. By the time he reached it, he hung in place and squinted with much stronger eyes at the waters within the circle it made.

Holding his breath, he dove between the pillars and felt the change upon his silver skin and within his giant, flared nostrils. Even the light was different, and though he felt a growing fear, another emotion drove him forward.

The world changed around him.

The ocean was suddenly larger, the air cooler, and when he came out of the other side of the pillars he looked up to see a blue-green moon hung in the sky beyond his reach.

He turned to take in the pillars, and even they had changed. Instead of a silver replica of Lasthome at their crest, a similar replica—but of the moon—spun slowly there in its place.

I'm home.

This, he realized, was Amylé's seaway. And he knew now what it was their mythology had called this.

The Moon Wizard's Ladder.

These waters were calm and devoid of light, unlike the waters that surrounded it on the moon, and he wondered at that.

But Nebios Whym did not ponder it long. Instead, he set out north and built speed until the air cracked again around him. He flew until at first islands and then a longer horizon took shape before him, and when the Churning Wastes unfolded below him, bathed in the bloody light of sunrise, he flew low to that blasted surface and inhaled deeply the smell of ancient shattered rock. He pushed until the Keeper's Wall rose up, and he raised himself up and over it without effort to take in the spreading forests that marked the edge of the Named Lands.

He flew to the center of that hidden place following the most recent scent of desolation and stopped to hang above the wide and silent grave of Windwir, where his journey had started what seemed so long ago. He turned and looked north to the Marshlands, east to the Ninefold Forest. Then, he banked south and once more broke the sky open as he sped for the seaway that had brought him home.

No, not home. This had never been his home.

He would return to the Firsthome Temple—his truest home, he knew—and tell Petronus what he'd found. Then, Nebios Whym would return to Lasthome and take back what he needed to finish his work upon the moon.

Rudolfo

Rudolfo winced at the pleasure and pain of Ire Li Tam's hand upon his bare chest as she dabbed salve onto his wound. He'd not been surprised by the sharp ache of it, but the stirring of desire he felt from it was an ambush he'd been unprepared for.

He lay slouched in a soft armchair in the corner of his bedchamber, and she had taken up a position on a cushioned stool across from him, leaning forward in a way that made it difficult for him to not notice the curve of her own scarred breast. He'd grown used to her scars, finding a certain beauty in them, knowing she'd taken them for the sake of her own family just as he had done. It was a powerful liqueur, and he suspected his desire built not just from her constant companionship but also because he often felt a slight arousal at the prospect of well-conceived violence.

Her fingers were strong, and he gasped when one touched the raw wound. "I'm sorry," she said. "I know it hurts."

He closed his eyes and settled back into the chair. "How old were you when you took your first mark?"

She traced more of the ointment along the edge of the wound. "This mark is always the first mark. I was twelve and an acolyte among the Daughters of Ahm. My grandfather had arranged it in secret. He had an ally there, though I never knew her name."

Rudolfo nodded. He knew little of Ire's life before she pledged her blades to him, but he knew it had been difficult. And he knew that as much conviction and power as the Y'Zirites had, there were still dissenters within their ranks and those who felt there was a better path than the blood of martyrs and sacrifices.

He had hoped against hope that his father was one of those, but in the end, he suspected that the best he could hope for was a father who believed collaboration and cooperation were the only path to assure his sole surviving son a place in the new world being born. And that was not enough.

Ire patted his chest, her hand lingering, and Rudolfo released his held breath. He'd not been with a woman since the night before his family left for the Machtvolk Territories. It was his longest stretch since an early age, and for the longest while, it had been because he wished to tend the love he had for his wife like a garden. He'd never imagined it would be a long-term choice—monogamy was certainly not an expectation in kin-clave, particularly for a king. But his bride, certainly for good reason of her own, had betrayed his trust, had fled from him with his son, and in so doing had violated their partnership. She was still the fiercest and most formidable woman he'd ever known, and he suspected that love still grew there amid the weeds that choked it into something smaller and weaker than it had been. But until he fully comprehended and accepted her choices, there would be a gulf between them that limited his affection for her.

So certainly, he could do as he wished now in this place. But he would not. Instead, he would accept the truth of what actually aroused his passion and seek that particular consummation.

He caught himself in a moan that wasn't pain, and he gently took hold of Ire Li Tam's wrist. "Thank you," he said. "I think it's time to dress for dinner."

"Let me bandage you," she said, turning to the small table she'd pulled closer. She replaced the lid on the jar of ointment and then took up the white lengths of cotton fabric.

Rudolfo leaned forward and stretched his hands over his head as she wrapped his torso.

The day had gone about as he'd expected. Despite arrangements made, none of the emissaries of kin-clave had stayed. They'd shuffled forward without eye contact to sign the fealty compact, and they'd vanished as quickly as they could. Philemus had lingered, and Rudolfo knew the man had wanted to speak with him, but he'd not dared to slip away with all eyes upon him. Instead, he'd arranged for Ire to pass him a brief and uncoded note that dealt with more trivial matters and thanked the man for representing the Ninefold Forest on Rudolfo's behalf.

Yazmeera had been perplexed by their unwillingness to avail themselves of the planned festivities, and inwardly Rudolfo had laughed at the blindness her convictions engendered. Outwardly, he'd smiled and nodded. "They do not yet see clearly a future they can embrace," he had told her.

"And what of you?" she'd asked him.

His smile had widened. "Oh yes," he said as he touched the blood-stained robe he wore at the time. "I see a very clear future that I can embrace."

He'd spent the remainder of the day resting in his bedchambers.

Ire was nearly finished wrapping him when she stopped. She reached into her shirt and drew out a small pouch that he recognized. One of Renard's men had left the fresh scout powders in the passage that led to the hidden door that opened upon his garden. She pressed the pouch against his chest at the uppermost edge of his wound, and he felt the ache of it.

"I'm putting it here," she said, "where reaching for it won't arouse suspicion." She wrapped the bandage twice more over it, leaving the looped end of the drawstring hanging out like loose threads. "Can you reach it?"

He reached over with his right hand and slipped a pinky through the loop. Rudolfo tried it a second time and then nodded. "Yes."

"You'll have to be fast. But not too fast. If this goes as you say it will, there will be a few moments of uncertainty that we can take advantage of."

He looked at her and their eyes met. "Are you certain of this?"

She shrugged. "I've done what I came to do," she said. "I need no certainty." Then, she smiled. "But I would see you safely to the completion of what you've come to do if we can stay alive long enough."

Indeed. He wasn't certain exactly how he would find his way to Y'Zir, but once this night's work was done, he'd take stock of his resources and plan his next steps. Returning to the mainland was a simple-enough task—he could do that in a rowboat. And once there, he'd overtake Philemus and his small party of scouts and start scheming what must surely come next.

Rudolfo stood and paid no mind to the woman as he slipped from his robe and went to the clothes she'd laid out for him. These were his own clothes, brought by Philemus, and they were welcome in his sight. Silk pants of a dark green that matched his forests; a silk shirt the color of rich soil, set apart by a yellow scarf. The soft low boots, made for affairs of state that might involve outrunning angry husbands, were comfortable and reminded him of other, less violent conquests.

When he was finished, she slipped into her own chambers and emerged quickly in a fresh uniform. Her own blood magicks dangled now from a chain around her neck, and her scout and ceremonial knives hung at each hip, ready to be drawn.

Rudolfo inclined his head to the woman. "I am ready."

She returned the gesture, and together, they left his borrowed house for what he knew would be the last time and walked slowly through the afternoon light to where the others had gathered. He took his time, feeling the ache in his chest and the sunlight on the back of his neck. When he entered the house and climbed the stairs to the rooftop where they would dine, he heard the sound of the gathering guests above and smelled the food. The dishes he himself had overseen dominated the air, their spices setting them apart.

Rudolfo reached the top of the stairs and waited at the entrance, looking out over the crowded tables. The Y'Zirite officers had traded their uniforms for bright-colored clothing that would've blended into his own feasts in the Ninefold Forest. The only uniforms present were the Blood Guard that took up stations around the room. He took them all in and knew the woman beside him did the same.

A woman in a deep crimson dress that clung to her sparse curves noticed him and stood. He nearly did not recognize Yazmeera until her face broke into a smile and their eyes met. "Brothers and sisters," she said in a loud voice, "I give you the host of tonight's feast."

The men and women gathered were on their feet, their faces bright beneath the silk canopies that shaded them from the afternoon sun. They applauded him, and Rudolfo felt his arousal shift now into an excitement that buzzed in his ears.

I am drunk on this moment, he realized, and thought perhaps he'd not felt so alive in more years than he could count.

Yazmeera met him and guided him to the master table, gesturing to his seat. He went to it but remained standing. Then, at her nod, he sat and they commenced to eating.

As they ate, he made small talk with his neighbors, answering questions and accepting their congratulations with a smile so practiced that it could never seem false. He explained the dishes he'd provided and listened to the explanations around the others. And when they'd passed two hours with ease, he sat back. He'd kept his portions small but had shown his gusto with how many plates he emptied. And when it was finished and they neared the final course, he met Ire Li Tam's eyes. She moved casually to the door as Rudolfo stood.

"In my Forest," he said, "our feasts and our toasts are famed throughout the Named Lands, and everyone drinks." He looked to the Blood Guard at their stations, then back to Yazmeera with a raised eyebrow.

She smiled and inclined her head. "One glass could not hurt."

Ire slipped through the doorway unnoticed by all but Rudolfo.

He grinned. "Men know to hide their wives from these events; and women have been known to sneak from their bedchamber windows to attend them." The room roared its laughter. "I hope that soon, those feasts and toasts will be famed not just here but also abroad. One day soon—maybe even tomorrow—I'm convinced that they will say 'none feast, nor toast, nor woo as well as Rudolfo.'" The room laughed again, and he laughed with them. He inclined his head, and the servants began moving amid the tables with their carafes, the condensation beading around the chilled peach wine they contained. As they moved, he watched and waited until everyone upon the rooftop had been served. "We have a saying here that my people have earned: 'If one must drink, drink deep as a Gypsy.'"

The glasses were full now, and Rudolfo held his aloft. The others followed his lead. Then, he looked to Yazmeera and raised his eyebrows. "But what to drink to?"

Her eyes twinkled with merriment, and with the earlier Delta wines they'd consumed. "How about the future?" she suggested.

"An excellent toast," Rudolfo said. "To the future."

And with his son's face behind his eyes and the mark of Y'Zir upon his heart, Lord Rudolfo of the Ninefold Forest brought the glass of chilled peach wine to his lips to drink deeply.

Then watched his enemies do the same.

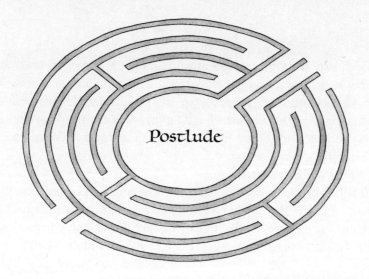

Postlude

The moon was high and hidden in clouds as they sat upon the rocky beach. They sat side by side upon a fallen log, and the girl held hands with her metal companion.

"What are we waiting for?" Marta asked.

Isaak glanced down at her. "I am waiting for transportation and for you to come to your senses and return home."

The others had left them, continuing on toward Caldus Bay. Isaak had led them here, his limp more pronounced since the earthquake that had marked his father's passing. They'd sat in silence but for the times he'd tried to convince her that she should leave.

"I could keep you from coming with me," he said finally.

She squeezed his hand, though she wasn't sure a mechoservitor could feel that kind of assurance and hoped her words would be enough. "You could try."

Isaak sighed and returned to silence.

Another hour passed.

"Is it a ship?" she asked.

Isaak shook his head. "No. Something . . . older."

Marta nodded.

It was past midnight when she heard it—a clanking and a chugging like the other metal men she'd met, only larger. And she heard water bubbling and splashing around it as it approached. When it rose up from the deep water just beyond the shore, she gasped.

Barely visible in the moonlight, she thought it must be a sea monster of some kind. But this one was metal, and as it pushed its way closer to them, the water of the bay receded behind it, displaced by its weight. Its mouth twisted open, and a dark red light spilled out from within it.

Isaak stood, and she stood too, taking up her pack. "What it is?"

"Behemoth," Isaak answered.

"Where will it take us?"

"It will take me to the staff of Y'Zir," he answered. "But first I must convince a friend to take a different path."

He's talking about me. And with the realization, she found herself blushing at the notion of being called his friend. "You're not going to convince me of anything."

Isaak laughed, and it was music by moonlight for the girl. "I know that already, little human."

"Good," she said.

"But you should still go home. Your father is worried for you. I saw him weeping in the dreamstone."

She noted the last words, marking them for later questions. Then, she focused on the others. "I will worry for you if I'm not with you," she said. "And that isn't my home anymore."

Isaak looked at her, his red eyes questioning.

"Silly metal man," Marta said. "Don't you understand that you are my home now?"

Isaak said nothing.

Then together they climbed into the mouth of the massive, waiting beast, and Marta smiled as the metal hand in hers squeezed back.

A Glossary of the Psalms of Isaak

A

Aensil's Hope: A Marsher village.

Aedric: First Captain of Rudolfo's Gypsy Scouts.

Androfrancine Order: Formed when the followers of the scientist-scholar P'Andro Whym and the behaviorist Franci B'Yot merged. The Androfrancines were the last bastion of order during the Age of Laughing Madness and led the settlement of the New World. The Androfrancines maintained strict control of the magicks and mechanicals they mined from the Old World.

Age of the Crimson Empress: The era of healing foretold in the gospels of Ahm Y'Zir.

Age of Laughing Madness: The 500 years that followed the destruction of the Old World by the Wizard King Xhum Y'Zir. This period was marked by chaos, anarchy, and an 80 percent insanity rate until the fourth generation of children. The madness was gradually eased among most peoples of the New World by the application of Franci behaviorism, though the Marshfolk are still considered effected by it.

Agnes: The Daughter of Ahm who Vlad meets in the Waste of Espira who was given charge of the Vessel of Grace.

Ahm: A land in the Old World ruled by the youngest of the Wizard King's seven sons. It was destroyed with the rest of the Old World by the Seven Cacophonic Deaths.

Ahm's Glory: Capital city of Y'Zir Empire. Home of the Crimson Empress and the Y'Zirite religion.

Ahm Y'Zir: The seventh son of Xhum Y'Zir, long thought dead. Spared by P'Andro Whym and smuggled out of the Homelands by the first

Rudolfo, he raised a hidden empire and created a faith based on his teachings. Alive but now mad, Ahm Y'Zir is sustained by blood magicks and preserved by technology scavenged from the Beneath Places.

Ahmir: Magister General of the Y'Zirite Empire.

Al Shadyk: The Y'Zirite name of Som Li Tam, leader of the Knives of Tam.

Alyn: A lieutenant among the gypsy scouts.

Amal Y'Zir: Younger daughter of Raj Y'Zir. Beloved of the Last Weeping Czar, Frederico. Her "fall" from the moon preceded the Moon Wizard's invasion. Later, she bargained alongside Frederico, with the last of the Elder Gods, that light once again be sown in the darkness.

Amara Y'Zir: The Crimson Empress and daughter of Ahm Y'Zir. Her union with the Child of Promise is prophesied to heal the world.

Amylé D'Anjite: The hidden daughter of the Younger God D'Anjite, a captain of the Younger God Whym's army during the Downunder War.

Anbar: A month in the Delta city-states calendar.

Andrys: A lieutenant of the gypsy scouts assigned to Winters after her exile from the Marshfolk and return to Rachyle's Rest.

Ansylus: The crown prince of Turam. Died during the Machtvolk attack on Rudolfo's Firstborn Feast.

Arch-scholar Ryhan: An arch-scholar of the expeditionary force during Petronus's papacy. Ryhan was involved in the discovery of the Seven Cacophonic Deaths.

Argum: A month in the Named Lands.

Aric: A Machtvolk priest.

Arys: One of Vlad Li Tam's aides.

Aubert: The Entrolusian overseer before Sethbert, and his father. A paranoid and problematic man, he was once removed from the papal palace for threatening the Pope's hospitality staff.

Aver-Tal-Ka: Last of the Keeper's Hatch, and last of the People's Builder Warriors. The Keepers were an arachnid human hybrid species genetically designed to help protect and care for the People on worlds made to serve them.

B

Balthus: A former gray guard, set to keep watch on Petronus at Caldus Bay after Sethbert's trial.

Bargaining Pools: The silver-colored blood of the earth in the Beneath Places. It is believed that blood and anguish could be used to purchase power and favor via these pools.

Barrens of Espira: The ruins of Espiria, where the Last Weeping Czar lived in exile before the Moon Wizard's invasion.

Baryk: Rae Li Tam's husband, a war priest of the southwest lands of the Emerald Coast.

Behemoth: The gigantic mechanical guardian of the Moon Wizard's Ladder. A segmented serpentine creature designed to carry passengers and cargo.

Ben Li Tam: Vlad Li Tam's father, who brought the worship of the Wizard Kings and their blood cult back to the Named Lands. When he realized he was wrong, he also initiated a plan to bring about an end to the Y'Zirite empire.

Beneath Places: The underworld of Marsher legend, where the dead wander in search of home. Based on the great labyrinth of the Younger Gods beneath the surface of Lasthome.

Benoit: Rudolfo's house physician, one of the Physicians of Penitent Torture.

Berende: One of the Entrolusian city-states.

Blood Guard of the Crimson Empress: The elite Y'Zirite imperial scouts, trained in hand-to-hand combat, blood magicks, and casting in the aether with dream-stones.

Blood Magick: Magick born in dark places, brokered and purchased with human blood mingled with the blood of the earth. Expressly forbidden in the Named Lands by the charter of the Androfrancine Order and the articles of kin-clave.

Blood Temples: The ancient houses of power that connected with the bargaining pools far beneath, allowing the Wizard Kings access for their magicks. In later years, the cuttings became more ritualistic in nature.

Book of Dreaming Kings: The cumulative history of the Marsh King's prophecies and revelation. It is over half a league long.

Brint: A city state guard at Windwir.

B'Rundic Script: A type of writing used during the Age of Wizard Kings.

C

Calaphia: One of the Entrolusian city-states.

Caldus Bay: The fishing town that Petronus grew up in and eventually returned to after faking his death.

"Canticle of the Fallen Moon in B Minor": Supposedly composed by Frederico, the last czar before the era of the Wizard Kings. In actuality, it is the Homeseeker's song, the People's Song of the Sowing, taught to Frederico by Ama Y'Zir.

Canimn powder: Used as a truth serum.

Carpathius: An artist of the first millennium who was commissioned to paint a series of paintings celebrating the settling of the New World and the great migration.

Carthos: One of the Delta city-states.

Cavern of Sleeping Kings: The catacombs where the Marsh Kings are buried.

Cervael: A minor noble of the Emerald Coast who conspired to destroy the second library along with Rudolfo and his family.

Chamber of the Book: The cavern housing the Book of Dreaming Kings.

Charles: Arch-engineer of Mechanical Science for the Androfrancine Order, and mechanical genius who was instrumental in recreating the mechoservitors from Ruffello's Notes and Specifications.

Charter of Unity: Founding document of the Entrolusian city-states.

Child of Promise: The Y'Zirite title for Jakob, the son of Rudolfo and Jin Li Tam.

Churning Waste: The ruined lands of what was once the Old World, before Xhum Y'Zir sent his death choirs singing destruction across the lands.

Compendium of Historical Remembrance: A companion to the Whymer Bible.

Congius: a unit of volume measurement that is approximately two liters.

Continuity Engine of the Elder Gods: A mechanism created by the People to keep their species alive. It shut down as a result of Y'Zir's uprising and the resulting Downunder War.

Cousin Wars: A series of wars amongst the People known as the Elder Gods after they left Firsthome.

Courtyard of Imminent Grace: In Ahm's Glory, the main courtyard of the city, at the east end is the great temple of the Daughters of Ahm, north is the military headquarters, west lay the imperial palace, and the south is open.

Crimson Empress: Amara Y'Zir, product of more than two millennia of careful breeding to produce the daughter of Ahm Y'Zir. Y'Zirite scripture prophesies that her union with the Child of Promise will heal the world.

Cyril: An arch-scholar of the Turam Francine House.

Czarist Lunar Expedition: A party sent to explore the moon, including the inventor Rufello and Lord Felip Carnelyin, that discovered the existence of Raj Y'Zir.

D

Daedrek: A Gypsy Scout.

Dagya: A friend of Marta's.

D'Anjite: A captain in the army of General Whym during the Downunder War. He left his sleeping daughter protected behind on the moon. After the death choirs of Xhum Y'Zir were sent into the world, the cataclysm supposedly awakened him and he placed a bridge across the gaping chasm so the fleeing survivors could arrive in the Named Lands.

D'Anjite's Bridge: The bridge placed by the Younger God when he awoke.

Danver: One of the Gray Guard in the Beneath Places.

Dayfather Ulno Shalon: A chieftain on one of the scattered isles that Vlad Li Tam initiated kin-clave with during his self-imposed exile.

Days of Gathering: The 500 years prior to the opening of the New World to the survivors of the Old by the Androfrancine Order.

Death Golems: One of the Seven Cacophonic Deaths.

Deepest of Deeps: Location of the last of the Elder Gods, place where Frederico and Amal bargained for the light to "once more be sown in the darkness that contains us all."

Detras: Arch-scholar of the Franci school.

Divided Isle: A divided island made up of independent counties, among the oldest non-Marsher, non-Gypsy settlements in the Named Lands.

Dragon's Spine: The wall of mountains that protects the Named Lands from the North.

Drea Merrique: Countess Merrique, the younger sister of Rafe Merrique and former ruler of Merrique County.

Dreaming Well: An access shaft to the Beneath Places hidden in the Churning Waste and containing Frederico's silver crescent.

Drusilla: A sister-mother of the Daughters of Ahm.

E

Earth Magick: Magicks created from what can be found on the surface of Lasthome. Defensive magicks (like scout powders) are only sanctioned during times of war, never to be used by the nobility in accordance with kin-clave.

Eastern Rises: The region of the Churning Waste where the last parchment containing the Seven Cacophonic Deaths was found.

Eastern Watch: The keep that protects the Whymer Way from the Wastes.

Edrys: A sergeant among Rudolfo's Gypsy Scouts. Present at the raid on the Papal Summer Palace. Later, first among the scouts at the Wall.

El Anyr: Emissary sent from Y'Zir to Rudolfo to bear the terms and conditions of the treaty between Y'Zir and Lord Jakob, Rudolfo's father.

Elsbet: Chief Mother of the order of the Daughters of Ahm Y'Zir. Assigned to Jin Li Tam as a tutor in language, history, custom, and eschatology; and spy and guide during her time in Y'Zir. A one-time lover of Ben Li Tam.

Eliz Xhum: Blood Regent of Y'Zir and entrusted with the throne of the Crimson Empress until her age of majority.

Emerald Coast: The region of the Named Lands known for a tropical climate, spicy foods, silks and independent city-states largely influenced by House Li Tam.

Enoch: A historian who wrote the largely apocryphal *History of the Wizard Kings* and also the designation of a first generation mechoservitor.

Erlund: Sethbert's nephew and the Entrolusian Overseer that took power from his uncle in a deal brokered by House Li Tam.

Errant Gospels: Gospels attributed to P'Andro or T'Erys Whym that contain information of an apocryphal or heretical nature.

Esarov the Democrat: An Androfrancine turned actor turned leader of the populist rebellion in the United City States of the Entrolusian Delta.

An Exegesis of Select Lunar Prophecies as Recorded in the Book of Dreaming Kings: Tertius's book from his time among the Marshers.

Exercise in Holiness: A papal decree closing Windwir to outsiders for a year.

Ezra: Keeper of the Book for Mardic and earlier his father's time. Herald of the Machtvolk Queen and prophet of the Crimson Empress.

F

Fargoer's Horn: The cape formed by the Keeper's Wall on the western side of the Churning Wastes that is occasionally sailed (illegally) by pirates.

Fargoer Station: The Androfrancine outpost at the Keeper's Gate.

Fargoer's Steel: The strange metal the Pope's ring is made of, also called Firstfall Steel.

Fargoer's Town: A waste village in the shadow of the Keepers Wall who had once traded with the Androfrancines.

Feris: A Gypsy Scout led by Jin Li Tam into the Machtvolk lands.

Final Dream: The pages cut from the Book of Dreaming Kings that together form the final Homeward Dream of the Marshfolk.

Firespice: A powerful liquor favored on the Emerald Coast.

First Assertion of T'Erys Whym: "Change can be forced by careful design and thoughtful effort."

First Gypsy War: Two hundred years after settlement, during which the Entrolusian city-states first united under an Overseer.

Firsthome: The world where the People first arose and set out for the stars.

Firsthome Temple: The name the Younger Gods attached to the structure on the moon that in current times is known as the Moon Wizard's Tower.

Firsthome Temple Sowing Song: "The Homeseeker's Song," also "Canticle of the Fallen Moon in the Key of B Minor," ascribed to Frederico, but far older.

First Precept of the Gospels of P'Andro Whym: "Change is the path life takes."

First River: The easternmost of the three delta rivers. Called the Rajblood among the Gypsies.

First Settler's Congress: The origins of the Charter of Unity and the Entrolusian city-states alliance.

Firstfall Axe: A symbol of the Marsher monarchy.

Firstfall Steel: Very silver and gives back a perfect reflection allowing even magicked scouts to be seen. Rumored to have been brought from the moon by Raj Y'Zir and his armies.

Fontayne: A charismatic mystic who attempted a coup against Lord Jakob which resulted in the deaths of Jakob and Marielle, and Rudolfo's early ascent to leadership. Later discovered to be the seventh son of Vlad Li Tam.

Franci B'Yot: Posthumous founder of the Franci Order and contemporary of P'Andro Whym whose correspondence influenced Whym. Eventually, the two movements merged and formed the Androfrancine Order.

Franci Orphanage: The Androfrancine orphanage where the children of the supposedly celibate priests are raised and trained in the ways of Franci B'Yot.

Francines: Slang for Androfrancines.

Frederico: Last of the Weeping Czars, who fell in love with Amal Y'Zir, the youngest daughter of the Moon Wizard, via a silver crescent that let him communicate with her on the moon.

Frederico's Bargain: An agreement made in the Deepest Dark, between Frederico, the Last Weeping Czar, and some great power in the Beneath Places, concerning the survival of the light and the People of Lasthome.

Freehold of the Emerald Coast: The loose confederation of independent city-states on the inner and outer Emerald Coasts.

Friendslip: One of the Ninefold Forest Houses.

G

Gaerrik: One of Winteria the Youngers Council of Twelve.

Galdus: Marta's father.

Gardens of Coronation and Consecration: The garden in Windwir where the new Pope is presented and named.

Garvis the Birder: The birder that served the seventh forest manor (at Rachyle's Rest) when Rudolfo was a boy.

Garyt ben Urlin: A grandson of Seamus set to guard the Book of Dreaming Kings by Ria, but who remains loyal to Winters.

Gath: A professor of human studies at the Franci school who taught Petronus the ways to read human intent in facial expression.

Geoffrus: A bandit leader in the Churning Waste.

Gervais: A playwright who wrote *4 Plays of the Early Settlement*.

Geryt: One of Sethbert's servants.

Ghosting Crests: The wide and dangerous sea east of the horn, supposedly haunted by ghosts and other creatures capable of sinking vessels.

Glimmerglam: The Gypsy King's first forest house and the location of the peach orchards.

Glossolalia: Escatic utterance brought about primarily by the Homeseeker's dream.

Gray Guard: The military arm of the Androfrancine Order. They guard the light "clothed in the ashes of yesterday's world" as dictated by P'Andro Whym.

Great Deicide: A Machtvolk reference to P'Andro Whym.

Great Mother: The Y'Zirite title for Jin Li Tam, the mother of the Child of Promise.

Gregoric: Rudolfo's closest friend and first captain. He died as part of Vlad Li Tam's shaping of Rudolfo.

Grun: A gypsy scout who followed Jin Li Tam into the Machtvolk lands.

Grymlis: A captain of the Gray Guard and friend of Petronus.

Great Library: The vast storehouse of knowledge that lay at the heart of Windwir and the Androfrancine Order. The result of 2,000 years of careful excavation and recovery from the ashes of the Old World.

Grun El: A legendary place famed for its cave castles.

Gulf of Shylar: Forcefully annexed by the Delta city-states.

Gustav: A Gray Guard scout attached to the Office for the Preservation of the Light.

H

Hanok: A Gray Guard attached to the Turam Bookhouse.

Hanric ben Tornas: Selected by Mardic to be Winter's Shadow, until she was old enough to rule in her own right. Killed during the slaughter Rudolfo's Firstborn Feast.

Harston Letter: A historical fragment of the Seven Cacophonic Deaths.

Headmaster Tobel: Administrator of the Franci orphanage.

Hebda Garl: An Androfrancine and arch-behaviorist of the secret Office for the Preservation of the Light. He is presumed to be Neb's father, and was believed to have perished in the fall of Windwir.

High Mass of the Falling Moon: Y'Zirite celebration of the coming of Raj Y'Zir.

Holga: The Bay Woman (in Caldus Bay) who prepares and dispenses earth magicks.

Homeseeker's Song or Sowing Song: The People's name for what is commonly called "Canticle of the Fallen Moon." The melody is coded with a dream that targets mechoservitors and contains instructions for the re-creation of Rufello's Ship that Sailed the Moon and for gathering the necessary components to command the Firsthome Temple once it is unsealed.

Hounds of Shadrus: Bred by Shadrus for House Y'Zir, used for hunting Younger Gods.

House Li Tam: A ship building and banking house known for its neutrality. A house without kin-clave, barring a secret relationship with the Androfrancine Order, this lack of kin-clave allowed it to broker information to the highest bidder. Secretly commissioned by T'Erys Whym to carry out his first assertion in the New World and shape the lives and history of the Named Lands intentionally.

House of Shadrus (Children of Shadows): An older name for the Marshfolk from their servitude to House Y'Zir upon the moon.

Hymnal of the Wandering Army: Three hundred and thirteen songs, which have never been written down, that describe the Wandering Army's strategies and tactics.

Hyran: Mayor of Caldus Bay and Petronus's closest boyhood friend.

I

Ignatio: Erlund's spy master and Y'Zirite agent, the illegitimate son of a Franci arch-scholar, killed by Lysias for his role in the death of Lynnae's child.

Ilyna: The wife of Kember, steward of Rudolfo's Seventh Forest Manor.

Imperial Archeology Society: An arm of the Y'Zirite empire.

Imperial Cutting Garden: An outdoor Blood Temple at the palace in Ahm's Glory.

Intellect VIII: An Androfrancine Pope centuries in the past who first gifted House Li Tam with the reconstructed golden bird.

Introspect III: The last Pope of the Androfrancine Order prior to the destruction of Windwir. Warned of the coming end, he allowed the destruction of Windwir that he might save the light as instructed by the Younger God Whym.

Ire Li Tam: The 32nd daughter of Vlad Li Tam and one of the Knives planted by her grandfather among the Blood Guard of the Crimson Empress.

Iron Armada: A fleet of iron ships built by House Li Tam according to specifications provided by the Androfrancine Order, to better allow them to protect the Order's wealth.

Isaak: Mechoservitor Number Three named by Rudolfo after being found in the ruins of Windwir. Also, Rudolfo's elder brother, poisoned by Vlad Li Tam as a part of Rudolfo's "shaping."

J

Jakob (the Elder): Rudolfo's father, Lord of the Ninefold Forest Houses and a secret Y'Zirite who negotiated a treaty with the Empire of Y'Zir that favored his family.

Jakob (the younger): The son of Rudolfo and Jin Li Tam, the Child of Promise according to the Y'Zirite gospels and prophecies.

Jamael and the Kin-Wolves: A bedtime story read to Winters by her tutor.

Jarvis: A former Androfrancine engineer who designed a bomb targeting Rudolfo, his family and the Forest Library.

Jarryd: A former Gray Guard dedicated to protecting Petronus.

Jaryk: A first lieutenant of the Gyspy Scouts.

Jeryg: A neighbor of Marta's whose wandering lamb she stole for Isaak.

Jin Li Tam: The 42nd daughter of Vlad Li Tam, the former consort of Sethbert, and wife of Rudolfo. She is the Great Mother of Y'Zirite scripture and the mother of Jakob, the Child of Promise.

K

Kallaberries: the dried berries of the Kalla plant, they have a calming and refreshing effect on the user. Can be smoked in dried form or ingested as an augmented, powdered mix called kallacaine.

Keeper's Creche: The scattered spaces of the world created by the Keeper to preserve human life on Lasthome during its various apocalypses and cataclysms.

Keeper's Gate: The massive locking gate in the midst of the Keeper's Wall that sets the Named Lands apart from the Churning Waste.

Keeper's Hatch: The offspring of the Keeper that are born during specific times to serve the People.

Keeper's Wall: The wall of mountains that protect the Named Lands on the East.

Keeper of the Book: The librarian and cataloger of the Marsh King's dreams and glossolalia.

Kember: Steward of the Rudolfo's Seventh Forest Manor. He and his wife are secret Y'Zirites converted by Lord Jakob.

Kendrick's Town: A town south of the ruins of Windir.

Kin-dragons: Legendary war beasts of the Younger Gods.

Kin-healing: The Y'Zirite rite of cleansing those who owe a blood debt and reuniting them with House Y'Zir and its faith.

Kin-wolves: Twice the size of timber wolves, intelligent and violent. Creation of the Wizard Kings.

Kin-ravens: Bred by the Wizard Kings as spies and messengers, larger and brighter than an ordinary raven. Thought extinct for more than 2,000 years until very recently.

Kinshark: Rafe Merrique's ship, which is cloaked by magicks that render it invisible.

Kinsman's Rest: A Marsher village.

Knives of Tam: The secret children of the Tam line set aside by Ben Li Tam for the time when they would be needed in the Y'Zir lands.

L

Landlish: One of the languages of the Old World that eventually became the common language of the New World.

Lasthome: The world of the Named Lands.

Lasthome League: A measure of distance, approximately 1.04 miles.

The Letters of Sister Alouise: A collection of letters by an early follower of Ahm Y'Zir's faith.

Library of Elder Days: The great storehouse of knowledge sealed within the Firsthome Temple, containing millions of years of the People's history and lore.

Lower Landlish: A variation of Landlish spoken on the Scattered Isles.

Lynnae: Jakob's Entrolusian wet-nurse and member of Gypsy King's household. Also, General Lysias' daughter.

Lysias: An Entrolusian general who fought against Rudolfo in the War for Windwir and later sought asylum in the Ninefold Forest, where his daughter resided. Lysias was tasked with creating the Forest's first standing army.

M

Machtvolk: "The people of power" once attached to the Firsthome Temple who later became the servants of House Y'Zir.

Magisters of the Knowledge of the Faithful: A Y'Zirite order dedicated to identifying, collecting, safeguarding and utilizing the magicks and mechanicals dug from the ruins and found in the Beneath Places.

Mal Li Tam: The first son of Vlad Li Tam's first son, and secret high priest of the Crimson Empress. Working for his grandfather, Mal ultimately betrayed Vlad Li Tam and brought about the death of most of his family. Mal was later killed by Vlad Li Tam in the basement of the Moon Wizard's Ladder.

Mardic: Marsh King and father of both Winteria the Younger and Winteria the Elder.

Markday: The day that a follower of the Y'Zirite faith takes the mark of House Y'Zir.

Marshfolk: The House of Shadrus, also known as the Machtvolk, former servants of the Wizard Kings. Seen as still affected by the Age of Laughing Madness, Marshers embrace superstition and mysticism and are not a part of the kin-clave of the Named Lands.

Marielle: Rudolfo's mother, killed in her sleep during Fontaine's uprising.

Marta (Martyna): A young girl who becomes the traveling companion to Isaak after his transformation. Her mother sold produce in Windwir and died in its destruction.

Mayhap Falls: A waterfall near the caves where Isaak hid after his battle without the Watcher.

Meirov: The Queen of Pylos who, enraged at her son's murder, eventually leads the conspiracy to kill Rudolfo and his family by bombing the Forest library. She is killed when Ria unleashes plague spiders upon the nation of Pylos, killing every man, woman and child.

Mera: A captain of the Y'Zirite who serves on the staff of General Yazmeera.

Micah: Lynnae's murdered son.

Moon Sparrow: An ancient mechanical bird used to bear messages for the Office for the Preservation of the Light in the Churning Wastes and where conventional messenger birds are ineffective or ill advised.

Moon Wizard's Ladder: See Seaway.

Moon Wizard's Staff: A relic tied to the Firsthome Temple and hidden by Amal Y'Zir and Frederico for the son of Whym as a part of Frederico's Bargain.

Moon Wizard's Tower: The visible structure on the moon's surface that was taken over by the first Y'Zir. Properly called the Firsthome Temple.

Myr Li Tam: Vlad Li Tam's 46th daughter.

Myra: A servant of the Ninefold Forest Houses.

N

Named Lands: The New World hidden behind the Keeper's Wall and deeded originally to the Marshfolk and the Gypsies by Xhum Y'Zir. Once the Androfrancine survivors arrived and settled, it became known as the Named Lands.

Neb/Nebios ben Hebda/Nebios Whym: The Homeseeker of Marshfolk prophecy. Thought originally to be the son of Hebda Garl, Neb is actually the offspring of the Younger God Whym. Neb was left by the Office for the Preservation of the Light to witness the destruction of Windwir, which awakened the latent gift within him.

Night of Purging: The night during which the remaining followers of Scientism and their allies, led by P'Andro Whym, overthrew and killed the seven Wizard King sons of Xhum Y'Zir in retaliation for the bloody suppression of the Scientism Movement.

Nightstone: Also called a dreamstone—an artifact of the Younger Gods which allows access to the aether and limited telepathic connection to others. It is believed to have been used to affect "group" dreaming in therapeutic, educational and recreation pursuits.

Ninefold Forest Houses: The nine forest manors that form the seats of government for the Ninefold Forest. The Gypsy King moves between the houses using a steward in each to administer in his absence between visits.

Niva: A captain in the Y'Zirite army that serves on general Yazmeera's staff.

Notes and Specifications: The great catalog of the notes and schematics of the science and secrets of the First World as compiled by Rufello. Deemed a forbidden text by the Moon Wizard and his descendants, only scattered pages and fragments remain.

O

Obidiah: Originally designated Mechoservitor Number Seven by Charles in his first generation of metal men, Obidiah was attached secretly to the

Office for the Preservation of the Light by Introspect and assigned to the Sanctorum Lux project. Exposure to the metal dream led to the new, self-assigned designation.

Office of Franci Practice: The Androfrancine office for behaviorism, analyzing, understanding and manipulating the pathways of thought and behavior.

Office for the Preservation of the Light: The secret office tasked by Pope Introspect with establishing Sanctorum Lux, and the preservation of the greater light, and assisting in the fulfillment of the Marsher Dream and the metal dream identified by the mechoservitors of Sanctorum Lux. Headed by Hebda Garl in the post-Windwir years.

The One Hundred Tales of Felip Carnelyin: A legend from the era of the czars, it tells the tale of a fabulous voyage to the moon, and how a daughter of the Moon Wizard fell in love and was spirited away from her home.

Orius: General and Commander of the Gray Guard before Windwir fell, charged with making sure the light survived. He retreated with a remnant of the Gray Guard and other Androfrancines into the Beneath Places to run intelligence and counter-invasion operations in addition to his work protecting the Office for the Preservation of the Light.

P

P'Andro Whym: The first offspring of the Younger God Whym to appear after the Downunder War. Whym's birthright was never validated in the Beneath Places; instead he was caught up in the growing Scientism movement. After the Wizard King Xhum Y'Zir and his seven sons destroyed the movement, Whym organized the Night of Purging, during which the Wizard King's seven sons were killed. His letters with Franci B'Yot would eventually result in the melding of the Whymer brotherhood and the Franci Order into the Androfrancine Order, which shepherded the survivors in the Churning Wastes for nearly five hundred years before settling the lands behind the Keeper's Gate.

Paltos: An Emerald Coast city-state and theistic society worshiping some of the more benevolent Younger Gods. One of the oft-avoided cities of the outer Emerald Coast, eschewed by the secular Androfrancines.

Panta Root: A Lasthome root that enhances strength, senses, speed, stamina when chewed.

Papal Summer Palace: The location of the Order's first attempt at settlement and allegedly a military stronghold to assist in containing the Marsher's "madness." It eventually became a retreat palace for the papal office and was destroyed in the Marsher uprising following the fall of Windwir.

Papal Unction: An irrevocable papal decree of the highest priority that must be adhered to.

Paramo: The third forest house of the Gypsy Kings. It has the rural charm of a logging village and is renowned for the wood products and workings that decorate the great houses of the Named Lands.

Parmona: An Entrolusian city-state.

The People: The name the Younger and Elder Gods call themselves, a species that originated on Firsthome.

Petronus: Also known as the Hidden Pope and referred to as the Last Son of P'Andro Whym. The youngest man ever selected Pope of the Androfrancine Order, he started in the Office of Francine Practice, and developed an eye and a reputation for always being able to perceive the thoughts of others in their faces. He faked his own death on the 19th of Argen in the 1966th year of settlement to go into a life of obscurity as a fisherman and returned to the papacy after the Fall of Windwir to preside over the trial of Sethbert and the dismantling of the Order.

Petros: An indentured man in the gospels of P'Andro Whym who served beyond the terms of his agreement. Also, the alias Petronus lived under after faking his death.

Phaerum: An Entrolusian city-state.

Philemus: The Second Captain of Rudolfo's Gypsy Scouts, valued for his willingness to question, and for his loyalty. Named Over-sheriff of the Forest in the wake of Rudolfo being named the Chancellor of the Named Lands.

Physicians of Penitent Torture: A Gypsy holdover from the era of the Wizard Kings. The cuttings now a redemptive ritual heavily influenced by the aberrant teachings of T'Erys Whym and Y'Zirite beliefs around the power of shed blood.

Plague Spiders: One of the Seven Cacophonic deaths, these large spiders multiply rapidly and carry lethal fever. They are used by the Y'Zirites and Machtvolk to destroy Pylos.

Port Charis: Old World city, birthplace of P'Andro Whym and location of Sanctorum Lux.

Prairie Sea: The ocean of grasslands that separate the nine massive forests that form the Ninefold Forest Houses from one another and the rest of the Named Lands.

Pylos: A nation in the Named Lands, located between Turam and the United City-States of the Entrolusian Delta.

Q

Queen's War: An ancient board game still played in the Named Lands, very similar to chess.

R

Rachyle's Bridge: The bridge that crosses the second river in the delta, connecting the United City-States of the Entrolusian Delta to Pylos.

Rachyle's Rest: The city growing up in the shadow of the new library at the site of Rudolfo's Seventh Forest Manor.

Rae Li Tam: The seventh and eldest surviving daughter of Vlad Li Tam. She is the wife of Baryk, a free city warpriest and the finest apothecary House Li Tam has ever produced. She disguised herself as a man and studied at the Franci school for three years.

Rafe Merrique: A pirate employed by the Androfrancine Order to run secret missions around the horn into the Wastes. Also was hired by Petronus to take him secretly to the Emerald Coast after his faked death. Rudolfo and Gregoric sailed with Merrique in their youth.

Raj Y'Zir: The Moon Wizard, who returned to Lasthome from the moon to revenge himself on the empire of Frederico, the Weeping Czar, who he blamed for the loss of both of his daughters, Ameera and Amal Y'Zir.

Rajblood River: The Gypsy name for the Delta's First River.

Regent of House Y'Zir: Eliz Xhum, Blood Regent of House Y'Zir.

Remus: Renard's father. Also a guide in the Waste frequently hired by the Androfrancines.

Ren Li Tam: Vlad Li Tam's 48th son, a skilled engineer.

Resolute: The falsely anointed Bishop Oriv, cousin of Sethbert. Resolute's suicide was faked by Grymlis and Lysias acting on behalf of Sethbert's nephew, House Li Tam and the remnants of the Androfrancine Order.

Restoration Scientifica Progrom: The uprising led by P'Andro Whym against the Wizard Kings which resulted in the deaths of Xhum Y'Zir's sons.

Reyjik: A neighbor of Marta's family who glimpsed Isaak in the woods.

Reynard: Son of Remus, a guide in the Waste.

Ria/Winteria the Elder: Mardic's eldest daughter.

Rites of Kin-Clave: The rituals and social rules which bind the Named Lands. Its origins lie in the years of Settlement following the Age of Laughing Madness.

River Woman: The herbalist/healer for the Seventh Forest House.

Rothmir: An Entrolusian city-state governor.

Royce: One of the two captains singled out by Lysias among the Ninefold Forest's new standing army to accompany him to the Beneath Places.

Ru Li Tam: Thirteenth son of Vlad Li Tam's twentieth son. He died upon the cutting table at Ria's command.

Rudoheim: One of the Ninefold Forest Houses.

Rudolfo (Modern): The Gypsy King, Lord of the Ninefold Forest Houses and general of the wandering army. A competent swordsman and brilliant strategist with the reputation of a womanizing fop, but can also be ruthless and always knows the right path to take. Rudolfo's life was shaped by the manipulations of House Li Tam largely following a secret Y'Zirite agenda.

Rudolfo (Historic): A desert thief with a band of Gypsy bandits in service to the Wizard Kings. Before the devastation of the Old World, Rudolfo led his bandits and their families west to the New World, granted access to the lands beyond the Keeper's Gate. He was also responsible for secretly smuggling Ahm Y'Zir away from the Old World.

Rufello: The Czarist scientist who spent his life studying the fragments and remains of the Age of the Younger Gods to better understand the scientific mysteries of the first world. Rufello designed The Ship that Sailed the Moon, which was used in the first Czarist Lunar Expedition. Apocryphal tales refer also to a resurrected Rufello working with Frederico and Amal Y'Zir as part of Frederico's Bargain.

Rufello's Grave: An Androfrancine supply cache in the Waste, just outside of what was once Ahm.

Rydlis: Arch-scholar of the school at the Franci orphanage during Neb's tenure.

Rylk: A Gypsy Scout killed by Archbishop Oriv.

S

Sadryl: An Entrolusian city-state.

Samael: An Entrolusian city-state.

Sanctorum Lux: Bastardization of Sanctuary of Light in a tongue from the earliest days of the Younger Gods.

Sasha: One of the soldiers of Esarov's Secessionist Union.

Scars of House Y'Zir: The symbol cut over the heart of a servant of House Y'Zir and a key sacrament in Y'Zirite faith administered to all practitioners that are twelve or older.

Scattered Isles: The various isles that are spread across the Emerald Sea southwest of the Named Lands.

Scientism Movement: During the era of P'Andro Whym, the Scientism Movement was eradicated as a threat by the House Y'Zir. It converted P'Andro Whym in his youth, and heavily influenced Franci B'Yot as well.

Seamus: The eldest of Winteria the younger's Council of Twelve.

Seaway, The: A path from the moon to Lasthome opened when the Firsthome Temple was reopened. In myth, it is referred to as The Moon Wizard's Ladder, but is actually an artifact of the Younger Gods.

Second River: The centermost of the three delta rivers.

Serendipitous Wind: Flagship of House Li Tam's Iron Armada.

Sethbert: The Overseer of the Entrolusian Delta city-states. He was manipulated by Y'Zirite influences, persuaded by paranoia and bad intelligence to destroy the Androfrancince city of Windwir. Ultimately tried and killed by Pope Petronus's own hand, invalidating his papacy.

Seven Cacophonic Deaths: The last great blood magick spell of the Wizard King Xhum Y'Zir, which legend claims he labored over for seven years to avenge the murder of his sons.

Shadrus (see House of): The leader of the Machtvolk during the time that Raj Y'Zir and his silver army left the moon and ended the Age of the Czars.

Shadrus's Dream of Unsealing: Also known as the Final Dream among the Marshers.

Shyla: One of the Crimson Empress' Blood Guard who tortures Neb in an attempt to locate the mechoservitors building the antiphon.

Som Li Tam: Vlad Li Tam's nephew, son of his brother Tarn Li Tam. Supposedly died at a young age but was instead sent to the Y'Zirite lands where he took the name Al Shadryk and leads the Knives of Tam.

Spirit of Amal: A ship of the Iron Armada.

Spirit of the Storm: A ship of the Iron Armada.

Steel Fold: The mechanical children of Brother Charles.

Stormwaters: The impassable oceans west of the Named Lands.

Straupheim Parchment: A historical fragment of the Seven Cacophonic Deaths.

T

Tal Y'Zir: Prime mover of the Downunder War, who led the rebellion against the Younger Gods and took the Firsthome Temple and moon from them.

Tamyra: The Y'Zirite name of Ire Li Tam.

Tarn Li Tam: One of Vlad Li Tam's brothers.

Tarviz: A colonel of the Imperial Regent's office assigned to Vlad Li Tam while he journeyed with the Daughters of Ahm.

Terick's Fall: A city in the Y'Zirite Empire.

T'Erys Whym: The brother of P'Andro Whym, and the leader of the Order until the Franci movement brought back reason as a central tenant. He was a mystic with aberrant beliefs, a poet, and for a short while, a pope.

Tertius: A renegade Androfrancine scholar and Marsher sympathizer who became Keeper of the Book during Mardic's reign and Winters' personal tutor. In fact, he was secretly a member of the Office for the Preservation of the Light assigned to study the Book of Dreaming Kings.

Thalnas: One of Marta's neighbors.

Third River: The westernmost river of the three rivers delta region.

Tormentor's Row: Where the prisoners under the care of the Physicians of Penitent Torture were housed and redeemed. Rudolfo tore down Tormentor's Row and used its stones to build his library.

Turam: A nation of the Named Lands.

Turik: The master of mines for the Ninefold Forest.

Tybard: One of the Captains selected by Lysais from among the Ninefold Forest's new standing army, to accompany him into the Beneath Places.

Tyrus: A miner from Rudoheim, part of the team mapping the Beneath Places under the Ninefold Forest.

U

United City-States of the Entrolusian Delta: the largest nation of the Named Lands and its economic center, though heavily dependent on the traffic from Windwir and the Ninefold Forest.

V

Valkry's Rest: A Marsher village.

Varn: A farmer from Kendrick.

Vas Y'Zyr: The third son of Xhum Y'Zir, and the Wizard King of Aelys. His left eye was replaced with an eye of nightstone that let him see into the Unseen World and to make pacts for his blood magicks.

Vesperleaf: A sleep aid.

Vessel of Grace: Chandra, the bride of Ahm Y'Zir, and mother of the Crimson Empress, whose union with Y'Zir and pregnancy with his blood-magick-induced child led to a terminal and painful illness seen in the Y'Zirite faith as "bearing the sins of the world." She was healed by Vlad Li Tam.

Vlad Li Tam: The current Lord of House Li Tam and direct descendant of Frederico, the Last Weeping Czar. His machinations and manipulations have shaped the Named Lands, including (in part) his unwitting participation in aspects of his father's secret collusion with Y'Zir, notably the events leading to the birth of the Y'Zirite Child of Promise. Tam surrenders his lands and assets to seek evidence of a foreign threat to the Named Lands and loses most of his family to the Y'Zirite kin-healing after his betrayal by his grandson. He meets the "ghost" of Amal Y'Zir and is led into his part of Frederico's Bargain, ultimately arriving in Y'Zir.

V'ral: One of the languages of the Old World, and the Imperial Tongue of the Empire of Y'Zir in the modern era.

W

Wandering Army: The extremely competent (and feared) volunteer militia of the Ninefold Forest Houses.

War of the Weeping Czar: Also the Wizard War, started when Raj Y'Zir and his silver army invaded Lasthome from the moon.

War Sermons of the Marsh King: The one Marsher voice heard during war, spouting prophecy and revelation based on the Marsher mysticism.

Wardyn: An Entrolusian general.

Waste Witch: A provider of magicks and powders in the Churning Wastes.

Watcher: An ancient mechoservitor in service to the Empire of Y'Zir and responsible for creating and assisting in the implementation of the Y'Zirite's complex conspiracy from his hidden cave in the Marshlands.

Watcher's Vigil: The fifty years the Watcher spent in the Named Lands preparing for the Advent of the Crimson Empress and the Y'Zirite invasion.

Watching Tree: A self-aware guardian created by the People to protect and care for them over vast stretches of time while they slept in the Beneath Places.

Western Steppes: The westernmost end of the Prairie Sea, near the border with the Marshlands and the Windwir Protectorate.

Wicker Throne: The throne of the Marshers, carried by each ascending monarch to the top of the Dragon's Spine for the proclamation.

Whym: During the era of the Downunder Wars, when the House Y'Zir first arose against the Younger Gods, General Whym led the armies of the Younger Gods. Now, he is the ghost of a Younger God, with three carefully placed offspring to save his people as a part of Frederico's Bargain.

Whymer Bible: The collection of teachings and writings that make up the Androfrancine scriptures, mostly written by P'Andro Whym or his earliest followers.

Whymer Maze: Popularized by T'Erys Whym during his brief papacy in the Named Lands, a circular maze that can only be solved by returning the way you came or enduring the pain and thorns to find its hidden center.

Whymer Way: The road leading from the Windwir to the Keeper's Gate, and past it into the Churning Waste.

Wind of Dawn: A ship of the Iron Armada.

Windwir (City): Home of the Androfrancine Order in the Named Lands, and home of the Great Library.

Windwir (Person): A poet, who became the first Pope in the Named Lands.

Windwir's Rest: The Machtvolk name for what remains of Windwir.

Winteria bat Mardic (the elder)/Ria: Winters' older sister, raised in Y'Zir and groomed to take leadership of the Machtvolk after Windwir's destruction.

Winteria bat Mardic (the younger)/Winters: The Queen of the Marshfolk forced to ascend the spire early when her shadow, Hanric, was killed. Winters also first recognized (and fell in love with) Neb as the fulfillment of Marsher prophecy. She was deposed in a coup led by her older sister and later returned with Jin Li Tam to ultimately bear the marks of

Y'Zir during the Mass of the Fallen Moon and lead a small remnant of her people out of the north.

Wizard Kings: The wizards that ruled Lasthome from the arrival of Raj Y'Zir with his silver army until Xhum Y'Zir and his seven sons.

Wizard Wars: The war that ended the reign of the czars and subjugated the world to the rule of the Wizard Kings.

Works of the Apostles of P'Andro Whym: A listing of the accomplishments of all of the Order's Popes.

Writ of Shunning: An order of the Androfrancine Pope that severs all ties of Kin-clave to whomever is named.

X

Xhei Li Tam: An early Lord of House Li Tam who was gifted the restored golden messenger bird by the Pope Intellect VIII.

Xhum Y'Zir: The Wizard King who ruled over, and eventually destroyed, the Old World. After the Night of Purging, when P'Andro Whym and his followers killed Xhum Y'Zir's songs, the Wizard King created the Seven Cacophonic Deaths and sent his Death Choir out to destroy the world.

Y

Yazmeera: The general in charge of the Y'Zirite invasion of the Named Lands.

Year of the Falling Moon: The year-long invasion of Lasthome by the Moon Wizard Raj Y'Zir; also an Androfrancine observance in which for one year, each century, a Pope would live beyond the comfort and shelter of Windwir and wander from city to city in recognition of the loss of the Old World and the world before as a result of the lunar invasion.

Younger Gods: The People—also called the Children of the Elder Gods— who settled Lasthome and were eventually driven to near extinction by Y'Zir's war on them.

Y'Leris: An ancient city of the Old World.

Y'Zir: The Empire forged by Ahm Y'Zir, the seventh son of Xhum Y'Zir who secretly survived P'Andro Whym's Night of Purging.

Y'Zirite Resurgence: Various emerging sects practicing the worship of the Wizard Kings, usually brutally and swiftly suppressed by the Androfrancine Order. Later resurgences appear to be the work of the Y'Zirite Empire.

Acknowledgments

Hello and welcome back.

Of all the books so far in the Psalms of Isaak, *Requiem* has been the hardest. It was written under some extremely difficult circumstances and a lot of folks rallied around to help get this book finally wrapped up after two years of work on it.

I've dedicated this book to those I've lost along the way. Over the course of the last five years, since just a month after Tor picked up the series, my wife and I have lost eight members of our family: four parents, a nephew, two aunts and a grandmother. Those losses, combined with the birth of my amazing wonder twins, made *Requiem* a very, very hard book to get written. So this one is for those I've lost—both recently and the long ago loss of my older brother, Rusty, when I was four.

Because this book was so hard, I am deeply grateful to all of the extra hands that helped along the way with so many things, from housework to babysitting to providing me writing havens. So big, big thanks to the following people:

First and foremost, thank you, Lizzy and Rae, for giving me the best two reasons to stay at the keyboard and write lots of books (because daycare is expensive). Daddy loves you.

As always, Team4J—Jen, John, Jay and Jerry—for amazing writing and life support. And right up there with them, Lisa, Melissa, Dale, Robert and Tracy for exactly the same thing (and Tracy, your work with me on the glossary is brilliant and much appreciated). And of course, I want to thank my agent, Jenn Jackson, for all your help keeping the business end of things sorted out. I'm amazingly graced by amazing people in my life.

A lot of folks came out and helped wrangle kids or helped with the house or brought meals . . . and every little bit of help let me go hide and find my words or helped Jen while I was off being writerly. I'm particularly grateful to Shauna, Victoria, Nadia and Scott for all you did. And to my brother and his wife, Jon and Carol, along with the West Clan (Kathy, Angela and Nick) for providing a place where the girls could go spend time while Jen and I caught breaks.

Vast thanks to Bob and Vivian for the use of their beach hideout. I'll leave of a copy of the book next time I'm up.

I also want to thank some of the local haunts here in Saint Helens where I escaped to work on the book. So here's to you, Joe, Tiffany and Melisa . . . and to your respective crews at the Village Inn, the Dockside and Plantation House. Thanks for great food, drink and space to create in. And thanks to Lori and her crew at the Saint Helens Bookshop for making sure people near and far had access to the series.

As always, big thanks to Beth and the fine folks at Tor for all their encouragement and help bringing this book into the world. You were all Very Patient with me while I pushed my way through this Very Late book. And Beth, as always, your eye on my writing makes all the difference in the world. I also want to thank Mel for her hard work getting things put together, Deanna for another great copyedit and Chris for another fine cover.

Usually, I save my Dear Readers for last but this time, second to last: Thank you, Dear Readers, for staying with the series and thank you for being patient. And thank you for writing in to let me know how much you're enjoying the books so far. I hope you enjoyed this one, too.

And last, for very special reasons, I'd like to thank Dr. Eugene Lipov at Chicago's Advanced Pain Management. Your work is changing and saving lives—including mine. Thanks, Doc.

Four down . . . one to go! Stay tuned for *Hymn*, the final volume in the Psalms of Isaak.

Ken Scholes
Saint Helens, Oregon
November 2012